This Is Why They Hate Us

This Is Why They Hate Us

Aaron H. Aceves

SIMON & SCHUSTER BFYR

NEW YORK · LONDON · TORONTO · SYDNEY · NEW DELHI

SIMON & SCHUSTER BFYR

An imprint of Simon & Schuster Children's Publishing Division
1230 Avenue of the Americas, New York, New York 10020

SIMON & SCHUSTER BOOKS FOR YOUNG READERS
and related marks are trademarks of Simon & Schuster, Inc.
For information about special discounts for bulk purchases, please contact
Simon & Schuster Special Sales at 1-866-506-1949 or business@simonandschuster.com.
The Simon & Schuster Speakers Bureau can bring authors to your live event.
For more information or to book an event, contact the Simon & Schuster Speakers Bureau
at 1-866-248-3049 or visit our website at www.simonspeakers.com.
Interior design by Hilary Zarycky
The text for this book was set in Berling.
Manufactured in the United States of America
First Edition
2 4 6 8 10 9 7 5 3 1

Library of Congress Cataloging-in-Publication Data
Names: Aceves, Aaron H., author.
Title: This is why they hate us / Aaron H. Aceves.
Description: First edition. | New York : Simon & Schuster Books for Young
Readers, 2022. | Audience: Ages 14 up. | Audience: Grades 10–12. |
Summary: Seventeen-year-old Enrique "Quique" Luna decides to get over
his crush on Saleem Kanazi before the end of summer by pursuing other
romantic prospects, but he ends up discovering heartfelt truths about
friendship, family, and himself.
Identifiers: LCCN 2021047131 | ISBN 9781534485655 (hardcover)
| ISBN 9781534485679 (ebook)
Subjects: CYAC: Bisexuality—Fiction. | Psychotherapy—Fiction.
| Dating (Social customs)—Fiction. | Friendship—Fiction.
| Family life—California—Fiction. | Mexican Americans—Fiction.
| LCGFT: Novels.
Classification: LCC PZ7.1.A2157 Th 2022 | DDC [Fic]—dc23
LC record available at https://lccn.loc.gov/2021047131

For Mom,
my first best friend

"I've learned that people will forget what you said, people will forget what you did, but people will never forget how you made them feel."

MAYA ANGELOU

This Is Why They Hate Us

My thumb hovers over the exit button on the remote, poised to strike as soon as I hear the jingling of keys that means one of my parents is home from work. Playing on our enormous flat-screen—easily the most expensive thing in our house because if there's anything my dad loves more than drinking beer, it's watching TV—is the end scene of a moody indie film about two white guys in love who don't end up together. Even though they're both bawling their eyes out at a train station, I can't help but envy them. "It's better to have loved and lost" and all that.

When the screen fades to black, I breathe a sigh of relief, switch over to my sitcom equivalent of a security blanket, and grab the bag of Hot Fritos on the glass-and-marble coffee table. Then I stretch out on the übercomfortable puke-green couch my mom inexplicably loves (possibly more than me) and start stuffing my face.

During the end credits of the first episode I watch, my phone lights up with a message. I sit up, suck chili powder off my fingers, and check it.

Hello!

Saleem. God I hate how much I love how formal his texting is.

sup, I reply.

Did you get home safely? he writes back almost immediately.

I smile and put my feet up on the coffee table. It only took one ride in Fabiola's truck for Saleem to realize that the fact that I make it home every day in one piece is a miracle.

nah i died

It amuses me to no end to respond this way. With every other person I text, I use adequate punctuation, but not with Saleem. It actually takes more of an effort to reply the dumb way—Autocorrect and I always get locked in a battle of wills as I fight to keep the first word of my sentence lowercase, among other things—but Saleem appreciates the chaotic energy I inject into his life. At least, that's what I tell myself.

Your fingers have remarkable dexterity for a corpse's.

wow dats deadist

I hope that makes him laugh. I can't say what I really want to say, which is "You wanna see how dexterous my fingers are, you sexy brown—"

The sound of keys makes me throw my phone across the room. When I look up, my mom's walking in, and she does not look happy.

"Bad day?" I ask.

She blows hair out of her deceptively young-looking face. *"There aren't enough cuss words."*

My mom works at the CVS down the hill from my school. Every day when she comes home, she goes off about an exceptionally stupid customer that she very graciously refrained from punching in the face. Unless she's too tired to do so, which looks like the case today.

She hangs her keys on the hooks beside the front door that she had my dad install because he could never find his keys in the morning before work, throws her purse onto the faux marble counter that separates the kitchen from the living room, and trudges past me to the hallway on the way to her room. But before she's all the way there, she backtracks until she's standing next to the couch, looking down at me.

"Why's your phone all the way over there?"

I look to the corner of the room where my cell is lying facedown.

"Uh . . . Fabiola just scored sixty points in Words with Friends."

"Triple word score?"

"Yup."

"Smart girl."

She glances at the TV, and my eyes follow hers. The episode currently playing features two lesbian side characters getting married. Shit. I usually skip this episode if my parents are home. But my mom doesn't say anything, just turns back to me and asks, "When you gonna ask her to marry you?"

This question has been a running joke from the time I was thirteen or so, but ever since I turned seventeen, my mom's been sounding less and less like she's kidding.

"We'd have to start dating for that to happen, Mom."

"Mm-hmm." I suspect she suspects we already are, but she changes the subject. "How was the last day of school?"

"That's tomorrow."

"Oh." She rubs her face and sniffs. "How was your second to last day of school?"

"Okay. Not too different from all the others."

"Only one year left."

"Yup . . ."

"Well, don't stay up too late, kid." She tousles my hair and goes to leave, but then stops. "Chips."

I grab the bag of Fritos from the couch, roll it up, and put it on the coffee table. She nods and is on her way to her bedroom again.

When she's gone, I retrieve my phone, and Saleem's message is waiting.

Is that a term for prejudice against dead people?

I reply with one (made-up) word.

jes

I will have you know that I have a number of close dead relatives, so it is impossible for me to be "deadist."

Oof. How am I supposed to respond to that? He's joking, but he's also not. . . .

As I often do when I don't know how to reply to someone, I shift my focus to something else in the hopes that a perfect response will pop into my head while I'm distracted. In this case, I actually start a game of Words with Fabiola. She completes her turn almost immediately.

After she wins, we start another game. I'm in the middle of putting down the word "gay" (for entertainment value, not point value) when my dad gets home. Despite toiling in the sun all day, he actually enjoys his work. I think he and his colleagues spend more time pranking each other than actually washing cars.

"Hey, Dad."

"Mijo."

He puts his keys on the counter, walks over to me, kisses my forehead, and then heads to the bedroom. I hear the squeak of springs as he falls onto the bed next to my mom.

I play a few more turns before I get up. First, I grab my dad's keys and hang them on the hooks. Then I head to my parents' room. Their door's open, and they're both passed out in their work clothes. I take off my dad's boots, then my mom's sneakers, and turn the ceiling fan on. As I leave their room, I glance at the Bible on my mom's nightstand and can't help but sigh.

In the living room, I flop down on the couch again and stare at the strip of wall next to the window. Hanging there are two framed decorative cards with my parents' names on them. Underneath the names, in parentheses, is their biblical meaning. My mom's card reads, *Maria (The wished-for child)*, and my dad's says, *Abel (Breath)*. I have a card as well, but it's hanging in my room. There is no Enrique in the Bible, so we had to cheat. My middle name is Luke, which means "light." I don't think that fits me at all.

My parents aren't the most religious people I know—we're those Christians who only go to church for Christmas and Easter—but they believe in God and grew up with ultra-conservative parents, which is why I haven't told them that I'm bi. Part of me is certain they'll still love me when—*if?*—I come out to them, but another part of me keeps saying, *You never know. . . .*

It's the same with Jesus. Most of the time, I know He loves me. I mean, that's what He's all about. But sometimes when I hear someone—my pastor, my grandparents, a random person on the Internet—say that God hates queers, I have to squash the tiniest inkling of doubt that worms its way into my chest.

My eyes travel to the coffee table, where my phone is flashing. I pick it up and see another message from Saleem.

Hey, are you still there?

yah sars

No need for (barely intelligible) apologies.

I smirk.

how tings wit aya

Saleem's sister Aya is just about the coolest person I know. I've only met her once, but I was stunned by her beauty and the confidence with which she carried herself. For some reason, though, whenever she comes home from film school in New York, Saleem gets a little weird about it.

They're going well.

Ah, a contraction. That means he's lying, but I'll let it go for now.

gude gude gude

Yes, "gude." Anyway, I wanted to ask if you happen to be free later tonight.

I sit up, my heart pounding because I know where this is going, and all I can think about is how the smallest act on his part—an accidental touch, a compliment, initiating a hangout—can send me reeling.

Having feelings for Saleem is one of the hardest things I've ever had to deal with because I know we can never be together. There are a lot of reasons why that's true (my own cowardice being one of them), but the main one is I did the math and calculated that there is—exactly—a 0.01 percent chance that he sees me the way I see him. I mean, why would he?

Saleem is thoughtful and kind and a much, much better person than I am. He never complains about his parents or fights with his sister like I would if I were him. He always holds doors open for old ladies and gives homeless people his change or at least apologizes to them when he doesn't have any. I bet he doesn't even do that thing where you break something at someone's house and only fix it enough so that it looks fine and the next person who breaks it thinks they did it. He has the sweetest, gentlest soul I've ever encountered, and I'm, well, me.

Which means I shouldn't tell him I'm free.

im free, I reply. *y?*

I was thinking of a late-night swim. Would you like to join me?

There it is.

hellz yeah, I write without hesitation. *gets hot af in my rume @ nite*

Great. I look forward to seeing you, 'Quique.

Ugh, he just had to add that sexy-ass apostrophe before my nickname. God I hate him. Except that I don't, never could. Short and handsome and smart and caring Saleem. He is my greatest source of joy, and despite all the possible complications, I need him in my life. I'm not going to ruin us.

I hope.

After I get his grammatically immaculate text saying I should head over at around nine o'clock, I go to my parents' room to wake up my mom and ask for permission to take her car.

She grunts in approval before turning over and resuming her snoring.

It takes twenty minutes or so to get to Saleem's. He lives equally far from school as I do but in the opposite direction. It's a quiet area with mobile home parks, shopping plazas, and similar apartment complexes to mine. I pull up to the gate where I usually punch in a code to get in, but the keypad isn't working, which is weird. I reverse back onto the street and park across from the complex.

After I jump the gate, I walk quickly to Saleem's apartment, noting that the entire compound is almost completely dark, which, again, is weird. Even the streetlamps are out. If this were my first time coming here, I would get lost as hell—this place used to be a maze to me—but now, even in the shadows, I know exactly where to go.

I hike up the stairs to the apartment but don't knock or ring the doorbell. I know Saleem can hear me arrive from any room inside his apartment. The few times I've been inside his place, I've found it grand yet homey. Everything (from the rugs to the curtains to the tapestries) looks handmade with rich colors and intricate patterns, and the now-familiar scent of cumin-forward Palestinian stews hangs in the air.

The door opens, and he comes out, forcing me to do what's become necessary for my survival: try my best to ignore everything about him that drives me wild. The smile that lights up his entire face. The black T-shirt that matches the single ringlet of hair dropping onto his forehead. The amber eyes that wait for me in my dreams.

"Hey," I say, "what the hell's going on?"

"Power outage," he replies, handing me a towel.

"Oh. That explains the gate."

"I should have warned you."

"Yeah, you should've, asshole."

He smiles, and we head to the pool. It's a considerable walk (because it's past all the apartments and across a parking lot), and walking in near-complete darkness makes it feel even longer. Every unexpected noise makes me jump.

"Are you scared?" Saleem asks with a laugh.

"No!" I say, with way too much defensiveness for him to believe me.

"That's Misty, Mrs. Jamreonvit's cat. You're not a bird, so you can relax."

"I am relaxed!"

I trip on a sprinkler head and almost go down.

"I can tell." I'm so glad he could only hear that. "I am still way too full," he says, most likely changing the subject to relieve me of my embarrassment. It's the kind of thing I'd never think to do because I'm way more comfortable having the upper hand in our conversations.

"Gluttony, my dear friend, is one of the seven deadly sins. Wait, is that a thing in Islam?"

"Not explicitly, no. They're not laid out in the Quran like that."

I should sit down and read the Quran one of these days. Most of what I know about it I've learned from Saleem. My friend/favorite source of pain is a faithful Muslim, which means he avoids pork and alcohol. He doesn't smoke weed. He prays five times a day while not at school (you can imagine how shitty the other kids would act if he did it there). He doesn't even cuss. And for the past month or so he's been fasting for Ramadan.

I've never asked him what the Quran says about guys liking guys. I kinda assume it handles the topic the same way the Bible does: ambiguously. Which means some people say it's unequivocally condemned while others disagree. When I Googled the topic, I found out that a lot of Muslims believe it's okay to have queer thoughts, but not okay to act on them. I wonder if that's what Saleem believes.

"They're actually not in the Bible, either," I say. "I have no idea where they come from."

"In any case," Saleem says, "I am not a glutton. You try fasting from sunup to sundown, and we'll see how much you eat when you're finally allowed to."

"I wouldn't last a day."

I catch a glint of moonlight coming off his crooked white teeth as he smiles, and it takes everything in me to stop myself from pushing him up against the nearest wall and mashing my face against the beard that's been coming in recently. In order to release some of my pent-up energy, however, I say something I know I shouldn't.

"But it's not like gluttony would be the hardest sin to give up."

There's a hitch in Saleem's regular footsteps, but his rhythm returns to normal before he asks, "Then which one is?"

I swallow. "I think you can imagine."

In the dark, it's hard to see the expression on his face, but I can tell he's nodding.

"I do," he says, almost solemnly.

Oh God.

"Yeah? What is it then?"

He turns to look at me and parts his beautiful lips. "Sloth."

And with that, he takes off across the parking lot, his sandals slapping against the asphalt. I shake my head, take a deep breath, and pelt after him.

I skid to a halt when I reach the pool. With my longer legs, it was pretty easy to overtake my vertically challenged friend.

"This is actually kinda dangerous," I say when I hear him approach behind me. I can barely make out where the water begins. "What if I belly-flop onto concrete?"

"Yes, well, at least we won't drown," he says, out of breath. "It's five feet at the deepest."

"You could still drown," I say.

He lets out a hoarse laugh, and that's it. I hate it. I mean, I love making him laugh, but the fact that he doesn't react in any other way makes me crazy (or craz*ier*, I should say). I wish he were the type to appreciatively slap me on the back or the type to playfully punch my arm, but he lets it go. Water off a duck's back.

We have the pool to ourselves because everyone in the apartment complex (including Saleem's family) has been avoiding it like it's infested with piranhas ever since a opossum drowned in it last summer. The time Saleem and I spend in the water is only for us. Well, mostly. There is the occasional visit from the old white dude in Apartment Forty-Three, who shows up to get away from his wife, Christine, but that's usually only during the daytime.

"Did Aya ask about me?" I say, pulling my shirt up over my head and throwing it onto a lounge chair.

Saleem snorts. "Sure, Quique."

I smile. "And how is it having her back?"

"Good . . . ," he says, taking off his shirt.

He's such a bad liar.

"Come out with it."

He sighs. "Fine. So every time Aya comes home, I feel like my parents forget that I exist, and I don't want to say anything because she was away for school, but it's hard being . . . forgotten."

It would be impossible for anyone to forget you, I say in my head, *you beautiful boy*.

"Or, not forgotten, but ignored a little bit. Sidelined. And then a part of me wonders if it's because I'm . . . boring. I know I'm probably being irrational, but . . . that's how I feel." He sighs again. "I'm being ridiculous, aren't I?"

"No," I say. "Not ridiculous at all." His face relaxes, and his shoulders drop. "But you are . . ." So many words hang in my pause. "Anything but boring, Saleem."

"Thanks, Quique." He clears his throat. "I think I only needed to vent."

"Of course."

My shorts are the last article of clothing to come off. Before, the reason I swam in my boxers was I kept forgetting to bring trunks, but at this point it's simply how I swim. I walk over to the pool before noticing that Saleem is still over by our clothes.

"What's up?" I ask.

"I forgot to change into my bathing suit," he replies, looking down at his shorts.

"Okay . . . Swim in your underwear like me."

He doesn't say anything. *Is he too shy for that?*

"I don't want wet underwear," he says finally.

"You can't tell in the dark, but I'm rolling my eyes. Let's go back and get your trunks."

"No, no, it's okay. I, uh, do you mind if I swim without . . . anything?"

I feel like I've been transported to another reality. My hearing seems to leave me completely. "Like, naked?"

"Yes . . . Would that be okay?"

I clear my throat. "Yeah, that's cool. I don't care. I can't even see anything right now."

"Neither can I," he says.

"In fact, that's kind of a good idea." *What the hell am I doing?* "Isn't skinny-dipping kind of a rite of passage?"

"I believe so," Saleem says evenly.

"I'll do it too, then."

"Okay."

There's nothing but the sound of crickets as we wait to see who's gonna go first. Then Saleem takes off what are presumably his shorts. After that, I strip off my boxers, place them close to the edge of the pool, and jump into the water.

Despite the shock of cold, I stay under for as long as I can. When I surface, I'm panting for breath, the smell of chlorine filling my nostrils. I glance where Saleem had been standing near the lounge chairs but can't make him out. Then I hear a splash not too far from me. I turn in that direction and, thanks to the moonlight, catch his curls breaking through the water.

"Oh my God, it's *freezing*," he says, out of breath.

"Yeah," I say, "but it feels good."

CHAPTER TWO

"Gay."

"Yeah."

"Like *super gay*."

"Yeah."

"And I know gay."

"That you do."

Fabiola's pickup truck comes to a stop, and she lowers her window. A McDonald's employee hands her a medium iced vanilla coffee and a grease-soaked bag. She thanks him, hands the bag to me, and then we're off.

"Damn right I do."

As I take a hash brown out of the bag, I think about how one of the major upsides of realizing I was bi a couple years ago was being able to come out to my best friend and find out seconds later that she had been keeping the same secret. I don't think either of us was too shocked considering we'd known each other since kindergarten, but the relief we felt was unmistakable. Any reaction other than complete understanding would have been devastating because from the time I met Fabiola, the two of us have always been scarily in sync, as if we had choreographed this life in a past one and were only now getting to perform it. In elementary school, it was my handing her the yellow crayon before she asked for it. In middle school it was her being able to tell when someone was aiming for me with a dodgeball and jumping in front of me to catch it. Right now, it's the way I can tell by the look on her face that her iced coffee isn't sweet enough.

"Gross, this just tastes like coffee."

Bingo.

"Anyway," she continues, pulling onto the street, "what happened after you got out of the pool?"

I take a bite of my hash brown. "We dried off, got dressed, said goodbye, and went our separate ways. The usual."

She takes another sip of her coffee and grimaces. "Except you two had just been naked together."

"Yup."

"For the first time."

"Yup."

Fabiola slams on her brakes as we get to a red light and holds out her hand expectantly. I place a hash brown in it, the one I make her order every time because even though she says she doesn't like to eat in the mornings she always ends up attacking my food.

"Did you see it?" she asks, taking a bite.

"Nope."

"How is that possible?"

"It was dark."

"Mmm. I bet he's packing."

I glance self-consciously at the car that pulls up next to us even though I know the elementary school kids in the back seat can't hear us.

"You think?" I ask when the light turns green and Fabiola peels off.

"Mm-hmm, it's always the quiet ones."

"But he's so short."

"Believe me, not always a factor."

"I mean I wouldn't care either way."

"Of course you wouldn't. You didn't even mind that the first boobs you handled were these lovely ladies." She swipes her hash brown–free hand across her chest.

Fabiola is the only person I've ever hooked up with because hooking up with people requires courage, of which I have none. Well, that's not totally true. I guess I can walk through a bad neighborhood with enough fake confidence to keep people from thinking I'm an easy target. But ask a girl to dance at a party? Impossible. Ask a cute guy if he wants to try stuff because that'd be kinda awesome? Even more impossible. Good thing Fabiola has always been extremely direct. Otherwise, I'd have never so much as kissed anyone.

"I love your boobs," I say.

"Mm-hmm."

"Didn't that seem like the case?"

She considers this for a second before moving her head from side to side. "Yeah, I guess."

Our brief encounter occurred at her fourteenth birthday party. It was fun. Really fun. She taught me how to kiss and then let me get to second base, so I'm not just being nice when I say her breasts are great. They're not big like she wants them to be, but they're these soft, brown drops of heaven. The night we fooled around confirmed that I did indeed like girls that way and Fabiola did indeed like boys that way.

We soon discovered, however, that the two of us were way better off as friends than anything else. That dynamic really works for us.

"You know who had great tits?" Fabiola says.

See?

"Mariana Quiñonez."

"Fucking Mariana Quiñonez." Fabiola takes a long pull of her coffee. "God, I miss that girl sometimes." She glances at me and must read the worried look on my face because she adds, "I'm not gonna get back with her, Quique."

"Let's hope not."

Mariana was Fabiola's secret girlfriend who she dated and broke up with countless times during sophomore year and the first half of junior year. No one knows about the romantic aspect of their relationship besides me (not even Saleem) because Fabiola was so terrified of her family finding out. It helped that Mariana goes to a different school.

"I didn't realize you hated her so much."

I nearly choke on my hash brown. "Fabiola, she showed up on my doorstep to try to seduce me in order to get back at you for forgetting the anniversary of the third time you two broke up. When my parents asked why I was slamming the door on the incredibly attractive girl on our porch, I had to tell them she was a Satanist. Which, now that I think about it, might not have been a lie."

"I'm still not sure how she found out where you live."

"I don't like to think about it."

"Well, anyway, our thirteenth breakup was our final one, I assure you. I'm done with all her crazy."

My stomach turns, and it's not because of the hash brown grease. Well, maybe it's *partially* because of the hash brown grease. Anyway, every time Fabiola uses that word, I think about how she'd react to hearing about my own struggles with sanity.

"Plus"—Fabiola's voice snaps me back into focus—"there may or may not be someone else I have my eye on."

"What? Really?" This is news to me. "Who?"

Fabiola barely makes a yellow light, and my seat belt digs into my collarbone.

"Molly Pham," she says.

"Ohhh. The Vietnamese girl whose 'beautiful, massive thighs' you always point out to me?"

She nods, her eyes taking on a dreamy quality. "For now it's only a crush and some casual DM flirting, but we'll see. And what about you? What's the next step in your plan to seduce Saleem?"

"I'm not trying to seduce him."

"You're right. The skinny-dipping was his idea."

"He's not trying to seduce me."

"Keep telling yourself that."

"I will! Because he is my friend—*our* friend—and I'm not gonna fuck it up."

"Mm-hmm. Well, you do have other prospects."

"Like who?"

"Uh . . . ," she says like it should be obvious. "Tyler 'The Bulge' Montana? Future Surgeon General Ziggy Jackson? Papi Chulo himself Manny Zuniga?"

I roll my eyes. "Sure, I've had, like, tiny, little crushes on those guys, but the way I feel about them doesn't compare to the way I feel about Saleem."

"Well, Quique," she says, pulling into the school parking lot, "if he's not an option, you might want to start exploring other avenues. At least give someone else a chance."

We finish our breakfast in the amphitheater. I collect all the wrappers and put them in the bag while Fabiola reclines against the giant concrete step behind her and surveys the clusters of people also hanging out here.

"Think about your summer," she says.

"What about it?"

"If you don't try anything with your non-Saleem prospects, then you're just gonna do the same things you did last summer and the summer before that and the summer before that and the summer—"

"I get it."

"I think we're both stuck. Me on Mariana and you on Saleem. Don't you think it's kinda weird that you've only ever kissed me, your best friend? That's already far more than any man deserves but still."

I push her playfully.

"Look," she says. "All I'm saying is he's leaving with his family tomorrow and won't be back for a month—"

"Three weeks and a day."

"Not at all creepy that you've done the math. Anyway, this is going to be the longest stretch of time that you've faced without him, so I think now's the perfect time to bring your browser history to life."

I laugh, but she might be onto something. Maybe pining for your close friend and suppressing your feelings for every other possible romantic interest *isn't* healthy. But how would I even begin to make courting my non-Saleem prospects a reality? What if none of them are into me?

"How do you know when someone wants you?" I ask when two goth kids walking down the steps are out of earshot.

"What?"

"Say I decide to give myself an actual chance to . . ." I look around to make sure no one is listening before continuing. "*Connect* with someone. How do I know if they want me?"

"How did you know I wanted you?"

I think back to her party freshman year. I was in the kitchen, doing my best to resist her cousin Cassandra's advances. Fabiola walked in. Then . . .

"You came up to me and said, 'Come to my room. I want you.'"

"Right. God, I love me."

"You're okay. But I'm serious. How?"

She sighs. "I don't know, Quique. You just gotta go for it if it feels right."

I consider the possibility of having such intense chemistry with someone that it's expressed physically and mutually, and I feel this literal ache in my chest that I get every time I'm talking to a guy who's nice and confident and athletic and everything else I'm not. It's like I'm a balloon being pumped with air and instead of the sweet release of bursting, I'm stuck with this horrible tightness in my chest. "What comes after?"

"After what?"

"After the first kiss, the first touch."

"Well . . . depending on the person, it turns into something deeper. Something even more intoxicating, even more thought disabling."

"Wow."

"Yeah."

"I want that."

I do. I can't even imagine what it would be like to fall in love. The light-headed, jumpy way I feel when someone I like is in close range is intense enough as it is. How can there be something better/worse than that?

"I want to take that risk," I continue, "make a change—"

"You're literally just quoting a Kelly Clarkson song."

"—be brave. The next time I have an opportunity to—"

"Tongue punch—"

"—*make a connection*, I'm gonna go for it, stop being a coward."

"That's the spirit," Fabiola says. "And I'll do it too. Molly's not gonna know what hit her."

I tilt my head to the side. "How have you not already made a move?"

Fabiola avoids my gaze, instead casting her eyes at the ground, and it's the first time in a while that I've seen her even the least bit sad. "I think things with Mariana kinda messed me up. In a real way. In the back of my mind I can't help thinking, *Molly seems normal now, but if we start dating, then I'm gonna realize she's actually crazy, then we're gonna break up, then she's gonna start mailing me her underwear. . . .*"

"Did Mariana do that?" I ask, concerned.

"But I need to get over that, Quique. Let's do the things that will lead to us becoming the people we want to be."

She extends her pinkie to me.

"That's actually a really solid goal," I say, taking her pinkie in mine.

"I try." We let go. "Also, I want all the dirty deets if you ever get laid."

"Deal."

I close my eyes and lay my head on her shoulder. It's as comfortable as they come. At least it is until it starts shaking.

"What are you doing?" I ask, eyes still closed. Then I realize she's laughing. I remove my head and look at her. "What's so funny?"

"Straight ahead, darling. A prospect awaits."

I turn.

Fuck. Me.

Coming up the steps is Tyler Montana.

Tyler is tall, muscular, and white, but his most notable features are his easygoing nature, kiddie pool–sized dimples, hip-hop obsession, and his . . . his, um . . . wait, what is it? What else does he have? Oh yeah, his ever-present, basketball shorts–clad bulge. I swear you don't even have to be a fan of penises to notice it. Anyone within a ten-foot radius can spot the flaccid monster inadvertently.

"Oh look, it's Tyler's penis," Fabiola says, "and he brought Tyler along."

"Fabiola, what do I do?" I ask, panic fraying my voice. Using Kelly Clarkson lyrics as a mantra is all fine and dandy until a cute boy who could ruin your entire life is in front of you. "He's coming over here!"

"Honey, you asked for this. The universe is rewarding you."

"I change my mind! I don't want to do this. I want to be alone and comfortable. Screw a connection!"

"Get your shit together," she growls as Tyler comes into hearing range.

"'Rique! Fabiola!"

Tyler holds out his arms, a big smile on his face. His backpack hangs casually off one shoulder.

"Heyyyy," I say.

"'Sup, Tyler," Fabiola says, standing.

Tyler wraps his arms around her waist and lifts her. "How ya doin', girl?"

"I'm all right, Montana," she says when he puts her down.

"Glad to hear it."

Fabiola and I got to know Tyler sophomore year in our Japanese class. He butchered the language, and Fabiola and I agreed that if he had one less inch (in terms of height) or one less pound of muscle, that would be a deal breaker. Alas . . .

He glances at her cleavage before looking at me. "I don't get a hug, man?"

Moments like these always set my gaydar off. Not his staring at Fabiola's boobs, obviously, but his blatant request for body contact. He's always been incredibly touchy with me, like when he picks me up for no reason like he did Fabiola. Or when he puts his hands on my shoulders and throws his head back, laughing, when I say something mildly funny. Or, my personal favorite, when he loops his entire arm around my neck and rests his hand on my chest as we walk and talk.

I stand up awkwardly. "I, uh, I was about to—"

"Nah, it's cool, man. Dap me up."

Ugh. I hate that I'm so attracted to this wanksta.

Tyler winds his hand back, and we slap, then clap each other on the back.

"Last day of school," he says.

"Yeah," I say. "This year flew by."

"No cap."

I smile awkwardly. I can sense Fabiola watching me, amused, and it makes me feel itchy all over. So I take a seat. I figured Tyler would sit next to me, but he remains standing, which means I'm face-to-face with his basketball shorts.

"Any summer plans?" his crotch asks.

I shake my head and look up at his face, which is a comparatively stimulating sight. He has beautiful blue eyes and perfectly straight teeth.

"Uh, not really. You?"

"My parents are dragging me to Barbados or the Bahamas or some shit for a week in July, but I rather just post up in my room and smoke, chill. You know how it is."

"Totally," I lie, "but I bet you look great in a bikini, though."

It's a weak joke but apparently not to Tyler. He bends over with laughter, one hand on my shoulder. "That's funny, dude." He returns to his upright position and then swivels his hips so that his ass is facing me. "Although I do get told that I have a pretty big booty for a white boy."

Fuck, he's right.

He laughs and swivels back.

"So, 'Rique, Fabiola"—I forgot she was here—"you guys down for a chill sesh sometime soon?"

Tyler looks at me for an answer, but I can't seem to find words. Fabiola subtly elbows me in the ribs.

"We're more than down," I say finally.

Tyler nods slowly, beaming at me. "Aiiiight." He turns to Fabiola. "It'll be lit."

"I don't doubt it, Montana," she says.

Tyler turns to me again and adjusts his backward baseball cap. A few locks of his copper hair fall out onto his forehead. "I'll see you there, 'Rique."

"Sheah. See ya."

He winks at me, waves to Fabiola, and continues walking up the steps.

Fabiola turns to me.

"Did you just say, 'Sheah'?"

"I meant to say yeah, and then I started to say sure."

"Smooth."

"I know."

"I don't know why you're so flustered by a white who says *'Rique* instead of Quique."

We watch as Tyler hikes up the amphitheater steps two at a time, his pretty big white boy booty straining against his shorts.

"Oh, right," Fabiola says, "because of that. Lord, if you don't hit that, I will."

I turn to her, dazed. "I think that might be best."

The weird thing is I can feel my desires so intensely some-times that they feel like needs, but in the moments when I'm actually faced with the objects of my desire, panic originating from deep inside my bones sets in.

"Dude, I'm kidding. Mostly. I'm focused on Molly, so that's all you. Well, not *all* you. I'll be here to make sure you don't chicken out."

"But what if I wanna?"

"Not on my watch."

When Tyler's at the top of the amphitheater, he turns and waves. I wave back and force a smile.

My mom has said that sometimes God lines things up for you in the exact way you want Him to because it's the best thing for you. Sometimes He does this because He's testing you and He wants you to practice overcoming temptation. And *sometimes* He does this because while the thing you want is ultimately bad for you, He wants you to go through with it so you can learn a lesson.

As of right now, I have no idea what God's plan is, and it has me feeling like I just woke up from a long, deep sleep and I don't know where I am, who I am, or what I want.

CHAPTER THREE

There is a universal law of time called The Last Period Effect that I have studied extensively during the past three years of high school. The Last Period Effect™ states that the passage of time slows down exponentially as the number of minutes until you're able to go home approaches zero. In other words, the last period of the day is always the longest.

This is especially true on the last day of the school year, when you're in a class with zero of your friends, and your teacher's handing back essays that were due the day of the precalculus final you studied really hard for but still ended up almost failing.

For the past few minutes, in order to take my mind off my essay, I've been writing a list in my notebook that no one would be able to guess the true significance of besides me:

- *hair*
- *eyes/eyebrows/eyelashes*
- *lips*
- *teeth*
- *skin*
- *arms*
- *hands*
- *butt*

For Dr. Frankenstein, this is a shopping list. For me, it's a list of things I love about Saleem Kanazi, who is, I remind myself, my friend. Just a friend. A good friend, but nothing more. Never anything more. Which is why I need the list. If I can distill all of the qualities that allow Saleem to reign over my thoughts, then I can find someone who has all the same features, and things can actually go somewhere with them. Maybe.

I sigh and put down my pencil—it has to be almost time to go. But when I glance at the clock at the front of the room, I'm proven wrong. I watch as the second hand ticks slower and slower until finally coming to a complete standstill five minutes before the bell's supposed to ring.

"You've got to be fu—"

My mouth snaps shut as Mr. Chastman comes into view.

"Clock's broken, Enrique," he says, expressionless, as he hands me an essay with a rude amount of green ink on it.

Mr. Chastman doesn't believe in red ink; he once told the class about a study that showed red ink causes infertility. Kidding, obviously. It just discourages students, traumatizes them or whatever. He cares about stuff like that, and it's his caring nature that makes him my favorite teacher. Well, his looks might also have something to do with that. Sure, he's handsome, but more than anything I'd describe his face as comforting. There's something so boyish about him, with his green-blue eyes and short blond hair and bright pink lips.

My heart races as I take the essay from him. I really enjoyed *The Picture of Dorian Gray*, but I wrote the second half of the paper a few weeks ago on my phone on the way to school as Fabiola drove even more like a maniac because she'd just choked down a *large* iced coffee.

"Don't worry," Mr. Chastman says, reading the panic on my face, "your analysis was impressive. It's those homonyms you need to watch."

"Oh shi—oot," I say, not quite catching my tongue in time. "Sorry."

"It's fine," he says. And as he walks away, "Autocorrect is not your friend."

Ugh. Of course he noticed.

I look over my essay and smile to myself. Sure, most of the corrections are extremely embarrassing (I, unlike my iPhone, know the difference between "it's" and "its," I swear), but there were certain sentences that he underlined and wrote "GOOD" next to. The positive feedback almost makes the circled "B+" at the top okay.

I stuff the essay into my backpack and go back to my list, which I'm only now realizing could apply to literally anyone. And Saleem is not anyone. If someone's going to take his place, then they need to provide me with something more affecting and intangible than a cute face and a nice butt. (But, like, in addition to a cute face and a nice butt.) So I guess I have to let myself add some stuff, some *real* stuff.

- *perfect grammar (read: nerdiness)*
- *perfectly crooked smile*
- *patience/kindness/general cinnamonroll-ed-ness*
- *adorably stupid ability to mishear song lyrics*
- *utterly sexy ability to speak Arabic*

- *the way he bites his lip when he's working on a math problem*
- *the line that forms between his eyebrows when he's reading*
- *how he makes me feel*
- *the person I am when I'm with—*

"Enrique!"

I look up, and I'm immediately blindsided by the sight of Ziggy Jackson. He's casually leaning against the doorway, his head nearly reaching the top, with a yearbook under his arm, and I can't seem to remember how to breathe.

Sigmund "Ziggy" Jackson is a tall biracial dude (his mom's Black and his dad's white and they're both hot) that I've known since the ninth grade when he transferred to our school. I had just joined yearbook club (because my freshman year English teacher, Dr. Bashir, was offering extra credit if we signed up) and I pitched a feature about the midyear transfer. Mostly because I wanted an excuse to talk to him. Ziggy, like his parents, is utterly gorgeous: thick eyebrows above green eyes, smooth mahogany skin, and an ass too impossibly round for a lanky boy like himself.

And he just said my name, so I should probably respond at some point.

"Heyyyy," I say.

Words are hard.

As he walks over to me, a couple of my classmates call out to him, and he acknowledges them with a raised hand and a politician-worthy flashing of teeth.

I can't help but envy him. I don't think anyone in this class even knows my name, and I've gone to school with most of them since, like, middle school. But they know Ziggy. At the end of freshman year, in a remarkable show of confidence for a new kid, he ran for school treasurer and capped off a funny, clever speech with the line, "There are three types of treasurers: those who can count and those who can't." It was a dad joke for sure—one I never could have pulled off—but all he did was flash a smile like the one currently possessing his face and voilà! Victory. When the yearbook came out the next week, my feature cemented his meteoric rise to high school fame. I'm lucky that, like a rapper at the Grammys who actually started from the bottom, he didn't forget the people who supported him before he was popular.

"Here you go," Ziggy says, handing me the yearbook. "Make sure to hold on to that. It'll be worth something someday."

"Thanks. I was starting to think I'd never get it back."

He throws a long-fingered hand to his chest and feigns a hurt look. "I took my time to write something heartfelt. Why are you throwing shade?"

"I'm not!" *Why does he have to be so cute?* I really hope I'm not blushing. "But it's been a while since I gave it to you."

"Mm-hmm."

We're both smiling, eyes locked, and I feel this, like, electricity crackling in the air. When Ziggy finally looks away, it's down at my notebook. I quickly close it.

"Anyway," Ziggy says, "I should head out before Mr. Chastman kicks me out."

"He wouldn't kick you out."

"Don't listen to him!" Mr. Chastman calls out from the back of the classroom. "You should be in your assigned class!"

Ziggy smiles.

"I swear he has, like, bionic hearing," I say.

"Yup. I really should go, though. I didn't do the homework for my SAT class."

I wish my parents could afford an SAT class. Then again, that would mean I'd actually have to attend an SAT class. I guess being solidly working-class has its perks.

"I'll see ya, Enrique."

"See ya, Mr. President."

He salutes me before walking off, and the sight of his gorgeous, plump posterior is almost enough to distract me from the fact that I called him *Mr. President*. Sure, he was recently elected next year's student body president, but the way I said it was just so . . . me.

As I watch him go, I think about the list I've been compiling. Ziggy certainly crosses off more than a couple items (and not only because he is a human being with a body). I'm sure if I got to know him better, I'd find that he met a lot of my "criteria." And that backside . . .

I cut my gratuitous staring short when I realize that there's a glitch in my whole "get over Saleem by bagging someone else" plan: I'm still me. I'm still the guy whose tongue seems to inflate to three times its normal size anytime I'm talking to a cute person. I'm still someone who hides parts of himself from everyone he knows so they don't realize I'm not worth all the trouble of caring about me.

How the hell do I fix *that*?

I open my notebook, flip past my original list to a blank page, and start writing.

- *Get hot*
- *Get cultured*
- *Get honest*
- *Get the guy*

Will this work? Will this force me to get over Saleem? Will it make me the best version of myself? Someone who actually lives life instead of waiting politely on the sidelines for his turn?

I picture myself at the end of summer, swaggering around school with a jawline sculpted from the flab around my chin, a worn copy of *Crime and Punishment* filled with all those colorful little sticky notes all the nerds use nestled under my bulging bicep. At lunch, I'm eating with Fabiola and Saleem, and everything is perfect. She knows I go a little crazy sometimes, and he knows I'm into dudes. But our jokes come just as easy because I'm not hiding something from her, and I'm no longer in love with him. Why? Because after lunch is over, I run into Tyler or Ziggy or Manny. We say a quick hello (a fist bump for everyone watching), but our eyes say, *See you tonight*.

Wow . . .

Okay. Maybe that scenario's not the most realistic outcome of this summer. But if I get anywhere close to that? Things would still be pretty damn great. Way better than they are now.

I'm about to go back to my fantasy when I hear the word that never fails to make my blood run cold when it's used so hatefully. It comes from a desk a couple rows back, so I slowly crane my head around and stare out of the corner of my eye. Then I hear it again.

"I'm not joking. It's some straight-up faggot shit."

I breathe a sigh of relief when I realize my eloquent class-mate is talking to his friend, pointing to the cover of his *Dorian Gray* book and not me. I glance at Mr. Chastman, who's on the other side of the classroom now, and I'm glad to see his bionic hearing didn't pick up the slur from over there. He'd probably keep the entire class after the bell to lecture us, and right now I just want to get out of here.

"Wikipedia said the guy that wrote it got the death pen-alty," my classmate continues.

He's wrong, of course. Oscar Wilde wasn't killed for being queer, but he was imprisoned. Apparently, nineteenth-century Britain wasn't a great place to be a guy who likes guys.

"That's what he gets if you ask me," his friend says in reply.

And neither is this school. We're surrounded by a quaint-ish LA suburb, but my high school is overcrowded and under-funded. Things slip through the cracks. At the beginning of the year, a senior named Arturo Peralta got jumped on his way home the day after he came out as gay on social media. I remember bumping into him a month later while with Fabi-ola, who had PE with him, and watching them talk for a bit before he made an offhand remark about his missing tooth. I hadn't heard about the attack yet, so I asked if he'd lost it "in a cool way" (because I'm an idiot).

"No, not in a cool way," he'd replied with a sad smile. "In a shitty way."

He transferred not too long after that.

I face forward completely, every inch of my skin suddenly on fire. Maybe I should say something, be brave about this for once in my life. But who am I kidding? I'm not the guy who stands up and makes an impassioned speech about equality that changes people's minds, who squares up when the remaining ignorant few still threaten me. I'll probably never have the courage to speak up for myself and people like me. I'm not even brave enough to tell my friend that I have feelings for him. I'm a coward, and I always have been.

The bell rings, and I nearly jump out of my seat. I throw my yearbook and my notebook into my backpack and rush out of the classroom, not caring if everyone is staring at me. I'm not going to waste another second here.

But as I enter the hallway, I still feel like shit for not saying anything. Though I can't say that I feel surprised.

CHAPTER FOUR

Pushing against the current of students in the main hall, who are fighting to get to the exit, is on par, I would imagine, with what the ancient Egyptians experienced when Moses and his crew had finished crossing the parted Red Sea and the water rushed back to its natural state, but my struggle is necessary. Surviving these next few minutes is essential to getting a ride home.

"Yeah, I can't give you a ride home," Fabiola says, opening her graffitied locker.

"What? Why?" I ask, my voice echoing slightly in the deserted hallway.

"Cass's birthday party," she replies, handing me a trash bag. "Remember?"

"Oh, right," I say, holding the bag open for her. She told me this morning in the amphitheater, but her voice was just white noise as I replayed the sight of Tyler's ass inches away from my face. *Ugh*. I hate Cassandra, and I thought Fabiola did too. "Can't you just, like, disown her?"

Fabiola begins tossing math tests and graded essays into the trash bag. "Believe me, I've thought about it, but I've come to the mature conclusion that even Geminis deserve love." She pauses. "In some cases."

I sigh and lean against the wall of gray-blue lockers.

"You can come, you know," Fabiola says. "Cass asks about you all the time."

She's now tossing an occasional package of rotten food out of her locker, and I'm trying not to gag for two reasons.

"Thanks for the invite, but the last time I went to one of her parties, she grinded on me so aggressively it hurt to pee the next day."

I look at Fabiola for a reaction, but she's too busy unfolding one of those carefully origamied love notes that only girls know how to make. She spreads the paper on the locker beside hers and starts smoothing it out.

I sigh again. "Late bus it is. Maybe I'll get to sit next to the guys who beat up Arturo. I can pull off a gap, right?"

"Stop being dramatic, Quique. No one knows you're into dudes besides me and you."

My eyes dart up and down the hallway, but there's not a soul in sight. I already knew that would be the case for two reasons: One, every year Fabiola's the only person who waits until the last possible second to empty out her locker, and two, she never would have said that if the coast weren't clear. But I still had to check.

"Yeah, but what if someone starts talking to me about Jason Momoa or Oscar Isaac and I get a boner and they see it and—"

She's not listening to me. She's reading the love letter. Or *lust* letter, rather, if it's from who I think it is.

"God," she says when she's finished. "I love the stuff you find once the school year's over. Look." She hands me the note and takes the trash bag from me. It's from Mariana, of course.

"Wow," I say when I'm done reading, "this is extremely graphic."

"I know," Fabiola says proudly.

I try to fold the note back into its original heart shape, but after several unsuccessful attempts, Fabiola takes it from me, does the job in two seconds flat, and puts it in her pocket. Then out comes her phone. She taps a couple times with her thumb and starts scrolling.

"How are your admirers?" I ask.

"You mean my *Faniolas*?"

"I've asked you so many times not to call them that."

"They're great. And growing faster than a middle school kid's pubes."

"Why must you—"

"I've gained almost a hundred followers since this morning when I slam-dunked on a Republican congressman."

My best friend is kind of a big deal when it comes to social media. She posts everything from political opinions to astrology memes to thirst traps to comments on her celebrity crushes' thirst traps to analysis of her favorite shows to thoughts on the Afro-Latina experience, and has gained an almost cult following along the way. One time she posted a video of us together with the caption *Me and the baby daddy*, and I started getting vaguely threatening DMs from hot girls with septum piercings.

"Can you hang out on Sunday?" I ask. "Or are your stalkers throwing you a virtual end-of-the-year party?"

"I gave them the Sabbath off," she says without looking up from her phone. "What do you wanna do?"

"What we usually do, I guess."

"Mall it is. I see you're not really taking my advice from this morning to heart."

"Well, it's just that . . . moving on from"—I glance up and down the hallway—"Saleem seems like more work than, like, actually telling him."

Fabiola slowly looks up from her phone. "You're gonna tell him?"

"Uh . . . I didn't say *that*. I—"

"Quique, I know what you're doing. You're gonna use a bunch of specious reasoning—"

"Specious, good word."

"—to somehow logic yourself out of pursuing anyone. But I won't allow it. This is your summer. This is your chance to figure your romantic life out. Whichever route you take, I'll support you." She puts her hand on my shoulder and looks me deep in the eye. "But you have to stop being a pussy."

I snort. "You're right."

"I always am."

"But isn't saying it that way internalized misogyny? Even though a vagina does not a woman make?"

"We both know it is. Which is why I feel comfortable saying it."

"Like how I call things gay in a derogatory way because we both know that queer stuff is better?"

"Exactly." She puts her phone back in her pocket and resumes trashing stuff. "Don't you have to clean out your locker?"

"Already did." I stop myself from adding, *Like everyone else . . .*

"Okay then can you do me a huge favor and take this?"

Fabiola pulls a bright orange precalc book out of her locker, unleashing a waterfall of papers, pencils, and other miscellaneous school supplies onto the floor, and hands it to me.

"But I might miss the b—"

"You'll make it! Just hustle. Here, actually, can you take these, too?"

She starts piling textbooks into my arms, and I start cataloging all the reasons I love her to keep from growling at her like the Rottweiler that lives across the street from me.

I let out a growl after I've dumped all of the textbooks into the outside book return. Our librarian must have been in a bigger hurry than I am because the library was dark and locked when I got here.

I turn around, about to jog to the bus stop, in this heat, because of Fabiola, when I bump into someone—an extremely solid someone—and lose my balance.

Tyler grabs my arms and steadies me.

"Long time no see, 'Rique!"

"Heyyyy."

Apparently, that's all I'm able to say around hot guys.

"Whatchu up to?" Tyler asks.

He's still holding me, which is highly unnecessary given that I righted myself seconds ago.

"Droppin' off some books for Fabiola at the last minute."

He shakes his head and smiles. "Headass."

It's easy to cringe (and I do) but only slightly because I'm distracted by his face. It's like the mismatch of his words and his . . . *self* is swallowed up by his dimples.

"Gotta love her though," he adds.

"Yeah . . ."

I wonder if he's into Fabiola. And by that I mean I wonder if he's into me. Sure, he could like us both—there's a couple in my grade that's been going out since middle school, and every time I see them making out between classes, my first thought is *Both*—but it's entirely possible that he's only into Fabiola and being nice to me to get to her.

"I really need to catch the bus," I say.

"Oh." Tyler lets go of me. "I'd totally give you a ride, but I'm on my way to the gym to meet up with the team and—"

"Totally cool," I say, interrupting him. Normally I'd be down to talk and try to get him to laugh at something stupid, but the Fabiola thing is throwing me. Plus, I really don't want to miss this bus. If I do, I'll be stuck walking home, roasting in the disgustingly hot Southern California sun. "But I, uh, gotta go."

"Aight. See ya, 'Rique."

"See ya, Tyler."

As I speed-walk away, I think about what it was like to be in Tyler's strong grip, and then I'm thinking about what he wrote in my yearbook, and that leads to thinking about what that kid said before the bell rang. And Oscar Wilde in prison. And Arturo and his missing tooth. And the kids I've read about in books who are forced to go to "pray away the gay" camps. If my parents found out about me, they would never send me to one of those—and for that I'm grateful—but if there were a cheap, painless, guaranteed "cure," I know they'd have no problem putting up the money for it. My mom would gladly pick up some extra shifts at CVS to pay for "Gay Be Gone" or "Queer Remover" or "Bye-Bye Bi" or whatever they'd call it. My dad would be okay with smiling extra wide at the white guy with the BMW to get a bigger tip at the car wash if it meant having a normal son.

When I reach the parking lot at the front of the school, the bus stop is in sight. All I have to do is walk around one side of the parking lot and I'm there. I check the time and find that I have a few minutes to spare, so I wipe sweat off my forehead, slow my pace, and try to will myself to stop sweating.

I'm glad the school's a ghost town. No one sticks around for even a second after the bell's rung on the last day of school except for me, Fabiola, and the basketball team, apparently.

Wait. Add to that list the guy standing between me and the bus stop, pulling a bottle of water out of a vending machine. *Who is that?*

I shield my eyes from the sun to get a better view, but his back is turned, and I can't see his face. Still, there's something intimately familiar about the shape of him, and even before he turns around, I know who he is. I'm surprised it took me so long to figure out.

Our eyes meet, and it's like a second sun has descended to Earth and is shining in front of me.

"Saleem!"

I can't keep the pure joy out of my voice, and the way he smiles as a response to it makes me smile. And this whole domino setup of happiness terrifies me because it all but confirms that trying to get over him will be a futile effort.

"Quique!" he says.

I stop a platonic distance away from him. Even though I'd love to, we don't hug or touch in any way. I saw him too recently for that. Despite how expertly and easily his entire being cracks though my hard shell, burrowing into the softest part of me, I have to pretend seeing him is an everyday occurrence. Which, yeah, it technically is during the school year, but I'll never get used to it.

"Water?" he asks, offering me the unopened bottle in his hand. It's tantalizingly coated in condensation, but even I'm not selfish enough to say yes.

"Uh, no thanks." He's finally able to drink water while the sun's out, and the first thing he does is offer it to me? "What are you doing here?"

"Waiting for my parents and Aya. We're going to my mom's best friend's house to celebrate Eid. You're welcome to join us."

He smiles at me, and I have to avert my eyes.

"I can't," I lie.

Ever since I started high school almost three years ago and my yearning for Saleem reached a newly urgent high, I've tried really hard to avoid spending more time than necessary with his parents. So far it's going well, with the thirty-second *Hi/ Hello/How's school?/How's work?* convos we have whenever we see each other, but I have to keep things this way because I'm petrified by the thought of them figuring out I'm lusting after their son.

"Oh," he says, "you have plans?"

I clear my throat. "Yeah. I, uh, I'm gonna go see a movie with my parents."

"I see." He uncaps his water and takes a drink. "How have you been?"

There are very few people in my life who ask that question and genuinely want to hear the answer to it—Saleem being one of them—but while I very much appreciate his sincerity, I am obligated to give him shit for asking it a few hours after we last saw each other.

"You mean how've I been since first period?" I ask.

Since Saleem's in all the smart classes, our schedules don't really line up, not even for lunch. I see him for an hour at the beginning of the day for Music Appreciation class, and it sucks. It feels like I last saw him a lifetime ago, but I can't tell him that. Instead, I have to pretend no time's passed at all.

"Well, yes, I guess." Saleem looks down and clears his throat, adorably flustered. "Your, um, mood can change pretty quickly, though, right?"

He looks up into my eyes, and I feel the familiar urge to reveal myself to him. Over three years ago, when I saw him in that eighth-grade classroom for the first time, my pubescent heart nearly broke for longing. He had (and obviously still has) the most beautiful eyes I've ever seen. They're honey colored, almost yellow, paler than his brown skin, and bright enough to light a fire in me that to this day has never died.

I want to tell him all of this. But I don't. The last time I gave in to that urge to confide in him, which was at the end of last semester during finals, I told him about The Breakdown, how I went a little, kind of, maybe, really insane and had to see a shrink for a while. I wasn't planning on telling him—or anyone other than my parents and Luciana, my therapist—but I didn't really have a choice after I sort of lost my shit at a math problem.

We had been studying in the library for our respective math finals—calc for him and precalc for me—when I reached a problem that I couldn't figure out for the life of me. I tried and tried, getting a different answer every time, but none of my solutions matched the one in the back of the book.

"Are you okay?" Saleem asked.

I looked up from my notebook and found him watching me, his pencil long abandoned. For a second I was confused, semi-terrified that he could read my thoughts and had been able to hear all the profanities I had hurled at my unsolvable problem, but then I realized, as I often do, that I had been expressing my inner turmoil externally without knowing it. My hand was clamped around my pencil so tightly it was a miracle it hadn't snapped in half, my jaw had been clenched so hard my teeth were starting to hurt, and I was inhaling and exhaling in ragged breaths. Saleem couldn't tell, but my heart was also beating way faster than normal. I was reminded of how I felt the day of The Breakdown.

"I, uh . . ." I didn't know what to say—I was definitely against telling him the truth—but his face said, *You can trust me*. So I did. When I was finished, I wondered if he would judge me, stop talking to me because I was crazy. Maybe part of me hoped he would, so my feelings for him could wither away and die. But he didn't. Instead, he leaned over and patiently explained where I was going wrong. When he was done, he looked at me with concern, and despite feeling relieved, I also felt incredibly embarrassed.

And it's that same concern I see in his eyes right now. He worries about me, and I'm touched. But I'm okay. I'm—

"I'm fine," I say.

He nods. "Good."

"And you?"

"Good. Aya drove me to school this morning. It's weird, but I always forget that she's on my side. It's easy for me to think that she's outshining me in some way that makes me invisible in comparison, but she's my sister, you know? We have so many inside jokes from growing up together, like how I thought the lyric in that one Green Day song was 'Sometimes I wish a mother bear will find me' instead of 'Sometimes I wish someone out there will find me.'" He laughs, and I do too. "She's one of my favorite people."

I clear my throat aggressively, and he smiles.

"And so are you, Quique."

"I wasn't fishing for that at all, Saleem." We smile, our eyes holding on to each other, and I think, *It's not* impossible *that he could like me, right?* I mean, we have fun together, we talk about serious stuff sometimes. I can't be 100 percent sure about his feelings. "You excited about New Jersey?"

Every year, once classes are over, Saleem and his family fly across the country to visit his mom's side of the family. Aya would have taken a bus or something and met them there, but she wanted to be in SoCal for Eid this year.

"Uh . . . yes," Saleem says. "I am."

"At least try to sound convincing."

He laughs. "Well, uh, it's probably going to be a little awkward."

"Why?"

"My aunt thinks one of my cousin's friends is quote, unquote 'perfect wife material.'"

I look down at my stomach because the sensation of being stabbed was so visceral, I have to make sure Saleem isn't actually twisting a knife in me as we speak. Nope. No knife.

I look up. "That *is* awkward," I manage to say.

"Yes, but she's great, though. I've met her." He adjusts his backpack straps. "Hey, um, if you can't make it to Eid, do you want to come over later and swim?"

I want to. I want to so badly. But won't that just make this harder?

"I, uh, I don't think I can."

"Oh, okay."

"Did you, uh, get your summer reading list?" I ask, knowing it's the best way to change the subject.

"Yes, I did, and I was surprised to see . . ."

And then he's off ranting about books, how he's already read half the list, how some of the novels are outdated and racist, how he wishes he could come up with his own curriculum. I'm in the middle of responding to that (by, of course, calling him a nerd and then mentioning how excited I am to steal all of his insights and say them in class so that I look smart) when my focus is momentarily pulled by the arrival of the late bus. I finish talking as it pulls up to the curb and stops, but I come to the realization that I'm not going to take it.

I know I have to move on from Saleem, but if this conversation is the last one I can have with him while pretending he could one day be mine, then I can allow myself this much.

I take my eyes off the bus and instead look at Saleem's mouth, where his words are spilling out like coins from a slot machine. A minute later, I'm only partially aware of the bus driving away in my peripheral vision, not feeling even an ounce of doubt about whether or not I made the right decision.

CHAPTER FIVE

I am in Manny Zuniga's car right now. Manny Zuniga is driving me home. There is a car, that Manny Zuniga is driving, to my home, with me in it.

And I'm not freaking out at all.

Minutes ago, as I began my walk home, having just said goodbye to Saleem and the last shred of hope I had for the two of us ever being together, Manny pulled up and asked me if I needed a ride, which I took as an (incredibly sudden) sign that moving on is what I'm supposed to do. And guess what? I totally played it cool. I didn't say, "Heyyyy," like an idiot. Why would I? When I'm with Manny, I'm a typical seventeen-year-old Mexican dude from East LA—I like girls and tacos. I like bottling up my emotions. I like imagining Manny pulling over so he can put his thick lips on every square inch of my skin. . . .

Okay, maybe I'm not so typical.

I stare out the passenger window of his freshly washed Mustang in an attempt to look casual, breathing in the scent of his cologne and watching as the manicured green lawns of the suburb where we go to school gradually transition into the shaggy, yellow lawns that signal the beginnings of East LA. Until I'm not.

Manny fiddles with the radio, skipping over some pop and

rock stations until he settles on the Latino one that plays reg-gaeton, not banda. It's only when he glances over at me that I realize I've been staring at him. In response, I snap my neck forward, blood warming my cheeks. I pretend to study a black plastic bag in the middle of the street, and out of the corner of my eye I swear I can see him smiling.

"I thought that was a dead cat for a second," I say.

"That woulda sucked," he says.

I only nod in reply.

There's a certain persona I adopt when talking to guys like Manny. The less you say the better, the less you react the better. See, Manny's basically the cholo-iest non-cholo in existence. Though we're both essentially from the same neighborhood, our lives could not be more different. His family, his friends, his home. They're all . . . *rougher* than mine. Instead of yellow lawns and faded mailboxes, his block has "Beware of Dog" signs and wrought iron gates.

So I don't say too much. I don't bring up the books I'm reading or the shows I watch. But I do hold my chin up higher and puff my chest out a little. It's not an act; it's just how you gotta be sometimes. This is me with Manny.

Not that he's ever made me feel like I can't be my actual self around him. For almost eleven years, we've had an easy, casual acquaintanceship, which happens, I guess, when you've gone to all of the same schools together since the first grade. We've never hung out outside of a classroom, but today changed that. Could today really be the start of a whole new kind of summer?

"You got any plans for the break?" I ask when I feel that

enough time has elapsed for me to still appear nonchalant.

Manny shrugs. "Getting fucked up with my cousins."

That makes sense based on my experience with Manny and his family. I went to his thirteenth birthday party and ended up being one of only three or four seventh graders attending (Manny, like me, mostly keeps to himself). His birthday was mostly an excuse for his older cousins to drink until they couldn't walk. Manny's dad is out of the picture and his mom's always working, so he and his cousins are kind of their own family, a pack. I wonder how they'd react if Manny were queer. Would they kick him out? Disown him?

"You?" he asks, glancing over at me.

I try to keep my voice steady. And deep. "Not much. Same thing as always: chillin' at home."

And by "chillin'" I of course mean doing my best to avoid another full-fledged mental breakdown like the one I had the summer after eighth grade, the one that only my parents and Saleem know about. For the past two summers, I've done so effectively, with minor exceptions.

"Left here," I say as we pass a cluster of beige apartment buildings.

He turns without acknowledging my direction or using his blinker.

"We're close, Quique," he says, meaning we don't live that far away from each other.

"Yup."

Manny may have just figured this out, but I've known this ever since the birthday party.

Without realizing it, I put my eyes back on him. I love how

he looks when he's driving: one hand on the wheel, so casual, so cool. With the AC blasting, his shiny, black hair blows in the wind. My eyes move lower, taking in his long, dark eyelashes and then his crisp, white T-shirt, which contrasts nicely with the cinnamon skin of his neck and arms. Underneath the shirt, I suspect, is at least one secret tattoo, something I'd very much like to see.

Suddenly, the car jerks to a complete stop, and I'm thrown forward. Before I can even process what's going on, Manny throws his arm out against my chest and pushes me back.

"You okay?" he asks.

"Uh . . ."

My mouth goes dry as I realize I could have smashed my head against the leather dashboard. I wouldn't have died, but it definitely could have been bad. A gash on the forehead or a broken nose or both. Definitely a lot of blood. Which isn't sexy at all. Well, scars might be. . . .

"Yeah, I'm fine."

We both take a moment to breathe before he removes his arm.

"What happened?" I ask.

He doesn't answer, just points his chin out the windshield.

Sitting in the middle of the road is a small black cat. It watches us with a look of condescending disinterest, like it wasn't a second away from being a furry smear on the asphalt.

I turn to Manny, who turns to me, and we laugh.

"Definitely not a trash bag," I say.

Manny shakes his head.

"Ey, get out the way!" he yells out the window.

The cat flicks an ear but otherwise doesn't move.

Manny makes a point of sighing loudly before he gets out of the car. I watch as he walks over to the cat (it still doesn't move a whisker), picks it up, and carries it over to the sidewalk. After he puts it down, he jogs back to the car and we're on our way again.

I want to tell him what I'm thinking, but that would be wildly inappropriate. The truth is I've always associated Manny with a cat. Not a *cat* cat, like the one we almost hit, but a big cat. A lion or a tiger or a jaguar or a leopard. It's all because of this one particular look he gives me every time I see him. It's a hungry look that I don't think he's aware of. It makes me feel like that massive chunk of meat mounted on a vertical rotisserie that taco guys shave to make tacos al pastor.

Manny's giving me the look now, and I wonder if he can tell that I like it.

"Right here," I say as we pass by my house. My neighbor's Rottweiler announces our arrival.

Manny stops the car and puts it in park. The fact that he didn't pull over to the curb displays a confidence that I'll never for the life of me understand. *Anyone driving down this street can go around me*, he must be thinking, *I'm not moving.*

I'm not gonna lie, it's a turn-on.

"Your place is nice," Manny says.

"Thanks," I say.

Objectively, I guess it's true. A cute white and avocado-green one-story with a low-key charm. But I only see the flaws. Outside, it's the grass, which my dad lovingly refers to as our "hay." Inside, it's the one bathroom that my parents and I fight over in the morning when I have school. Manny doesn't know about the latter, and he must be ignoring the former.

"So . . ." I don't know what to say, but I don't want to get out of the car. Away from school, with my parents still at work, and no one else around, things can happen. "I'll . . . see you around?"

"Bet."

He holds out his fist, so I bump it. And that's it. No meaningful look or promising words. Just a mashing of our knuckles, the indisputably least sexy parts of the human body.

As soon as I'm out of the car, the sun's on me like it's been lying in wait. Walking to the front door, I pray that Manny can't see the sweat already pooling on my lower back. At the same time I fit my key into the lock, I turn around to look at him one last time. He's already driving off, and I feel stupid for not inviting him in or asking him to hang out some other time.

Once inside, I hang my keys up. Then I walk over to the counter and start leafing through the mail. I don't really have a reason for doing so—no one but my grandma sends me stuff in the mail, and Easter (*real* Easter, not that "pagan rabbit mierda") has already passed—but that doesn't stop me. For some reason I'm always holding out hope that I'll receive a letter that changes my life for the better. A million-dollar check from a distant dead relative wouldn't be too shabby. But of course there are only bills in the pile, so I head to my room.

My room's the hottest in the house because why would it not be. In a vain effort to combat the sunlight slicing through the thin curtains covering the window above my bed, I turn on the ceiling fan and the box fan that sits on the sand-colored carpet. All the quizzes, essays, and notes from this past year that have accumulated on the floor, under my bed, and on top of my dresser start flying around the room. I'm about to do something about that when my phone rings. I immediately know it's Fabiola because she's the only person I know who calls without warning, or at all. She says texting inhibits her "undeniable charisma and charm."

"Hello?" I say, dropping my backpack to the floor.

"Are the 'shrooms I took last week finally kicking in, or did I really see you getting into Manny Zuniga's car as I left school?"

I can hear music in the background. She must have just gotten to Cassandra's party.

"The latter," I reply, closing my door.

"Wow. I can't take you home one day, and you just jump into a car with someone else?"

I laugh and walk over to my bed. "I'm always a slut for a ride home, what can I say?"

"So." Her tone is semiserious. My heart rate instantly sky-rockets. "I guess we're going with Operation Not-Saleem."

"Uh . . ." I picture Saleem's face, the light in his eyes, his smile, and I almost say no. But then I picture him with his "wife," and soon enough I'm seeing them ten years older with cute little Arab babies in their arms. "Yes. Yes, we are."

"Okay then. I hope you set things up nicely with Manny."

"I don't think I did," I say, pushing a pile of clothes to one side.

"What happened?"

"I got in his car, he drove, we almost killed a cat, we got

to my place, we fist-bumped goodbye, and that was it."

"I really hope you're holding out on me, Quique. I tell you everything."

"I know," I say, sitting. "Too much, actually. But I assure you, I'm not."

"Disappointing. He gave you a ride. You could at least return the fav—"

"I don't know if he's into me."

"Unlike Tyler."

"How do you know Tyler likes me?"

"Didn't he write in your yearbook that he wanted to 'loosen' you up, or something equally homoerotic?"

After Tyler signed my yearbook a week ago, I immediately showed it to Fabiola, so we could dissect it to death.

"I mean, yeah," I admit, "but you know he didn't mean it like that."

"Ugh. You're exhausting. Why do I care more about this than you do?"

"That's not true. I'm all in on this plan, I swear."

"Prove it."

"I need to do some more recon. Manny probably only gave me a ride because he felt bad for me because you *abandoned* me."

"Que dramático."

"And Tyler's always friendly. Maybe he was just maintaining his reputation as everyone's bro. I mean what would we even do together?"

"Literally exactly what he said. First, you two would play with each other—"

"Please don't say that."

"*Basketball*, sweetie. He'd make you play a game with him and his friends where the two of you are on the same team, so he can volunteer to be skins. And then every time he'd make a shot, the two of you would give each other a sweaty chest bump and—"

"You've thought about this a lot."

"I have."

"As lovely as this conversation is," I begin, kicking off my shoes, "I'm gonna have to let you go. I have something to do."

"Yourself. You have yourself to do. Because you spent the past ten minutes in a confined space with Manny, and he most likely touched you in some innocuous way that sent your cute, li'l libido reeling, and now you have to let some of that pent-up energy out before you do something you might regret. Like . . . doing something you won't regret."

"Enjoy the party, Fabiola."

"We'll plot on Sunday, sl—"

I hang up before she can finish. I hate that she's right. But I also love how well she knows me. At least, I love how well she knows this side of me, the one I don't share with anyone else. I should probably open up to her about the mental stuff sooner rather than later, but I can never bring myself to do it. It's not that I don't think she'd understand. It's that . . . she's the one person who can always make me smile no matter what, and if she knew how weird my brain got sometimes, she'd change how she treated me. She'd start overthinking everything she said to me, and the last thing I want is a best friend who censors herself because she thinks I'm "delicate" or whatever.

I sigh and put my phone on my nightstand. Right now I only have one task to accomplish to clear my head.

My mom calls it "playing with yourself," which is indisputably the worst name for it. I'd call it "jacking off" if I didn't associate that nomenclature with white guys who drink Monster and wear weed-embroidered socks. "Beating your meat" would be a front-runner if sexual euphemisms implying violence didn't make me uncomfortable. "Masturbating" is too standard. "Choking the chicken" and "spanking the monkey" are for middle school kids.

I guess I don't call it anything. I just make a dry fist around my dick and go up and down until every muscle in my body tenses, then untenses, and I have to get up and dispose of the evidence. It's mechanical, as "scratching an itch" as you can get. I try not to think of anything as I jerk off (*eh*), keeping it purely physical, because that's when I feel the least shame. According to a Bible verse my grandma threw around when I was growing up, "touching yourself" (*God no*) is a sin.

I lie on my unmade bed, still fully clothed, daring not to move because of the stifling heat, and stare up at the popcorn ceiling, thinking about the implications of my sexuality, which only revealed itself to me in full when puberty arrived. I'd get my ass kicked at school for sure if someone found out I like guys. My family would pretend everything is okay, but they'd cry in private and ask God to rescind what is obviously a cruel punishment being inflicted upon them. Imagine the shame of having a queer son or grandson or second cousin once removed. But that's not the only thought that keeps me up at night. My fear is I'll never know what it's like to kiss a dude.

And I don't know why a kiss is such a big deal, but it is. I get the balloon sensation, and it won't go away until . . . up and down, up and down, rinse and repeat.

But I guess if I'm being completely honest, the balloon feeling doesn't always go away when I take care of the physical part. No matter how many times I . . . clear my head (*that one's not so bad*), I can't erase the longing Saleem elicits from me. And I need to stop thinking about him.

I drift back to Manny's sudden stop and relive it so vividly I can *feel* his arm across my chest, strong and protective. What would have happened if, after that, when he tried retracting it, I had reached out and held him, instead of letting him go? Would I have seen that hungry look in his beautiful brown eyes? What if I had pulled him toward me, close enough that I could feel his hot breath on my face, close enough that I could touch his pillowy lips with mine?

This feels real.

Could that really happen?

Not just with Manny. With Tyler? Or Ziggy? Or would they back away, shocked by what I just did. Would they cuss at me? Hit me? Sound the gay panic alarm? Am I willing to risk having that happen?

It would be so much easier not to feel anything for anyone at all. The problem is I feel so much.

CHAPTER SIX

Saturday morning, I wake up thinking about the truth of the words "easier said than done." My "get over Saleem" initiative is going to force me to expose what I've kept hidden for years, but it's so hard to even think about shaking off the resolve I've had for so long: go with what's comfortable, stick with what's safe, and don't disrupt the lives of the people who care about you because they deserve peace. If I make a move on a guy, I'm not the only one who'd feel the effects of that.

I forcefully push these thoughts to the back of my mind, so I can clear my head, mentally and physically. I keep my eyes closed tightly the entire time, my mind as blank as possible, and it's over before I know it. Then I hop in the shower to wash all the sticky off me (dried sweat, not what you're thinking).

I'm giving myself until Monday to start working on my plan, so after I get dressed, I pour myself a bowl of cereal and make my way over to the living room to eat it. I flip through channels until I land on one of those crime shows where women kill their husbands. It's all my mom watches these days, which makes my dad a bit nervous, but I'm pretty sure she doesn't want to kill him.

My parents aren't the most compatible couple at times— they once fought for an hour about who was going to be the designated driver at my cousin Julio's graduation party—but when they're happy, they're *really* happy. I don't quite believe in the "two halves of a whole" idea of soul mates, but they've shown me that it's possible to find someone who appreciates your own particular brand of weird. My mom cries from laughing every time my dad scrunches up his mouth and does this nasally voice that's supposed to be an imitation of their old geometry teacher, and my dad never fails to stare at my mom with a pervy admiration every time she takes a shot and makes it look like she's tossing back water.

After half an episode, I get a text from Saleem telling me he's arrived in Jersey. He and his family left early this morning. I tell him to have a *gr8 trip* and push my phone in between the couch cushions, so I won't be tempted to continue the conversation. That's when my mom enters the room, yawning. Her hair's a mess, and she hasn't completely opened her left eye yet. She always looks like this at eleven a.m. on weekends.

"Morning, sunshine," I say.

"Morning, brat," she says. "Want chorizo?"

"Sure."

"Then go make some."

I smile. "Do you really want to eat my version of chorizo con huevos again?"

The three of us were chomping down on eggshells every other bite the last time I made breakfast.

She rubs her eyes. "You make a good point. I'll make it, but get your bowl off my couch."

"It's empty."

"Don't care."

My parents and I eat together, and by that I mean the three of us sit on the couch and watch TV, shoveling food into our mouths. During a commercial break, my dad briefly brings up the possibility of going to Vegas for our family vacation, but I know it probably won't happen. We haven't done that since the summer after seventh grade because my dad's a coin-happy gambler and that meant I was always stuck watching my mom suck down three-foot-tall piña coladas at Caesars Palace. Before yesterday, I didn't expect anything from my summers. The best I could have hoped for was a party or two before the summer ended. Maybe an amusement park visit. But given my and Fabiola's vow, something life-changing has to happen, right? There's no way she's letting me back out. I mean I pinkie swore!

Speaking of the devil, I get a message from her in all caps. The only time I get texts from her is when the topic is queer related and she knows I'm with my parents. I'm about to reply to it when my mom looks over at me and asks, "Who's that?"

"Fabiola."

My parents share a look, the one I see every time I bring her up. It says, *We know where this is headed!*

"How is she?" my mom asks.

The truth: She's freaking out because "*MOLLY HASN'T REPLIED TO MY LAST TEXT (YES WE'VE MOVED ON TO TEXTING SHE GAVE ME HER NUMBER LAST NIGHT) AND ITS BEEN HOURS AND SHE HAS HER READ RECEIPTS ON SO I KNOW SHE SAW IT!!!!!!*"

My lie: "Good, Mom. She says hi." I look at my dad. "To both of you."

"Well, tell her I say hi back," my mom says.

My dad just puts his hand up, meaning, *Me too.*

After I text Fabiola back (*Calm down. She'll message back*) and my mom clears the dishes and gets ready, I join her on her weekly Target trip. When we get to the store, we split up at the dollar section because that woman can be there for hours.

I make my way to Electronics, more specifically the music section. Most people would say CDs are obsolete, but I love 'em anyway. Nothing beats the physical presence of music in my hands. Plus, my mom's car is so old it only has a CD player.

I pick up a random album and look at the cover art: a jacked white guy sitting on a tractor with a guitar resting on his lap. I'm torn because on one hand he looks like he's the team captain of the Klan's softball team, but on the other? Save a horse ride a—

"Finding everything okay?"

I slam the CD back on the shelf and whip around to find a tall Target worker standing next to me, a wide smile on his face.

"Oh my God," I say, my stomach flipping when I recognize him. "Arturo?"

What is he doing here?

"Hey, Enrique."

"Since when do you work here?"

"I just started actually. Gotta do somethin' in between graduation and college."

I nod, my mouth hanging open. What do I say? The last time I talked to him I made a complete ass out of myself. I can't do that again. But my brain is blank and this silence is deafening. I look at his smiling face and say the first thing that comes to mind.

"Your, um, your tooth grew back."

"What?" he says in disbelief.

Without thinking, I point to my own upper canine as an explanation.

"Teeth don't . . . grow back," he says.

"I know," I say, suddenly aware of what I said. "I just . . . I don't know. Please ignore the words coming out of my mouth."

He shakes his head, laughing. I'm lucky he finds me funny instead of infuriatingly stupid, which is how I find me right now.

"Dentist put in an implant a while back," he says. "The only problem is it's so much whiter than the rest of my teeth."

He pulls back his lip to prove his point, and I laugh.

"Look, I'm really sorry I keep saying the wrong things. I don't know why I—"

"It's okay, Enrique. I know you don't mean any harm. You know, I've always been disappointed by the fact that we didn't talk all that much when we were in school together."

"Yeah?"

He nods.

Something about the way he's looking at me and what he's said makes an alarm go off in my head, one that screams, *He knows he knows he knows!* But do I need to be worried about coming up on his gaydar? He of all people wouldn't out me, and it would be a huge relief to talk to someone other than Fabiola about my "boy problems."

"I always wished we were friends too," I say. "Especially now because I happen to be going through . . . some stuff at the moment. Stuff you might know a lot about."

"What kinda stuff?"

"Well . . ." How do I say this so that he doesn't assume I'm hitting on him? As cute as Arturo is with his lankiness and his wavy white-boy hair, I don't find him attractive. I turn to the CDs. "Let's say that ever since I was little I've listened to female artists. But then when I was thirteen or so, I started realizing that I wanted to listen to male artists, too. And now I know I like all singers, but lately I've been incredibly drawn to one artist who . . . sings in Arabic. But he's . . . streaming only."

I turn to Arturo, who looks like he's trying to multiply 9,293 by 12,566 in his head.

"Does that make sense?"

"I think so," Arturo says.

"So since his music is streaming only, I've been eyeing some other male artists." I motion to the CDs, my hand ending up right in front of tractor guy.

"Really? Even Captain Confederate?"

I snort. "What?"

Arturo points to the CD. "I call this guy Captain Confederate because he looks like Captain America if he were pro-slavery."

"That's hilarious."

"Thanks. Anyway, how's the . . . listening going?"

"Okay. I mean, the albums are great—and Fabiola's doing her best to get me to blow out my speakers with them—but what if I don't get over the first album?"

Arturo nods. "First of all, I miss Fabiola so much. She's the best. Second, this metaphor is getting way out of hand.

And third . . . if you can't be with the first guy, then there's no shame in getting to know the other guys. I mean, if anything you get to learn stuff about yourself and what you want from other people."

"Whoa, whoa, whoa. Who said anything about dating guys?"

We both laugh. "Right, well, I'll just say it worked for me. When I first agreed to go out with Guillermo, I didn't think anything would come of it, but then . . . he surprised me. Sometimes people surprise you."

"And Guillermo is your boyfriend?"

"Yup."

"Huh, a relationship. I should get me one of those."

Arturo smiles. "I mean, what's stopping you from trying?"

"You done, Quique?"

I rip my eyes away from Arturo and find my mom standing at the end of the aisle, a mountain of useless tchotchkes in her cart.

"Yeah, I'm coming!" I turn back to Arturo. "Maybe I'll surprise myself."

"I hope you do."

I practically jog over to my mom.

"What was that about?" she asks, pushing the cart forward.

"He thought I was shoplifting."

"I taught you better than to get caught," she says without missing a beat.

After my dad and I put away the groceries and my mom puts them away again (this time in their *proper* places), we gather on the couch to watch TV. Yes, that is all we do together. This time, though, we're watching the news.

"Oh my God." My mom sighs. "Saturdays disappear faster than your father's Coronas."

I laugh, and my dad tips the bottle currently in his hand at her.

She works Sundays, so her Saturdays are, well, Sundays.

"I have to go get my clothes ready."

She gets up and walks to her bedroom, and for some reason the silence that follows is more pronounced than the one a minute ago when the three of us were in the room not saying anything. I love my dad, I do, and I know he loves me. But I'm not gonna lie, there's always been a distance between us.

I watch him out of the corner of my eye, looking for any sign that he feels it too, but he just sits there like always. Drinking his beer. Staring at the TV.

It didn't help when I had The Breakdown. Telling my parents that I had to go to the doctor even though I hadn't, like, cut myself with a knife or gotten hit by a car or something was super hard. They took me because they're good parents, but ever since then, the wall I felt when I was younger only grew.

" . . . sending it over to Dante Kruger for the sports report," says the older male anchor.

Dante, my love. I could listen to him go on forever about sports stuff I don't understand because all I'm doing is staring at his mouth and his wide shoulders and his cro—oh no. Here comes this week's episode of "Pretend Not to Be Out of Breath Because There's a Hot Guy on TV and Your Dad Is Sitting Next to You."

"Psh," my dad sneers. "He's full of shit."

I have to stop myself from firing back with something stupid, something like, *Dad, leave my ridiculously buff, ethnically ambiguous husband alone! He looks like all the hottest characters on Shonda Rhimes shows blended together and poured into a thousand-dollar suit!*

That's when my mom reenters the room. She plops down on the couch and takes a deep breath. I put my hand on hers, and she smiles at me.

I hate that she and my dad work on Sundays. How is that at all fair?

If I could make one wish, I know exactly what it would be. I would ask the genie/fairy/leprechaun/unicorn/phoenix/ whatever for a talent or skill that I could use to make enough money to be able to tell my parents to quit their jobs. I constantly imagine what their faces would look like, how fucking happy they'd be. But then I crash back down to reality, and I realize I can't save them.

Not that they expect me to. Ever since they found out I was crazy, they haven't wanted to put any pressure on me whatsoever. Everything I do is "good enough." Even waking up in the mornings is seen as an accomplishment. Which, I guess, sometimes it is. But now I wonder if they've given up on me.

"Thank you, Dante," says the young female anchor. "Coming up next: the tragic story of a nine-year-old boy who committed suicide after coming out to his classmates. After the break."

It's like a giant fist has just slammed into my chest. My heart stalls, and I have to fight for breath.

"Oh my God, that's horrible," my mom says.

My dad just shakes his head.

I nod, when what I really want to do is scream.

Why is the world like this? *How* is the world like this? How is it that humans have created a society that allows a child to come to the conclusion that they would be better off dead than alive because they like the same sex?

"I gotta pee," I say, and before my parents can say anything, I hop off the couch and hurry to the bathroom.

When the door's closed behind me, I inhale as slowly and fully as possible. Then I exhale the same way. I do this for a while until my heart stops hammering in my chest. It's still pounding, but I don't feel like it's going to explode anymore.

I can control myself. I can get over this. I can push down this panicky feeling that makes me feel hot and cold at the same time, push it down until it's buried.

So I do.

And I feel better. Because I feel nothing.

CHAPTER SEVEN

"You're awfully quiet today."

Fabiola stops in front of a cellphone case kiosk, zeroing in on a bedazzled rose gold monstrosity, and I almost crash into her.

"Oh," I say. "Sorry."

"Why?" she asks, staring at the phone case.

"Why am I quiet?"

"Why are you sorry?"

"Oh, uh, I don't know."

When she's done convincing herself not to buy the case, we continue on.

"Are you gonna tell me what's up with you?" she asks.

I sigh. "Just something on the news yesterday. I can't stop thinking about it."

"The gay kid who killed himself?"

"How did you know?"

She gives me a look that says, *Do you really have to ask?*

I take a sip of my Cappuccino Chiller, the coffee-flavored frozen drink we always get at the mall that's approximately 120 percent ice cream. Then I change the subject, though not completely if I think about it long enough.

"You'll never guess who I ran into yesterday at Target."

"Morgan Freeman?"

"What? No. Why would he be—doesn't matter. Arturo Peralta."

Her eyes go wide as she sips her own Cappuccino Chiller. "O-M-G! Arturo! I miss that homo."

"He said he misses you, too."

"Aw."

We walk in silence for a while before I speak again.

"Do you think it's smart for me to pursue guys right now?"

"Well . . ." The serious look on her face quickens my breathing. "No."

"What? Why?"

"Because boys are the worst. If I could choose not to be attracted to them, I would."

I laugh, and my breaths come easier. "I mean—"

"I know what you mean. I don't think it's stupid or wrong to pursue who you're feeling. Are you even into any non-dudes right now?"

"Besides Aja Naomi King, Salma Hayek, or Lucy Liu?"

"You definitely don't have a type. Anyway, yeah."

"Uh . . . no."

"Then you're shit out of luck."

"Yeah . . ."

We stop in front of a clothing store, so Fabiola can stare at something else she'll never buy. It's a low-cut navy blue dress in a window display that I can tell she'd say she "doesn't have the tits for."

"Are you gonna come out to your parents this summer?" she asks, moving on.

There's an Asian family waiting in line for pretzels, all wearing crucifixes—not crosses, *crucifixes*—so I wait until we're far enough away to answer.

"That's part of the plan."

"What plan?"

"Oh, um, the plan for the summer. Bag a dude and come out to people who aren't you."

And tell you about The Breakdown, I add in my head. I also don't mention the "get hot" part of my plan. It's too embarrassing.

Fabiola nods and takes a long pull of her Chiller. "How do you think your parents would react?"

Now it's my turn to windowshop, mostly because I'm avoiding Fabiola's question.

"Quique, you're not a snapback guy and you know it."

I should have known she'd see right through me.

"I could be, though," I say, turning to face her.

"Absolutely not."

"Yeah . . ."

We continue walking.

"I've imagined it a million different ways," I say. "I never know which one's gonna be the closest to reality. What about you?"

"I can't tell them."

"Ever?"

"Maybe. It's funny, I feel like I'm living an entirely different life online and stuff. I can express myself however I want to. I can be thirsty and angry and dumb and funny. I can be me without worrying about what my parents or my aunts or uncles will say. I wish I could be like that all the time."

We reach a dark wooden bench next to a charging station and sit. Fabiola's phone is almost always about to die.

"Me too," I say.

Fabiola takes out her charger and plugs in her phone.

We sit for a while, drinking in silence, until we both finish our Chillers at the exact same moment and toss them into the nearest trash can in a near synchronous motion.

"Which one of your prospects do you like the best?" Fabiola asks.

My first thought is Saleem, but he's not a prospect. "I don't know," I say when the abuela shuffling past us is out of earshot. "They're all hot, but they make me feel good in different ways."

"That's not gonna get complicated."

I smirk.

"Thank God I've only got two things on my mind, and they belong to the same person," Fabiola says.

"Molly's thighs?"

"Molly's thighs."

"I knew it."

"Okay, maybe Ziggy's on my mind too."

"Huh, why?"

"Because he's headed in our direction."

I follow her eyes and find my lanky prospect hopping off the escalator, holding shopping bags in both hands. He hasn't seen us yet.

"I'm gonna throw up," I say. I'm supposed to start Monday. I'm not prepared for this!

"Quique, be cool. You got this."

"Got what?"

My voice is so high-pitched I barely recognize it.

Ziggy still hasn't noticed us, but he's strutting in our direction, presumably to the beat of the song playing on his headphones.

"All you're gonna do," Fabiola says calmly, "is act like a normal human being. Is that too much to ask?"

"Yes."

"Too bad." Her hand shoots into the air, and she starts waving at Ziggy. "Yo, Ziggy!"

He spots us, breaks into a surprised smile, and quickens his pace.

"Showtime, Quique."

Melted ice cream sloshes in my stomach as Ziggy stops in front of us and puts his bags down.

"'Sup, Fabiola!" he says, lowering his headphones onto his neck.

"'Sup, Ziggy!"

He turns to me, and I can hear the faint sounds of Beyoncé coming out of his headphones. "Hey, Enrique!"

"Hey," I say. "I—Wait. Are you listening to 'Baby Boy'?"

"Oh!" He quickly hits a button on the side of his headphones and the music stops. "Yeah, I, uh . . . was."

"You don't have to be embarrassed," Fabiola says. "The five or six joyless people in the world who *don't* listen to Beyoncé should be embarrassed."

Ziggy nods but looks mortified. I try not to think about that time Saleem said he thought Sean Paul was saying "Tortilla," on the track instead of "Dutty, yeah."

"How are you guys?" he asks.

"Good," Fabiola says. "Enjoying our freedom. Right, Quique?"

"Yeeup. Fuck school, am I right?"

"I actually like school," Ziggy says. "I miss it during the summer."

Damn it, I'm already screwing up. Wait, what if I pretend I'm talking to Saleem?

"Fucking nerd," I say.

Ziggy's thick eyebrows shoot up, and his mouth drops. I feel Fabiola stiffen beside me. But then he laughs, and we all relax.

"Guilty as charged," he says.

And suddenly it feels like these balls of energy are pinging back and forth between us, creating an almost tangible friction. A good kind of friction.

"What do you have there?" I point to one of his bags.

"Oh!" He reaches into it and takes out a thick, forest green sweater that has no business being sold during summer in Southern California. "Nice, right?"

"Yeah, it's beautiful," Fabiola says.

"I'm volunteering at my dad's practice this summer," he says. "I want to look professional. And he always keeps the thermostat at a crisp thirty-two degrees."

Ziggy's dad is a doctor, but not just any doctor. He's the Internet's "Hot Doctor." I met him sophomore year when Ziggy and I were lab partners in chemistry and I had to go to his house a couple times to work on stuff together. I was physically unable to speak to Dr. Jackson, despite his being the nicest man I've ever met, so it was no surprise when this past year a picture of him went viral and made him a minor online celebrity.

I glance at the price tag on the sweater and become uncomfortably aware of the fact that despite hanging out at the mall all the time, Fabiola and I never actually buy anything except our four-dollar Cappuccino Chillers.

I push those thoughts to the back of my mind before saying, "You should model it for us."

Ziggy snorts, and I'm able to see a hint of a color change in his cheeks.

"Maybe some other time. Although I did post a photo from the dressing room on my Insta story."

"Hmm," I say, reaching into my pocket and taking out my phone. "I don't think I follow you."

"Oh, word? And why the hell not?"

"I hardly ever use this app," I say clicking on the icon. "But here, follow yourself."

He takes my phone, types a little, taps a few times, and then hands it back to me.

It's open to his profile, but the box below his bio still says "follow" instead of "following."

"I didn't do it myself," he says. "It has to come from you."

I nod and finish the job.

"Done," I say.

We stare at each other until Ziggy says, "Well, I gotta go, but I'll see you two around. Hopefully, not just digitally."

Fabiola and I voice our agreement before he picks up his

bags, dips his head in farewell, and continues past us.

"How do you feel, Quique?" Fabiola asks when it's safe.

Good question.

"I feel . . . not like everything has changed . . . but like something might."

CHAPTER EIGHT

I'm in the middle of a luxurious stretch, about to melt into another couple hours of peaceful slumber, when I suddenly bolt upright, my brain screaming at me that I either slept through my alarm or forgot to set it. It's only as I'm frantically pulling a T-shirt up my leg that I realize it's summer vacation. I groan, toss the shirt aside, and crawl back into bed. Waking up on the first Monday following the end of the school year is always a rough adjustment.

I try my hardest to go back to sleep, but that hope dies at the hands of the adrenaline still coursing through my body as well as the aggressive amount of sunlight pouring into my room. I attempt to fight it by covering my face with my pillow, but I almost end up smothering myself. Admitting defeat, I reach under my bed, grab my yearbook, and head to the living room. Here, the thick floral curtains protect me from the sun.

I place the yearbook on the coffee table and begin to flip through it, scouting for guys with The Look. The Look™ is the almost indescribable quality of a person's face that lets people know they're queer. My main criteria for identifying queer guys might be *Do they look nice?* Because straight boys are not nice. They are not considerate. They don't do anything for you unless they want something.

I grab a Sharpie from the coffee table and start circling all three of the diverse, pants-tightening boys who've been flustering me everywhere they show up. Ziggy's photos come up a couple of times because he's in track and student government. I keep seeing Tyler because he plays football and basketball. Manny's only in here once with his standard portrait, so I flip to that page. Next to his picture I write a note about his lifesaving arm interference. I start doing this for all of my prospects, writing in the margins all the possibly flirtatious things they've done with me. My last entry is my and Ziggy's prolonged eye contact yesterday. The entries aren't exactly smoking guns, but it's not like any of these guys are doing Pride parades anytime soon.

I go to the back of the yearbook to reread the messages they wrote me.

Ziggy's reads:

> *To Enrique,*
> *Another school year, another year of your mem-*
> *orable misadventures. I'll never forget getting*
> *stranded on the roof of H-Building and having*
> *to save your life, helping you put Mr. Stewart's*
> *stapler in Jell-O and receiving my first ever*
> *detention, or "borrowing" that security guard's*
> *golf cart and fleeing the scene after we crashed it.*
> *Thanks for all the teen movie antics.*
> *–Ziggy*

I smile reading it.

After the roof incident, and many other entertaining screw-ups, Ziggy told me that I lived my life like I was the main character in a teenage comedy. If we are indeed in a teen movie, I hope it's a rom-com. If I don't get to kiss him at least once, I think I might die.

Manny's is short, but what it lacks in words, it makes up for in heart.

> *Kiké,*
> *Let me know if anyone ever messes with you I'll*
> *fuck em up.*
> *Manny*

I really enjoy the imagery of it. Like we're at a party and the dude from my English class calls me a fag or something, so Manny lays him out and then tips his head down the street and is like, "Let's go get some tacos, vato." Wait, would he say vato? Vato's what he calls his cousins sometimes. Maybe it would be something more like, "I'm feelin' some al pastor right now. You comin', baby?"

That would be . . . stimulating.

Tyler's message is lengthy, exactly like his you-know-what. He doesn't seem to have any regard for basic grammar, but that means I can easily read it in his voice.

> *To my main man Rique, had an awesome*
> *time with you this year dude don't ever change*

haha. Remember how everyone used to write that in middle school? Anyway it's true man you're the best. The funniest guy I know keep it up. We should chill more outside a school next year play some pickup, smoke a fatty, the usual haha. You always look like you could use some losening up haha. Anyway man I hope you have a great summer (with me in it duh) see ya duuuuuuuuuuuuuuuuude Ty

Like Fabiola said, the "loosening" line sounds pretty homo. But sometimes it's the straightest, most masculine guys who show the most appreciation for other men, something about being secure with themselves and the pedestal they're placed on in society.

I almost close the yearbook but freeze when I think about Saleem's picture. It's not the best photo of him in existence—his curls are kinda flat, and he looks too tired to smile properly— but . . . it's him. So I can stare at it all day. But I won't. Right? There's also the note he wrote me that I haven't read yet. I was too scared it would disappoint me, or worse, that it wouldn't.

I shake my head, and some will to move on that I didn't know was in me forces me to snap the yearbook shut, pick up my phone, and start drafting a message.

As I do so, I think about my two biggest fears. The first is, of course, what if Tyler isn't into me, and I end up outing myself to one of the most well-known guys in school? The second is what if he *is* into me and what if as soon as he pulls his

Dodger Dog dick out of his shorts, a hole opens up in the sky and it starts raining fire?

I hesitate before pressing send.

Hey Tyler, what are you up to today?

Oh my God. Oh my God. Oh my God. I sent it. I sent it. I sent it.

And now there are those three little dots that mean he's typing.

One sec, he writes.

Wow, he actually answered me. Sure, it's not the most promising reply, but it's something. Then I get another text from him, but this time it's in a group message with Fabiola and two other numbers I don't recognize. What the hell?

Sup y'all wanna link up tonight?

Um. That's not a great sign, is it? He probably doesn't want to hang out with me alone. Fuck, this sucks.

But then I think about my conversation with Arturo two days ago. How he said people can surprise you, and the fact that despite this world being a shitty place he's still out there living his life the way he wants to. So I begin typing out a message. I start with, *Thanks for the invite* . . . And then I'm stuck. That's not how a bro responds. Who even says "invite" anymore? I have no idea how to do this, and I'm sure everyone else in the group chat is seeing my three dots.

Then, it hits me. The perfect response. A delicately crafted affirmative. As I type it out, I smile, profoundly proud of myself for coming up with something so flawless.

Sure

A few seconds later I get a response.

Litty

From Tyler.

I grip my phone so hard I wonder if I might actually crush it. I did it. I'm amazing. A true queer icon.

Then a new message:

See ya there!

From Fabiola.

Which means she'll be calling in three, two, one—

"Hello?" I say.

"The blue-heather T-shirt, the black jeans that make your butt look good, and the Vans you wore to my birthday party. If they're still in good condition."

"Huh?"

"Don't use gel but take a shower and comb your hair right after."

"Fabiola—"

"We're going for a 'chill, guy next door' look."

"I—"

"Trust me, I got this."

"Okay then."

"You're gonna make a move, right?"

"Yeah, definitely, for sure. If the opportunity presents itself, ya know?"

"Quique, opportunities do not 'present' themselves. You have to pursue them. Like I did."

"Oh, so Molly finally texted back?"

"No, she didn't. She probably isn't interested, but at least I tried."

"Oh. Um. I'm sorry. Do you want to talk about—"

"Blue shirt, jeans, Vans. Got it?"

"Fabiola—"

"Do you doubt my fashion advice?"

"No, but—"

"Then do what I say."

I sigh again. "Okay, I will."

"Good boy. I'll see you tonight."

Because it's only the beginning of the week, my parents don't immediately pass out when they get home around five o'clock. Instead, they join me on the couch, where I've been the entire day, save for the few times I got up to eat, go to the bathroom, and briefly work out.

We watch an episode of my mom's "women who kill" show, and my dad flinches every time my mom reaches for the remote to lower the volume during commercials. When it's over and another one begins, I finally ask if it's okay if I hang out with Fabiola tonight, and my mom says yes.

Asking for permission to leave the house is a formality at this point. The only way I'd get a "no" is if my parents were both using their cars. I feel somewhat lame for wishing sometimes that they'd press more, do what my other friends' parents do: ask questions on questions on questions. *Who are you going with? What time? What are you going to do? Will there be adults there? What are their Social Security numbers?* But really, how annoying would that be? I lucked into the position I'm in. . . . But maybe a *Did you eat?* would be nice every once in a while. But then again, I'm almost legally an adult, and I know how to feed myself.

After my parents and I find out that Anelise Bur-gess-Cañón's sister Maria Cañón helped her murder Victor Burgess, Fabiola texts me that she's outside. As I climb into her pickup truck, which has seen more days than either of us, my parents wave from the porch. Fabiola waves back, beaming, and then takes off.

The whole ride to Tyler's, I really want to ask her about Molly, but I can tell she doesn't want to talk about it. The only thing she says while we're in the car is "You look good. It's so hard being right all the time."

And she doesn't even know that I exercised today. Right after I ended my call with her, I did about a million jumping jacks, a shit ton of squats, and four and a half push-ups.

When we arrive, the two of us get out of her truck and take a minute to admire Tyler's neighborhood. All of the houses are elegant two-stories with lawns so lush they look more comfortable than my bed. The make of the cars parked in the driveways ranges from Mercedes to Lexus to BMW.

"I didn't know he was *rich* rich," Fabiola says.

"I didn't either," I say.

She turns to look at me. "Do you think we'll ever live in a neighborhood like this?"

I smile. "You will, and I expect a room for me to stay in."

"Psh. If you don't think I'm replacing you with an actor who looks just like you who obeys my every whim without objecting, you're dreamin'."

We enter through the side gate like Tyler told us to, both of us a little on edge because we're two brown people entering a white person's property in a very affluent, very Caucasian neighborhood.

We walk around the house and come to the garage, which looks like a second, smaller house. Fabiola knocks on the door, and we wait. There's a bit of commotion coming from inside, like Tyler's running an obstacle course to get to the door. When it finally opens, out comes his red face.

"Hey, guys!" he says, dimples deep as ever. "I hope you don't mind, but I started getting high without you."

Tyler's "man cave" is exactly how you're picturing it: huge leather sofa in front of an enormous flat-screen (bigger than the one in my living room), a dusty black drum set on the right, king-sized bed in the left corner. Trap music bumps from the TV speakers.

"Take a seat," he says.

Fabiola and I sit on either side of the video game controller resting on the center couch cushion. Tyler picks up the controller and sits in between us.

"Locked and loaded," he says, holding up an expertly rolled joint. He offers it to Fabiola, and she accepts. She holds it to her mouth as he lights it for her, then takes one long, deep hit and slowly exhales.

"Wow," Tyler says approvingly.

Fabiola hands him the joint, and he holds it out to me. My hit's only a quarter as big as Fabiola's. When I'm done, I give the joint back to Tyler, who hits it and then puts it down. He leans back and puts his arms around my and Fabiola's shoulders.

"So . . . ," I say. "Who were the other two people in the group chat?"

"Aaron and Michael," he says. Two guys on the basketball team. "Why do you ask?"

"Just wondering," I say. Tyler picks up the joint. "When are they getting here?"

He takes a drag. "Oh, they're not coming."

"Oh, uh . . . what happened?"

Tyler laughs. "I forgot," he says, then laughs again.

"That's okay," Fabiola says. "I'm sure Quique and I are much better company. If I do say so myself."

Tyler nods, his tongue sticking out of his mouth slightly, like he's unaware of it. "I'm sure you are."

He offers her the joint, and she takes it.

The three of us smoke and talk for ten minutes or so before Fabiola gets up to the use the bathroom. When she's gone, Tyler offers me the last hit of the joint, and for the first time I decline, even though I'm not high yet. You never know how potent California weed can be, so I'm exercising a little caution.

Tyler finishes it instead, puts the roach down on the table in front of us, and spreads out on the couch on his side. His head goes where Fabiola had been sitting, and he rests his legs on me. In this position I can't see his most noticeable asset, which makes me realize I haven't seen it since we got here. Did he tape it down because he was having company?

Tyler lets out a soft moan.

"You going to sleep?" I ask.

He smiles, eyes closed. "No, man, I'm just comfortable. Is there anything better than being comfortable?"

He's definitely high, but he's not wrong. Nothing's better

than being comfortable. Being comfortable is . . . it's . . .

"Being comfortable's the best," I say.

Wait. *Am* I high?

"Whatever feels good is good," he says.

We're quiet for a bit, unmoving. And then, I don't know why—okay, that's a total lie, I definitely know why—I start to rub his legs. Nothing obscene, only shins and calf, you know how bros do. I try not to look at them so that way it's only something I'm doing, a mindless action, casual. Eventually, though, I have to look down to confirm my suspicions.

"Dude," I say.

"What?" Tyler says.

"Do you shave your legs?"

He laughs. "Nah, man, I'm naturally smooth."

"Bullshit."

He opens his eyes. "No, really!" He rolls onto his back and lifts up his shirt. "Look, see?"

"Uh . . . yeah. Not a hair in sight."

I don't care about hair right now. I'm focusing on trying not to drool as I stare at his six-pack and pecs.

It's then that the bathroom door swings open and Fabiola hops out.

"Am I interrupting something?"

Tyler pulls his shirt down. "Guy stuff."

"Of course." She walks over to the couch. "Am I supposed to sit on your head, Tyler?"

"I wouldn't mind," he says with a smile. But always the gentleman, he takes his legs off me and jumps up. For the first time today Tyler Jr. makes his appearance. Tyler

Sr. takes a seat on the couch, not in the middle seat like before, but on the other end. Fabiola sits in between us before stretching out on top of us. Her head rests in Tyler's lap, and her legs rest on mine like his were a minute ago.

"This is nice," she says.

"For you," I mumble.

"What do you—"

"I need some air." I push her legs off me more forcefully than I mean to, stand up, and head out the door.

I'm high, really high, but that doesn't mean I can't feel furious at the same time. I thought Fabiola was supposed to help me out, not snag Tyler for herself. I don't care if Molly ghosted her. My mind was just altered enough to make a move! Maybe.

I walk over to the pool and sit down. It's kidney shaped with a hot tub at the other end. I stare at the reflection of the moon on the water, the smell of chlorine in my nose, for what might be twenty seconds or twenty minutes, both relieved and disappointed that neither Tyler nor Fabiola comes out to see what's wrong. At some point, I reach into my pocket and take out my phone. I'm unaware of who I'm calling until he answers.

"Hello, Quique, what a nice surprise. What's going on?"

"Oh, nothiiiing," I say.

"Okay . . ."

Neither of us says anything for a while.

"Are you okay?" Saleem finally asks.

"Uh . . . yeah. I think so. Nothing's broken, nothing's bleeding."

"That's good. Are you . . . Have you . . . Um, how do you feel?"

Oh fuck. He doesn't know if I'm drunk or high or in the middle of a meltdown, and he doesn't know how to ask. And I'm so embarrassed I can't say anything.

Luckily, he takes it in a direction I can work with.

"Are you under the influence of something?"

I laugh. "Oh, yeah, definitely. I'm high as fuck, dude."

"I see. So I'm to assume that I'm not supposed to take anything you say too seriously then."

"Yeah, exactly."

"I can do that pretty easily. You sound . . . peculiar."

"God I love you."

"What?"

I stand up.

"The way you talk, the words you use. They're so you." I start walking around the pool. "And I love that. I love *you*, Saleem. We should be able to say that, right? As friends? We love each other, and there's nothing wrong with that. Right? I love you, Saleem."

He clears his throat. "I love you too, Quique."

"I love you too, Saleem."

"You said it fir—"

"Ugh," I say. I've started getting closer to the perimeter of the pool, one foot in front of the other like when you're a kid walking on a curb. I stick one arm out to keep myself balanced. "I even love your name. Saleem, Saleem, Saleem, Saleem—"

"Are you sure you're okay?"

"Yeah, man, I'm great. Are you sure *you're* okay?"

He laughs at that. "Yes, Quique, I'm fine."

"How's your wife?"

"My wife? What do you—oh." He laughs. "Well, like I said, Ahed is pretty cool. She writes poetry, in Arabic first, and then she translates it into English before she posts it online. She says she usually doesn't show it to people in real life, but she's read me a couple poems. They're beautiful. And she's really happy that she doesn't have to translate them for me."

Everything's blurry. For a second, I think it's the THC, but then I realize I have tears in my eyes.

"That's awesome," I say. "I love that for you. For her."

"Quique, where are you? Are you alone?"

"Tyler Montana's house. And yes. I needed some fresh air."

"I see."

"He has a pool. It's really nice." I stop. The left side of my left shoe lies past the concrete edge, over the water. "I wish you could see it. I wish you were here."

"Really?"

"Yeah."

"I'm sure we'd have fun."

I pause. "Why? What would we do?"

"Swim, Quique, what else?"

I laugh and keep laughing, and eventually he joins me. Even though I'm high, I can kind of tell that it's not exactly a *haha, that's funny* laugh.

"Ugh," I say, "I should go."

"Okay," he says too quickly. "If you think you should."

"Bye, Ssssaaaalllleeeeeeeemmmm."

"Bye, Quique."

And he hangs up. Almost immediately.

I take a last look at the water and head back to the garage. I open the door and look around inside, finding Tyler and Fabiola tangled up together on the bed. They're both asleep and fully clothed, but Fabiola has her hand down Tyler's shorts.

"Fantastic," I say.

I walk over to the couch and lie down. Hopefully, I can fall asleep before they wake up, even though I don't feel tired.

CHAPTER NINE

Fabiola spends the whole next week apologizing to me via text. I think she's too ashamed to do it over the phone. Her defense is she was sad about Molly, and when she came out of the bathroom, she was so high that all she could think about was "a handful of that pink dick." I say I forgive her, but I don't know if that's true. Yet.

I'm on my way to Target with my mom, which is how I know it's Saturday. I haven't made much progress on The Plan. I've been exercising but haven't seen any changes in my body. I haven't texted Tyler because I'm terrified he'll tell me he's into Fabiola. And I've been texting with Saleem more than I should be, slutty temptress that he is.

"What's up with you?" my mom asks, pulling into a parking spot.

"Nothing," I say.

She gives me a look.

"Really, nothing."

When we enter the store and I catch sight of the dollar section, a hot flash of annoyance spreads throughout my body. Before I can stop myself, I say, "Do we really need to come here every week?"

My mom slowly cranes her neck to look at me, eyebrows raised.

"You don't have to come with me," she's quick to point out, grabbing a shopping cart. "I don't need your negativity when I'm in my happy place."

My anger drains out of me, suddenly replaced with amusement. I pull a sanitary wipe out of the red container in front of me and hand it to her.

"Seriously, what's been up your butt this week?" she asks, wiping the handlebar of the cart.

My heart jumps at her choice of words and how they relate to the elephant in the corner of the room that I'm trying desperately to cover up with all the clothes in my closet.

"Like I said, nothing."

"Fabiola?" she asks.

"Uh . . . Yeah."

It's the most I can tell her without lying.

"I see. Well, you two always work things out. I swear you two are like me and your father."

She pushes the cart to the dollar section, and I stand there watching her. She knows Fabiola and I aren't together, but she makes comments like this all the time, comparing the two of us to a married couple, like we simply haven't "figured it out" yet. Imagine if I told her that the reason I've been acting weird is I'm mad at Fabiola for cockblocking me when I was high and ready to pounce on my school's star athlete. Imagine if I told her that one of the reasons I came with her today was so my queer ass could talk to another queer guy about another guy. She doesn't mind too much if I drink, if I stay out too late, if I have a life. But if I fell in love with a boy? She wouldn't know what to do with that.

I catch up to her and let her know I'll find her later. She waves me off as she catches sight of a plastic Disney princess cup, as well as the five-year-old girl also staring at it who she's going to have to fight for it.

Like last time, I stand in the music section and stare, but this time I'm not browsing. I'm fully aware of my surroundings. If a certain güerito came up to me, ready to hear me vent about my boy problems, I would launch into a recap of what happened at Tyler's.

But Arturo doesn't show up. I keep giving him one more minute and one more minute and one more minute until I accept that he's not coming and go look for my mom. At this point in her shopping, she should be in the chip aisle grabbing her favorite flavor of Doritos (spicy nacho), but when I arrive there she's nowhere to be seen. There is, however, another familiar face in that aisle.

Manny rests his hand on his chin, surveying Target's extensive Flamin' Hot selection. He still hasn't noticed me, which means I have time to slip away, but that would be a wasted opportunity to advance The Plan.

So I sidle up to him and say, "Hot Cheetos are obviously the GOAT, and I have a soft spot for Hot Fritos. But if you wanna get really crazy, there's the Hot Funyuns."

He turns to me with a look on his face that says he's going to slug me, but it melts away when he realizes who I am. Then it's time for the *I've been trapped in the jungle for eight days without food and my tour guide is starting to look like a slab of carne asada* look.

"Quique, wassup, homes?"

Quick handshake and two-armed hug. Much better than a fist bump.

"Not much, Manny. Just at Target with my mom on a Saturday. Like all the other cool kids."

Manny smiles and licks his lips. "I love this place, man. And you're right about the Funyuns."

He grabs a bag and starts walking to another aisle. I follow, and we end up in front of a wall of Pop-Tarts. He grabs a box of the cinnamon ones without hesitation. "I grew up with this shit," he says.

I smile at him. "Hey, so, Manny."

"Yeah?"

What am I doing?

"What are you doing later tonight?"

"Who's asking?" he says, an edge to his voice.

"Uh . . . me." I laugh uncomfortably. "I thought we could . . . hang."

His face softens into a look that says, *Don't mind me while I cover your entire body in Tapatío.* "Aight, let's do it."

"Cool. Uh . . . what should we . . . do?"

His mouth twitches. "Meet me at the park by the library at ten o'clock. Bring your car."

"Oh, okay. I'll see you there."

He walks away without another word, and all I'm left thinking is *What the hell did I agree to?*

For the rest of the day, I'm nervous about my "date" with Manny. I'm only now starting to realize how weird his proposition was. First of all, who meets up with another dude at a park? That's right, sexual delinquents. And while I know I'm very much down for guys, I don't think I want to start off by jumping into the deep end and seeing if I can learn to swim. Second, why does it have to be so late? Parks get pretty dangerous once the sun goes down.

As the minutes tick by and the hours inch their way to ten o'clock, I'm getting more and more anxious. My mom's already asleep, which is good because at this point, she'd know something was going on. My dad, on the other hand, is clueless.

As we sit on the couch in silence, watching baseball, he displays zero indications that he senses my body's about to tear into two at any moment due to severe mental discord, and I'm glad he's so magnificently obtuse when it comes to my emotional state. In the past, his obliviousness in this regard has enabled me to avoid accidentally coming out via my fury every time he makes an "I bet he secretly likes dick" joke about politicians he hates. And for now, it means I get to avoid questions about my Manny-related anxiety.

When I ask him to borrow his car, he simply nods without taking his eyes off the TV screen.

It's odd, but I kind of wanted him to stop me. My mom might've if she were awake because she can tell when I'm distraught. But that's why I didn't ask her. It's odd, but I definitely don't want her to stop me.

"Want a beer?" my dad asks.

Normally, I'd say yes and then we'd drink and I'd stare at baseball butts and he'd yell at the TV and it would be some quality bonding time. But it's nine forty-five, and I've got someone to meet.

"Can't," I say, getting up. "I'm heading out."

"Responsible. I raised you right."

"Yup." I fail to mention the fact that he just offered his underage son alcohol. "See ya, Dad."

"See ya, son. Protect yourself."

He means driving-wise, but my brain goes in a different direction. It's funny how everything's a double entendre when you're living a double life.

I hate driving with a mini tempest of conflicting emotions going on in my stomach, but here I am. I turn into the parking lot at the north end of the park and pull into a spot, thinking about how I'm never this nervous when I'm meeting up with Saleem. A little bit, sure, but not, like, nauseated, which I am now. I keep my headlights on and scan the landscape for Manny but don't find him. Looking back, I should have asked for a meeting spot, but it all happened so fast.

I finally turn off the engine and get out of the car, heading to the playground because it's the most obvious place to go to in a park.

As I hurry over to the swing set, I start having all sorts of paranoid thoughts. *What if Manny set up an ambush because he secretly hates me? What if he set up a gang initiation because he actually likes me and wants me to be his homie forever? What if he invited me to, like, a secret, gay, hood, Chicano orgy?*

That last one might not be the worst.

I finally get to the swing set. I look around and still don't see Manny, so I head over to the monkey bars and climb onto the top. I figure this is the best vantage point and an easily defensible fortress of sorts.

Despite my superb tactical thinking, however, I'm still caught off guard when I hear "Why the fuck you up there, bro?" from down below.

Manny laughs as I start and almost fall off. "You scared the shit out of me," I say, jumping down onto the wood chips.

"Thanks for meeting me here," he says.

"No problem," I say.

"Is that your car?" he asks, pointing to where I parked.

"Yeah."

"Good. Mine's in the shop. Yours should come in handy."

Huh? How's it gonna come in handy? Are we gonna mess around in my dad's car? I think about the strong signature scent of his cologne and start to panic.

"Come with me," Manny says.

Luckily, he leads me in the opposite direction of the car, into the heart of the park.

We walk for a bit on the concrete path before he stops at a tree with sprawling roots and an expansive network of branches. He puts his hand on the lowest branch. "Remember climbing these shits when you were little?" I nod, even though I wasn't much of a tree climber as a kid. "It was like a competition to me. I always had to go higher than everybody else." He smirks at me. "And I always did."

He puts his foot on a knot in the bark and hoists himself up onto the branch. "The only problem was," he continues, "I was a dumbass."

I laugh.

"I'd keep going until I was so high looking down made me dizzy. I couldn't act afraid, though, so I sat there like I just liked the view, like I had all the time in the world." He laughs and looks down at me. "Get up here, Quique."

I step on the foothold and try to pull myself up. I'm not entirely successful, so Manny has to help. He has a strong grip.

"You still haven't asked why we're here," he says.

I clear my throat. "Yeah, I, uh, thought this was, uh, a hangout."

"So," he says, "a guy you barely know asks you to meet him in the park in the middle of the night, and you do it? Just like that?"

He stares at me, and I feel so incredibly stupid.

"I kinda know you," I say.

"That's what you *think*."

I'm feeling an incredibly strange but pleasant mix of terror and anticipation. I still don't know if he's going to punch me or kiss me. Whatever's going to happen, I want it to happen now.

"Then tell me," I say. "Why am I here? Why are *you* here?"

He smiles. "You really wanna know?"

"Yes. I do."

"Then I'll tell you." He licks his lips. "Or do you want me to show you?"

I swallow hard. "The latter."

"Huh?"

"Show me."

He doesn't move, so I inch my face toward his. But just as

he starts leaning in, his head snaps in the other direction, and he whispers, "Did you hear that?"

"What?"

He shushes me and we listen. Sure enough I hear someone walking down the park path toward us. *Shit.*

"What do we do?" I ask.

"He's early. I gotta take care of something real quick."

"Huh?"

A figure comes into view. It's a kid around my and Manny's age. He doesn't seem to notice us at first, but when he does, he freezes. Without any warning, Manny jumps down and absolutely *launches* himself at the guy. It takes a while for the other kid, who looks to be a lot taller than Manny but skinnier, to realize what's happening and run. He only gets a few strides in before Manny crashes into him and they land in a heap. They wrestle for a while until Manny's on top. Then the guy starts screaming.

"I'm sorry! I'm sorry! I'm sorry!"

"Too late, motherfucker," Manny says.

And then he starts pummeling the guy, his fists flying impossibly fast. I'm frozen where I am, my hands clutching the branch underneath me for dear life. *WHAT. THE. FUCK. IS. GOING. ON????*

"Hey, man!" I realize Manny's calling out to me. "You want in?"

Again, what the fuck?

"No! We need to get out of here!"

Manny looks down at the guy, who's shielding his face beneath him. "Never again, fucker." And then he jogs over to me.

When he reaches the tree, he yells, "What are you doing? Let's go, dumbass!"

I jump down, not at all gracefully, and he helps me up. We streak to the car, and before I know it, I'm speeding back to our neighborhood.

"Dude," I begin, "I'm only gonna say this once. What. The. FUCK?"

He gives me a self-satisfied smirk. "The look on your face, foo. It's priceless."

"I mean it! You owe me an explanation. Who was that?"

"My ex-novio."

I nearly slam on my brakes. "Really?"

He laughs. "No, stupid. But that look."

I laugh purely out of awkwardness. Did he just come out, or was he making an always hilarious *I'm so straight, wouldn't it be funny if I were gay* joke?

"Then who was he?"

"My little prima's boyfriend."

I give him a look.

"*Ex*-boyfriend. He cheated on her."

"Oh."

That's not . . . excusable, is it? I'd definitely never do it (at least I don't *think* I would; I don't have a female cousin), but does that mean it's wrong? Maybe.

I look over at him, and I think he can tell that even if I don't *condone* what he did, I get it. He smiles at me, and I wish I weren't so turned on at the moment. Any time he smiles it's unfair. The lips, I'm telling you, the lips.

I turn my eyes back to the road, knowing I shouldn't take

them off it like my dad taught me to, but I use my peripheral vision to monitor what's happening around me, also like my dad taught me to. Manny's looking out the window now, his right hand gripping his chin. I think he's still smirking.

This is when my imagination begins to run wild. *What if he reached over and squeezed my thigh? What if he told me to pull over? What if he put his hand on the back of my head and started running his fingers through my hair?*

Because I'm starting to think those are the "hints" that would make it okay for me to put myself out there, to step onto that high branch swaying in the wind. Manny said he pretended not to be scared, but I don't know if can do that. At least not yet.

"Quique, stop sign."

"Oh shit!" I slam on my brakes, both hands gripping the wheel. "Sorry!"

"It's okay, man. Relax."

He reaches over and pats me squarely on the sternum a couple times. The weight of it causes my pulse to skyrocket even more, and it feels like I have two hearts in my chest, both beating for different reasons.

My dad's car is technically still moving when Manny gets out. He walks around to my side and motions for me to roll down my window. I do so, and he leans in.

"Remember," he says, "we spent the whole night together. At your place. Got it?"

I nod.

"Our little secret," he adds. He kinda gives me a once-over

before saying, "All right then, I'll see ya, man." And with that he leaves. He walks over to the entrance of his gate, opens it, and disappears. From what I can see through the black bars, his house is the same as it was four years ago. There's the main house in front, and then an addition behind it for his abuela, and behind that an additional addition for some other relatives.

I sit there in the car for a while, watching, not completely believing what happened tonight. Watching Manny throw hands at a guy I'd never met was the last thing I could have predicted. Then there's all the sexual tension between me and him that I don't think I can deny is reciprocal anymore. . . . All my wires are crossed right now.

I take a deep breath before taking off. When I'm barreling down Whittier Boulevard, I roll down all the windows and turn on the radio. I'm not going to lie, I feel dirty . . . but alive.

CHAPTER TEN

As I eat my quesadilla in the kitchen (burning my tongue in the process because it's fresh off the comal), I have a realization that may or may not be influenced by the fact that I haven't left the house since my meetup with Manny five days ago: I'm done with people. People are exhausting. Sure, they can be fun sometimes; they can "open you up to new experiences" or whatever. But the anxiety leading up to spending time with them and the emotional drain afterward make them not worth it.

Even Saleem. *Especially* Saleem. With him, it's simple: his presence (virtual or otherwise) brings me actual physical pain. He sent me a picture of him with his sitti this morning, and my stomach twisted so violently I ran to the bathroom. I love him, and I want him. And he genuinely cares about me, but he doesn't want me. Yes, he's, like, literal sunshine, but you know what happens when you're in the sun too long? You burn.

Then there's Fabiola. She pushes me to do things I don't want to want to do, which is super annoying in and of itself, but then she has the audacity to do the thing she was pushing me to do that I didn't want to want to do! That thing being Tyler.

Speaking of, Tyler is a cartoon. He's this, like, golden

retriever puppy who doesn't know what he's doing or what damage he's causing. Sure, he's cute, but he's destructive.

Which fucking reminds me: *Manny*. Who the fuck has someone accompany them on a mission to exact revenge on an unassuming kid in the park? He's reckless. And I'm stupid for going along with everything.

So today I'm gonna take charge and spend some quality time with myself. Today's about me, about getting *in touch* with me. And no, not in that way. Although, I have done that two times already. I've spent the past few days on autopilot, like I'm a figurine in a claymation movie being manipulated by some giant invisible director. I haven't exercised at all, and I've been listening to music that reminds me of Saleem on repeat. I need to do something that'll get my summer of self-improvement back on track, and I know exactly what that is.

When I'm finished eating, I wipe my hands on my shirt, head to my room, and grab some cleanish basketball shorts from the floor. Then I cram my oafish feet into my slightly too small running shoes before looking in the mirror.

I've learned over the years that avoiding my full reflection is the best way to prevent a body image–related spiral, but if I'm going to track how my body changes, I have to know my starting point, right?

I have what some would call an hourglass figure, which, because I'm a seventeen-year-old boy, I would not consider a compliment. I pinch the fat on my hips, then press my hands against my chest like that'll permanently flatten it. My eyes travel down to my mini beer belly, which doesn't give me that much anxiety because at least that I can suck in. My gaze inches farther south until I'm looking at my legs. If it weren't for them, I think I'd hate every part of my body that isn't my face. They're tan and muscular. Not bad for never working out.

My one positive thought soon gives way to another insecurity, this one more intangible, something ingrained in me by a society that prides itself on hate, but I can't help it. I look at my reflection and ask myself, *Do I look queer? Can people passing by me on the street pick up on the forbidden desire? Can they see it in my face? Can they hear it in the way I talk? Can they sense it in the way I move?*

I don't know. And I don't care. At least, I'm trying not to.

It helps to focus on yet another fragile part of my masculinity: my dick. I'm no Tyler Montana. Quique Jr. doesn't stretch out for all the world to see. He just peeks out, like he doesn't know if it's safe outside yet. Now, he's not always like that, he can . . . take up space, when he wants to. But sometimes it takes a lot to coax him out of his cage. He needs to feel a firm but gentle touch. He needs patience, time, understanding. He needs to hear soft words and the right music. So before I leave, I sort of tuck him out of sight so he can rest until he's needed, which, if I'm being optimistic, will be at some point this summer, and if I'm being realistic, will be no time soon.

I finally peel my eyes off the mirror and take out my phone. I make sure I've downloaded the latest pop masterpiece by an indie female artist (peak queer male culture), so that I have a soundtrack for my run. It's been a while, so I pray I don't end up passed out on the street.

• • •

I'm zipping down Whittier Boulevard, past palm trees and birds-of-paradise, past our taco place and our tamales place, getting tons of weird stares because no one jogs here, but I don't care. I love running. It's as close as humans can get to flying. And when a bomb-ass song is playing? Heaven. Sure, it doesn't take all that much time for me to feel like I'm gonna yak on the side of the road, but still, for half an album or so, I feel on top of the world.

I stop at a park (one where I've never seen anyone laid out by Manny) to sit on a bench and try to catch my breath. Then I hear something over my music, so I hit pause on my phone. The sound doesn't repeat, so I look to the side and find an older white dude staring at me while holding an iced coffee from Starbucks. Wait, not just any white dude—

Mr. Chastman. *What is my English teacher doing here?*

"Oh, hi, Mr. Chastman."

"Enrique."

This is going to be awkward. But not as awkward as it would be if one of my other teachers were here. Mr. Chastman's objectively the easiest to talk to.

"Did you say something?" I ask.

"Yeah," he says with the subtlest hint of a smile. "I was admiring your dance moves."

My face gets hot. "Dance moves?"

"You were groovin' in your seat."

Fuck. I didn't even notice.

"Um, thanks," I say.

I want to die.

"Thought I'd add a little bit of awkwardness to your day," he says, sitting next to me on the bench. "It's been two weeks since I've had the opportunity to humiliate a teenager without meaning to."

I smile slightly. "You don't mean to do it at school?"

I love Mr. Chastman, but he does have a reputation for roasting us. Most of the time it's playful and funny, but sometimes he goes for the jugular when a student's said something horribly offensive. When it was the latter case, I always had to stop myself from jumping up and trying to Z-snap in support.

"Sometimes I do," he admits. "Most of the time, though, I say things without thinking and hope you guys aren't paying attention."

"So that doesn't go away with age?" I ask.

"Oof." He puts his hand on his chest like he's been shot, and I realize he and Ziggy share that mannerism. I don't know what to do with this information. "How old do you think I am?"

"You're thirty-one," I reply with absolute confidence.

He looks slightly terrified, and I'm glad the tables have turned for the moment.

"How do you know that?"

"I'm very observant."

"I'm well aware, but what did you observe?"

"Sophomore year, I delivered something to the main office and saw a cake for your thirtieth birthday, so that makes you thirty-one."

He sips his iced coffee and raises his eyebrows. "Well done, kiddo."

"Thanks."

I was actually very happy with the information. I'm bad at guessing people's ages (especially white people's), so Mr. Chastman's had been a mystery. Still a mystery that I wonder about: his first name. By the time I saw the cake, the pieces with his name on it had been eaten. Maybe God knew I would have been overwhelmed if I had learned that, too.

"Well," Mr. Chastman says, standing up. "I better head out before I see another one of my students here. I ran into Mr. Jackson a few minutes ago."

"Ziggy? You saw Ziggy here?"

"Yes, I did." He raises an eyebrow. "Do you two not get along?"

The opposite, Mr. Chastman, the complete opposite.

"From what I remember," he says, "you two seemed to be having the time of your lives on top of H-Building."

My face gets hot again. I forgot it was him who "saved" us.

"I, uh, just hate seeing people outside of school. It throws me off."

"Tell me about it." He tosses his cup into the trash can. "All right, I'll see ya, Enrique. Hopefully at school next time."

"Yeah. Bye, Mr. Chastman."

I make sure he's out of view before I jump up and run in the opposite direction, out of the park. I can't see Ziggy today. Today is about me, remember? Today is about self-fulfillment! Today is the day of self-completion! NOT LIKE THAT.

With newly revitalized energy, I round the corner and sprint home.

It's only as I come into view of our yellowed lawn that I realize I may have overreacted a bit. What would have been wrong with bumping into Ziggy? He's a nice, pleasant guy. It's not like I would have had a Tyler-like or Manny-like disaster on my hands. I'm not terrified of my feelings for him like I am with all of the other guys. And even if this day is about me, I can surely make room for other people, as long as I let myself dictate what happens between us.

But then I remember his eyes. Those piercing, gorgeous, emerald motherfuckers. And the brows. Ugh, I'd do anything for them. I'd forget myself in an instant if I saw him today. And that makes me wonder, *Why is it so easy for me to discard myself for someone else?*

Anyone: Jump.

Me: How high?

Anyone: Run.

Me: How fast?

Anyone: Swallow.

Me: Hur mur?

I shake my head. God, I'm right back to square one.

The first thing I do when I'm in my house is take a shower, give my mind a chance to turn off for a bit. Once I'm clean and nearly dry, I get dressed in comfy clothes and curl up on my bed. It's three p.m., but time is a construct.

I don't know how to move forward at this point. Here I am, like always, waiting for life to happen. And yeah, no one can fix that but me, but it's still tempting to think that there's someone who can show me what else is out there, what I'm missing. They say you need to love yourself before you can love someone else, but I feel like I need confirmation sometimes, that I'm someone to love.

I want a person to demonstrate that it's possible to love me, no matter what. And those three words are so important: *no matter what.* I want someone to love me unconditionally. I want to be certain that nothing I could ever do would make them stop. But right now, I don't feel like anyone in my life fits that bill. I mean, I'm hiding a part of myself from everyone I love, too scared to show myself in my entirety because maybe then they'd leave.

Wow, this train of thought is thoroughly depressing.

But it's comforting to know that I can't possibly be the only one who feels this way. I've read enough books, seen enough movies, listened to enough music to know that the human species is decidedly a lonely one. Sure, what sets us apart from animals is our superior social and communication skills, but we're the only species that's left alone with our thoughts. Our minds are truly the one place where no one else can follow us. Even if we try, if we constantly express every thought that comes to mind, if we exist as a walking stream of consciousness, we won't be able to convey everything that's going on. There are emotions and feelings and sensations that we'd never be able to articulate.

I say simply, *Ugh.*

I'm just going to listen to music until I fall asleep or snap out of this contemplative funk. No more femme power pop, though. Happy music never makes me happy when I'm sad.

It's time for something moody and depressing. I need to match how I'm feeling, like how you're supposed to steer into the skid when you're driving and you hit a patch of ice and start spinning. That's when I don't feel so alone.

CHAPTER ELEVEN

I wake up around midnight, disoriented by the lack of light and noise in the house, which is usually what happens when I go to bed super early because I can't nap like a normal person. As I rub my eyes, I think about the dream I just woke up from. I was in Rome, and an alien ship attacked with a green blast of energy that gave me superpowers. There was a dream before that, too. One about having an estranged older brother who showed up on my birthday to give me a letter . . . And there was one more before that. It's all a little fuzzy now, but I know I was high up, on a bridge or something, with someone else. Someone I know from my actual life . . .

I rest my hands under my head. Who was he? I run through all the people I've seen recently, but none of them ring a bell. It was someone tall and lanky but not Arturo. Someone with brown skin but not Manny or Saleem . . .

Oh.

Ziggy. Duh. I was on a bridge with Ziggy Jackson when he suddenly sprouted eagle wings and flew off without me. Because it makes perfect sense that—in addition to cockblocking me—my subconscious would associate him with heights.

Months ago, I very stupidly (or ingeniously based on the events that followed) got both of us stuck on the roof of the tallest building at our school after Homecoming. As editor in chief of the yearbook, I was at the game cheering on my school's team, the Amphibians, as they took on some school from West Covina, as well as making sure my photographers got everything we needed, namely, copious snapshots of Tyler Montana. Ziggy was there campaigning for student body president and, at the end of the game, stuffing a churro in his mouth like he hadn't eaten in weeks.

"Impressive," I said as I approached him, my relative boldness a result of the fact that I was a little drunk on all the festivities . . . as well as a big swig from Mariana's flask when I visited her and Fabiola in the stands. This was during one of their brief but numerous reconciliations.

Ziggy laughed, his mouth full, and wiped cinnamon sugar from his mouth.

"I can't control myself around these things," he said. "I have to thank you on behalf of your people."

"I accept. And I'd like to thank you on behalf of all your ancestors for . . . um, all of America?"

Ziggy laughed again, and my heart pounded in my chest.

"You're welcome," he said, dusting his hands off. "Though, that's only my mom's side. Please don't thank me on behalf of the ancestors on my dad's side."

"Oh, you mean for the whole Indigenous genocide/slavery/white supremacy thing?"

"Yeah, that whole *thing*."

Ah, the electricity. I felt a small spark of it then, and I'd feel it in full force if he were lying down next to me right now.

"Hey, would you mind going with me to my locker?" he

asked, pointing his thumb in the opposite direction of the football field. "I forgot to grab my biology book earlier."

"Yeah, sure."

How could I say no?

"So," I said to Ziggy as we walked to H-Building, "why'd you want me to come with you?"

"This place is kinda scary at night," he replied. "Don't you think?"

I looked around. The concrete pathways from building to building were usually swarming with angry, depressed, horny teenagers. But now they were empty, and the buildings stood tall and austere in the dark of night. Away from all the action, I could see what he meant.

"You think I'd be able to protect you?" I asked.

"Oh yeah. Definitely."

"Or do you need someone slower than you who the murderer can kill while you get away?"

His hand flew to his chest. "You got me."

We both laughed, coming up on the door to the stairwell that leads to the second floor of H-Building, where our lockers were.

"Shit," Ziggy said.

"What?"

He pulled the handle, but the metal door didn't budge.

"It's locked."

"Oh. We can go find someone to—"

"Here, give me a boost."

"Uh . . . why?"

"If I can stick my arm down behind the door, I can push the metal bar and it'll open from the inside."

"Oh."

I remember thinking, *God, he's smart.*

I knelt down and cupped my hands. Ziggy took a quick step onto them and swung his arm through the bars of the door, near to the top. It's then that I realized how heavy he was. He was thin but tall, and while I considered myself at least somewhat sturdily built, I wasn't used to this kind of exertion. My arms were already starting to wobble.

I held my position, though, my stamina stemming from my fear of disappointing Ziggy, and eventually he said, "Pull me back!"

I did as he said, and the door came with him. When it was open wide enough, my hands let go without consulting my brain, and he fell to the ground.

"Enrique!"

"Sorry!"

Then the door began to close on its own, so I ran forward to stop it, barely catching it in time.

"Success!" I yelled.

Ziggy looked up at me from the floor, tipping his head to the side with a look that said, *You really think so?*

"How'd you do on the last test?" I asked a few minutes later as Ziggy took his bio book out of his locker.

"Ninety-four," he said, winking at me.

"Impressive," I said. "At least, it would be if I hadn't gotten a ninety-eight."

Ziggy laughed. "I kicked your ass on the one before that, though."

"True."

Ever since freshman year when Ziggy and I both kept acing our geometry quizzes, we've had a little competition going in whatever classes we had together. For the most part it's harmless fun, but when I was really struggling with a class, it was incredibly embarrassing. Ziggy didn't seem to notice that I only did well in English and any class that only requires memorization. That's why I'm good at biology and geometry, but chemistry and Algebra 2 were a shitshow sophomore year. He was always low-key encouraging when he knew a subject was kicking my ass, but I still felt small, wondering why he got to be good-looking and rich and popular *and* smart.

Ziggy closed his locker, and we started back to the stairwell.

"Wait," I said.

"What?"

"Look."

I pointed to an open door that was always locked during school hours.

"What is it?" he asked.

"The way to the roof!"

"Oh, sure, *that* door's unlocked."

"Don't you get it?"

"What?"

"We can go up there!"

"Uh . . ." Ziggy raised an eyebrow. "Why would we do that? You know there's not actually a pool up there, right?"

At our school there's a tradition of upperclassmen trying to convince freshmen that there's a pool on top of H-Building that you can only gain access to when you're a senior.

I rolled my eyes. "Yes, I know that." My dad claims to have started the rumor when he went here. "But I still want to go."

"Why?"

"Because!"

"Convincing."

"Ughhhh. It's not something I think I can explain."

How could he not see the appeal? Going to the roof of H-Building was forbidden and wrong and, therefore, exciting. He and I could be alone. Really alone.

"We can check it out," Ziggy said, "if it means that much to you."

"It does."

"Then let's go."

His amused exasperation made my feet feel especially light as I bounded up the stairs.

Upon arriving at the top, I found that my suggestion was, in fact, genius. Especially considering I was trying to impress Ziggy. The view that welcomed us was almost breathtaking, the tiniest bit romantic. It wasn't the New York skyline, but it was our school, and beyond that our town, miniaturized yet vast, and beyond that the lights of Downtown LA, distant yet bright.

"Not too bad," Ziggy said, coming up behind me.

"Right?"

We stared for a while in silence, the static electricity present and intensified, until we heard a loud slam.

"What was that?" Ziggy said immediately.

"I don't know," I said.

But I did know. There was no doubt in my mind that that was the sound of the door below shutting on us, the sound of our doom. I just didn't have the balls to tell him that.

"The door!" he screamed.

Turns out I didn't need to.

Ziggy turned on his heel and ran to the steps. I followed at a slower rate, already sensing the futility.

Once he was at the bottom of the stairs, Ziggy began pulling at the door handle, but it didn't budge.

"Hello?" he called out, banging on the door. "We're here! We're stuck! Help us!"

He paused for a moment, and we listened for a response. Nothing.

"Aggghhhh!" Ziggy pounded on the door again. Then we waited.

Still nothing.

"What the fuck are we gonna do?" he asked, his eyes wider than I'd ever seen them.

"Calm down," I said. "We'll figure it out."

We stood there for a couple minutes, waiting for the other to do so.

"Enrique—"

"Come with me."

I grabbed his arm and led him back up the stairs, all too aware of our skin touching. When we got to the top, I let go.

"Take out your phone," I said, doing the same. "We can call someone and tell them to come get us."

He did as I said.

"Who's at the game that we can call?" I asked. There was only one person I could dial, and she wasn't very reliable.

A smile crossed Ziggy's lips as he stared at his phone, but it was twisted, almost menacing.

"Principal Ramos, Vice Principal Kuo, Mr. Chastman—"

"Oh my God," I said. "That's perfect! Any one of them can help us."

"Yes, they could," he said, acid in his voice, "if my phone weren't dead."

"Fuck."

"What about you?"

"Fabiola."

"Call her."

I began scrolling through my contacts, hoping against all odds that she wouldn't be too distracted to answer my call.

"She didn't pick up?" Ziggy asked when I lowered my phone.

"No," I said, trying to remain calm for his sake.

"Oh my fucking—"

"I'll try again. She'll answer, Ziggy."

But she didn't. Not the second call, or the third, or the fourth.

"We're fucked," Ziggy said. "In the a—wait. What about Saleem?"

"What about him?"

"Is he here? Call him!"

"He's not here."

Ziggy's sexy eyebrows knitted together. "But you two are always together."

"He doesn't really like . . . big social events."

"Ugggghhhh."

Ziggy closed his eyes, put his hands on his hips, and craned his head back in frustration while I tried not to let on that I was flattered that he paid close enough attention to me to notice how close Saleem and I were.

"You don't have any of the faculty's numbers memorized?" I asked.

"Of course not!" he said, his eyes flying open. "This is the twenty-first century!"

"Right. Well, I guess there's only one thing left to do."

"What?"

I walked over to the edge of the building, leaned over the railing, and yelled at the top of my lungs, "HEEEEL-LLLPPPP!!!!"

"ENRIQUE, STOP! GET AWAY FROM THERE!"

I turned around.

"What's wrong?" I asked.

Ziggy's eyes were bulging out of his skull. "You're gonna fall over! And die! Your death isn't something I can have on my conscience!"

I snorted. After the metal railing came two solid feet of concrete. I could conceivably climb over it and stand there without being in any real danger.

"Ziggy, I'm not gonna fall. Do you think I'm stupid?"

"Just move back. Toward me."

His hands were spread out in front of him, and he spoke in a controlled, calm voice, like he was talking someone out of committing suicide.

"So you don't want me to get any closer," I said, a bit of mischief seeping into my blood.

"No," he said evenly.

I lifted myself up on the railing, my body hoisted about a foot off the ground. "So I shouldn't do this?"

I tried not to the let the strain enter my voice. I was heavy.

"Enrique, stop. *Now*."

He was backing away from me, like I would take him down with me if I fell.

"Or this."

I kicked my leg over the railing.

"ENRIQUE!" His high-pitched shriek sounded like a death scream in a horror movie.

"I definitely shouldn't do this, huh, Ziggy?" I called out, straddling the railing.

At this point, I was terrified. I obviously wasn't as afraid of heights as Ziggy was, but I knew I was being completely reckless. I knew one small variable that I didn't take into account could knock me off the building. But I'd never felt more alive than in that moment.

I smirked at him devilishly, and then my risk paid off. Ziggy ran toward me, and before I could move, he grabbed me by my left bicep and yanked me down. I fell to the ground on the nonlethal side of the railing, and I actually did take him down with me. He didn't end up on top of me, though, which is, of course, what I would have preferred, but he did end up lying at my side, his eyes penetrating mine. When he was angry their green hue seemed to change, melting into the lime-green color I associate with villains in Disney movies.

The two of us were breathing heavily, him because of fear and anger and me because our faces were so close together.

It was a shame they never touched.

A second or two after we hit the ground we heard someone coming up the stairs, and that sound, of someone coming to save us, gave me an odd feeling. It was the least relief anyone's ever felt when being rescued.

CHAPTER TWELVE

I must have fallen asleep again after reliving the roof incident because I wake up around six o'clock in the morning, feeling better than I did after my run. Turns out fifteen hours of sleep can do wonders for your mood. My mom's already up, getting ready for work, which means my dad'll be up in a bit to tell her to hurry up and finish showering.

You'd think I'd be well rested now, but I still feel groggy. I consider going back to sleep, but just because I don't feel awake doesn't mean that I'd be able to. What else is there to do at this hour?

I guess I can catch up on everything that happened yesterday while I was in a mentally induced coma. I root around under the sheet I use as a blanket during the summer, looking for my phone.

No one's texted me since the last time I looked at it, which is a source of both relief and disappointment. One by one, I check all of my social media accounts and scroll through them. Apparently, yesterday was not a day for new things to happen—everyone did what they always do.

I'm about to close one of my apps when I see a picture Aya posted. It's her and some other girls around her age on a wicker bench in someone's backyard. There's only one boy, on one end of the bench, and that is of course Saleem. Now *this* is a great picture of him. His happiness looks genuine, and his eyes didn't disappear when he smiled (like mine do).

And that's when I notice his arm around the shoulders of the girl sitting next to him.

"Oh, hello, Ahed," I say out loud for some reason. "Nice to meet you."

My eyes go back to Saleem. "Traitor."

I go back to looking at Ahed. I inspect every pixel of her, and when I'm done, I have to admit, she's *gorgeous*. And now comes the feeling that only bisexual people are lucky enough to know the true horror of: wanting to make out with the person who's stealing the person you also want to make out with.

Disgusted with myself, I digitally fling the picture away with a dramatic swipe. I land on a photo of the sun rising over a pool posted a few minutes ago. The caption is "Cameras never do this view justice." I roll my eyes and look at the poster.

Ziggy. I almost laugh. Instead, I click on the message icon and draft a well-thought-out greeting.

Hey, I write.

Hey, he responds, almost immediately. *Why are you up so early?*

My pulse quickens. *I should ask you the same question.*

Don't. Just answer mine.

I raise my eyebrows. Since when is Ziggy so . . . commanding?

I'm about to start replying when he shoots me a couple of quick messages in succession.

Sorry.

That sounds rude.

Must be the sleep deprivation.

In my experience, being sleep-deprived is kinda like being drunk, so I think about what I'd say if my mom's favorite tequila were flowing through my veins. Hmm. I type it out and it doesn't look *that* bad. But I'm not actually gonna send it, right? That would be dumb. So dumb. Like really dumb. It would be fantastically, horribly dumb—

I hit send.

And oh shit. Just like that my message is staring up at me from my phone. Which means Ziggy's looking at it too.

It's okay. Don't apologize. I like being told what to do.

I'm breathless now, which is tragically pathetic. How long will it take him to—

I take back my apology, he writes. *Tell me. Now.*

Oh boy, no turning back.

That's more like it. I went to bed really early yesterday. Wasn't really thinking about my sleep schedule.

Ah, I see. I spent all of yesterday trying to tire myself out so I wouldn't have a problem falling asleep. It worked perfect obviously.

I flip over onto my stomach so I can type faster.

*perfectly, smart guy. You really do need some shut eye.

Oh shut up. And it's "shut-eye" if you mean sleep.

Did you just start a sentence with "And"?

Shut uuuup. Stop torturing me; I'm dying here. :(

I swear I'm not trying to torture you but did you just use an emoji?

An emoticon, but yes. Textual communication is hopelessly inadequate at conveying emotions.

I see. Well, I thought this conversation was going great.

Oh, but it is. Watch— :)

Mmm. Very convincing.

My thumbs are a blur now because each of my replies is exactly what I'm thinking. I hope Ziggy is smiling as hard as I am on the other end of this conversation.

Not the same as the real-life Ziggy Jackson million-dollar smile, I add.

My what now?

You read me.

Haha. I wasn't aware.

Mm-hmm.

Really, I wasn't. I got a nice smile?

Yes. You haaaave a nice smile. Although "nice" is putting it lightly.

But I don't got anything like them trademark Tyler Montana dimples.

WHO ARE YOU???

Haha. You don't know me, Enrique.

Maybe not but I'd like to.

I sit up now. How's he going to reply to that?

Fair enough.

I'm drawing a blank. How do I respond to that? What can I say to "fair enough?" This is his fault, right? He threw a conversational roadblock into our chat. What do I say? I guess I could change the subject, mention something else that's been on my mind. But what would that be? "Hey, Ziggy, do you wanna sit on my lap and let me open eye kiss you until I die?"

Ugh, what if I—

New message.

Yo, what are you up to right now?

Wow. That comma after "yo" is doing things to me. Also, he has great timing because I was about to spiral.

Uh . . . nothing. It's six in the morning so I'm still in bed.

Right.

What are you doing?

Talking to you. In between push-ups.

Fuck me.

I reply.

One of us is considerably more evolved than the other.

Very true, he writes. *But don't rub it in. ;)*

Okay, we are in dangerous flirt territory. This is like code red, or whichever color is like really serious but not the most serious. I take a deep breath. Now or never.

Don't play, Jackson. Anyone with eyes can see it's you.

I'm not, and they wouldn't. You got something all your own. If only you'd stay out of trouble.

I reply simply: *Make me.* Perhaps the most immature yet sexually charged thing you can say to someone. I wait a second or two for his response.

Then: *Can I come over?*

Alarm bells start going off in my head. How did I get here? Where am I? *Who* am I?

This is the feeling I had in the park with Manny. This is the feeling you get when you're on a ride and you reach the absolute top, right before you drop. And I'm going for it.

Sure. I'll let you know when my parents leave for work.

He replies almost immediately.

See ya then. ;)

Oh my God. Am I really going through with this? I think about his face. Yes, apparently, I am.

What feels like hours later, my parents finally head to work, but before I hit up Ziggy with my address, I have to squeeze a few things in first. I take my morning dump, shower (meticulously), get dressed in casual, semi-flattering clothes, and run a comb through my hair. I look at myself in the mirror and mouth shrug. I don't look too bad. Then I send Ziggy my address before I can convince myself not to.

If I thought the wait for my parents to leave the house was long, this one is several consecutive eternities. After I sent Ziggy the message, I threw my phone across the room, so I wouldn't have to look at it. For all I know he could have messaged back with "Actually, you're disgusting. I'm not coming over after all."

I pace the living room, refusing to check my phone. He knows where I live. If he wants to come over, he can. If not, then he doesn't. No games.

But what if something legitimate came up? There are two roads with my street name. One's actually a street and the other's technically an avenue. What if—

And then I hear it: a knock on the door. For a moment I consider running to the bathroom and shitting again, but I'm pretty much empty at this point. It has to be the nerves.

I take a deep breath and try to convince myself that Ziggy is human. I mean, *remind* myself that Ziggy is human.

I walk over to the door and open it.

"Hey!" he says.

Oh no. He's shirtless. And sweaty. And smiling. And his teeth are so, so white.

"Heyyyy," I say, feeling like someone squeezed the air out of my lungs.

He leans in, and we hug, like actually hug, which is an extremely bold choice considering the glistening layer of sweat that's coating him. I wonder if he knows I'm the opposite of grossed out. I wonder if he knows how good he smells after a run. How is that even possible?

When we break away, I say, "Come in, come in," and close the door behind him.

He stands in the center of the living room and surveys the house, fists on his hips. He nods slowly.

"Nice place."

"Thanks." I don't know how he can say that. The room suddenly feels cramped to me as I think about Ziggy's mini mansion, the one that stands not too far from Tyler's now that I think about it.

Ziggy wipes his forehead, and the sight of his armpit hair makes me shiver.

"Want something to drink?" I ask too loudly.

I know *I'm* thirsty as fuck.

"Yeah," he says, "some Gatorade would be great."

"We're a Powerade family."

He laughs, and a ball of electricity grazes the top of my right ear.

"All right by me."

I walk past the counter into the kitchen and open the fridge.

"What flavor do you want?" I call out.

"Which do you have?"

"Red, yellow, and blue."

"I'll take the blue."

I grab a bottle for him and a red one for myself, then walk back into the living room.

"Thanks," he says as I hand it to him. He cracks open the cap and says, "Cheers."

"Cheers."

We clink and drink.

As he lifts the bottle to his lips and takes several, long gulps, I catch every movement of his upper body. The way his bicep bulges, the up and down of his Adam's apple, even the slight in and out of his stomach muscles.

He lets out a satisfied gasp, the bottle half-empty now. "Thanks, man, you're a lifesaver."

"No problem." I lead him over to the couch, and we sit, putting our Powerades on the coffee table. Well, on coasters on the coffee table. I would prefer it if my mom didn't kill me.

"How's your summer been?" he asks.

"Fine," I say. "Haven't been doing much. You?"

"Good, good. Except for the whole insomnia thing."

"Oh right. What's going on?"

"Nothing big. I . . . well, remember how I told you I'm working with my dad at his practice?" I nod. "Well, I love it. I know I'm supposed to be like, '*This isn't my dream, Dad! It's yours!*'" I laugh, smitten. "But I really love volunteering there."

"That's good."

"Yeah."

"But."

"But my dad's patients aren't always . . . They kinda . . ."

"Ziggy, what is it?"

He sighs. "Every time my dad introduces me to one of his white patients, they're surprised. And, like, I don't really fault them for that. But some of them are so nice."

"Assholes," I say without thinking.

He smirks. "No, like, in a fake way. Like they're looking for a way to mention that they really love Jordan Peele movies."

I laugh.

"And yeah, that's better than the patients who won't make eye contact with me or assume I'm the janitor before my dad introduces me, but still. Last night I couldn't stop thinking about . . . all that."

"That sucks."

He leans back against the couch and sighs. "Yeah."

He must be so exhausted. In a lot of ways. What should I do? Or say?

I put my hand on his shoulder. He looks at it and smiles. That's a start. Then I change the subject.

"I assume you ran all the way here?"

"Yup," he says, sitting a little taller. "You're only six miles away, which is my sweet spot."

"Dear Lord."

"What?"

"I did a half-mile run to Saybrook Park yesterday, and I had to stop there for like ten minutes."

He laughs, but then tilts his head to the side. "Wait a minute, I was there yesterday."

"I know."

He gives me a weird look. "Were you stalking me?"

"Obviously. But also Mr. Chastman told me."

"Ohhhh. Yeah, I ran into him there."

"Me too. It was awkward."

"At least you weren't shirtless." He takes a drink of Powerade. "I'm assuming."

"I wasn't."

"You should try it. It's really freeing."

"Ha, no. I don't want to subject innocent bystanders to that."

"Ah, come on. I'm sure you look great."

"I, uh, I don't." I quickly grab my Powerade and chug a little. The static crinkles. I hope he can't see me blushing. "You though." I motion to his torso. "I know you're usually in shape for track, but you look, um, you look . . ."

"Bigger?"

"Yeah."

"Good. I've been trying to bulk up since winter break. It's hard with all the cardio, but I've been eating everything in sight and lifting almost every day."

"That's cool. Hard work pays off, I guess."

"Thanks, man."

We sit there and smile at each other. When I feel like we've been making eye contact for too long, I glance above his head at my parents' name cards. I quickly look away. My heart's racing, but I'm sure his is beating at a leisurely thirteen bpm or some shit. Then, it happens.

I don't know who starts it (probably Ziggy because he ends up on top of me), but all of a sudden we're kissing. And . . . I can't help but compare him with the only other person I've ever kissed.

Fabiola's lips were delicate but in control, like she was a sushi chef crafting a tray of carefully prepared rolls. One slight movement of her tongue involved my lower body in a way that seemed to defy human physiology. Ziggy's kiss is so aggressive I keep imagining two circles of teeth bumping against each other.

Fabiola also visited other parts of my body. She kissed my neck, licked along my jawline, and when she started on my ears, God Almighty, I felt things I never could have imagined. She bit my earlobe, and my entire body reacted like every cell was at a concert and they were all jumping up and down and singing in unison. Ziggy keeps his mouth pressed hard against mine and his eyes shut tight.

But it's not all bad, obviously. I like how much bigger he is. Especially when it comes to his hands. He's got one on my face and the other on my throat, and it's vaguely threatening, but I'm not *not* into it. I start poring over his long torso with my fingers. It's all so new because I'm not used to hard bodies; I'm used to my own.

I remove my mouth and hands for a moment, and Ziggy opens his eyes.

"What's wrong?" he asks, for some reason sounding hopeful.

"I wanna take my shirt off."

"Oh, okay."

He climbs off me, and I remove it. A new confidence takes over, and I don't care what I look like in comparison. I want my skin on his skin.

I climb on top of him, and we start kissing again. Suddenly, there's a new, urgent intensity to what I'm doing, so I shove my tongue into his mouth.

"Whoa, whoa, whoa."

Ziggy pushes me away, and I immediately back off.

"I'm sorry," I say. "Was that terrible?"

He clears his throat. "It's fast, don't you think?"

"Yeah," I say. "Definitely. I just, uh, I'm sorry. You're really attractive. Not that it's your fault. I'm not blaming you. I should've asked."

He clears his throat again. "I think I'm gonna go."

"Oh, okay."

He gets up from the couch and strides over to the door. I follow him.

"See ya," he says, opening it.

"See ya."

And then he's off. And I have no idea how to feel.

CHAPTER THIRTEEN

I wish I could focus on the monumental shift that's just taken place in my life. The fact that I kissed a guy for the first time. The fact that the guy was fucking gorgeous. The fact that I overcame my self-consciousness to enjoy it even more . . .

But then there's that awful, abrupt ending.

What if Ziggy realized what the consequences of kissing me would be? What if he freaks out and tries to turn this all around on me, saying that I used some, like, gay wizardry on him?

No. He wouldn't do that. He's not a malicious guy.

Which means I must have done *something*.

I keep replaying his words in my head. *It's just a little fast, don't you think?*

Wait, that's not exactly what he said. His exact words were *It's fast, don't you think?* The "just a little" would mitigate some of the blame. . . .

Ugh, I was actually making progress on my journey to transform myself this summer, and now it's all gone. Classic me.

It's only been an hour or so, and I'm still trying to decide if I should message Ziggy or not. If I offended him and don't check in on him, then I'm the worst. But what if he hasn't figured out how he's feeling yet and needs some time to reflect? Maybe *he* isn't even sure what happened. That doesn't seem likely, though. He ran out of here so fast. . . .

Then again, he did run *to* my house.

Ugh, fuck it, I'm messaging him.

And now comes my next dilemma. If I keep it too casual, I come off as callous and obtuse. If I'm too dour about it, he might think I'm dramatic and annoying.

I end up typing *Hey, you home?* It's simple, straightforward, and it'll let me feel things out. So I hit send.

My biggest fear is having to wait an agonizingly long time before I get a reply, but thank God his response is almost immediate.

Yeah, just arrived.

Those four words do little to help me suss out his mood.

How are you? I ask.

Good, you?

Ugh. That has to be the vaguest answer possible. He had his sweaty body on top of mine not too long ago, and that's the best he can do?

I'm also good.

Let's see how he responds to my vagueness.

Cool.

With more vagueness. Awesome. Should have expected that.

I type *Dude*, but delete it. This is not a "dude" moment.

Ziggy, we've been friends for a while now and I'm new to all this and I don't really know what's going on. I just really need to know if we're okay, if you're okay.

It takes a minute for him to reply.

We're cool. I'm cool. Don't worry.

You sure?

Yes.

I'll need proof.

We're cool. :)

I breathe a big sigh of relief. I know there's still something unresolved, something he's not saying, but I trust that it doesn't necessarily have to do with me.

That's a relief, Jackson.

Happy to oblige.

I'm still dying to know why you left tho.

A conversation for another time. Trust me.

I pause before I reply. *Fair enough.*

I'm still not sure exactly what to do with my day. I feel like I've lived an entire lifetime since waking, and it's not even eight o'clock. Sleep is out of the question because now that the awkwardness with Ziggy has been (somewhat) cleared up, I keep replaying the good parts of this morning and getting myself worked up.

I decide I need to tell someone about it. I can't keep the information to myself or it'll kill me. Obviously, my best option is Fabiola, but it takes me a few minutes of staring down my phone before I finally admit that I'm not mad at her anymore and call her.

"Hello?" she says groggily.

"Come over," I say.

"Quique, it's . . . seven fifty-five."

"Would I be waking you up and telling you to come over at this hour if it weren't warranted?"

Silence on her end. The last time I did this it was because I had stayed up the entire night finishing her favorite book (a novel called *Notes of a Crocodile*, which is about a lesbian going to college in Taiwan) and needed to talk to her about it immediately.

"I'll be there in fifteen," she says.

I wait until we're sitting on the couch before I tell her that Ziggy and I kissed. Her reaction is exactly what I thought it'd be.

"HOLY SHIT!" The drowsiness instantly vanishes from her face. "Really? Right here?"

I nod.

"Woooooow." She starts smoothing out her curly hair, which is wild right now. "Wow. Wow. Wow. I didn't even think Ziggy was into dudes."

"Really? He was my top prospect." Which isn't exactly true, but who cares. I'm actually really proud of my gaydar right now.

"I can't believe it. You did it. Without my help."

"I know, right?"

"And with Ziggy Jackson no less. Hmm, maybe I should have given more thought to my first guy-kiss."

"I was your first guy-kiss."

"Yeah . . . Wait, so how far did you guys go?"

"So we kissed for a while, and then I stopped to take my shirt off—"

"Yaaa—"

"—and then I climbed on top of him—"

"—aaaa—"

"—and started, like, grinding against him—"

"—aaas—"

"—and sticking my tongue in his mouth—"

"—ssss—"

"—and then he pulled away and said we were going too fast."

"—ss. Oh."

"Yeah."

"How exactly did he say it?" I tell her. "Hmm."

"So then I messaged him." I show her the conversation. "What do you think happened?"

"Hmm." She looks deep in thought. "Maybe . . . Maybe he didn't want to have sex."

"Huh? He thought we were gonna have sex?"

That hadn't even occurred to me honestly. The whole kissing-a-guy thing was milestone-y enough for a first-time encounter.

"I mean you did start thrusting into him like a mostly clothed porn star, didn't you?"

"Um, *sure*, but I wasn't gonna take it any further. I think."

"Well, he definitely didn't know that."

"I guess."

"You need to learn to control your white-hot sexual charisma."

"Ha. Ha."

"Does this mean you're ready for Tyler?"

"Oh, are you done with him?"

She looks guilty. "I know you mean that mockingly, but yes, I am."

"Well, thank you, I appreciate it," I say sarcastically.

She clears her throat. "And I'm actually really sorry, Quique."

Seeing the pained look on her face and knowing it's there because of me (even though I have a right to be mad or hurt or whatever) is too much for me. I hate when things between us are heavy.

"I know," I say. "So we're good."

"Fantastic, because this whole Ziggy thing is a big step, Quique. I remember after I kissed Mariana I felt so . . . I don't know, *free*. Because the whole world didn't end because I kissed a girl. And liked it."

She smiles at me, and I smile back. I feel exactly how she did.

"I'm glad I forced you to come over," I say. "For some reason, I took the Tyler thing pretty hard, and I was pretty pissed at you."

"I could tell," she says, putting her hand on mine. "We've barely even been texting since then."

"Yeah . . . Which sucked because I've been dying to know if Molly ever answered you."

She doesn't say anything right away, and I can tell from the look on her face that she's trying really hard not to reveal how she's feeling.

"Oh, come on." I say, "Out with it—"

"She wrote me a letter!"

"What?"

"Her parents took her phone away because she snuck out of the house for a concert—baller move, I might add—so she couldn't text me back. And since they also disabled the Wi-Fi, she had to write me a *fucking letter*."

She reaches into her pocket, takes out a folded-up piece of paper, and holds it to her chest.

"You have it?" I ask, surprised.

"Yeah. I've sort of been keeping it on me ever since I got it."

I wait for her to hand it to me so I can read it, but she doesn't. She must realize what's unsaid because she clears her throat and starts lowering the letter to her pocket, trying to look nonchalant.

"That dirty?" I ask.

"Uh . . . no," she says, sliding the letter into her pocket. "It's . . . I don't know. It's kinda personal. Like between us."

Oh. Usually "us" means, well, *us*.

"That's cool," I say, trying to mean it. "It's your relationship. Or whatever."

I force a laugh, and she smiles at me awkwardly.

But why is this awkward? I mean, I'm not entitled to reading the letter. Fabiola doesn't have to share *everything* with me. But I guess it still stings a bit knowing there are some things I won't be privy to when it comes to my best friend.

"No matter what," Fabiola says, looking at me earnestly, "we have to promise to never let anyone come between us again."

Oh thank God. An assurance.

"You got it," I say.

We pinkie swear on it, and I feel stupidly relieved.

"Especially because you're about to go on slut safari," Fabiola adds.

I laugh. The truth is I do have a newfound self-assuredness that I'd like to test out. Not only on Tyler, but Manny too.

"Oh my God," I say.

"What?" Fabiola says.

"I didn't tell you what happened with Manny!"

Fabiola and I spend the next hour or so hanging out the way we always have.

Her: "Listen to this song. I know you'll love it. The artist is Dominican, and I think she's singing about how the person she's with smells like weed and she likes it."

Me: "My mom's doing okay, I guess. She said she almost lost her shit with an old white lady who refused to understand that her coupon had expired. My dad actually did lose his shit the other day because the Dodgers lost."

Her: "Look who followed me after I made a meme of him. God, he's so funny. I wish he were into women."

Me: "Yeah, WebMD was like, *It's definitely an STI*, and I was like, *But I haven't had sex! How is that possible?* Turns out it was a pimple. Apparently, you can get those down there."

I hadn't realized how much I missed her, and I'm so glad that the me-and-her "us" is still alive and kickin'.

"All right, I gotta go back to sleep," she says finally, stifling a yawn.

"Thanks for coming over."

She gets up and walks over to the door.

"Keep me updated."

"Will do. You too. As much as you want."

She nods and smiles.

Once she's out the door, I spread out on the couch. Even though this is usually the time when I wake up, I'm starving (which makes sense because I haven't eaten since the quesadilla from yesterday). I don't want anything in the house at the moment, so I decide to put on some shoes and head to the nearest burger joint.

I order Pogo's number six combo, a pastrami burger with zucchini fries, and find a booth. I stare out the window until one of the workers, who's around my age, brings it over. He's not cute, but he's not ugly. I say thank you as he puts my food down, and he leaves without saying you're welcome. Definitely straight. Which makes me think about the question I asked myself in the mirror yesterday. Is it even more obvious now? Did finally kissing a guy emblazon an invisibly visible scarlet letter on my forehead?

I'm too hungry to care, which is a relief. I don't feel bi or queer or gay or straight or poly or pan or anything. For now, my sexuality is my attraction to the food in front of me, and I feel like I'll die if I don't go HAM on this hamburger in the next five seconds.

CHAPTER FOURTEEN

Saleem gets back from his trip in four days, which, obviously, I don't care about at all. In fact, I'm sitting on my bed updating my yearbook with what happened between me and Ziggy a couple days ago. I flip to where there's a picture of him giving an election speech, and think, *God, he looks good in a suit*. Then I click my pen and record what occurred as succinctly as I can next to the picture.

MO.

Made out.

It feels supremely anticlimactic, but it's undeniable proof that I'm getting on with my plan.

I'm about to close the yearbook when I decide to flip to the varsity sports section. Thanks to me there's a well-executed action shot of Tyler at the peak of his layup. I remember seeing the picture on my photographer's camera and thinking, *He looks like a totally different person*. The look on his face is so foreign to me because his eyes are focused and determined, and his dimples are nowhere to be seen.

I thumb through a couple sections to get to the junior class photos. Very nearly to the end of it, I find Manny's portrait. You'd think a guy like him wouldn't care about looking good for it, but the picture says otherwise. He's got a fresh fade, diamond studs, and a smile that wouldn't need any substantial words behind it to convince me to rob a bank with him.

"What are you up to?"

I look up, instinctively slamming my yearbook shut.

"Oh, hey, Mom." She's standing in the doorway, one eyebrow raised. "Just, uh . . . lookin'."

"At what?"

"Myself."

"You're just like your father. He cares way too much about his looks."

"He does?"

"Let me see."

She walks into my room and holds out her hand. My grip tightens on the yearbook, but there's no way out of this. I relax my fingers, open to where my photo is, and hand it to her. As she inspects the picture, I pray she doesn't turn the page in either direction. Ziggy's portrait is on the page before mine.

"You used too much gel," she says.

I laugh. "Yeah."

Her eyes scan a bit and stop. "*Aw*, Saleem." She looks up at me. "He's got some eyes on him, doesn't he?"

My mouth is suddenly very dry. "I, uh, haven't noticed."

She nods, closes the yearbook, and hands it back to me.

"When does he get back?" she asks.

"This Saturday."

"We should have him over for dinner. Fabiola too."

"Uh, yeah, that would be cool."

"Ask them when they're free."

"Okay, I wi—" My phone dings, and I glance at it.

"Him or her?"

"Uh, him."

"His ears must have been burning. What'd he say?"

I open the text.

Quique, why have you let me believe for so long that Beyoncé's singing, "My c***'s waiting on the phone" in "Suga Mama" when the actual lyrics are, "My ACCOUNTANT'S waiting on the phone?!"

I try to hold in a snort, which makes me swallow wrong, which turns into a coughing attack. When I'm able to breathe, I say, "Nothing, Mom. Something really stupid."

She's reading my face, but since I'm not actually lying, she says, "I see . . . Well, let him know about dinner when you can."

"Will do."

As she walks away, I take a deep breath and reply.

U stupit idiot

I'm so happy to hear from him that I hit send before I could uncapitalize the *u.*

AYA AND ALL OF OUR COUSINS ARE LAUGHING AT ME. I SAID IT WAS INAPPROPRIATE TO PLAY THAT SONG IN FRONT OF OUR SITTI AND THEY ASKED WHY, AND I SAID IT HAD THAT WORD, AND NOW THEY'LL NEVER LET ME FORGET IT.

I'm smiling at the beginning of the text, but I stop at the end when a thought crosses my mind. He's not just talking about Aya and his cousins. He probably means Ahed too.

I let out a huge sigh and fall back onto my bed. Moving on feels easy (enough) when one of my prospects is in front of me (or under me), but Saleem doesn't even mention her, and

I start to spiral? I've been improving. I've been focused. I've been making progress. And yet . . .

I'm back in the car. It's last summer. My arm's hanging out the window, and I'm singing along to the radio as a stray bottle rocket explodes in the sky. The sun is setting, and I'm driving toward it. I'm on my way to Saleem.

From late June to mid-July in East LA, it's Fireworks Season, because my people (Mexicans, not queers) care less about the exact date of Independence Day than we do about colorful explosives. For this reason, as I drove to Saleem's apartment complex, I felt like I was living someone else's life.

I reached the gate at the entrance and punched in the code before I drove in. I parked across the street from his place and got out. Before I could even start walking up the stairs, Saleem exited his apartment with our towels in hand. He was wearing trunks.

"Hey!" I said.

"Hey," he said.

Then he smiled at me, but it was tempered by something. I assumed at the time that he was simply readjusting to being back home because he'd just gotten back from a week in Jersey.

When he reached the bottom of the stairs, we hugged awkwardly. Before we pulled away, a burst of yellow fireworks exploded above us.

"Happy First of July," he said sarcastically.

I forced a laugh. Okay, there was definitely something off about him.

We walked to the pool in silence, and I did my best to not

keep looking at him. When we arrived, he took off his shirt, and I stripped down to my boxers before we dove in. Well, he dove in; I just kinda walked until there was water instead of concrete beneath my feet. Saleem did a couple laps while I floated on my back like a starfish, gazing up at the sky. There was an occasional burst of chemically bright color against the natural, soft pink/purple/blue of the sunset.

Saleem took a seat on a ledge not too far from me.

"Quique?"

"Yeah?" I asked, not turning to look at him.

"What part of Mexico is your family from again?"

"Uh . . . I don't know."

"Oh. I thought you mentioned a state before."

"Nope. It was my great-great-grandparents who immigrated, and I've never really bothered to ask anyone where from."

"I see."

I turned my head slightly. "Why do you ask?"

"No reason."

His voice was higher than usual with the kind of overdone nonchalance characteristic of a parent trying to pry into their kid's social life.

"Are you wondering where you came from?" I asked. "I mean, I know you and your parents were born here, but are you, like, curious about where your family's from?"

He skimmed his fingers over the water, just barely breaking the surface tension.

"Yes. Seeing my older aunts and uncles and grandparents always makes me wonder what life is like there. I have no idea.

The only time I see Palestine in videos or pictures is when something horrible has happened.

"But I want to know everything about . . . everything. Like what their schools looked like and the subjects they learned. Who their friends were and if they had stupid inside jokes. What it smelled like at dinnertime. What the adhan sounds like there. How they celebrated holidays. The family they left behind . . . And not just the ones who survived."

I listened to the gentle lapping of the pool water before I spoke.

"Why don't you ask them?"

He was quiet for a second. "I don't think they want to talk about it. I get bits and pieces, but then they start thinking too much about it and change the subject."

I let myself sink so that my feet touched the bottom of the pool. I finally faced him.

"Too painful?" I asked.

He nodded.

I thought back to the year I met Saleem, particularly to one of the most uncomfortable things I've ever seen happen to him.

"Do you remember . . ." I cleared my throat. "Do you remember the thing with Ms. Gray? The globe thing?"

Saleem's eyes drifted away from mine, until he was looking over my shoulder at a particularly intense fireworks display I could only hear.

"Yes, I do."

We were in middle school and he had only been there for a few months at that point, but I had already become enamored with him from afar. Our teacher, Ms. Gray, was a young, sweet, well-meaning white lady, and one day, she had the idea to make everyone in our class find their country of origin on the globe she'd placed at the front of the room. It was her way of celebrating our classroom's diversity and I don't blame her for what happened, but what resulted still makes me cringe every time I think about it.

Ms. Gray herself was the first to do it. She pointed to Ireland and talked a little about her great-great-great-grandfather, or whoever, coming to America in the 1800s. Then she had each student come up and show her where their ancestors came from. For the most part, we stuck to the Western Hemisphere, given that Mexico and a good number of Central and South American nations were represented.

Then it came time for thirteen-year-old Saleem to go up.

"I remember walking to the front," Saleem said, still not looking at me, "knowing that the globe wouldn't have the name on it because I had already checked the first day of class."

Of course he knew. That explains the stiffness in his young shoulders and how slowly he walked, like he was hoping a fire alarm or a meteor or something would interrupt class.

"A lot of the kids actually needed help," I said, "but you knew exactly where to point."

Saleem's eyes came back to mine. "The only thing missing was the name of the country."

"Which one are you pointing to?" Ms. Gray had asked. "Jordan?"

Middle School Saleem shook his head, picked up his finger, and pointed again.

"Israel?" Ms. Gray said.

"Palestine," Saleem said.

Her face turned violently crimson, and she spoke quickly. "Oh. Thank you, Saleem. So, everyone, it's silent reading time!" Sixteen-year-old Saleem shook his head, smiled a sad smile.

"I was so humiliated. All the whispering that broke out after . . . I hurried back to my seat and spent the rest of class with my eyes on my book, but I wasn't reading."

It's true that the rest of us were initially confused by what had happened and speculated about it, but we forgot all about it when we engrossed ourselves in our Percy Jackson books right after. I only started to understand the significance of that moment about a year later when Saleem opened up about his family history (in the pool, naturally). All he said was his grandparents fled Palestine during the sixties because things turned ugly, but that led to me learning from Google about the Six-Day War, when Israel went to war with a bunch of Arab countries and violently seized control of even more Palestinian land, and a lot of other pivotal moments in Palestinian history. I kicked myself for not doing my research right after the globe incident.

There was another school incident that I didn't need to ask if he remembered, considering it had happened a few months earlier.

Saleem and I were in the same world history class, and our teacher was Mr. Stewart, who told us on the first day of school that the United States was the best country in the world and his favorite president was Reagan. One day, late into the year, we covered the aftermath of World War II and the founding of Israel, and after about twenty minutes of him going on and on about how because of the atrocities the Jewish people had suffered, they deserved a safe haven, their own country, Saleem spoke up for maybe the third time that year (despite the fact that he knew everything, he'd always been shy).

"And who was already there?"

Mr. Stewart immediately stopped talking and gave Saleem a puzzled look. Everyone's eyes fell on Saleem.

"I beg your pardon?" Mr. Stewart said.

Saleem had had his eyes on his textbook when he interrupted Mr. Stewart, but he looked up before he asked, again, "Who was already living in Palestine before 1948?"

Mr. Stewart's mouth hung open, but no words came out. I thought all of us in that classroom were going to live in that silence forever.

"Oh . . . Uh . . . Well, there was a small Arab population, but they—"

"Were killed," Saleem finished for him. "Or beaten. Or kicked out of their homes. It's called the Nakba, and it never really ended."

"Now, now, that's ridiculous. Both sides—"

"It's true," I said finally. Saleem looked at me, and I held his gaze, scared but braver when I looked at him. "I see it all the time on the Internet. Israeli people just taking people's homes or Palestinians being forced to demolish their own—"

"Well, if it's on the *Internet* it must be true," Mr. Stewart said with an eye roll.

"My grandfather still has a key to his childhood home," Saleem said. "His father gave it to him before he died. He thought eventually they'd return."

Saleem waited to see if Mr. Stewart would respond to that and continued when he didn't.

"Ever since those colonizers started settling in Palestine, there have been countless human rights violations. 'Israel' kept invading, seizing, and occupying Palestinian land and homes, killing Palestinian people, jailing us, controlling our movements, our access to water—"

The bell rang then, and Mr. Stewart, being the upstanding intellectual he prided himself on being, said, "That's all the time we have for today. Tomorrow we start on the beginning of the Cold War."

After class, Saleem and I walked to our next period in silence because I didn't know what to say. He was obviously upset but trying hard not to let it show, and I felt helpless to make him feel better. Months later, in that pool, looking at my friend, directly into his tawny eyes, I felt that way again.

"I wonder what it would be like," Saleem said.

"What what would be like?"

I expected him to say something like, *I absolutely abhor the fact that the English language allows for that grammatical construction to exist,* but instead he said, "Growing up surrounded by . . . my people."

I understood (as much as I could) where he was coming from thanks to a conversation I had with Fabiola not too long before that. She had confided in me about how being Afro–Puerto Rican/Cuban meant that she didn't always feel welcome in Latinx spaces, that there were things I'd never understand about her experience with Latinidad. I remember feeling hurt when she told me that. Or not hurt, really, but discomfort, a selfish kind of discomfort, and I felt that way again in the pool. Like last time, I tried to hide it.

But Saleem must have seen it in my expression—or my silence—because he said, "I mean don't get me wrong. I love it here. I relate to the South Asian Muslims here and the other Arabs, but based on how excited I get when I meet another Palestinian at masjid, I fantasize about what it would be like to live in a place where I'm constantly interacting with people who share my exact culture and history. I wish I could have been born in Palestine and raised there, even for a couple years or so. But I can't exactly tell my parents that because I know my grandparents must have sacrificed so much for us to be born here. But it would have had to have been meaningful."

Another grammatical disaster he did not comment on.

A breeze drifted past us, and we listened to the rippling of the water before Saleem spoke again.

"I feel like a zoo animal sometimes. You know how they talk about a tiger that's born in captivity but still yearns for the wild? It feels like I'm that tiger, as if I were born in a cage, but I still feel the jungle beneath my feet, as if it's ingrained in my DNA."

He gave me a look that begged me to understand him. It was the only thing that kept me from making a joke to cut the tension.

I ended up putting my hand on his bare shoulder.

"I don't know what that's like, and it kills me that you feel that way."

"Thanks," he said. From what I could tell he didn't look disappointed or relieved. Which, to be quite honest, is the best-case scenario for when I comfort someone. "It doesn't help that everyone thinks I'm weird. Or worse, dangerous."

And once again I thought about middle school. Most of the Latino kids assumed Saleem was one of us, but when they realized he wasn't, when they found out his name or he talked about his religion, they said horrible, terrible, racist, hateful things. And I didn't stop them. I pretended not to hear.

I squeezed his shoulder.

"Saleem, I know I didn't stand up for you like I should've back then—"

"It's okay. We were all young and . . ."

"But I'm here now. And believe me when I say this: From now on, if *anyone* tries to hurt you or say something shitty about you . . . I will *literally* fight them."

I'd never said anything like that before, but I had just realized something: You can't love someone if you're not willing to fight for them. And boy did I love that boy in front of me.

My heart was beating fast. It was hard to breathe. Our eyes locked onto each other's, and I felt myself slipping into his. If I could've spent forever like that I would've.

He swallowed. "Thank you, Quique. That means a lot."

His voice sounded unsteady.

I removed my hand and cleared my throat.

"That's what I'm here for."

And I meant it.

I still mean it. I sit up, pick up my phone, and stare at Saleem's contact photo. I think about what would happen if someone hurt him and what I would do, and I feel zero doubt about whether or not I'd have his back.

CHAPTER FIFTEEN

Sometimes I get Saleem hangovers, which is what I call what happens after I experience a particularly intense flood of emotions related to how I feel for him, like I did yesterday. It's almost identical to an actual hangover—I spend the next day curled up in bed with a pit in my stomach, regretting all or most of my decisions—which sounds a bit dramatic, but I happen to be a bit dramatic. Also, I'm not the best at expressing my emotions, so they make a habit of manifesting as physical symptoms.

It's the Fourth of July, so my mom and dad are off today. They've been checking in on me, but I keep telling them I stayed up really late last night and need sleep. I love that they know me well enough to trust me. They know if things get bad enough, I'll ask for their help, like I did three summers ago. See, my parents make it clear that they're there for me but give me the alone time I so desperately need, or think I need.

But would it help to tell them about the reason behind The Breakdown? It would be weird. It would be awkward. It would be irreversible. But can I carry the weight of this secret on my own?

I try to picture exactly how they'd react.

Me: "Mom, Dad, I'm into guys. I'm not gay, but, man, am I into men."

My mom: "Is Saleem your boyfriend?"

My dad: "So you take it up the ass?"

I shake my head violently. Is that actually what they'd say? No. Let me try again.

Me: "Mom, Dad, I like girls."

My mom: "Are you sure?"

My dad: "Do you really though?"

Me: "Yes and yes. But I also like guys."

My mom: "There it is."

My dad: "I knew it."

Me: "Wait, so you're okay with it?"

Both: Laugh.

My mom: "Of course not!"

My dad: "You think we want a faggot for a son?"

I slap myself. Also not a possibility. They love me. A lot. They know no one's perfect. They know I'm a good person. They also saw that scene in *Captain America* where Chris Evans emerges from the body-transforming machine.

Me: "Mom, Dad, I'm bisexual. Not gay, or straight, or confused. Bi."

My mom: "Okay . . . Thanks for telling us, honey. We still love you. Not that you should have ever questioned that."

My dad: "Your mom's right. You'll always be my boy."

There. That feels right. But would it be perfect? No. Would they say that I should marry a woman? Probably. Would they tell me to keep it among the three of us and never tell another soul because *those* people might not be as accepting? Yes.

And so I don't want to tell them. Not yet, anyway. It's my gay and I can keep it to myself. For now.

I eventually get out of bed around three o'clock and do all the things that normal people do without effort: shower, dress, eat. I'm in the living room with a bowl of cereal, watching Netflix, when my parents come in. They look surprised to see me. More than that, their hair is disheveled, and their faces are flushed. I'm pretty sure they just had sex.

My mom recovers quickly enough.

"Move over," she says.

I do and she sits next to me. My dad sits on the other side of me.

None of us say a word, and I know we're all trying really hard to focus on what's going on on-screen, which is unfortunate for me because I'm watching a mockumentary about a high school that's plagued by a series of poop-related pranks.

"Now that's just gross," my mom says.

"I'm gonna put something else on."

I switch over to cable because I don't want my parents to see a bunch of gay shit in the "Watch it again" section. I made them each their own profile a while back to avoid discovery.

"So," my dad says when I've settled on a real documentary about dolphins, "your mom wants to go out for dinner tonight. You up for it?"

I swallow the cereal in my mouth. "Uh . . . Yeah, sure."

"All right then," he says. "You're DD."

I smile.

Even though it would be hard to accuse my mom and dad of being the "friend" type of parents who don't let their kids know who's in charge, I've always enjoyed the freedom I've felt as a result of the fact that they have, between the two of them, a life. They are each other's best friends (most of the time), so I'm a welcome addition, not a necessity.

Some parents pin all their hopes and dreams on their children, and as a result, those kids feel all kinds of pressure to be some sort of familial savior destined to achieve greatness and keep their extended family from drowning. And while I feel that pressure even without their showing it, I know my parents are happy as long as my head's above water. Which, for now, it is.

An hour or so before we're supposed to leave for the restaurant, my mom and dad start getting ready. They upgrade their clothes, do their hair, and shave (different areas of their bodies). This makes me feel obligated to put on some pants and a non-T-shirt shirt (specifically a brightly colored Hawaiian grandpa shirt that my mom jokingly bought for me—it was eight bucks at JCPenney—that I ended up loving).

Then we head out. My dad drives *to* the restaurant, narrating everything he does so that I'm aware of all the "subtle, skillful things" a great driver like himself does that go unnoticed to the untrained eye. He quickly pulls into a parking spot near the front, getting there just in time to beat a car trying to get to it from the other direction.

"Not today, cabrón!" he calls out gleefully.

My mom laughs and slaps his arm. I place a hand on my chest and feel my heart pound against my rib cage. I'm glad I'm driving home.

There are about a dozen or so parties waiting inside the restaurant to be seated, but my mom somehow gets the hostess to promise to seat us within the next few minutes. We wait in the outside seating area where they serve before-dinner margaritas. My parents each order one, and they seem to materialize in seconds. They're disappearing almost as quickly.

"Agghh," my dad groans, holding the right side of his face. "Brain freeze."

"That's why I get mine on the rocks instead of blended," my mom says. She's nearly drained the giant glass in her hand.

"They help me pace myself," my dad says.

My mom puts down her margarita glass, which has nothing but ice in it, and holds up her hands. "Well, *excuse* me. Mira 'pacing myself.'"

My dad laughs. "You'll be sorry when you're hungover tomorrow. You need water, and you choked that down before the ice could even melt."

My mom looks like she has a response locked and loaded, but she glances at me and all she says is, "We'll see, Abel."

The hostess, true to her word, comes to seat us before my dad can finish his margarita. He leaves it outside.

El Pez is a Mexican seafood place with an obnoxiously big and bright neon sign on the outside. On nights like tonight, the inside looks more like a club. There's a section of the restaurant that's just a bar and an open area for dancing. The hostess takes us to the other side, where she seats us at a table for four. My parents sit together, and I sit across from them.

"What are you getting, Quique?" my dad asks when our hostess is gone.

"Same thing as always," I reply.

"Chiles rellenos," my mom says.

I nod. I'm not one to change up my order.

"I'm getting camarones a la diabla this time," my dad announces.

He, on the other hand, is.

"You're gonna regret it," my mom says.

"My tongue can handle it."

"Your mouth isn't the end I'm worried about."

They stare at each other before they bust out laughing. I join them.

My parents have another margarita before they get their dinner, a margarita while they eat their dinner, and a margarita after they finish their dinner. As the waitress takes their credit card, my mom sucks the last few dregs of her glass while my dad has a stare down with his, willing it not to give him any more brain freeze.

"He damn sure wasn't the smartest guy after me," my mom slurs at the end of her "how me and your father got together" story. "Or the handsomest." She swirls her ice with her straw. "Or the tallest. Or—"

"Just the best in bed," my dad says, interrupting her.

I expect my mom to hit him or laugh or joke about how small his penis is, but she shrugs. I shake my head, trying to erase these past few hours. All throughout dinner, I've been hearing the same stories I've heard my entire life, but with new details added due to both of my parents' advanced inebriation. This new detail I did not need to know. But go Dad, I guess.

Before we leave, my dad finishes his margarita in one long pull and grimaces all the way to the car. On the ride home, he passes out in the back seat while my mom turns up the radio and sings to every song that comes on, even if she doesn't know the lyrics.

When we get home, my dad goes straight to bed, while my mom, still in party mode, breaks out the tequila.

"Have a shot with me, son."

"Huh?"

She grabs two shot glasses from the kitchen and comes back to the living room.

"It's the Fourth of July." She sways as she talks. "Independence Day. Independence for who, I don't know. But we're gonna use this day as an opportunity to drink. So drink with me, mijo."

She hands me the Disneyland shot glass and keeps the Las Vegas one for herself. Then she fills both of them up with tequila.

My parents have always been pretty chill about alcohol. Over the years they've let me sample various beers, wines, and mixed drinks, but I've never taken a shot with one of them before. My mom must be really hammered.

"Cheers," I say.

"Cheers," she says.

And we both knock 'em back.

"How was that?" she asks.

"All right."

"Do you want another one?"

Is this a trick question? She doesn't look like she usually does when she's laid a trap for me. . . .

"Only if you think I can handle it, mamacita."

She refills our glasses. "You're my son. Of course you can."

We once again down them together.

"Okay," she says, "that's enough. Otherwise, Child Services'll be knocking on the door any second."

She goes back to the kitchen, puts the shot glasses in the sink, and takes a swig of tequila straight from the bottle.

"Do something about the music situation," she calls out.

I walk over to the stereo system next to the TV, turn it on, and connect it to my phone. I know exactly what kind of music my mom likes, so it's not too long before she's dancing around the house to an eclectic array of multi-genre bops. (At one point she busts into her bedroom and dances on the bed, her legs on either side of my dad, who groans, turns over, and covers his head with a pillow.) I'm not buzzed enough to join her.

Before I know it, she collapses on the couch, whether from drunkenness or exhaustion, I can't tell.

"Quique," she says, "come over here."

I obey and sit down next to her.

She puts her hand on my face, her eyes looking intense but also far away.

"You're a person," she says.

"Sometimes, yeah."

"I created you. For seventeen years of my life you didn't exist, and then one second you did. And now you're a whole human being. With a life and a personality. It's so weird."

"I can only imagine."

"And I'm so, so relieved you came out how you did. You're my favorite person."

I smile, my eyes watering a bit. "Thanks, Mom. You're mine."

And in this moment, it's true.

"I did good with you. Even though I'm a mess."

My first instinct is to deny it. "You're not a—" But then I stop.

"I am," she says.

"You kinda are," I say.

We both laugh.

"But I've always loved you," she says, stroking my cheek. "*So* much. And I always will. No matter what."

And she's said it. Those three magic words. *No matter what.*

She drops her hand, and I say, "Mom?"

"Yes, Quique?"

"What would you say if I told you I'm . . . that I . . . that I'm kinda really . . ."

"Kid, you have five seconds to tell me whatever it is you want to tell me because I am fading, honey."

I swallow hard and clear my throat.

"I think I'm in love with Saleem."

I didn't mean to say it like that. It just came out that way. *I* just came out that way.

I wait for her to respond, but her face is blank, like she hasn't heard me. This is worse than what I imagined. Silence is worse than anything she could say. Why did I do this? Why did I think this would work out? This was a mistake. I should've—

"Does he love you back?"

"Huh?"

Why would she ask that?

"Is Saleem in love with you, too?"

I shake my head. "Uh, no, he's not."

"That must hurt."

My face gets hot, and for the first time in a long time I feel tears forming.

"It does," I manage to squeak out.

She reaches up and holds my face. "I'm so sorry, honey. I really am."

I nod, not able to speak at this point. I can feel it now. The tears are definitely coming.

"Come here," she says.

I lie down next to her and curve my body into hers. I'm sobbing now, my entire body shaking.

"Shh, shh," she says, holding me.

We're like that for a while before I stop crying. At some point, I notice that her grip around me has loosened. Then I realize I can hear her snoring softly in my ear. I unwrap her arm from around my waist and slide off the couch. I check to see if I woke her, but she's still completely unconscious.

I grab a sheet from the hallway closet, cover her, and leave a glass of water and a bottle of Advil for her on the coffee table. Then I retreat to my room. It feels like one big weight has been lifted off my shoulders, but another one has been added on. Part of me wants my mom to wake up tomorrow and remember nothing, like when I was ten and I broke her favorite shot glass (a plain glass one that she won in a drinking contest at some bar) while she was drunk and she woke up the next morning and assumed she did it. But that's all up to chance. And neurochemistry, I guess.

I lie on my bed and stare up at the ceiling, feeling like the room is spinning, knowing it's not because of the alcohol.

CHAPTER SIXTEEN

Earlier this morning, my mom knocked softly on my door, and I pretended to be asleep when she opened it. Why? Because it's time to initiate Avoidance Mode™.

Right now, I can hear my parents' voices sound from the kitchen, and I worry that at this very moment my mom is telling my dad exactly what I told her last night. I hear my dad's laugh and realize that can't be the case. He's a fan of gay jokes but not *our son literally likes dudes* jokes. I wish they were going to work today, but they always take the fifth off knowing they'll be hungover, which makes sense because I think I'm meant to face my problems head-on today. God is clearly telling me to clear the air and deal with the consequences.

And that is exactly what I'm *not* going to do.

Instead, I take out my phone and text Fabiola. She will be my saving grace.

Fifteen minutes later, I hear the doorbell. My dad answers the door, and I hear his voice higher than usual as he exclaims, "Fabiola! How nice to see you!"

She says something I don't catch in reply.

Then I hear my mom saying hi and something about how long it's been since she's seen her. A low-volume conversation follows, and before I know it, someone's banging on my door. I close my eyes as it opens.

"Quique!"

It's Fabiola. I open my eyes and do my best to pretend I've just woken up.

"Fabiola? What are you doing here?"

My parents are standing behind her.

"Picking you up, idiot!"

"For what?"

"My hairstylist's cousin's quince! What else?"

"Ohhhh," I say. "I totally forgot."

"I figured. Okay, well, I'm gonna have breakfast with your parents while you get ready. Then we're off! Okay?"

"Okay."

"Hurry up!" she says, and closes the door.

God I love that girl.

We're in Fabiola's pickup on our way to nowhere in particular. After I got dressed earlier (in a suit because Fabiola just had to pick a quince as the fake event she was taking me to), I said a quick goodbye to my parents before peace-ing out. I take off my jacket and begin unbuttoning my dress shirt.

"So, what do you have planned for today?" Fabiola asks. "We're gonna have to stay out of town if we're gonna avoid running into your parents."

"Uh, I haven't really thought about it. Although, I guess I'll have to buy a new pair of shorts right about now. I'm not gonna walk around all day in a T-shirt, Chucks, and dress pants."

"How were you able to remember to bring a change of shoes but not a change of pants?"

"I don't know how my brain works, Fabiola, you know this."

"Right. So, first stop: the mall."

"Yes. But not the one—"

"Not the one we usually go to. Duh, I'm not stupid, Quique."

"Of course not. Would a stupid person invent their hairstylist's cousin's quinceañera?"

She smiles. "It's not made up. My hairstylist's cousin is actually having her quince today."

"You're joking."

"Nope! I like to ground my lies in reality."

"Crafty."

She checks her blind spot and then merges into the right lane. I've always admired her ease while driving. Even though her style is borderline dangerous, she's always in control. She has a Manny-like confidence that's still characteristically her. Watching her, in her red sundress with black and white flowers on it, with her so-dark-brown-they-look-black eyes, with her no makeup, I'm a little . . . turned on.

"Quique, why are you staring at me?"

"I was checking you out."

"Oh. I charge, you know."

"Add it to my tab."

She smiles. It didn't occur to me to lie to her. About that.

"Here," she says, handing me her phone. "If I look hot right now, the least you can do is snap a picture and send it to Molly."

I do as she says, varying the framing and the angles.

"Gimme," she says when I'm reviewing the pictures.

"No."

"Quique."

"You're driving, I gotchu."

I select what I feel is the best pic—the one that accentuates the pure volume of her hair, the curve of her chest, and her manicured fingernails on the steering wheel—and send it to Molly. I get a reply almost immediately.

"What did she say?" Fabiola asks.

"Um . . . She . . ."

"Come on, tell me!"

"Quiet, I'm counting."

"Counting? Why—"

"She responded with sixty-nine heart-eye emojis."

"Nice."

Indeed. I'm trying really hard not to be envious. But I so am.

"So," Fabiola says, "you *really* told your mom about Saleem?"

"Yup."

"Wow."

"I know."

"That's ballsy," she says as she merges onto the 60 ramp. "If my parents ever found out about my bi ass they'd freak the fuck out."

Like my mom and dad, Fabiola's parents disapprove of certain "lifestyles" despite their life-of-the-party lifestyle. Fabiola has an older male cousin who she used to hang out with all the time before he came out as gay. After that, her parents wouldn't let her be alone with him and were super awkward around him at family parties.

"Thanks," I say. "And I'm sorry."

"No problem. It's cool. I mean, it's not, but it is."

"They love you, ya know." I'm almost certain that Fabiola's parents wouldn't react the same way they did with her cousin. I can tell by the way they look at her, like she can do no wrong. "Like a lot. I've seen it."

She sighs. "I know but . . . I wouldn't come out to them unless it was necessary, like if I ended up wife-ing Molly or something. I don't want to . . . burden them. You know what I mean?"

I picture myself in my room at age fourteen, soaking wet from head to toe with sweat, gasping for breath. I had just spent ten minutes running in place, my knees practically hitting my chest, in an attempt to diffuse all the manic energy that had hit me like a school bus as soon as I woke up. It was summer, and the sweating wouldn't stop. My vision kept going black. I walked slowly to the bathroom and crumpled to the cheap tile my dad put in himself. I crawled over to the tub, got inside, and grabbed the showerhead. I turned on the cold water and sprayed myself in the face with it until I came back.

"Yeah," I say, swallowing hard, "I know what you mean."

I find cheap, acceptable shorts at H&M and wear them out of the store. Fabiola wolf-whistles at me when she sees them. They're a little more revealing than my usual cut.

"Damn, baby," she says, handing me a Mocha Milkshake,

this mall's version of a Cappuccino Chiller. "Who knew you had cake like that?"

"Everyone who's ever touched my butt. So . . . you."

We start walking.

"And Ziggy," she says.

"No, actually."

"What? He didn't grab your ass?" I shake my head. "That's straight-up disrespectful! What is wrong with that boy?"

I shrug. "Not to be weird, but what me and you did was so much better."

"It'd be weird if you didn't think that."

I laugh.

The mall we're at is a lot nicer than the one back home. It's got four floors instead of two, with glass elevators and high-end stores. As we go down the escalator, I take a sip of the Mocha Milkshake, and I gotta say coffee-flavored ice cream–based drinks are the one area our mall's got this one beat.

"Tyler would have the common decency to grab your ass," Fabiola says. She drinks from her own Cappuccino Chiller knockoff. "I say that based on personal experience."

"Sore subject."

"I thought we were over that little incident."

"Best not to test it."

"Well, it's a good thing we probably won't see him here. Can't have that li'l wanksta breaking up our friendship."

"Mm-hmm. Although, with my luck we're still bound to run into someone from school despite being an hour away."

"You think?"

"Yup." I take a quick look around. "I've seen more of our

classmates in public spaces in the past three weeks than I ever have before that. It's uncanny."

"Well, who do you hope it is? Do you want to clear things up with Ziggy in person? Do you want to see Manny in a place where he's not very likely to attack someone?"

I sigh. "I don't know, Fabiola. This is all exhausting. I just want to live my life without thinking about my romantic prospects all the time."

"Are you giving up on the plan already? Is it because Saleem's coming back soon?"

"No. Not at all. I just want to be able to focus on . . . on, um, my . . . I want to focus on . . ."

"On what?"

"I have no idea, but isn't sex stuff trivial nonsense?"

Fabiola purses her lips, thinking. "On one hand, yes, but on the other, who cares?"

"Huh?"

"If you let something unimportant in your life become really important then that's not healthy," she says as we get off the escalator. "But you don't need to cut it out completely. And for now, for you, exploring your blossoming queerness is something you want to do, so I say do it. But if it takes over your life then it's not worth it, and you should consider buying a chastity belt."

I laugh, and we walk for a bit in silence before I say, "So, uh . . ." I scratch the back of my head. "I don't mean to pry, but, uh, is the . . . physical stuff the same with Molly as it was with Mariana?"

Fabiola's kept me somewhat updated on her and Molly's

Sapphic rendezvous (which occur mostly at night in Fabiola's truck), but compared to what she used to tell me about her previous girlfriend, it's been pretty Disney.

"Huh," Fabiola says, lifting her straw in and out of her Mocha Milkshake.

"What?"

"I don't think about it like that."

"Have you guys really only made out?"

Fabiola looks down like she's embarrassed. I figured she was leaving stuff out in that department like she did with the letter, but that might not be the case.

She continues doing the straw thing, so I put my hand on hers.

"Stop. It looks like you're pleasuring your cup. Especially with the dome lid."

"Yeah, we've only ever kissed," she says.

"So does that mean you were more into Mariana?"

"Definitely not."

"Then why—"

"With Molly the excitement doesn't come from how far we go. It comes from . . . her. When she puts her hand on my hand it gives me the same feeling that Mariana's hand did when it was . . . other places."

"Wow."

"Yeah."

"I guess I get that. I don't know if I ever told you this, but whenever I really like a guy there's like this literal pain in my chest and—"

"You feel like a balloon, I know." She throws her cup into a trash can. "Look, in your case you need to relax a little, explore. Don't force things. Go with the flow."

She undulates her arms to emphasize her point.

"Easier said than done," I say.

"Well, don't forget our pinkie swear. I'm in this with you, so I'm your teacher in all things sexy and chill—OH FUCK!"

Fabiola grabs my arm and drags me behind a huge decorative plant.

"What are you doing?" I say.

"MARIANA'S HERE!"

"*Mariana* Mariana?"

"Yes!"

I smile. "Why don't we say hi? It's been too long."

"Quique, I swear to God I will kill you if you in any way alert her to our presence."

I laugh. "See, when it's *your* issues they're so sensitive. But when they're *mine*—"

"Quique, you know this could not be more different. That girl out there is a *psychopath*, and we actually dated. And it did not end well!"

"You know, someone really smart once told me that if a guy calls their ex 'crazy' then he's probably a shitty dude. So if I apply this logic to you, then it makes sense that you're probably—"

"What's going on here?"

Fabiola and I freeze and turn around slowly. Standing in front of us is Mariana Quiñonez. Despite giving Fabiola a hard time, I know that Mariana is indeed actually wicked in addition to being wickedly hot. I'm terrified and turned on just looking at her.

"Mariana," Fabiola says evenly.

"Fabiola," Mariana replies.

They lock eyes.

"I'm here too," I say.

"Shut up, Enrique," Mariana says.

"Oh how I've missed you."

"So. Are *you two* finally dating?" Mariana asks.

"No," Fabiola says. "Though Enrique and I would be less of a train wreck than we were."

"Thanks," I say.

"Because he's boring," Mariana says.

"Hey!"

"Enough!" Fabiola says. "This is why we broke up. You're vindictive and cruel."

Mariana looks hurt for a second before she gets angry. "Would a vindictive person do this?"

She grabs the bottom of her top and lifts it up, exposing her breasts. But not, like, her bare breasts. Though, that might have been kinder because the bra she's wearing is an impossibly sexy black and pink one with lace and a little bow and—

She pulls her top down. "Huh? Would they?"

"That has nothing to do with being vindictive!" Fabiola yells.

"Well it's the first thing I thought of!" Mariana yells back.

"Why would she admit that?" I mumble to myself.

"Go away!" Fabiola says.

"Fine!" Mariana says. "You drive me crazy!"

"Don't blame me for that!"

And with that Mariana storms off.

"What? If we don't have it at Target, it [doesn't] exist."

"So . . . A lot's happened since the[n]. I kinda haven't processed it all."

"Ah, okay, I see. You wan[t] [to talk to a] fellow sodomite."

I choke on my spi[t].

"Yeah."

"All righty then. You can [come] to the store tonight at eight o'clo[ck.]"

"Huh?"

"Pick me up when my shift's over [and you] can tell me all about your baby gay proble[ms.]"

"Oh, okay. That sounds—"

"Quique?"

My mom. Just like last time. Except for the weir[d ex]rently on her face this time. Normally, I'd be able to p[lay the] *Mom, I'm straight* card, but now I'm not so sure I can.

"Thanks for all your help!" I say to Arturo, sticking my hand out.

"All in the job!" he says as we shake.

We let go, and I walk over to my mom.

"He looks familiar," she says as we walk away.

"That's Arturo," I say.

"He go to your school?"

"Used to."

"I see. . . ."

I look her dead in the eye. "Can I borrow your car tonight?"

"For what?"

Fabiola and I stand there in silence for a [bit. Then a thoughtful lo]

"Wow," I finally say.

"Yeah."

"I . . . wow."

We don't say anything for a bit. Then a thoughtful lo[ok] appears on Fabiola's face.

"Was I . . . Did I . . . Was I too mean to her?"

"What?"

"I was a little harsh with her. Should I go say sorry? I'm sure there's some stuff we haven't worked out yet and—"

"Fabiola! Molly!"

She shakes her head. "You're right. Huge momentary lapse in judgment. That girl . . . does things to me."

"Understandable."

"Maybe we both need chastity belts."

"I'm sure they have some here. I want one like Mariana's bra."

"Shut up," Fabiola says, smiling.

"I just wanna feel pretty!"

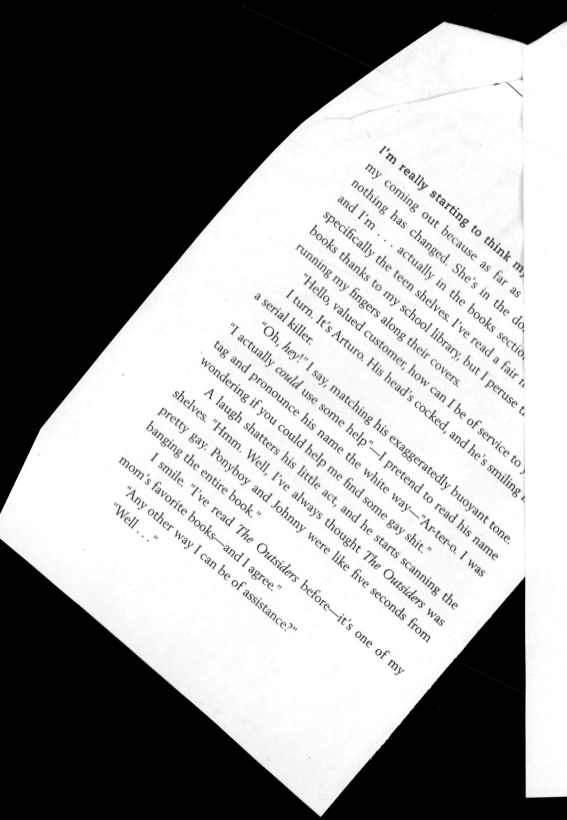

I'm really starting to think m[y] my coming out because as far as nothing has changed. She's in the do[...] and I'm . . . actually in the books sectio[n] specifically the teen shelves. I've read a fair [...] books thanks to my school library, but I peruse t[...] running my fingers along their covers.

"Hello, valued customer, how can I be of service to y[...]

I turn. It's Arturo. His head's cocked, and he's smiling [...] a serial killer.

"Oh, hey!" I say, matching his exaggeratedly buoyant tone. "I actually could use some help"—I pretend to read his name tag and pronounce his name the white way—"Ar-ter-o. I was wondering if you could help me find some gay shit."

A laugh shatters his little act, and he starts scanning the shelves. "Hmm. Well, I've always thought *The Outsiders* was pretty gay. Ponyboy and Johnny were like five seconds from banging the entire book."

I smile. "I've read *The Outsiders* before—it's one of my mom's favorite books—and I agree."

"Any other way I can be of assistance?"

"Well . . ."

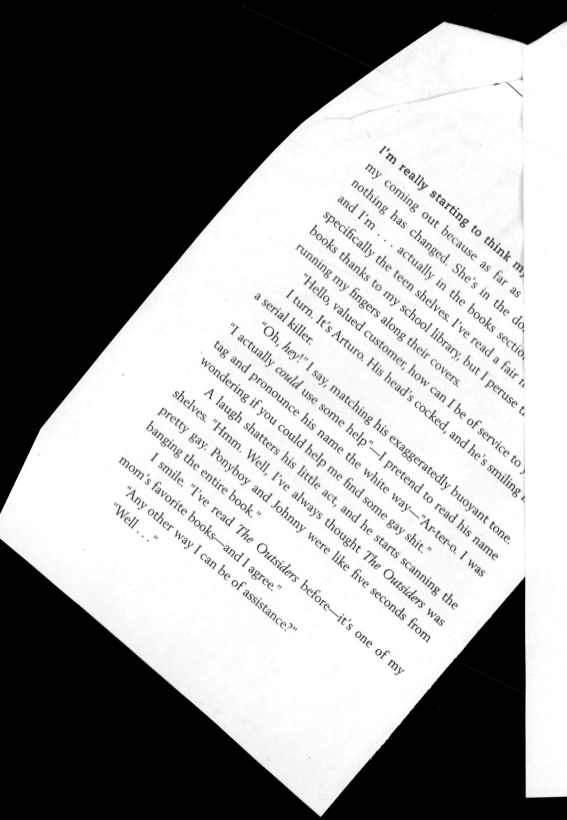

·I say the first lie that comes to mind. "Saleem's getting back tonight. We're gonna hang."

Oh shit. If she remembers what I told her, she probably won't want us to.

"You didn't remind me he was getting back tonight. When does he want to come over?"

Oh shit and that, too.

"Tomorrow."

"Jeez, Quique, thanks for the heads-up."

"Sorry."

"It's okay, but as punishment you're coming with me to the grocery store."

"They don't have a dollar section. I'll live."

She laughs.

"And, uh, I can borrow the car to see him?"

"Yeah. Go see your friend."

The way she says it makes it seem like she for sure forgot about my coming out. Or maybe she remembers the part where I told her that Saleem doesn't like me back. And for the very first time in my life, I'm thankful that he doesn't.

It's only as I pull into the Target parking lot for the second time today that I realize I have absolutely no idea where Arturo and I are gonna hang out. I can't really take him to places I go with my parents for fear of being outed to them sometime in the future. I park near the front of the store and try to think of something, but I can't settle on a spot.

I guess I'll have to ask him about it.

When I check my phone and see that it's 8:10, I start to

worry that I either got here too late or something came up and Arturo's not coming. I wish we had exchanged numbers, but that would have been difficult with my mom staring at us like she'd caught me with my hand down the front of his khakis. Maybe I should ask Fabiola if she has his number—

Wait, there he is. He just exited the store wearing a tight blue T-shirt and shorts. I laugh to myself (because our outfits are almost identical) and honk my horn to get his attention. He spots me and heads over.

"Hey," he says, getting in the car.

"Hey," I say. "You hungry?"

"Yeah, starving."

"Cool. There's this place called Pogo's"—Yeah, I decided to go with my go-to—"that's really good."

I thought about what I'd like to share with Arturo, and I want to share the number six with him. Plus, my parents don't go there because they say it always gives them "the runs."

"Sounds good," he says.

When we get to Pogo's, we go up to the counter to order. Arturo does so in perfect Spanish, joking around with the cashier like she's his sister or something. That leaves me in the awkward position of ordering after him in English. When we've been given our drinks, we head over to a booth in the corner.

"It's funny," Arturo says as we sit, "looking at us, people would assume you're the one who speaks Spanish, and I'm the one who can't."

"Yup."

"I love when people start talking shit about me, assuming

I don't understand them. They nearly shit themselves when I respond."

"Must be nice. Mostly people get mad at me for not being able to speak Spanish and then proceed to talk shit about me right in front of my face, but I can't say anything because I don't know exactly what they're saying."

He laughs.

"So," I say, "how's the boyfriend?"

"Guillermo's good. He just got a job at Walmart. Even though he's the one who got me the Target gig."

"Ooh, scandalous. Like a modern-day Romeo and Juliet."

"Romeo and Romeo."

"Homeo and Juli . . . Eh, there's nothing there."

Arturo takes a sip of his Orange Bang. "So, Enrique, I've been wanting to know . . . Are you *bi* bi or . . ."

"What's the alternative?"

"Using that label as a stepping-stone before coming out as gay."

Oh. My first real life encounter with biphobia. I've read all about it, but I've never actually experienced it.

"I'm bi," I say. "I assumed I was straight as a kid. Then when puberty hit and I started feeling things for guys, I assumed I was gay. But then I saw a character from one of my TV shows say she was bi, and it clicked. Fit me like a glove."

"That's great. I was just wondering. You only mentioned guys when you did the whole CD code talk thing."

"Right. Well . . ." How do I address this? I know I'm not gay as easily as I know I'm not straight. But he's not wrong when he points out that I'm all in on guys right now. "Okay, so, it's like this: Say you're at a wedding, and it's dessert time. There are two options: a slice of tres leches or a piece of tiramisu."

"I actually hate tres leches."

"Exactly. So a lot of people would choose one or the other."

"But you would definitely eat both."

"Yes, I would go to town on both. But it's more complicated than that. Let's say that because you were born Mexican, people assumed you wanted tres leches and pushed you to eat it, and you were like, 'Um, cake, okay, lovely.' But then you realized you wanted tiramisu, too, and at first you did your best to ignore it because you knew you weren't supposed to and because, again, cake is amazing. But then when you accepted that you craved tiramisu and any dessert that isn't tiramisu, you started seeking out other people who liked the 'wrong' dessert. So then you found them and saw that throughout all of history they've existed, and not only that, they've, like, given up *everything* to eat tiramisu: They've been beaten, imprisoned, killed . . . All because the bride said you can only like tres leches. But a weird side effect of learning all that is that you can't help but think, *Holy shit, tiramisu must be, like, the best thing ever*. And even though you wish you were at a wedding where dessert selection wasn't such a contentious subject, that's not the case. And now there's so much . . . weight assigned to your desire for tiramisu. And it'll always have this extra decadence because it's forbidden, ya know?"

Arturo doesn't say anything in response to my rant.

"Was that too much? I—"

"You really like your metaphors," he says.

I laugh. "There are a lot of people who don't understand

people like me, and a lot of the time I find myself practicing how to make it simpler for them. I spend a lot of time trying to explain . . . me."

He nods slowly, as the same guy who served me the morning of my make-out sesh with Ziggy delivers our food. Arturo says thank you, and exactly like last time, the guy walks away without saying you're welcome.

"Rude," Arturo says.

"Yeah," I agree. "I've stopped trying with him."

"He must only like tres leches."

I smile.

"Wow," Arturo says. We're in my mom's car, parked on a hill near my school with a view of Downtown LA. The windows are down, so along with a warm breeze, the sound of crickets fills the air. I just told him everything about Ziggy and Saleem and coming out to my mom. "When I saw you a couple weeks ago," he continues, "I didn't think you were that close to coming out."

"I didn't either."

"I don't know why I say it like that."

"Say what like what?"

"I referred to one coming out. Like a straight person. There's never just one. I did my best to make sure I only had to do it once with my cross-platform announcement, but I'll be coming out for the rest of my life."

I nod. "Arturo?"

"Yeah?"

"I don't like to bring it up in case I, like, retraumatize you or something, but . . . are you okay? Like considering everything that happened after you came out?"

He clears his throat before speaking.

"It was really shitty. Obviously. For a while after, I'd wake up with the pain, which would remind me of what happened, which would remind me that people suck, which would remind me that I could have kept my mouth shut . . . But."

"But?"

"But I was also really proud. Of myself. It was fucking terrifying, but I did it. And as for the consequences . . ." He looks me in the eye. "I hope you don't think I went down without a fight."

He glances down at his knuckles. There's zero evidence there now, but when I think back to when Fabiola and I saw him a month after his attack, I remember they were still bruised. I had assumed that was the result of something inflicted by his attackers. But now I know. He fought back.

"I'd still be proud of you if you had just curled up into a ball, armadillo-style," I say, "but I have to say I'm impressed."

Arturo smiles a sad smile. "I hope you never have to, but if you do have to fight . . . I know you have it in you."

"Thank you. I hope you're right."

"Are you gonna come out to Saleem?"

I sigh. "I . . . I think so. Eventually. I didn't think I'd tell my mom, but in the moment it felt right. But the thing is, even if I tell him, that would feel like a cop-out without adding the whole 'you're the one who made me realize I like guys' thing. Omitting my feelings for him would feel wrong, but I don't think I'll be ready for that until . . . I really don't know."

Arturo nods. "And what about the remaining dudes?"

"I don't know. They're all fun and attractive and when I'm with them I can forget about Saleem for a while, but I think I'll always come back to him."

"Maybe you're not giving them a chance."

"Maybe."

We sit there for a while, listening to the crickets, the lights of the city in the distance.

I drop Arturo off a block away from his house. After I make sure he's safely inside, I leave. On the drive home I can't help marveling at how light I feel, like Arturo and I are both carrying our burdens together. Even though everything's still up in the air when it comes to navigating my bottomless ocean of desire, I feel like I'm at least stepping up as a worthy captain.

My mom's in the living room watching TV when I get home. I'm surprised she's not already asleep.

"Hello," I say.

"Have fun?"

"Yeah."

"How's Saleem?"

Her eyes haven't left the screen.

"He's good."

"Good."

There's a tone. She has a tone. Does she know I lied? Or does she think something happened with Saleem? Or does she feel differently about me now, like I've become a different person?

"Well, uh, good night," I say.

"Night," she says.

I hang the car keys on the hook and head to my room. After I shut the door behind me, I exhale so fast my lungs hurt. I didn't realize I'd been holding my breath.

I don't feel light anymore. I feel heavy, like I'm attached to a sinking ship, waiting for it to pull me under.

CHAPTER EIGHTEEN

The last time I hung out with Fabiola and Saleem at the same time was at school, which was about a month ago. They get along great, but they don't, like, hang out just the two of them. I feel bad for being more than okay with that. They play such different roles in my life that sometimes it's weird for me to have them interact independent of me. I also feel like I'm a completely different person with each of them, so it's hard trying to be both versions of myself.

I often ask myself who, between the two of them, I think gets to see the "real" me. On one hand, I'm incredibly open with Fabiola. I tell her about everything, especially sexual things and queer things, but I've never been "deep" with her about my mental stuff. Saleem, on the other hand, knows about the hard stuff. He always listens to my non-romantic emotional problems with a calm, receptive face and does his best to comfort me. But there's an entire thread of my identity that he has no idea about. And since I've been pulling on that thread more and more lately, I feel like there's going to be some distance between us. Plus, I haven't seen him in almost a month.

Whatever the case, I will see both Fabiola and Saleem tonight. This will be Fabiola's millionth time coming over, but it's only Saleem's third. His first time was a couple months back when my mom found out his parents were out of town visiting Aya.

It hits me around lunchtime that I used Saleem as an excuse for my meetup with Arturo, and I am, therefore, screwed. When I use Fabiola as a cover-up for something I'm not supposed to be doing, all I do is give her every detail I gave my parents, and she backs me up immediately, even throwing in a few embellishments that amuse her and make me bite my nails. But with Saleem, things are going to get awkward.

First off, he's extremely bad at lying. Second, if I ask him to lie for me he'd ask what I was really doing last night, and I wouldn't be able to tell him about Arturo without his asking hard-to-answer follow-up questions. And third, well, this is going to be the first time I see him since he left, and I wish I could just let myself welcome him home.

So I call Fabiola to see if she knows what to do.

"Here's what we do," she says, "I tell Saleem that you went out with me yesterday night, and we were doing something your parents wouldn't want you doing, like sneaking into the public pool or something. I'll ambush him before he sees your parents."

I heave a sigh of relief. Thank God for her.

"That's great, Fabiola."

"I know, I know."

"Wait."

"What?"

"That means Saleem still has to lie to my parents."

"Oh yeah, huh. Hmm. What if we say that I joined you and Saleem unexpectedly? Then I can take over all the lying for him. Anytime your parents ask him a question, I can jump in and answer for him because he's a pushover and I'm obnoxious."

I laugh. "He's not a pushover. He's . . . considerate."

"Sorry, Quique. Didn't mean to insult your man."

Silence. Sore subject.

"Sorry," she says, seriously this time. "I also didn't mean—"

"I know. It's cool."

"Okay. We have a plan. Don't worry, it'll all work out. You know, your parents might not even ask about last night."

"Let's hope so."

Hours later, when my parents are home and cooking in the kitchen, the doorbell rings. I go to answer the door, but somehow my mom beats me to it.

"Fabiola! Saleem!"

Fabiola beams at her from the porch, looking like her normal self. Saleem, meanwhile, is standing there crushing a pink dessert box in his hands, looking like he just shit himself and he's trying not to move around too much. Even being tangentially involved with a cover-up story is freaking him out.

"Hello!" Fabiola says, hugging my mom.

Saleem hands my mom the dessert like a robot.

"From my parents," he says quickly.

"They're too kind," my mom says, hugging him. "Please tell them thank you."

"I will," Saleem says.

"Come in, come in," my mom says.

My dad walks into the living room, and the greetings start

all over again. Then my parents excuse themselves to finish preparing dinner.

I want to rush Saleem, grab him and wrap my arms around him and never let . . . him . . . go . . . as a *friend*, but I can't because I saw him last night, remember?

"Hey," I say to him.

"Hey," he says.

Fabiola makes her way over to the couch, patting my shoulder on the way.

"You, um, you look different from last night."

"I do?"

"Yeah, your, um, your beard is, uh, thicker."

"I guess it is."

I clear my throat. "Let's sit."

We walk over to Fabiola and sit on either side of her.

"So far, so good," she says, her voice not as loud as it usually is so my parents don't hear.

"Well, I'd hope so," I reply. "It's only been five seconds."

Saleem sits rigidly, breathing very deliberately.

"Sorry about all this," I say.

He slowly turns to me with a strained look on his face. "It's okay."

Like I said, he's a terrible liar.

"In the future I'll use Fabiola as an excuse without fail."

Saleem's eyebrows knit together. "I've been wondering . . . Why would Fabiola be an excuse if you were actually hanging out with her? As in, why didn't you tell your mom that you were hanging out with Fabiola in the first place and not tell her what you did?"

A good question.

"Uh . . . well, Fabiola likes to keep her lies grounded in reality. I like to go as far out as possible. Makes it easier for me to remember."

I smile at him, and he decides not to push it.

"Dinner's ready!" my dad calls out. "If you like the beans, they were all me. If you don't, Maria made 'em!"

"Let's get this over with," I say, getting up from the couch.

"I'm actually looking forward to this," Fabiola says. She's not kidding.

"I was too," Saleem says.

His use of past tense breaks my heart.

We're eating at the kitchen table (a first for me and my parents this summer), halfway through the meal, when my mom brings up my hangout with Saleem (or Fabiola, if you're Saleem; or Arturo, if you know the truth).

"What'd you two get up to?" she asks Saleem.

He's (relatively) calm on the surface, but I know him well enough to know he's a ball of nerves right now. There's a sheen of sweat on his forehead, he's scratching his face more than usual, and he's barely touched the chiles rellenos my mom made especially for him. He clears his throat to speak, but Fabiola interrupts him.

"The usual stuff."

My mom turns to Fabiola. "Oh, you were there?"

"Mm-hmm."

"I didn't know that."

I chime in. "She invited herself over."

"Yes, I did," Fabiola says. "You two just stand around in the pool for a couple hours when I'm not there!"

"But that's exactly what we did!" *Why is this coming out so easily?*

"I know, but with me there it's an *experience*."

"Whatever you say, Fabiola."

Seriously, I feel like I'm starting to believe our own lies.

"It was fun," Saleem says. His speech was labored, but he relaxes a bit after saying it, proud of his contribution.

"I'm glad you all have each other," my mom says before taking a sip of wine.

"Me too," I say. "Me too."

After dessert, my friends and I offer to clean up the kitchen while my parents go relax in the living room. Fabiola washes the dishes, Saleem dries them, and I put them away.

"I think that went well," Fabiola says in a low voice.

"I think so too," I say.

Saleem dries a plate in silence. The look on his face has me concerned.

"You did all right," I tell him.

He looks up. "Thanks." He doesn't sound like he means it.

"You could use a little more practice though."

He hands me the plate. "I never want to do that again."

The intense way he says it makes my stomach drop. I don't know what to say.

"From now on we'll keep you out of our shenanigans," Fabiola says, handing him a glass.

"That would be appreciated," he says.

I watch with a sinking feeling as he dries the glass, not taking his eyes off of it. *What have I done?*

The three of us eventually join my parents in the living room. I should feel happy and calm with my chosen family and my actual family in one room together, but I can't get the look Saleem gave me, the one before he started avoiding eye contact altogether, out of my head. He's angry with me and, worse, hurt.

"He deserved it," Fabiola says.

The narrator of the show just revealed that the reason Jessica Allard-Keleman killed Calvin Kelemen was that Calvin married Jessica for her money and was trying to run off with her fortune and a much younger person.

"Agreed," my mom says.

"Why did he say *person?*" Saleem asks.

"Did he?" my mom says.

"Who exactly was Calvin Kelemen's significantly younger paramour?" the narrator asks. "*His* name was Ali Caplain, and he's a community college student where Calvin teaches oceanography."

The living room rings with silence.

Why? Why did this have to happen now? I've seen a hundred episodes of this show and this is the first time anybody's ended up gay. Or bi or queer or whatever. I try to remain calm as blood rushes to my face. No one knows but Fabiola. And possibly my mom.

"Well," my mom says, "he still deserved it."

We all laugh. True equality, I guess.

When the show's over, Saleem says he should be going, and Fabiola agrees. My parents hug them and say goodbye before I walk them out. We head over to Fabiola's truck first.

"All right, Quique. Till next time."

We hug.

"Bye," I say.

She hugs Saleem. "Nice seein' ya, cutie."

"It was great seeing you, too, Fabiola."

They break apart, and she gets into her truck. I walk Saleem over to his parents' gray sedan.

"Sorry again," I say.

"It's okay."

"Is it really?"

He pauses. "It will be."

"I hope this night wasn't all bad."

"It wasn't," he says.

We look at each other.

"I promise I won't do it again."

"I know you won't," he says.

"And, uh, we obviously need to hang out again really soon, so you can tell me about your trip. Looks like you had a great time."

"I did. I really did."

"I'm glad." And I mean that. But those two words scraped my tongue on their way out.

We stand there for a while, and then, after a moment of hesitation, he hugs me. It's unexpected, and I almost stumble back but manage not to. Instead, I wrap my arms around his waist, and breath him in. Stealthily. I don't know how to describe his scent, but it always serves as a trigger for the phantom smell of a pool. I wish I could somehow engineer the combination in a lab and make it into a candle. Creepy, I know, but that thing would always be burning.

Saleem finally pats me on the back and pulls away. "It's good to be back."

"Yeah . . . I kinda missed you, Saleem."

"Likewise. But I'll see you soon."

"Yeah. Bye, Saleem."

"Bye, Quique."

He gets in his car and starts the engine before I turn and walk away, the ground beneath me suddenly feeling unstable.

When I enter the house, I find only my mom sitting on the couch, scrolling on her phone. I'm about to walk past her to my room when she says, "You didn't smell like chlorine."

"Huh?" I say, halting.

"Usually when I'm awake and you come home after going swimming with Saleem, I can smell the chlorine. Last night I couldn't."

"Oh."

She doesn't look up from her phone. What else am I supposed to say? She's hasn't accused me of anything, and I can't take back everything Fabiola and I said tonight.

"Okay then," I say. "Good night."

"Night."

I walk into my room but don't close the door. Closing the door is what guilty people do. Instead, I flop onto my bed facedown and turn my head to the hallway. I feel exposed.

CHAPTER NINETEEN

I had an . . . interesting dream last night. It was, uh, stimulating. Physically.

And it had nothing to do with Saleem, which is good. Sex dreams without the guy you're trying to get over, who you had a charged moment with the night before, are good.

Although, I'm not completely sure you can call it a sex dream. For one, I don't know if it was a person in the dream (and no, that doesn't mean it was an animal, gross). It was an . . . entity. A body made of, like, clouds or something. And I didn't have sex with it . . . exactly. I remember kissing the being and things feeling really intense and then . . . emission. Nocturnal. The leading cause of laundry loads consisting of exactly one article of clothing.

I love wet dreams, though. All of the orgasming, none of the shame-feeling. And this dream in particular was oddly satisfying. I feel rejuvenated and clearheaded, like there's this whole arena of life I don't have to think about anymore. And without Saleem or any of my actual prospects taking up valuable real estate in my mind, I can focus on something more important.

But what more could I do to improve myself? I think about my list. I've been exercising (sorta). I kissed Ziggy. I came out to my mom (sorta). There's only one thing I haven't really tackled yet, and that's the whole *Get cultured* thing.

But how do I actually accomplish that? How can I expand my mind? Fully realize my potential? What useful creation can I breathe life into and gift to the world?

I have no fucking idea. I am good at nothing. Seriously. I can't paint or draw or act or sing or write or dance or snap my fingers. (Yeah, that last one isn't particularly useful, but I really can't do it.) I'm doomed to a life of zero self-expression. Which might not be the worst thing. Maybe I could focus on something practical. What if I started studying for the LSAT today? I could be a lawyer, right? In college all of my prelaw friends would be freaking out about the test, and I'd be like, "Well, I'm fine. I've been studying for it since I was seventeen." Then I realize I should actually be studying for the *SAT*, and that sounds boring and stressful so that idea's out.

Ugh, why does summer break even exist? Why would the US educational system give teenagers two and a half months a year with no structure? No purpose? I always ask these questions when I'm on break. Then during the school year all I do is curse the fact that school's mandatory.

Hmm, well what do I like about school? Besides lunch. Mr. Chastman. His English class. Reading. Books. Queer books.

Yes! That's it! I remember feeling good about being able to understand *The Picture of Dorian Gray* in a way that my fellow classmates didn't. I need to chase that!

But first: laundry.

When I was a kid, I always used to wonder how it was possible for older people to get winded from riding a bike. Back then it seemed like I could pedal for an eternity, never approaching a physical limit. I do not feel that way now.

The library's about twice as far as the park where Mr. Chastman and I talked almost two weeks ago, and with a high of ninety-something today, I'm ready to pass out on the lawn when I get there.

I enter the building drenched in sweat, hoping the air-conditioning can dry me off quickly, and take a good look around because it's been a while. I spot the teen section but don't walk over. For some reason I'll only get that stuff at my school library or Target. I don't like the section here. It's pandering, like, "Oh yeah, teenagers'll definitely want to read about other teenagers." But no, not me. I'm heading for the classics. I'm going to expand my mind today, really think about human nature and all of its endless permutations. God, I hope I find some gay shit.

Dorian Gray is Oscar Wilde's only novel, so that makes things difficult. Who else writes queer literature? I don't really want to ask a librarian, so I guess I can just browse. I certainly have time on my hands, and it won't be too difficult to read summaries until I find something like *Life becomes an enigma for the aristocratic James Chatterby when he befriends a lowly shopkeep by the name of Lawrence Watershy on a cloudy morning in Cardiff, Wales, in 1897. James must soon choose between his heart's truest desire and the life he thought he was destined to live.*

I get through the As without finding anything, but at the beginning of the Bs I find something promising: *Giovanni's Room* by James Baldwin. Why is the author's name familiar? I have no idea. But the blurb on the back mentions being "caught between desire and conventional morality," "the mystery of loving," and controversy, so I'm pretty sure some dudes are smashing in it.

When it comes time to check out the book, I keep expecting the cute, chubby librarian to give some indication that he knows what the book is about, but he remains impassive as he scans it and does that rubby thing that lets you get past the metal detectors without them going off. I also expect him to ask for ID for some reason. It's weird to me how every movie that comes out has a suitable-age rating but books don't. I read so many books as a kid that if adapted into movies would be slapped with an R.

"Have a nice day," he says as he hands me the book.

"Thanks," I say. As I walk away, I think about how I always forget to add, *You too*. I need to get into that habit because I don't want people to think I'm rude. Especially cute people.

I ride my bike to the park, not because I need a rest (though that's definitely a contributing factor), but because I thought it would be nice to read while sprawled out on the grass in the sunshine. I'm of course wrong on both accounts, but it takes me a while to admit it. Turns out grass is itchy, and even when I'm not riding a bike, the sun bearing down on me is enough to make me sweat like a whore in a church full of parishioners who care more about judging people than spreading Jesus's actual message of love and acceptance.

I close *Giovanni's Room*, get up, wheel my bike over to a bench in the shade of a tall tree, and sit down. Much better. I open the book again and continue. I was right, this Giovanni guy's gonna get railed.

"I thought we agreed the next time we'd see each other would be at school."

I look up. It's Mr. Chastman.

"Oh, hi," I say.

He sits down next to me. "Whatcha readin'?"

I show him the cover. He raises his eyebrows.

"Have you read it?" I ask.

"Yes," he says. He takes a drink of his iced coffee. "A few times."

There's a silence that follows, and I clear my throat. I just realized that queer book probably means queer boy. So now he knows about me. But wait, that means . . . I think Mr. Chastman and I both like men.

I flash back to all of his classes, and it makes perfect sense. First off, he's nice. Second, he's incredibly intolerant of homophobic/transphobic/sexist remarks. And third, whenever someone asks him if he has a girlfriend, this wry smile appears on his face and he just replies, "No," every time.

"When was the first time?" I ask. He gives me a look. "That you read the book."

He almost laughs. "College." And there's the "girlfriend" smile. "I'm glad you're reading it now. It's nice to know your generation finds these things sooner in life. Great literature, I mean."

"Of course."

The way we're talking reminds me of my conversations with Arturo. Why do we always have to speak in code?

"What else would you recommend?" I ask.

"Hmm. Well, normally I'd say *The Picture of Dorian Gray*, but I know you already read it."

"See, that's where you're wrong. That was all SparkNotes."

He smiles a normal, non-girlfriend smile.

"No, it wasn't. Trust me, I can tell. Anyway, I'd say *Maurice* by E. M. Forster would be in line with what you're reading now."

I take out my phone to type the name into my notes app. "Anything else?"

"Let's see how you like that one first," Mr. Chastman says.

"Okay."

He stands up. "I should get going. Can't spend my whole day reading in the park like some people."

"Oh, please. Teachers get the summer off too."

"That is true. But we overthink it. We start making all these plans and coming up with ideas for the next year . . . It's terrible."

"You guys don't have a monopoly on overthinking," I say.

He mouth shrugs. "Maybe not. All right, Enrique, I'll see you."

"Bye, Mr. Chastman."

"At school next time!" he calls out as he walks away.

As I watch him go, I realize I'm envious of him in a lot of ways. He's an adult, a real person. He can make decisions for himself; he doesn't have to answer to anyone. He's free. The way I want to be.

I turn to my book for comfort even though it's not exactly that. Whenever I read queer books, there's always the initial relief I get from confirming that I'm not, in fact, the only one who feels the way I do, but then comes a certain cloud of melancholy that settles around me shortly after when I think about the fact that I'll always be fighting myself in a way. In *Giovanni's Room*, the main character, David, has a crisis of courage that inadvertently leads to the detriment of those closest to him. Now, I know what that should mean to me, the reader—that I should live life with honesty and integrity, that I must be true to myself and never waver, fuck what everyone else thinks—but there's a danger lurking in that message that scares me. What if David had been brave, what if he had forsaken everyone but himself and followed his heart? Would he have found a happy ending? Would everyone else?

I don't think so. Sure, things would have turned out differently, but he still would have caused hurt. That's what I've always been afraid of. I don't want to hurt those close to me just so that I don't feel held back by anything.

I close my book and get up from the bench. I'm trying not to think too much, but attempting to shut down the thought factory that is my brain doesn't always work. Sometimes it makes things worse.

I hop on my bike and try to focus on not getting killed. I'm riding a little faster than usual because I think I'm trying to fly; I'm trying to be free. Mostly I'm trying not to feel like a bird in a cage.

CHAPTER TWENTY

Today I woke up at eight o'clock (yes, a.m.), went for a bike ride, showered, dressed, made myself eggs for breakfast (I only bit into an eggshell once), biked to the library, returned *Giovanni's Room*, checked out *Maurice*, biked back, and finished half the book while drinking tea.

No, really! I did!

I may have been all gloomy two days ago, but yesterday I started feeling better, and today I feel on top of the world! I am thuh-riving. My summer of improvement, what my biographer will call the Renaissance of Enrique, is in full swing.

When I'm done washing my tea mug and setting it to dry on the dish rack, I decide to reach out to all of the people on my mind today, just to let them know I value our relationships.

To Fabiola I write: *Thanks for always being there. You're hilarious and smart. Irreplaceable. Love ya.*

To Saleem: *totes gr8ful your in my life have the bestest day*

To Ziggy: *Hope you're doing well and not stranded anywhere particularly high up.*

To Tyler: *Hey man, hope you're having a great day because you make everyone else's days great.*

To Manny: *Hope you're doing well and staying out of trouble.*

Over the next few hours, as I clean my room and do laundry, the replies roll in.

From Fabiola: *Thanks. I already know that but it's nice to hear it/read it/whatever. Love you too, bb.*

From Saleem: *Thank you, 'Quique. I am certainly glad you are in my life as well.*

From Ziggy: *Haha. I am safe for now. #noanticszone :)*

From Manny: *You know it homes my nose couldn't be cleaner if I did lines of detergent*

I smile at all of these messages but don't really feel the need to reply. Right now, everything feels balanced. Well, except for things with Tyler. I can't believe he didn't text me back. Actually, I can. He probably got high and fell asleep.

When my room is a-sparkle, I turn my attention to the rest of the house. I already know my dad's going to come home today and accuse me of doing cocaine for the first time.

I'm in the middle of scrubbing the bathtub when I get a new message on my phone. It's from Tyler.

Awwww thanks man hope your day's the shit

I take off my yellow rubber gloves to text him back.

Thanks. What took you so long to reply?

I fell asleep after I got high

Of course.

But then he writes:

Jk I was playin a game w some of the boys from the team

Sorry I missed it, I write sarcastically, which means I'm begging to be misinterpreted.

Hey man I'm sorry your welcome next game

See?

Nah, it's okay. I'm getting my life together. Kinda.

Oh that's great man!! Well when you need a break come over

Huh? Like to his house?

I ask him as much.

Yah fo sho, he replies.

Uh . . . This has Ziggy's early-morning-visit-to-my-house vibes. Do I want that to happen? I try to gauge how I'm feeling at the moment, but it's hard. My heart and mind are racing, which is usually a bad sign, but it could just mean that I'm bad at handling excitement. It's good that Tyler makes me nervous, right? I wouldn't want to be with anyone who doesn't give me butterflies in my stomach. Although, the discomfort I feel makes me wonder if there's a swarm of angry wasps in there rather than a kaleidoscope of monarchs.

(And yes, the official name of a group of butterflies is called a kaleidoscope. I found that out a year ago after fact-checking a *Simpsons* episode that claimed a flock of crows is called a murder. The show writers were right, and I'm glad to say there are plenty of strange collective animal names. A squad of flamingos is called a flamboyance! How wonderfully gay! A clique of frogs is called an army! Who are they fighting? I don't know, but I support them!)

What do you have in mind? I text back.

It's kind of a useless thing to ask. It's not like Tyler would ever preemptively text something like "We're gonna hook up dude!! Make sure to shower really well lol."

He messages again.

Idk whatever you wanna do smash bros?

I take a deep breath, only now realizing how suggestive the title of that game is. But Tyler and I are just gonna be two dudes sitting next to each other on a couch and staring at a screen, hands occupied by button mashing, right? I'm sure nothing else is going to happen . . . but if something did . . . well, then that wouldn't be the worst thing. Especially with Saleem back in town. I need to forget about that hug, keep movin' on, ya know? I mean, it was a *hug*. A good hug. A comforting, warm hug from someone whose smell sends a spark up and down my spine. But still, a hug.

I text Tyler back.

Ok let's do it.

Tight see ya soon dude

See ya soon. Just gotta shower.

Really well.

Unlike this morning's bike ride, when my mind was unburdened by homoeroticism, my current rush-hour ride is turning slightly dangerous due to the fact I'm having a little trouble staying focused on not dying. I fly past an elote man who cusses at me because I clipped his cart and shake my head. I hope I survive this trip.

When I reach the outer limits of Tyler's neighborhood, I slow down considerably. I don't want anyone here to call the police and tell them I've probably just come from robbing a bank or something. Despite the decrease in physical exertion, my heart only begins to beat faster now as I navigate my way to Tyler's. The sight of his house nearly sends me into cardiac arrest.

As I make my way to the side gate, I try to control my breathing, wondering if one day I'll stop being such a total neurotic mess. I open the gate and walk my bike into the backyard, then head over to the garage and knock. Like last time, I hear a lot of commotion as Tyler makes his way to the door. There's the small click of the door being unlocked and then nothing.

I stand there for a few seconds, wondering what the hell just happened. Then: more thumping and Tyler calling out, "Come in!" I open the door and find the man cave empty. Is he hiding somewhere, waiting to jump out and scare me? That would be a totally Tyler thing to do.

Then he exits the bathroom, cleaning his ears with a Q-tip, a dimpled smile on his face.

"'Sup, 'Rique!" he says.

"'Sup," I say.

I'm surprised I'm able to get that three-letter word out.

Tyler's in a towel. Just a towel. A white towel. A white, fluffy towel. But I'm not really looking at the towel. I'm looking at his well-muscled torso, from his traps down to the well-defined V of his hips. The white makes his skin look less pale than usual and the fact that he's slick with water means he's glistening.

"Glad you made it," he says.

"Of course," I say, forcing myself to look at his face.

He throws the Q-tip in the trash.

"Sorry I don't have clothes on. I fell asleep after I texted you and woke up feeling musty. I was actually in the shower when you knocked, so I had to run out, unlock the door, and run back in here to grab a towel."

I smile and nod. He was naked with only an inch or two of door between us. He's still kinda naked. I hope he's really bad at tying towels.

"Go 'head and sit," he says, pointing to the couch.

I do as he suggests and set my eyes on the TV. He's watching some reality show where Americans spend ninety days with foreigners they want to marry before their visas expire. I pretend to watch the show, but I'm actually watching Tyler out of the corner of my eye. He goes back into the bathroom, grabs a small towel, and walks over to me. He stands in front of the couch and dries his hair.

"I'm addicted to this show," he says. "It's so crazy. The American dudes are usually these old weirdos trying to marry young foreign girls."

"Oh, so that's what you're into?" I manage to joke.

He laughs. "Totally."

And then he sits, putting the towel he used to dry his hair on the armrest. We both keep our eyes on the TV.

I know what this looks like—every queer boy's fantasy—but that's exactly why I can't make a move. This is too good to be true. If I so much as hinted that I was attracted to Tyler, he'd be up in arms and would probably never speak to me again . . . Right?

"Oh, but this guy's fine."

I swear I hear a record scratch.

"Huh?" I say.

Tyler points to the TV where a young Black dude is talking about his French Internet girlfriend.

"I said all the dudes are creepy, old weirdos, but this guy's young. Hot."

I swallow and slowly turn my head.

"Is he your type?" I ask.

Tyler looks me in the eye. "I ain't got no type," he sings, badly.

I almost laugh at him, but the look on his face and the tone of his voice is playful, inviting, *seductive*. I don't want to dispel that.

"Me neither," I say.

He nods. "Cool."

We continue to stare at each other.

Ah, fuck it.

"Can I see it, Tyler?"

A puzzled look appears on his face, and he half laughs in surprise.

"What?"

No backtracking now.

"Can I see it?"

"See what?" I look down at his towel and then back up at him. "Oh. Do you really want to?"

I nod.

"Okay then."

He stands up and turns to face me. And then with one fluid motion, he unwraps his towel, and it hits the ground.

Now, I'm not going to say I'm unimpressed; I'm just going to say it's what I expected. All these years of basketball shorts viewings mean there was little left to the imagination. The only thing that's news to me is the color. I know Tyler's white, but wow.

"Do you want to touch it?"

I look up. He's serious.

"Can I?"

"Yeah," he says. "Some guys only wanna see."

I raise my eyebrows. "Which guys?"

He smiles and shrugs. "Some guys on the team."

I laugh. "Wow. I didn't know you guys got down like that."

"We don't. Mostly. Like I said, they mostly just wanna see it. They're curious."

"Oh."

"But you're not, right?"

"At this point, no. I'm more than curious."

"Then go ahead."

I stand. There's exactly an arm's length between us. I want to kiss him, but I feel like that isn't what this is about. This is different from what happened between me and Ziggy. I reach out and wrap my hand around it.

It's soft. Unlike me, he probably uses lotion every time he clears his head. I'm proud to say it's thinner than what I'm used to handling, which is good because the length spilling out both ends of my fist is considerably more than I'm used to handling.

Without thinking, I start stroking. It's only natural when you've been . . . clearing your head for years and have a dick in your hand, even if it's not yours. Tyler lets out a small grunt.

"Is that okay?" I ask.

"Yeah, dude."

I continue.

After a minute, Tyler pulls away and walks over to his bed. I follow. He spreads out on it with his hands behind his head, and I lie next to him. We don't make eye contact; his eyes are cast downward. I think again about kissing him, but his body language says, *Get back to it*. So I do.

He comes a minute or so later. I get hard watching. I've seen videos like this before, and I'm not a fan. Solos never get me off. But in person it's hot. I like the noise he makes. He was mostly silent throughout, but at the end he can't help but moan. I think my favorite part, though, is the fact that his arm shoots out and grabs my shoulder.

When his body's done convulsing, he lies back, blissed out.

"Can you grab the washcloth for me?" he asks.

"Sure."

I get up and grab the small towel he used to dry his hair. I wipe my hand off before walking back over to the bed and giving it to him. He takes it and starts wiping his six-pack and chest. At this point it's pretty obvious there will be no reciprocation, but I still stand there like an idiot, waiting for him to say something.

All I get is "Thanks, man," as he gets up. He walks to the bathroom and closes the door.

I guess that's my cue to go.

All the way home, I hope for a buzz in my pocket, a text from Tyler saying something like, "Hey man where'd ya go?" but it never comes.

When I walk through the front door, my dad's on the couch with a beer. He must have left work early.

"Hey!" he says as I enter the living room. "The house looks good, Quique. You try coke for the first time?"

I flash him an insincere smile. "Yup. Great stuff. Love it. I get the hype now."

He laughs. "Do you wanna watch the game with me?"

"Can't."

I walk to my room before he can say anything else. I close the door behind me, climb into bed, and wrap myself up in my blanket.

Why am I acting like I'm depressed? I'm not depressed. Today was productive! Today was fun! I have no reason to feel sad! But do I feel sad? No, I guess not. The feeling isn't sharp enough.

I feel . . . used. Yeah, I feel used.

CHAPTER TWENTY-ONE

It was only a hand job. It was only a hand job. It was only a hand job.

Wait, why does that sound like the world's worst Killers song?

Ugh.

Jerking Tyler off yesterday shouldn't have been a big deal, and it certainly shouldn't *still* be a big deal. I mean the only record of it is a "GH" (gave hand job) next to his layup picture, and what could be a smaller deal than that? It wasn't even technically sex (right?). What's with the dramatics? I'm an adult (almost) and I did an (almost) adult thing. This is a step forward. This is me finding myself. This is me overcoming a lifetime of religious and societal oppression. This is . . . pointless. I feel the way I feel, and I can't change that.

I went over to Tyler's place, got him off, and now I'm nothing to him. Or, if not nothing, a new notch on his bedpost. A half notch.

I want to talk to Fabiola about it, but I can't for two reasons. The first is she's been hanging out with Molly all day and I don't want to burst their little bubble with my overreaction. The second is I still feel a bit awkward talking to her about Tyler considering her history with him. Okay, I know they only hooked up once and all they did was make out but . . . but . . .

That's exactly it. That's why I feel this way.

When Fabiola and I hung out with Tyler, we actually hung out. I mean, he brought out the weed and we talked for a while. And then? He made out with Fabiola (meanwhile there is no MO next to his GH in my book). She got into his pants (basketball shorts). And then? They slept together (literally).

What was different with us? Is it possible Tyler treated me this way because I'm a dude? God, that would suck. Not that guys have a hard time treating women like sex objects. Fabiola has assured me, and I agree, that sexism against men isn't a real thing, but this could very well be a homophobic thing. Maybe Tyler thinks that if his encounters with dudes mean nothing to him then that means he isn't actually queer. . . .

Whatever the case, I need to try to move on somehow, and that usually starts with getting out of bed.

After I rationalize not having to shower (I'm gonna get sweaty from my bike ride anyway), I put some clothes on and bike to the park to read.

My book is supposed to take my mind off everything, but it's only making things worse. The titular character, Maurice, reminds me of myself because, well, he's a piner. And another character, Clive, reminds me of Tyler because of his casual disregard for Maurice's feelings. There's a seed of anger in my stomach that keeps growing, and I don't know how to kill it. It doesn't help that I sat down on my usual bench before realizing it was soaked from the sprinklers, and now I feel like I had an accident in my pants.

I won't admit it to myself, but I'm hoping Mr. Chastman shows up today. I love the idea of getting a grown, gay guru to help me navigate the mess that is currently my life. He has to have seen it all. I bet he's happily married to some good-looking stockbroker who has a killer sangria recipe or something. Ugh, I'm not focusing anymore, who am I fooling?

I look up from my book and see a guy and a girl spread out on a blanket in front of me. They're sunbathing with their faces close together, talking softly and smiling.

And all of a sudden, I'm struck with a robust surge of envy, the magnitude of which I've never really felt before. I'm almost scared of how intense it is. I've of course been envious before (it's an emotion I know well), but usually I know what it's about. The couple's just lying there, wrapped up in each other, not a care in the world. Why am I reacting so strongly? I try to pinpoint the exact reason I'm this insanely resentful of them, but I can't. Neither of them is particularly attractive, so I'm not bitter about their individual and collective hotness like I usually am. So what is it?

I don't know. And I shouldn't care. Because this is exhausting.

I'm tired of being envious of people. It's a never-ending list. I'm envious of people with tanner skin, people with non-brown eyes, people who are musically talented, people who are athletically talented, people who are dumber than me and don't have to think, people who are smarter than me and do everything with ease, people with normal brains who don't lose the ability to function at the drop of a hat. Sometimes I'm envious of straight people and white people and rich people.

I'm envious of guys who are taller than me, guys with bigger dicks, guys with better asses, guys who are hairless, guys who are hairier. I want to be anyone who isn't myself. I want to be the hot guy with the hot girl jogging through the park, the hot girl with the hot guy jogging through the park, the pop princess who could have any guy (or girl) she wanted, the stadium-touring stand-up comedian hearing the thunderous applause of a sold-out stadium. I'm envious of (most) presidents, famous poets, famous writers, famous actors, famous "social media stars" with zero talent but mountains of money. I'm envious of kids who are younger than me and have more time to figure their lives out, older people who have their shit together and live how they want to live. Most of all, I'm envious of people who aren't envious.

And that's when I realize why I hate the couple in front of me: They're happy. They've achieved happiness. Sure, the fact that they're white and presumably hetero means they haven't had to deal with everything I have, but I'm sure they've had hardships. The difference between them and me, however, is that they've overcome those hardships. They are living, not just surviving. And I *hate* them for it.

And I hate myself for hating them for it.

These people have done nothing to me. They're not even being loud and obnoxiously in love like other annoying couples. They're just . . . content.

Why does it hurt so much to see other people happy? Is it because happiness is my first love who never came back? Seeing her (because, let's be honest, if we had to assign happiness a gender, it'd be female) shine in other people's lives reminds me that she left me, and all I can do is wait and hope she'll eventually find me worthy enough to be with again.

I try to go back to my book, but I can't. I can't distract myself from this feeling; it's all-consuming. I get up from the bench, grab my bike, and walk it out of the park. Once I'm on the sidewalk, I mount and start riding, not knowing where I'm going. I just hope *this* dissipates, like a dark cloud blown away by a strong wind.

As I ride, I try to ignore an incredibly hard-to-ignore thought in the back of my head. It's morbid and terrible and incessant. My brain keeps telling me to swerve. Into traffic.

It's not that I want to die. I think. It's that I don't want to feel right now. I want a break from all this, a brief respite, so I can be better in the future. I know what these thoughts are called: suicidal ideation. My (former) therapist Luciana used that term once. It's basically the lowest-grade suicidal behavior. Not as uncommon as you'd think. But right now, I'm scared that I'll give in. I never have before, but who knows what could happen now. All it would take is some steady pressure from my right arm. I'd watch my wheel lean farther and farther to the left, until I felt a sharp jolt from behind. I'd fly over the car, tossed off of it like a bull rider, and hit the ground. Hard. And then I'd be dead. But at least I'd have flown.

It'd be silly to think I'm having these thoughts solely because of Tyler and/or hetero park couple. These . . . *episodes* of mine are a result of my brain's well-trodden path to total meltdown. Sure, there are triggers, but this is who I am.

It's what I deserve.

That thought prompts a voice in my head, probably

Luciana's, to disagree. But as hard as I try, I can't make out the words; I can't create the counterargument. And that's how I know I have to go back to therapy, that I shouldn't have stopped seeing her in the first place. I guess I assumed that I had gotten better. I knew I wasn't "fixed," but I didn't think it could get this bad again.

It always happens in the summer. People are supposed to get sad in the winter, but for me it's always the summer. There's too much time. Too much time to think. Too much time to feel.

I stop at a random street corner. Or rather, my body does. I was in no way in control of it. I'm breathing heavily and coated in sweat. I feel like I might pass out. But that's just my body. In my brain there are sensations and combinations of emotions that I can't begin to understand.

I feel useless and used. I feel hot and cold, empty and bursting, raw and hardened, vulnerable and vengeful. I feel full of shit and gilded in gold. I feel everything, and I don't know how to make it stop.

CHAPTER TWENTY-TWO

"Hello, Enrique. It's nice to see you again."

She hasn't changed at all except for her hair. It used to be long, straight, and almost blond. Now it's short, wavy, and chestnut brown.

"Nice to see you too, Luciana."

"Please, take a seat."

I do as she says, on one of those couches that have the cushions built into them. Not very comfortable. I learned last time that you're not supposed to lie down during these sessions. That's only in the movies.

"How are you, Enrique?"

"Uh . . ." I resist the urge to say good. I would not be here if I were good. "Okay. I mean, not great."

"Why do you say that?"

"I had the thoughts again. Yesterday. The ones about killing myself. They weren't super serious. I want to die, but, like, I don't want to go through the process of dying, ya know?"

"We discussed this a few years ago. After you had a manic episode, you contemplated drowning yourself in your bathtub."

"Yeah . . . I guess I've never been a very happy camper."

She smiles at me, the therapist smile, the one that says, *I know exactly who you are, and I am so fucking tired of trying to pull the truth out of you when you and I both know exactly what's wrong with you.*

"Can you take me through yesterday? Step by step?"

I do my best, omitting anything Tyler-related.

"You were disappointed that Mr. Chastman didn't show up?" she asks.

"Yeah. I, uh, I thought he could help me."

"Help you with what?"

Ugh. Now's the part where I tell her about Tyler. She doesn't even know I'm queer. I hadn't come out to myself last time I was here.

I tell her everything. About Tyler, about Ziggy and Manny and Saleem, too. I even tell her about Fabiola. She nods the whole time, impartial and accepting, and it makes me want to scream. What is it about shrinks that make clients crave strong reactions? I want her to high-five me or call me a slut. I want her to call her friend up and say, *Girl, I have this client here who's gonna make you spit your drink.* But all she does is nod.

"Let's take these relationships one at a time. Let's start with Fabiola. What is she to you?"

I clear my throat. "My best friend. My least complicated relationship with anyone."

"But you two were physical."

"Yeah, but that was one time. It doesn't mean anything anymore."

"I see. Let's move on to Saleem."

"Probably my most complicated relationship. Because of the whole *I can't stop falling in love with him* thing."

"And this love isn't platonic?"

"No. I mean, part of it is, but it's also very, very not platonic."

"I see. Does he know?"

"No. God no. Are you crazy?"

She seems genuinely amused by my reaction. "What do you think would happen if you told him?"

"That I'm into him?"

"Not necessarily. Just that you . . . are . . ."

"Bi."

"Bi. What would happen if you told Saleem you're bisexual?"

"Um . . ." I can't answer her question seriously. I keep imagining biblical-style natural disasters resulting from my coming out to him. "I don't know."

"What do you fear will happen?"

I know the answer to this one.

"That he'll stop talking to me. That he'll go away. I wouldn't survive that."

Luciana writes something down. I've never been bothered by that. People always want to know what their therapists are writing, but I don't care. She's making notes, not writing, *Man this kid's a shithead.* I hope.

"We'll come back to that, but let's move on," she says. "It seems as if you lump your other friends"—she looks at her notepad—"Ziggy, Tyler, and Manny into one group."

"Well, I don't know if I'd call them friends."

"Why not?"

"Because of the sexual stuff. I almost kissed Manny, and I hooked up with Ziggy and Tyler."

"And Fabiola."

"Uh . . . yeah. But that's different."

"Enrique, do you notice that you tend to see things in black and white? Especially with relationships. You have two categories: friends and . . . romantic interests? 'Prospects' I believe you called them. Saleem is in the friend category, and the other three are prospects. The only person who seems to transcend these categories is Fabiola, but even then she neatly fits into the friend category because you downplay your . . . interaction with her as a one-off."

"It was."

"I'm not saying it wasn't. I'm simply suggesting that moving forward, you allow all of your relationships to be multifaceted. If you feel unsatisfied by your relationship with Tyler because there's no companion aspect, you can change that. Either by talking to him about it or, if you must, ending that relationship. Same with Ziggy. Perhaps you two could enjoy each other's company somewhere there's no pressure to be physical."

Here's the thing about therapists: I always know what they're gonna say. I know how I *should* be, how I *should* feel, what's "healthy behavior." But there's a reason I don't always go in that direction. When you're poor and overworked you don't go to the grocery store after your shift ends to shop and then go home to slave over the stove, even if that's the healthier, more cost-efficient option. When you're poor and overworked you go to McDonald's, and even though you already feel guilty for ordering a large Big Mac meal, you throw in a strawberry shake because there's a chance that fucking shake is the only thing standing between you and death. Well, a faster death.

I bite my lip. "Luciana."

"Yes?"

"Can I be real with you?"

"Of course."

"I want healthy relationships. Everyone does. But that's not always easy. I am a malleable person. Who I am and how I act depends on who I'm with. If they give fifty percent, then I give fifty percent. If they give a hundred, then I give zero. If they give zero, I give a hundred. I don't like this about myself. In most of my relationships I either feel like I'm selfishly taking from people who truly care about me or giving everything I have to someone who couldn't care less about me. And it sucks. Sometimes it makes me the most self-centered bastard you've ever met, and at times it makes me a pathetic, groveling moron.

"And it's hard, so hard, to change that. Because if I stop doing all the work for someone else then they leave, and if I try to match someone who loves me I will fail. Because I'm tired. All the time. Not just physically, but mentally and spiritually. I'm so, *so* tired."

Luciana stares at me for a while, processing, before she speaks again.

"You mentioned feeling tired the last time you were here. We focused on the manic episode and the suicidal ideation, but you also described times when you would feel . . . 'paralyzed' is the word I believe you used, like you felt trapped in your body. Do you still have those moments?"

I forgot I used that word, but it's accurate. Sometimes I lie in bed, unable to move despite trying my best to do so. I stare at the wall or the ceiling and run through all the things I could be doing if it didn't feel like my limbs were made of lead.

"Yes, I do."

"So to review: For the past three years at least, you've experienced suicidal thoughts, occasional instances of both manic energy and extreme lethargy, and I would venture to say anxious, obsessive thoughts."

She looks at me to confirm, which I do with a glacial nodding of my head.

"Enrique, have you ever considered the possibility of taking medication?" She must see my jaw drop because she hastily adds, "Once we've reached a diagnosis. And it would be in addition to our sessions. How would you feel about that?"

"I, uh, maybe. I'm not against it, but . . ."

"What are you worried about?" she asks, leaning in. "A lot of my patients find it helpful to voice their worst fears and interrogate their likeliness."

"What if it changes me? Permanently. What if meds alter my brain chemistry in a way that can't be undone? I'm not particularly fond of the brain I have now, but it's at least familiar. I've figured it out. Mostly."

"I understand your concerns, but medication is definitely something to consider given your condition."

"Condition?"

She puts down her notepad. "Enrique, in all likeliness you have multiple disorders. Namely, anxiety and depression. Possibly a mood disorder."

"Oh."

My hands, which have been gripping my knees the entire time I've been sitting here, relax. She didn't diagnose me with anything last time. But I always knew. It's hard not to notice. But hearing it out loud is . . . comforting. Kind of. I lean back, letting my shoulders sink into the couch.

So often I blame myself for being lazy and dramatic, and while I'm sure I can't blame everything on my mental ill-ness(es), I just don't want to be making it all up.

"Medication's not a miracle solution," Luciana continues. "You'll still have to come to therapy and do the work, but it could help."

I sigh again. "Okay, I'll consider it."

"That's all I ask. Now, I want to point something out that you may or may not have noticed. Your mood, on any given day, can depend on a plethora of different factors: whether you've eaten enough, slept enough, whether you've exercised or socialized, whether your hair looks good that day. Whether someone you like likes you back or not."

Oof.

"A lot of those stressors are external: They come from the outside world. But there are also internal stressors, which are sources of stress that come from your thoughts, from your way of thinking."

Again, *oof.*

"It sounds to me as if you have no shortage of stressors in either department, and my best advice to you, for now, is to talk about your problems with someone."

"Isn't that what we're doing?"

"Yes, but when was the last time I saw you?"

"Touché."

She smiles. "It sounds like you're lucky enough to have people in your life who love you, Enrique. You might want to trust in them more."

Easier said than done.

"Can you do that?" she asks.

"Yes," I say. Get honest was on my list, but it was a lot easier to pursue guys, read books, and work out than tell everyone in my life the things I don't want them to know.

"This is all a process, Enrique. You've already taken a huge step by admitting you need help. Okay?"

"Okay."

"We're going to continue, but before that I want you to take a deep breath."

I stop myself from rolling my eyes, but I think she can tell because she smirks and says, "Never underestimate the power of a deep breath."

My dad drives me home without a word, stealing glances at me when he thinks I'm not looking. This is the part I hate. These awkward silences always make me feel volatile (or worse, fragile). Now is when I start to ask myself why I can't just deal with my problems on my own like everyone else. What makes me so special (or worse, weak) that my parents have to pay for someone to help me live my life?

Before we get out of the car, my dad puts his hand on my shoulder and squeezes. *Good job, son,* he's saying. I'm utterly drained from talking about my problems for an hour, but I somehow manage a smile.

My mom's in the living room when we enter the house. I hate that she took today off for me. Her and my dad.

"How'd it go?" she asks.

"Okay," I say. After a pause, I add, "She dyed her hair."

"Lighter or darker?"

"Darker."

"Thank God," she says. "I always said the blond made her look washed out."

I smile, and she smiles back.

I'm thankful for this moment. I don't know how she did it, but she made me feel okay again, even if it was only for a second.

CHAPTER TWENTY-THREE

I'm tired of thinking. It's Friday night, and I had to have an emergency therapy session this morning. I don't want to use one more neuron today, and that's why I'm calling Fabiola. Luciana said to trust the people who love me, and I trust Fabiola to help me stop thinking.

"Hello?" she says.

"You. Me. Debauchery. Leggo."

"Ooh, I'm loving the attitude, Quique!"

"Thank you."

"But I can't."

"What? Why?"

"That's Enrique?" I hear a voice say. "Tell him I say hi!"

Oh.

"Molly says hi."

"Cool."

Silence. Horrible, grating silence.

"Oh, right, tell her I say hi."

"Quique says hi!" Fabiola calls out. "She really wants to meet you, ya know. She says you guys had health class together freshman year but never got to know each other."

"Yeah, that's true. . . . So, uh, you guys are hanging out tonight?"

"Yeah . . ." She sounds guilty. "I'd ask you join us, but we planned—"

"Oh no, it's fine. I'm busy anyway."

Shit, why did I say that.

"Quique, you idiot, you called me to hang out."

Ugh, I'm so stupid.

"I know. I'm just . . . I don't know."

"Quique, it's me. You don't need to put up a front."

If only that were true.

"Let's hang out tomorrow, though," she says. "Molly can get discount Six Flags tickets, and even though she won't join us because she's a fucking chicken, we can go. Sound good?"

"Yeah."

"Okay, lit, see ya tomorrow."

"See ya."

"Bye, Enrique!" I hear Molly call out.

"Bye . . ."

I hang up quickly. God, that was awkward. I'm sure I'll like Molly because Fabiola does, but there's a weird tension I feel with her. Maybe I'm a little jealous. Not just of her for stealing my best friend, but of Fabiola, too, because she has someone. And of course this isn't the first time she's been with someone while we've been friends. But things were different with Mariana. When they were together, I never felt like the third wheel because they were always at odds, but I feel like one now and I haven't even met Molly properly.

Ugh. I really need to get out of my head. I need someone wild and exciting and—

Oh. Duh.

I pick up my phone and dial. I don't care if his plan is to beat someone up. I need to live more than a little right now—I need to live a lot.

"'Sup, Quique," he says.

"Manny."

"Whatchu up to?"

"Nothing," I reply. "Absolutely nothing. How are you gonna change that?"

Despite not being able to see him, I know for a fact that he's smiling on the other end of the phone.

"I got somethin' in mind," he says.

My heart beats out of my chest the entire ride to Manny's. I'm not quite as worked up as I was when I met him at the park, but I'm still nervous. Especially because I lied to my parents. I told them I was going to have a very relaxing night with Fabiola planning our Six Flags excursion tomorrow. Instead, I parallel park right in front of Manny's house. Before opening his gate, I admire my work. I'm usually so bad at parking.

A split second after I knock on the front door, Manny opens it.

"Come on," he says, walking past me.

"Where are we going?" I ask.

"My cousin's having a party."

"But my parking job!"

He stops in his tracks and turns around. "Huh?"

"Nothing."

He looks at my car, realizes what I said, and smiles.

"We're walking, Quique. He lives a couple blocks away."

234 • AARON H. ACEVES

"Oh."

"We don't gotta mess up your perfect parking."

I love the look in his eyes, like it's Christmas morning and I'm a puppy with a bow around my neck.

"Vamos," he says.

Like I mentioned, even though it's not too far from where I live, Manny's neighborhood is considerably scarier looking than mine. I'd probably be fine on my own, but I'd be discreetly looking over my shoulder a lot. With Manny next to me I don't really give it a second thought. There is something that I give a second (and third and fourth) thought to, though: holding his hand. Not as something that I would ever possibly do, but rather as a thought experiment.

If I reached out and took Manny's hand and he let me hold it, intertwining his fingers with mine, how long would it take for us to get jumped? I guess it depends on who's on the streets right now. Older men would probably just call out slurs for the sake of their religion and what they see as the crumbling of traditional male society. It would be the younger dudes who'd encircle us, feeding off the strengthening savagery secreted by each other, and beat us to a pulp, their manhood intact.

Oh how I love thinking about fun stuff like this. It's who I am.

"Just a heads-up," Manny says when we're almost there (I can tell because there's a house a block away blasting music that I can make out from here). "Don't do any of the coke there. It's cut with some scary shit."

I laugh, but I'm also mildly horrified. "I thought I had to

be scared of other drugs being laced with coke. What's more dangerous than cocaine?"

He smiles. "You're cute."

I come to a complete stop right outside the house. Manny hops up the steps, not noticing. He turns around.

"You comin'?"

I nod, not able to form words, much less sentences.

As we enter the house, Manny immediately begins greeting people. Slaps and claps for the guys, hugs for the girls. He introduces me as his "homes Quique," and I stick out my hand and shake like I'm at a job interview.

He leads me to the kitchen where there's an entire liquor store's worth of, well, liquor.

"What do you drink, Quique?" he asks, motioning to the glass bottles lined up on the counter.

"Uh . . . tequila."

"Classic. I like it. We'll take the Patrón 'cause we're special, 'kay?"

"We're Special K?"

I'm only 60 percent sure that that's a street name for a drug.

He laughs and grabs a clear, squat bottle.

"Yeah, we are," he says, looking at me. "'Cause we'll fuck a bitch up."

"Yup. Like we did at the park."

"You really beat that fool's ass."

I snap finger guns at him. "Damn right I did."

We gaze at each other for a while, and I feel hot all of a sudden. Luckily, our staring match is interrupted by two people entering the kitchen.

"Gonzoooo!" Manny yells.

Manny and the dude who walked in perform an elaborate handshake before embracing each other. He looks vaguely familiar. I may have seen him back when he was skinnier, with hair and fewer tattoos. Manny hugs the girl who came in and kisses her on the cheek.

"Hola, Luz."

"Hola, guapo," she says.

Manny turns to me.

"Quique, this is my cousin Gonzo and his wife, Luz. Gonzo, Luz, this is Quique."

"Hi," I say, extending my hand to Luz. She slaps it away and hugs me.

"Manny's friends are our friends," she says into my ear.

I turn to Gonzo, and he holds out his heavily tattooed hand, but not for a normal handshake. It's at shoulder height, so I grasp it before we give each other a one-armed hug.

"She's right," he says. "Anyone who's cool with Manny is cool with us."

"Cool," I say.

"We're gonna go up," Manny says, heading back to the living room. I follow him.

"Be safe, boys," Gonzo calls out after us.

As Manny and I push through the crowd, I wonder if he meant that how I think he did.

Once upstairs, Manny opens a door, and we enter a bedroom so nondescript that it must be a guest room. He closes the door behind us, walks over to the bed, and sits.

"All right, Quique. Let's do this."

"Do what?"

He pulls the cork out of the tequila bottle and starts chugging.

Oh.

I walk over and sit next to him. When he's done drinking, he hands me the bottle.

I roll my head around my shoulders, steeling myself. I'm well aware of the desperate need I feel to impress him right now, to show him that I'm a part of his world, that I'm not cute or innocent or soft. So I put the bottle to my lips, tip my head back, start chugging, and . . . almost immediately begin choking.

Manny laughs and pats me on the back as I wipe tequila off my face, my eyes tearing up.

"Easy there," he says.

"It's the fucking lipped bottle!" I yell.

"What in the fuck?"

"It's curved!" I say, running my finger along the opening of the bottle.

"Whatever you say. Did you at least get a little in you?"

"Yes. I'm pretty sure it's even in my lungs."

"Good. Now you can come out."

I swear I hear a record scratch, like I did when I was at Tyler's last time. Then I hear it again. Oh wait, that's the song playing downstairs.

"Come out?" I repeat.

"Yeah," Manny says. "I wanna see the real Quique come out."

"Oh." My heart, my poor overactive heart. "You don't think you've seen the real me?"

"Nope. I think there's a lot I don't know about you. That I wanna know."

"Yeah?"

"Yeah. So tell me what's on your mind right now."

I look into his eyes and debate whether I should actually say what I'm thinking at the moment. All it takes is him batting his deadly eyelashes at me before I decide to do it.

"Do you have any tattoos?"

He looks surprised by my question, like he didn't actually expect me to speak up.

"Uh . . . yeah, I do. One."

"Well then let me see."

"Aight."

He gets up from the bed and grabs the bottom of his black T-shirt. He lifts it up to his neck, and I see it: blue-black ink blooming beneath his smooth chest. It looks like an Aztec queen mixed with a bird. Her arm-wings are fanned out, framing his pecs.

"Cool," I try to say casually, resting the bottle of tequila on my crotch. I'm hard. Not all the way, but enough. "Why, um, why there?"

"Easy to hide," he says with a smile. He drops his shirt, demonstrating. "My mom would kill me if she knew."

"Oh."

"But it was in honor of her. Even showed the tattoo chick a pic of her."

"That's sweet."

"Soy un buen hijo."

Oh God. I can't handle this. I feel like I might vomit.

Mostly I just feel the need to expel something from my body. I'd kill for a sneeze right now.

"It reminds me of Adam Levine's." I'm just saying the only thing in my brain that isn't *I want you in my mouth*.

Manny makes a disgusted face, and I laugh. "Actually, it looks a lot like Rihanna's."

"I'll take that," he says. "She's hot. And a fucking boss."

I imagine the two of them together. Tattoos and brown skin. Manny's smooth, expert strokes . . . And now I'm at full mast, almost impossible to hide.

Manny's right in front of me now. I hadn't noticed him coming closer. I look up and our eyes meet. He's either going to kill me or kiss me. The least I can do is try to get him to execute the latter before the former. I put the tequila bottle on the nightstand and reach for his belt. God, I love guys who wear belts. I'm about to get it off when his hands close around mine and stop me. I look up.

He shakes his head.

Oh shit. I misread. I'm stupid. Fuck. Is he gonna deck me?

Instead of hitting me, he gently releases my hands and kneels in front of me, not letting go of my eyes for a second. Then he reaches for my zipper. Oh God, this is happening. I help him lower my pants and underwear until they're around my ankles. Then he puts his mouth on me.

It's evident within the first two seconds that not only has he done this before, he's a fucking pro. This can't be real. How is this happening? How am I this lucky?

I stay on that train of thought for about five seconds. Then I start thinking about how this can all go wrong. *Is Manny going to run away like Ziggy?* That doesn't seem like a possibility given his . . . enthusiasm. *Am I going to feel shitty afterward like I did with Tyler?* Well, I guess that's always a possibility. I mean—

Manny snakes his hand up my shirt and starts rubbing my left pec (not that I have *pecs* per se, but you know what I mean), and I'm surprised by how good it feels. *He's into this. He's into me.* This isn't what happened with Tyler.

I relax a bit and close my eyes for a second, really letting myself enjoy it. That's when another boy pops into my head: Saleem. And I know I should immediately banish his face, let go of his gaze with my mind's eye, but the image of him with the physical sensation—

"Manny, I'm about to—I'm gonna—I—"

He doesn't take his mouth off me, and then . . . it's over. My first time. Right? I'm assuming if the act has the word "sex" in it, then it is indeed sex.

Manny rises up, planting his palms on my thighs. Then he leans in and kisses me. He's already swallowed, but I can still taste something I've never tasted before.

"How was that, papi?" he asks.

What he just said and the way he said it are almost enough to get me hard again.

"That was . . ." I start laughing. "I can't even describe it." He smiles. "Do you, do you, um, want me to—"

"Nah," he says, interrupting. "Let it be what it be."

"Okay."

I'm glad he doesn't see the need for reciprocity. I wouldn't be able to live up to his expertise. He sits next to me, and for a while we listen to the West Coast rap blasting from the speakers downstairs. The entire room is vibrating from the music and everyone's dancing.

"Who else have you been with?" Manny asks, looking down at my junk.

"Uh . . ." I pull up my pants. I hadn't even realized I was still exposed. "How do you mean?"

"Who have you done stuff with?"

"Oh, um. I mean I made out with Fabiola a long time ago, got to second base."

"Nice. She's cool."

"Yeah, but we're just friends."

"Anyone else?"

I should probably say no and respect the privacy of my past partners, even if it means Manny would see me as a loser, but I know he's not a chismoso. He wouldn't gossip about them with his friends because they'd probably find it suspect that he cared about other guys hooking up.

"I, uh, made out with Ziggy Jackson."

Manny nods in approval. "He's hot. Didn't think he was into dudes, though."

"You're not the first person to say that. And, uh, last but not least, I gave Tyler Montana a hand job."

He makes a face again, the same one he made when I mentioned Adam Levine. "That wanksta?"

I laugh. "Yeah. He's hot though. Objectively."

"I'm not big on white dudes."

"I've guessed as much."

"They do nothing for me. Their dicks freak me out too. They remind me of pan crudo."

"Raw dough?"

"Yeah."

"So . . . How many guys have you been with?"

He shrugs. "A couple here and there."

"How do you find them?"

"App."

"But you're seventeen. Don't you have to be eighteen to use those?"

He shrugs again. "I say I'm twenty. No one really questions it. They just want some head."

"Oh, so you're a big fan of . . . of, um . . ."

"Giving, yeah. I blame my cousins. They shouldn't have made fun of me for having DSL."

We both laugh, and Manny grabs the tequila from the nightstand, takes a swig.

"I don't think I could use an app," I say as he offers it to me.

"Why?"

"Well . . . ," I say, taking the bottle. "There's the age thing."

"I told you no one asks—"

"I know," I say before taking a small sip. "But they're still breaking the law. I don't think I could lie and put someone in that position."

He doesn't say anything.

"And even if I were eighteen it still freaks me out. I'd assume everyone was gonna murder me. And if they didn't, they'd only want sex, right? What if I'm not ready for what they want to do?"

"Not everyone wants sex." He puts his hand on my thigh. "Some people are weird and just want to talk."

We laugh, and he starts rubbing my thigh with his thumb.

"I like talking. With you."

"Yeah?"

"Yeah."

He squeezes.

"Then let's talk."

I have a feeling I'm not going to get that much sleep tonight.

CHAPTER TWENTY-FOUR

I can't stop thinking about Manny, and not only in a sexual way. I can't stop thinking about how much taller I walked when we left Gonzo's party last night, how easy it was to be myself around him after he . . . broke the ice.

"What's with the . . . happiness?" Fabiola asks, not looking up from her phone in the passenger seat.

"Uh . . . life, ya know?" I answer, switching lanes because our exit's coming up. I'm driving her truck because she was so distracted by messaging Molly this morning as she arrived at my house that she drove into our trash cans. I'd rather not die after finding out how much there is to live for.

"Mm-hmm," is all she says as she fires off another text.

I want to tell her in person about Manny—the only one I've told so far is my yearbook, where there's an "RO" (received oral) next to his class picture—but haven't had the chance yet, and I'm definitely not doing it with Saleem in the car.

I check him out in my rearview mirror. He's serenely staring out the window, wearing a dark gray T-shirt that hugs his modest but noticeable biceps. His hair seems extra curly today, and I bet it smells like coconut. His beard also looks denser. I wonder if—

"Did either of you bring sunscreen?" Fabiola asks, snapping me back to reality.

I shake my head and focus my eyes on the road again. As I take the exit, I think about how I should maybe cut her some slack for the trash cans. Distractions happen.

"Nope," I say.

"Here," Saleem says, holding out a bottle.

"Thanks, love," Fabiola says. "You're a lifesaver."

"Always prepared," I say.

"Not for today," he says, a grim look on his face.

This is the first time the three of us are going to Six Flags without it being a school event, and I'm so glad Saleem agreed to come despite his embarrassing lack of chill when it comes to roller coasters. Fabiola and I scream because it's acceptable roller coaster behavior. Saleem screams because he's genuinely terrified to the core. We've seen it year after year on field trips, and it's a riot.

"Oh, you'll be fine," I say. "You're facing your fears! Becoming a man! Conquering the world!"

"Oh, shut up."

Fabiola and I turn to each other, our mouths open in amused shock.

"See!" Fabiola says to Saleem. "You're changing right before our very eyes!"

He shakes his head but smiles.

Good on Fabiola for convincing him to go last night after she hung up with me. Even if it was probably her way of saying sorry for not hanging out. The only thing that could make today better is if we took a school bus back home like we usually do.

I normally hate buses, but the post–field trip bus is an entirely different animal, a magical place. It's nighttime and everyone's tired but still buzzing with excitement. People are sharing candy and playing games of Would You Rather or Truth or Dare. And then, at a certain point on the ride home, the entire bus goes quiet as everyone crashes from a long day in the sun. It's just you and your seat partner, the person who—if you're lucky—you tried your hardest to sit next to.

On our last trip, the person sitting next to me was Saleem, obviously, and at that special time of night, rumbling down the freeway with only the periodic flash of highway lights illuminating our faces, Saleem asked if I wanted to listen to music with him. I of course said yes, so he handed me an earbud, and we listened to his music the entire ride home.

The song I remember best is the one he played last. It was this moody indie rock track by a Lebanese band he loves. It's got these beautiful strings and synths, and the lead singer has this strong, sexy voice that immediately transported me to the inside of a dark club where neon lights sliced through fog, and there was only one other person there besides me. I imagined us walking toward each other and meeting in the middle. We kept getting closer and closer until I could feel his hot breath on my skin and the smell of chlorine washed over me.

And then the bus stopped, the lights turned on, and I was cruelly awakened from my trance.

As I pull into the Six Flags parking lot, I look at Saleem in my rearview mirror. He glances up at the tallest roller coaster with a look in his eyes reminiscent of when you're four years old and staring up at your mom after you've done something bad. It's heartbreakingly cute.

"Today's gonna be fun," I say.

"I hate you," he says.

I smile.

We start off easy: fast rides with twists and turns, but no drops. Fabiola and Saleem sit together for these rides. I'm fine with looking like a third wheel, and plus I get a better view of Saleem screaming his head off.

"Is anyone else hungry?" Saleem asks after we exit "The Orphan Maker," the remnants of a grimace still on his face.

"You need a break already?" I say.

"I didn't eat breakfast! Fabiola, are you hungry?"

"Actually, now that you mention it, I am, Saleem. Let's go grab something."

Saleem juts his head forward and shakes it, a nonverbal *See? I'm not only asking to get out of going on any more rides for the moment!*

I get a burger. Fabiola and Saleem both get a turkey leg. I get slightly aroused watching them eat. When we're all done, Fabiola heads to the bathroom.

"So," I say as Saleem and I walk over to the trash cans with our trays. "Tell me about Joisy."

He laughs, pushing his food against the swinging flap. "Well, my family and I didn't do a whole lot besides catch up and eat. We did go to New York for an afternoon, went to The Met. You would have been so bored."

"You know me well." And that fact kills me in a way that it probably shouldn't if what happened between me and Manny last night had actually made me move on from him. I shake the thought from my head.

"Too well," he says as we walk back to the table.

I take a deep breath before I ask the question I need the answer to. "And, uh, Ahed?"

"What about her?"

We sit.

"I saw her on Aya's Insta. She's, uh, she's pretty."

He clears his throat. "You think?"

"Yup. Don't you?"

"Of course. She's gorgeous."

Gorgeous. She's gorgeous. Saleem thinks she's gorgeous. Not *pretty* but *gorgeous*.

"So didja pop the question, then? Pick a date?"

A coaster of screaming people flies over our heads. Saleem waits for them to disappear before he answers.

"No, Quique." He sounds almost annoyed, so I quickly glance at his face. His mouth looks small, tight. "My family doesn't actually pressure me that way."

"Yeah, I know your aunt was, like, half kidding about her being your future wife. I was fully kidding. I'm sorry."

"It's okay. I, uh . . . Yeah, it's okay."

"So how did you leave things?"

"We decided we're gonna get to know each other as friends before, uh, anything else."

"Oh. That's good. Smart."

He nods.

We haven't made eye contact since Fabiola left, but when he looks at me, I stare back. He's so close I can smell his sunscreen, and yet every cell of me is telling me to get closer. It's like I've been dying of dehydration in a jungle, and even though river water is flowing over my hands, it won't matter until I cup my hands and bring it to my lips.

"What next?" Fabiola says.

Saleem and I whip around to see her approaching, a two-foot-long churro in her grasp. She takes a park map out of her pocket and spreads it on the table, leaving greasy fingerprints all over it.

"Drop tower," I say immediately because it's the first thing I thought of.

"How about something that won't make us throw up immediately after riding it," she says. "How about . . ." She scans the map. "That raft ride where we all get in a circular boat and one person keeps getting soaked while another person stays completely dry?"

"Sold," Saleem says.

"Leggo," Fabiola says.

As Saleem and I get up from the table, I glance at him, trying to get a read. He doesn't look my way.

The ride attendant helps Fabiola into the boat, then Saleem. I hop in without any assistance. The three of us place our belongings in the center storage space, cover them with the plastic top, and we're off.

"I hope it's you," Fabiola says.

"Who gets soaked?" I ask.

"Mm-hmm."

"Why?"

"Because you deserve it the most."

I laugh. "That may be so, but life isn't always fair."

As if to confirm that point, our boat takes a really fast turn and Saleem is slapped with a gush of water.

"See?" I say.

"Aw, pobrecito," Fabiola says. She means it. It's hard not to feel protective of Saleem with his big eyes and compact body.

He laughs, though. I guess he's just grateful he's not being tossed around while fifty feet in the air.

As the ride progresses, Fabiola's theory proves mostly true. Saleem's sopping wet before we're halfway through, and I've remained almost completely dry. Fabiola's somewhere in between.

As our boat climbs the final drop of the ride, she says, "This is it, Quique. This is when you get what you deserve!"

I shrug.

"I don't mind getting wet. It's actually really hot right now. I could use a refreshing blast of water."

"You'll get it," she says. "Oh, you'll get it."

Our boat tips over the edge, and we plunge down to the bottom. As we float back to where we boarded the boat, Saleem and Fabiola gape at me incredulously.

"You motherfucker!" Fabiola says. "You're drier than a lesbian watching *Magic Mike*!"

I look down and see that it's true.

"That's not fair!" Saleem says.

I smile.

"When you're a saint like I am, God rewards you."

"That's it," Saleem says, reaching into the water.

"What are you doing?"

"This." He brings his arm up, aiming a handful of water at me. The only problem is the boat just so happens to turn at the exact right moment and Saleem ends up splashing Fabiola instead. She yelps as the water hits the side of her face.

"I'm so sorry! I was trying to get him!"

Fabiola's mouth is open in shock, a few curls plastered to her cheek. "Oh my God!"

And then she starts laughing. And then I do. And then Saleem.

The same attendant who helped us board earlier helps us disembark.

"That was hilarious," Fabiola says.

"I am still so sorry," Saleem says.

As they keep talking, I feel like a creep because I can't help ogling them. Fabiola's wearing a white tank top and her purple bra is visible underneath. I think about what Luciana said about how what happened between me and her didn't have to be a "one-off," and I realize that if not for Molly it might be true. My gaze travels over to Saleem, whose T-shirt clings flatteringly to his body. I notice his nipples sticking out, and I feel faint. Being bi is torture.

"You ready?" he asks.

"Yeah," I say, shaking my head to clear it. "Let's go."

When we exit the log ride, we're swept up by a crowd going the same way as us, and as we walk deeper into the park, I keep bumping into people's sticky skin.

"Ugh," Fabiola says, next to me. "Why can't my dad be the Afro-Latino Tom Cruise and rent out this whole place, so I don't have to deal with all these people!"

Saleem and I laugh.

"Tomás Cruz," I say.

"You ever notice how the only time we see this many white people is at amusement parks?" Fabiola continues, ignoring my brilliant joke.

"Yup."

"Amusement parks and college campuses," Saleem says.

Fabiola and I nod. Then her finger shoots up into the air.

"Next stop!"

I look up and spot the drop tower in the distance. Then I look to Saleem.

All the humor has vanished from his face. I'm about to make an alternate suggestion when he swallows hard and says, "Yeah, let's do it."

I'm both surprised and impressed.

Saleem sits all the way at the edge, I sit next to him, and Fabiola sits next to me. A group of five strangers sits to her left.

"You ready?" Fabiola asks Saleem.

He nods, gripping his shoulder handles as hard as he can.

"You can do this," I say. I feel such a tender compassion for him right now. I know he'll be okay, but I don't want him to be scared.

"I know," he says, releasing the handlebars. "I will be fine."

He remains calm as we start to ascend, but when we're about fifteen feet in the air he frantically checks to see if his seat belt is secured before grabbing his handlebars again. Then he starts gulping down air.

Usually free falls are the only rides that sort of freak me

out, but by the time we all get to the top of the ride, I can only worry about Saleem. He turns to look at me and finds that I've had my eyes on him.

"Quique, we're gonna die."

"We're gonna be fine, Saleem. Inshallah."

He smiles. "Inshallah."

"This'll all be over soon. I promise."

We stare at each other silently, both taking deep breaths.

"Woooooooo!" Fabiola screams. "These bastards *looooove* keeping us up here all day! Bring it on, bitches!"

We hear a clicking sound like the ride's about to drop, and Saleem's hand shoots out and grabs mine. We look at each other, and realizing what he did, he tries to pull away. But I don't let him. Before he can ask me why I won't let go, the ride drops, and we're too busy cursing at the top of our lungs to say anything else (yes, even Saleem).

Seconds later, he and I sit there, suspended one foot off the ground, breathing heavily, still holding hands. At the same time, we both slowly start to let go.

"That was . . . something," I say, flashing him a manufactured smile.

"Yes, it was," he says, his face blank.

There's a tension between us now, unmistakable and unwelcome.

A belt of shiny laughter hits my ear, and I realize Fabiola's been having a loud conversation with the blond guy sitting next to her. She's cursing and joking, and he looks smitten. Poor guy doesn't know he doesn't stand a chance.

She turns to me.

"Hey, let's hang out with these guys," she says. "They're cool. Plus, even numbers are better, right?"

"Yeah, I guess," I say.

"Fine with me," Saleem says.

The three of us integrate into their group effortlessly. Fabiola and the blond guy, whose name is Ben, continue to hit it off, while Saleem and I both start talking to the two single girls. The last two people in our group of eight high school kids are a PDA-loving couple named Jason and Jennifer.

My companion for the night, Olivia, is pretty and actually really cool—when I'm not sputtering like an idiot we manage to find that we've read a lot of the same books and like a lot of the same music—but I can't get Saleem out of my head.

As Fabiola and Ben lead the group, each eating a churro (Fabiola's second and most likely not last), Olivia and I walk behind them. She's talking about this really cool concept she has for a song she wants to write, and all I can think about is what Saleem's talking about with his date. I'm trying so hard to focus, but I can't. Instead of listening, I'm obsessively replaying the moment Saleem and I shared at the top of the ride, our heads almost literally in the clouds. I swear I can still feel his hand pressing into mine.

CHAPTER TWENTY-FIVE

Two nights ago, after we dropped Saleem off at his apart-ment, I ended up telling Fabiola about Manny as she drove me home. She screamed after almost every sentence.

"I'm so sorry," she said, "but I am so going to beat off to that tonight."

"Ew, please don't say it like that.'"

"Why, 'cause I'm a girl?"

"No, because I hate that expression."

"Whatever. I'm doing it, and there's nothing you can do to stop me."

"What about Molly?"

"You think I'm not allowed to fantasize because I have a girlfriend?"

"You, um—she's your girlfriend now?"

Her eyes flitted to me for a split second.

"Oh yeah. We, uh, had the talk. So yeah."

"Cool. Congrats."

"Thanks." She cleared her throat. "Anywayyyy, how big's your dick again? I want my fantasy to be accurate. No, wait, don't tell me. You might spoil it."

"Thanks for the confidence."

"No prob. When are you gonna see him again?"

"I don't know."

"Dude, you should be, like, texting him every second if he's as good as you say he is."

"I don't want to come off as desperate."

"Better than not interested."

"I know. But then there's this whole thing with Saleem—"

She lifted an eyebrow. "What are you talking about?"

"He held my hand on the ride."

"And?"

"I think it meant something."

"It didn't."

"How do you know?"

"Because I'm a realist. I know I encouraged you to pursue him before, but now you have other viable options. Saleem was scared. People do crazy things when they're scared."

"I know but—"

"Quique, you need to focus on Manny. He should be your top prospect. Better than 'freaks out for an unknown reason' Ziggy or 'doesn't hit you up anymore' Tyler." I still haven't told her that I jerked him off. "Even Olivia's a better option. Given you didn't fuck things up with her tonight by obsessing about Saleem."

"That's a big given."

"I know. But, anyway, this Manny news is great! The summer of Quique is finally here!"

Now I'm lying in bed, getting pummeled by sunlight, gathering my strength to live today. If school were in session right now, I would have skipped, given myself a three-day weekend. This isn't quite a Saleem hangover—it's not *that* bad—but still.

The only thing on my agenda today is biking to the library to return *Maurice* and borrow its replacement. I'm glad it had a happy ending, unlike *Dorian Gray* and *Giovanni's Room*. Apparently, E. M. Forster was very conscious about that. He thought us queers deserved a break from the usual morose tragedies that befall non-straight fictional characters.

I finally had the foresight to Google popular novels featuring MLM (a term I just learned that stands for men who love men) beforehand, so after entering the library, I head straight (ha) to contemporary fiction. This week's book is *Call Me by Your Name* by André Aciman. I find it within seconds of beginning my search.

I once again have the feeling that the cute, older librarian is going to comment on my book selection—it's not hard to see a rainbow-colored pattern at this point—but he doesn't. He simply hands me my book and says, "Have a nice day."

"Thanks," I say. I'm about to walk away when I add, "You too."

He smiles at me. Small victories.

I allow myself to go to the park. I'm in a much better mood than I was last time I was here, and I believe in my ability not to lose my shit when I see a happy heterosexual couple.

I plop down on my usual bench and begin to read. For the next hour, I do nothing but. During the first third of the book I'm shocked and later terrified. My secrets are being exposed on every page. How had this author gotten everything so completely right? It's as if he cracked open my skull, scooped out my most intimate thoughts, and squashed them between the pages of a book. I feel like Lauryn Hill in the Fugees cover of "Killing Me Softly."

The main character in the book is a bi seventeen-year-old kid (like me) named Elio who becomes infatuated with a twenty-four-year-old grad student named Oliver, and so far Aciman has described his longing with such an impossible familiarity that I half expect to turn around and find him watching me from behind a tree, writing down everything I do in a notebook. I legitimately have to stop reading because I feel so naked.

When I'm home, I splay out on the couch and start again. I house within me the all too familiar competing desires that come with reading a great book: On one hand, I want to go as slow as possible, savoring it like a well-cooked meal, and on the other, I want to rip through it as fast as I can to see what happens next, devouring it like I haven't eaten in weeks. I guess it's true that us queers are starved for stories that mirror our lives. I can't remember a time when I saw a queer person in a movie or TV show or book that I didn't have to actively seek out myself. (Except for, of course, Calvin Kelemen and his college lover from my mom's murder show.)

I don't know how to feel when I finish the book. Actually, I could rattle off a list of emotions I'm feeling—it's just that they're all jockeying for control. I guess the feeling that's pressing on me the hardest is . . . *yearning*. I'm not going to say I'm horny because it's not only that. What I'm longing for right now, what I'm dying for, is a strong, undeniable connection. I want to be in love. And yes, I also want to physicalize that love in a series of reckless, diversely debauched ways.

I text Manny to see what he's up to, but I know he mentioned going on a trip around this time. Sure enough he texts me back letting me know he's in Vegas with his cousins testing out his new fake.

I think of who else I could reach out to and run through a list of names in my head: Fabiola (no), Saleem (no), Ziggy (no), Tyler (no), Arturo (no), cute librarian . . . no. Olivia would be a yes if she didn't live an hour's drive away.

I'm out of options.

I guess I'll just be insanely lonely today. Like always. But this loneliness is different. I don't think I've ever experienced this type of deep-seated yearning before. I can feel it in my bones.

I turn on the TV to try to take my mind off it, but it doesn't help. Apparently, today is *reruns of every "they will" episode of my favorite "will they/won't they" shows* day.

At some point I get up to eat, but then it's right back to kissing in the rain, passionate, unexpected declarations of love, and meaningful hookups. Will that ever be me one day? Will anyone ever tell me I'm the one?

I can't take it anymore. I'm doing what I know I shouldn't, what Manny does—I'm downloading the app.

It takes a few seconds to load before I open it. I make an account, and then it starts asking me questions about myself. How old am I? Twenty-one, obviously. Height? I'll tell the truth. 5'10". Weight? I have no idea. Body Type? I don't know, so I put "normal." Race/Ethnicity? Latino. Position? "Big spoon" isn't an option, so I don't put anything. Looking for? All these questions are so hard. I check everything on the list except "networking" because I doubt I'll get an internship on here.

Now I have to come up with a username and a bio. God, this is a whole process, isn't it? I don't want to use my actual name obviously. What do I want guys to know when they see my name? Hmm . . . Oh, wait, that's perfect. I smile as I type in "Everygay."

For my bio I'm straightforward. I write, *New to all this. Don't really know what I'm looking for. Hopefully someone who can talk books or shows about women who "snap."* There. That sounds good! I'd hit on a guy with this bio.

Now for the picture. Hmm, I know I'm not going to use my face (because who knows who's on here), but what else can I use to show who I am? I save my incomplete profile and go on to the sea of profile pics of guys in my area. Some of them are blank, some of them are faces, some of them are various landscapes, but most of them are torsos. I can't upload a photo of my torso because I'm guessing teenagers with dad bods aren't in high demand in the queer male community.

I decide to present my possible suitors with my current view. I put my feet up on the coffee table and snap a picture. If there are any guys with weird foot hang-ups on the app, I'm golden. But non-weirdos can probably appreciate it too. Who doesn't like a guy with nice legs?

I upload the picture and wait for it to be approved. Even before that, my phone buzzes and a little red dot appears on my messages. I switch over and find a message from "down arrow emoji." He's forty-seven. I click on the message and immediately wish I hadn't.

I grimace before blocking him. Not exactly a great start.

After my profile pic is uploaded, I start getting more messages. Two are from blank profiles that say *hi*. The third is a dick pic from a guy so close to me he must be down the street. I reply to the blank profiles with *Hey, how are ya* and block dick pic guy. I may have stared at it for a while, but that's not what I'm looking for right now. One of the blank profiles replies, *horny u?*

I can see everyone's pretty direct on here.

You could say that, I write.

Host?

"Host"? What does that mean.

Can we do it at ur place

Uh . . . I didn't think about this part. I mean I guess I imagined heading over to someone's house. But now that I stop to weigh my options I'm stuck with a dilemma: Do I want a dude from this app to come to my house and kill me? Or do I want to go to his house and have him kill me there?

I shake my head. I could never bring a stranger into my house to bone. And plus, no one on this app is going to murder me. . . . Right?

I type, *No, I can't host*, and hit send.

It takes a couple minutes for me to realize he's not going to reply. So much for our magical connection.

For the next few hours, all of my conversations go one of several ways. There are of course the unsolicited, graphic photos, which I block right off the bat (until I run out of blocks). There are guys who find out I can't host and stop talking to me. And then there are guys who ask for pics (more often than not spelled with an *x*) and stop messaging me when I ask, "Of what?"

It's a lot of effort for a lot of rejection, and I consider deleting the app almost every five seconds. I don't get how Manny does it. Well, I guess offering head might make some guys keep the conversation going.

I'm about to log off when I get a message from a torso with the name "Starbucks Lover." It'd be redundant to say the torso is white.

I check his message instead of his profile. I'll do that later.

What are you reading currently? he asks.

Wow, someone who actually read my bio. Someone who actually wants to talk about non-sex stuff. Someone with good grammar. Someone who cares, maybe?

Nothing, I reply, *but I just finished* Call Me by Your Name.

Mmm. What'd you think?

I loved it. Have you read it?

Yes. I have some . . . thoughts.

Oh yeah? Good or bad?

We'll have to discuss it in person.

My heart starts beating really fast. Is he for real?

When? Where?

Well, usually I like to go out for a glass of wine when I meet up with someone.

Oh shit. I can't meet him at a bar. Hmm . . .

Why don't we have a glass at your place instead? I write.

He doesn't reply right away, and I'm afraid I've scared him off—but then he writes back.

I'll pick up a nice Merlot.

Holy shit. This is happening. But I still don't know if he's being genuine. I don't even know what he looks like.

That sounds lovely. I have to ask though. Why no face pic?

Once again, I wait anxiously for his reply. After a minute I add, *I understand the irony of my asking that.*

He replies finally.

My job requires some discretion in this matter. Also, you must have had a really good English teacher because your use of the possessive case before a gerund is impressive.

Haha. Thank you. I did. And I don't need a face pic. What matters is you're a person. An actual person. At least, that's the impression I get.

Glad to hear it. I won't ask you for one either. I also make my decisions with my head more than my eyes, and I've enjoyed our convo so far

"Convo"? You're getting very familiar, Mr. Starbucks Lover.

Thought I'd mix things up a bit. Might even mention that your face doesn't matter too much because I'm a sucker for quads.

Quads? I'm guessing those are my thighs?

Haha, yes. Your gym teacher wasn't as good as your English teacher.

Apparently not. But if my face cancels out the thighs you can slam the door in my face later.

Haha, I wouldn't do that.

Such a gentleman.

I'm showing my age. Guys your age sometimes have trouble seeing the people on here as human beings.

Oh, he's older. You wouldn't be able to tell from his body, though. Starbucks Lover keeps it tight.

So when can I see you? I'm in a weird mood today and could use some good "convo" and company.

You're cute. How about in an hour? I'm finishing up some errands.

Oh my God. This is going better than I ever could have hoped. An older guy with a nice body and an even better personality is inviting me to his home to have wine and talk. I feel like I've skipped a decade or so of my life. I'm on fire!

I'll be there. Send me your address when you can.

He does. And adds, *Is that too far for you?*

I look it up on my map app.

Nope! Only two miles away.

All right, Everygay (you'll need to explain that when we meet), I'll see ya in a bit. Can't keep messaging on this app in the grocery store, or I'll never leave the cereal aisle.

See ya, SL. Looking forward to meeting.

Likewise, EG. :)

Wow.

Wowwww.

I should have done this a long time ago. This is working out spectacularly. I guess these types of apps just give you what you ask for. I should go get ready. I'll leave for his place early, so I don't have to ride too fast and undo my shower.

Before I know it, I'm on my way. I feel so light it's like I can't even feel my bike under me.

I'm on track to get to his place earlier than expected, so I stop at the park for a little bit. I open up the app and start checking out his profile, noting all the stuff I missed before. He's gay, a huge Taylor Swift fan, and he's looking for something meaningful. I reread our conversation twice before getting on my bike again and heading to his place.

He lives in a cute one-story house with a porch swing on the patio. I can't help picturing the two of us sitting on it. It's morning and we're enjoying some coffee before we start our day. He rests his hand on my thigh (because he's always been a sucker for quads) and we lean in to kiss. . . .

Wow. What's going on with me? I'm seventeen for fuck's sake. I'm most likely going to lose one of my virginities to this guy and never see him again. But it will be a tender, memorable moment.

I take a deep breath and knock. This is it, the moment of truth. I hear him walking to the door. Whether he's handsome or ugly doesn't matter. What matters is his face is one I'm going to remember for a long, long time. I see the doorknob turn and I wonder for a split second if I can run away. I wonder why. Maybe this is too much for me. Maybe I shouldn't have—

And there he is. For a moment nothing registers. Then I realize he's handsome. But he's not just good-looking; his face is . . . comforting. And then the realization hits me.

The phrase *Oh dear God* repeats over and over in my mind.

I shake my head, trying to dispel this obvious hallucination but nothing changes. So I stand there, unable to speak, feeling like the universe is against me and life is one big joke.

CHAPTER TWENTY-SIX

"Mr. Chastman," I'm finally able to say.

"Hello, Enrique," he says calmly. For a moment I wonder if he somehow knew it was me he was talking to on the app, but then he asks, "What are you doing here?"

He hasn't made the connection yet. He thinks I just so happened to come here right before his date tonight. I don't want to see the moment he realizes the truth, but it's coming. I wish he'd slam the door in my face right now.

Mr. Chastman furrows his eyebrows. "How do you know where . . . I . . . live . . ." There. There it is. The look of horror that comes with knowing. "Oh my God. Are you . . . are you . . ."

I wince. "Everygay? Yeah . . . I'm Everygay."

"Oh dear God."

We both stare at each other, not saying a word, not moving a muscle.

"Mr. Chastman? Are you okay?"

He swallows. "But you—you—you said you were twenty-one on the app."

My face gets hot. I don't think I've ever been this completely, utterly embarrassed before.

"I, uh—they don't let you on the app unless you say you're at least eighteen. . . ."

His face darkens, and I'm actually a little scared he's going to hit me.

"I wonder why that is," he says sardonically.

I can't help it, I laugh.

His face softens a bit. "Well, this is a new one."

"Really? This is the first time you've arranged to meet up with a student you talked to on a hookup app?"

He almost smiles. "Believe it or not, yes."

"Mr. Chastman, I know this is really, really, unbelievably awkward, but can we make the best of it? Can I come inside?"

Alarm registers on his face. He's probably about to say something along the lines of *Are you fucking kidding me?* when I interrupt him.

"I don't mean it that way. I . . . I need to talk to someone, and I think you'd understand."

He gives me an odd look.

"Nothing inappropriate," I say. "I swear."

He folds his arms, and my guess is he isn't going to budge. Maybe I can bait him.

"I guess if you can't control yourself around me, I understand. . . ."

He rolls his eyes. "Okay, fine, Enrique. You have some explaining to do anyway." I smile as he steps aside. "And no wine obviously!" he adds as I walk in.

True to the stereotype, Mr. Chastman has decorated his place impeccably. At least, it all looks fancy to me. Black-and-white photographs of people smoking in European cities hang on the walls. There's a grandfather clock next to the fireplace. And most importantly, his bookshelves are built into the wall, like a mini version of Belle's library in *Beauty and the Beast*. I resist the urge to check out his collection and instead walk over to his brown leather couch and sit. There are two glasses of red wine on the dark wood coffee table. Oh how differently this evening could have gone if I weren't seventeen. Or if Mr. Chastman weren't my English teacher.

He closes the door, walks over, and sits next to me.

"I guess these are both for me now," he says, grabbing the glasses of wine.

He downs one entire glass (impressive), sets it down, takes a sip from the other, then exhales.

"All right," he says. "First question: How long have you been on the app?"

"Like five hours."

"All right that's good. I think. Second: Have you met up with anyone besides me?"

"No."

"Good. Have you gotten . . . pictures?"

"Yes."

"Have you sent pictures?"

"No."

"Good. You know that's illegal, right? That you and the person you sent them to could go to jail for that?"

I nod, my face on fire, as he takes another big sip of wine.

"I'm sorry, Mr. Chastman. I really am. I wasn't in the right state of mind."

He sighs. "Apology accepted. This just . . . This could have gone so badly. It's obviously not ideal, but I'm a little glad you ended up here."

"What do you think could have happened with someone else? I mean I assumed there was a chance I'd get murdered tonight. But what else?"

He smiles, then frowns.

"It's not only murder you should worry about. You're seventeen. You're a kid. So many horrible things could have happened."

"I'm not a kid."

"Okay, maybe not, but you're still so very young. And I'm sure you're even younger in terms of . . . your sexuality."

"Yeah . . . This is all new."

"How are you . . . getting along?"

"It's okay. I mean . . ." I look at him. How much can I tell him? "I guess I'll take it from the night before the last day of school. Saleem texted me. . . ."

Apparently, I can tell Mr. Chastman everything. He's a great listener. He's a teacher so he won't repeat anything I say. He doesn't interrupt. He laughs at the funny stuff and makes disapproving faces when I talk about the hurtful stuff. At one point he says, "Wow, I didn't think Ziggy liked boys," and I reply, "No one does." And when I finish, he says, "This has been an . . . *eventful* summer for you."

I laugh. "I didn't want it to be all about books."

He smiles. "That's right. You said you read *Call Me by Your Name*?"

"Yes, and you said you had *thoughts*?"

"I do."

"Let's hear 'em."

He takes a sip of wine. "Listen carefully. This is going to be relevant to our situation. *Your* situation. So, first of all, Elio is seventeen, like you, and he has a romantic relationship with a twenty-four-year-old—"

"But—"

"No 'buts.' I don't care if they were in love. I don't care if it's legal in Italy. I don't care about everyone around them in the book condoning it. It's wrong. Predatory."

The corner of my mouth twists. "I just . . . I don't feel that young. I know technically I am, but I feel like I know what I want. I know that I'm lonely. And if I want someone and they want me and the only thing standing in our way is our age, then it shouldn't matter. Right? If I want what Elio got from Oliver, then I deserve it. Right?"

I look at Mr. Chastman, really look at him. He's smart and handsome and kind and familiar. And I realize I would have gone through with it. If he hadn't objected, if he hadn't made a big deal about it, I would have done whatever he wanted me to do.

He sighs. "Enrique, I'm not saying you don't deserve love at your age. And I'm not saying that being lonely doesn't make you do things you're not proud of doing." He motions between us as an example. "I only want you to be safe, and I want you to experience love and relationships when you're old enough not only to legally consent, but understand how to protect yourself."

I don't think I've ever seen him this sincere before. He cares about me; I know he does. And that's why he won't kiss me. Even though now I'd give everything I have at the moment for it to happen.

"Mr. Chastman." I shouldn't ask it. I know that much. But I'm so insanely curious. "If I were eighteen—"

"Nope."

"Why?"

"You'd still be my student. And eighteen is still incredibly young. I had a mini crisis over messaging a twenty-one-year-old."

"Who's the twenty-one-year . . . oh. Duh."

He shakes his head and takes a long slug of wine.

"From now on," he begins, "I'm only dating men twenty-five and older. No, that's still too big a gap. Twenty-six sounds about right."

I sigh. "I thought you'd at least have it all figured out by now."

He laughs and shakes his head again. "My mother says the same thing."

I laugh. "No, what I mean is you're older, with a job and a house and a . . ." I decide to embarrass him. ". . . Tight body."

He snorts. "Enrique!"

"So I thought you'd be able to get everything you want."

"Even at my age, with everything I have, I still get dicked around."

"But that's what I want!"

"I'm this close to kicking you out of my house," he says, his index finger and thumb a nanometer apart.

I'm not gonna push my luck. "Anything else wrong with the book?"

"Yes, there was a plethora of fucked-up elements."

"Like?"

"Well, there was the girl Oliver slept with who was also Elio's age."

"Chiara, I think."

"Yeah, her. And there was that incredibly racist San Clemente sequence with the old, white poet sexualizing the entire country of Thailand and talking about the presumably gender-queer concierge in the most offensive ways possible."

"Huh . . . I did find that part really weird."

"Yes, it was fetishistic and fucking gross."

"Why don't we talk about books like this in class?"

"AP graders don't look too kindly upon use of the f-word."

"A fucking shame."

"Agreed." He drinks. "Where'd you get your username?"

"I came up with it."

He raises his eyebrows. "Oh, really."

"Yeah. It was actually inspired by *Call Me by Your Name*."

"How so?"

I sit up straight, cross my legs, and form a triangle with my hands (my impression of a snooty college professor).

"You see, Mr. Chastman, my dear friend, after reading a whopping ten or so queer books over the course of my life before this one"—he laughs—"I'm starting to see a pattern. These books all center around a shy everyman character—the Everygay—who comes into contact with the Better Man. The Better Man is usually attractive. He can also be tall, smart, rich. But above all he must be confident. Because above all else queer men crave confidence, correct? It's what we're taught not to have. We're instead taught shame and fear. And hate."

The gravity of my words hits me, and my posture returns to normal before I continue.

"We're supposed to . . . be ashamed of who we are, fear anything that could out us, and hate the things we fear. That's why we don't really have the luxury of being carefree or whatever. If anything, we overcompensate with actions that'll . . . hide us."

He nods slowly. "I can see that."

"But maybe I've just seen too many Everygays like myself. You see, the Better Man is never the protagonist or the narrator. He's a plot device who's meant to draw out the Everygay and make him experience life for once. More than love, a lot of the books I've read focus on idealization and idolization. Which, of course, I have experience with."

"Do you, now?" he says after sip of wine.

"Yes. But I don't have a singular Better Man. I have three. Four, if you count Saleem. Ziggy and Tyler are the quintessential Better Man. Manny has that wild confidence that comes from growing up in his hypermasculine environment. And Saleem has a quiet kind of confidence that comes from knowing who he is. He'd never embarrass himself to follow his base desires like me. Even though he hasn't even kissed a girl yet, I feel like one day I'll wake up and he'll be married with children, and I'll be 'Daddy's old single friend who always stares at him for just a second too long.'"

Mr. Chastman drains his wineglass and puts it down on the table.

"Do you really feel like an 'Everygay,' Enrique?"

"Well . . . I mean, for starters I'm not gay."

"Bi? Pan? Queer? Sexually flu—"

"All of the above, I think. But bi is the first label I ever found that fit. I use gay a lot because everyone else says gay when they're referring to more than gay guys."

"Bierasure."

"Right. And, like, biphobia in general sucks because it's not just someone else's way of thinking. It's . . . mine too. I don't always believe in it, but I've heard enough of it to, like . . ."

"Internalize it."

"Yeah, exactly! It's like this thing I learned about in my psych class called stereotype threat. You internalize an idea about yourself and it starts affecting how you act and you end up with a self-fulfilling prophecy. So I'm constantly doubting my attractions, my actual feelings. I'm gaslighting *myself*. Because the message I've gotten about guys who like guys *and* girls is that we're faking, that we couldn't possibly be attracted to girls if we're attracted to boys. Bi girls get the same thing, but for them it means they're perceived as straight and for us it means we're perceived as gay.

"So I'm kind of terrified that whoever I end up with is going to be determined by how other people see me."

I take a deep breath and wait for Mr. Chastman to respond, searching his face to see if he understands me.

"Whomever," he says finally.

"What?"

"It's 'whomever I end up with' because the person is the object of the preposition."

I stare at him, annoyed that he completely missed the point, until he laughs.

"I'm kidding, Enrique."

"Oh."

I manage a smile.

"Maybe it's only me," I say. "Maybe I'm the lucky one who gets to obsess about my every action and impulse. Maybe I know nothing."

"I'd never say that you know nothing. You're an incredibly bright kid, and the pure volume of your thoughts on your experience as a bisexual person is as impressive as it is worrying. And I have to say, your thoughts on queer literature are especially of interest to me as your English teacher. I don't think I could have ever quite conceptualized the 'Everygay' and 'Better Man' archetypes the way you did. But I will say that you need to cut yourself some slack and allow yourself to learn and grow. You're not an 'Everygay' in a host of ways."

I know I shouldn't say it, but right now I want to reach him. I want a poignant moment between the two of us, something that forces all the air out of the room.

"You know, Mr. Chastman. Your username should be Better Man."

He sighs and then smiles a sad smile.

"No, Enrique, it shouldn't. I'm not a Better Man."

"Well you're definitely not an Everygay."

"No. I'm not. I'm just me. We're not literary archetypes, Enrique. We're two men, or one man and one boy, rather, who are trying to change their lives for the better."

"I think you could make my life better."

"Enrique, stop."

He says it firmly, and I have to wonder, *Is the reason he*

keeps telling me to stop because I might be able to convince him? Is he scared of being swayed by me?

"Why?"

"Because," he says, "every time you try to tell me you and I would be a good idea you seem even more naïve and it makes me worry even more."

Oof. Reality check. Much needed but still, *oof.*

"I'm sorry," I say. "I . . . can we start over? Can we have a one-hundred-percent-platonic, one-hundred-percent-appropriate queer teacher–queer student relationship?"

He thinks about it. "Sure. That sounds like it could work. What do you hope to gain from it?"

"Book recommendations, life advice, extra credit, and wine."

"No extra credit. No wine."

"Deal."

I smile at him, and he smiles back.

We talk for a while. He makes me delete my profile and the app and promise not to download it again until I'm at least eighteen. As I get up to leave, I wonder if he'll contact someone else tonight. Since I can't be his sangria-loving stockbroker, I hope he finds someone else who can as soon as possible.

"This is going to sound really sketchy," he says, "but don't tell anyone about this, please. I'm mortified as it is."

"I won't."

"Good, and we'll just go back to the way things were at school."

"Agreed." I can't resist teasing him one last time. "I'll make sure not to wear my newest pair of shorts. They show off a bit of my quads, and I wouldn't want to make you uncomfortable."

He puts his hand to his forehead and squeezes it.

"I can't wait until you're older and look back on this moment and cringe at everything you've said."

"You know you're not that old yourself," I say. "You're the same age as the guy who played Oliver in the movie."

"Oh my God. Tell me that's not true."

"It is."

"It was bad enough when he was twenty-four."

"If you were twenty-four—"

"All right, bye, Enrique." He closes the door in my face.

Okay, so maybe Mr. Chastman isn't my Better Man, but maybe I don't need a Better Man after all. Maybe I am both the Everygay and the Better Man. Maybe I'm neither. Maybe I'm enough for myself. Maybe.

On the ride home, I find myself not thinking, and it feels right. I'm not going to lie, I feel weird, but I also feel . . . well, hopeful.

CHAPTER TWENTY-SEVEN

My mom's ready to leave for Target, and I have no idea if I want to go with her. What if she catches me talking to Arturo for a third time and assumes we're flirting? What if she uses her weird mom ESP and figures out we've seen each other since the last time I saw him in the store? What if—

"Do you wanna go or not?" my mom says, blocking my view of the TV. "I don't got all day."

"I'll go," I say, getting up from the couch. "Gimme five minutes."

I find him in the video game section testing out a new racing game.

"They pay you for this?" I ask, standing beside him.

He glances at me and then looks back at the screen. "Snitches get stitches."

"I ain't no snitch."

He hands me a controller and starts a new race.

"What's been going on with you?" he asks as he peels off at the starting line.

"A lot, actually." My car politely eases onto the track as I try to figure out what the buttons on my controller do. "I've started going to therapy again—"

"I thought I was your therapist," he says, not taking his eyes off the screen.

I laugh. "I found out that Mr. Chastman is gay—"

"Duh."

"How did you—he never—doesn't matter. I had sex for the first time."

"Oh shit."

He glances at me.

"Yeah," I say. "And I, uh, think I understand you now."

"How so?"

Arturo is in first place. I'm second to last. My shiny blue race car is getting splattered with mud as I struggle in the grass off to the side of the track. I wait until I'm back on the road before I answer him.

"This summer I've been realizing that even the most important people in my life don't know me completely. I've kept different parts of myself hidden from them and offered up a version of me that I thought they'd like, that they would feel comfortable with. And lately, that's become utterly exhausting. Because I'm tired of people loving pieces of me. I want them to see me, in full, and celebrate me for who I am."

I manage to pass a few cars, and I've never been so grateful to be in thirteenth place.

"Which they can't do if I'm not being honest," I say. "But the only thing keeping me from being completely honest is fear. Fear that everything will change."

Neither of us says anything, and the race ends with Arturo as the winner and me in fifth place.

He hangs up his controller. "Whatcha gonna do?"

I hang up mine. "I don't know."

He nods.

"How've *you* been?" I ask.

"Guillermo broke up with me."

"What?" I practically scream.

"Yeah . . ."

"Why?"

"I don't know."

"What did he say?"

"That's the thing." Arturo smiles bitterly and shakes his head. "He didn't say anything. He just . . . stopped. Stopped texting, stopped calling, stopped caring."

"What a dickbag."

Arturo laughs. "Yeah. I went to Walmart a week ago, fully intending on kicking his ass in front of his coworkers, but he wasn't there. I imagined him spotting me on the security cameras and taking his lunch. Or seeing me walking down an aisle and hiding behind a display until I passed by. But then on the drive home, I figured he probably wasn't there, and I wasn't meant to see the guy who ghosted me. Because maybe I wouldn't have kicked his ass. Maybe I would have fallen down at his feet and begged him to take me back."

"Wow. I . . . I'm so sorry."

"Thanks. And I feel especially bad because I sort of knew that you looked at me like I had everything figured out, and I didn't want to disappoint you. And I know I should say something wise about how that's life and at least I tried and it's better to have loved and lost and all that shit, but . . . I just wanna say life sucks." He sighs. "And so does this game. It lacks imagination."

"It really does, and I'm not just saying that because I'm horrible at it."

We stand there for a while before it occurs to me to put my hand on his shoulder. When I do, he looks behind us, searching for something.

"What?" I say.

"I expected your mom to pop up out of nowhere."

"She does have a habit of materializing without either of us noticing. . . . But now that you mention her, I should probably go find her."

"Yeah."

I remove my hand. "I'll see ya, okay?"

"Yeah. See ya, Enrique."

As I walk away, I tell myself that he'll get over this in no time because he's strong. But if I were in his position? Who knows if that's true.

My mom pushes her cart down the pasta aisle while I absent-mindedly throw things into it.

"You don't eat gluten-free mac and cheese," she says.

I look down at the cart.

"Oh, my bad."

She watches me as I take the box out and replace it with actual mac and cheese. "You okay?"

"Never better," I reply, faking a smile.

As we exit the parking lot, we pass by the strip club across the street.

"Is that Dad's car?" I ask, fake shock on my face.

"You still think that's funny, huh?"

"I do," I say, forcing myself to unwrap my Snickers. I'm trying to act normal, so my mom doesn't ask me what's wrong.

"What's wrong?" my mom asks.

I must be a terrible actor.

"Nothing," I say.

She stops at a red light, silent for a moment.

"Did you see him today?"

I jerk my head to look at her. "Who?"

"The cute Target kid."

Oh my God. I was right about her thinking Arturo and I have been flirting. I'm dead.

"I don't know who you're talking about," I say, turning away from her.

"Come on, Quique. Be honest with me."

How? She'd be ashamed.

"I don't want to."

She laughs as the light turns green and steps on the gas. "Try it. You might like it."

I take a bite of my Snickers before I speak.

"We're not into each other. But, uh, he helps me with stuff. He understands me in a way that no one else really does."

"I see."

"So . . ." I turn my head slowly. "You remember the Fourth of July?"

"Yes," she says, making eye contact with me before looking back to the road. "Tequila didn't save you this time."

We laugh, thinking about the broken shot glass. I confessed a couple years ago that I was the one who broke it.

"And you never said anything?" I ask.

She shrugs. "I knew you needed time."

"Did you tell Dad?"

She shakes her head. "That's all you, kid."

"Yeah . . ."

She checks her blind spot and merges into her left lane. "So I'm guessing you're not over Saleem?"

I can't help but laugh.

"I'll take that as a no."

"I thought I could get over him, but now I'm not so sure. He's perfect."

"He shits like the rest of us, kid."

"*Mom.*"

"All I'm saying is he's human. He isn't worth every other person in your life. He's a sweet boy with a beautiful soul, but so are you. Don't sell yourself short."

Ugh. I hate when people exaggerate how "amazing" I am. The distance between my perceived self and the person they claim to see grows so large it becomes unbelievable. Why don't they keep it realistic and call me an "okay" person? *That* I'd accept.

"Where were you the night you said you were with him?"

I don't answer her right away. "I was with Arturo."

"Talking."

"Yes, Mom. It's really not like that."

She nods. "I believe you."

We ride in silence for a while before I speak again.

"Hey, Mom."

"Yeah?"

"Thanks for being so cool about all this."

She looks at me, her face twisted up a bit, like she's trying not to cry.

"I love you, kid."

"I love you, too."

"I don't like you lying to me, though. We'll come back to that."

"Fair enough."

She pulls up to the curb outside our house. "Quique, one other thing."

"Yes?"

"Don't let your father see my Doritos."

I curl up on the couch after I help my mom put everything away. I'm not really tired, but the next thing I remember is waking up from a nap, not knowing what month we're in or my last name.

"I said move over."

My dad flicks his hand at me, and I slowly sit up. The TV's on. He takes a seat next to me and starts flipping through channels. He lands on a baseball game, but it immediately goes to commercial. An ad comes on that I know very well.

I'm not actually sure what it's for (travel company maybe?) because every single time it comes on I'm not listening to what the spokesman is saying; I'm thinking about the things he'd do to me. Because that's how it would go. He looks . . . dirty. Yes, very dirty. He's like the human version of the purple devil emoji. And *he* would do things to *me*, not the other way around.

"Quique!"

I shake my head. "What?"

"I said your name like five times," my dad says.

"Oh, sorry."

"Do you want a beer?"

"Uh . . ."

"It's a crime to watch baseball without a beer."

"Well, if it's a crime. . . ."

He smiles in such a loving way that it does something to me. A tectonic plate shifts inside my chest and with that comes a release of pressure. My dad loves me, and maybe he'd add a "no matter what" to that.

He starts to get up, but before he does, I say, "Dad?"

"Yes, mijo?"

"I, uh . . . I like guys."

He freezes, palms on the couch cushion, midway through pushing himself up.

"I already told Mom." I look at his face. Unreadable. "I just, uh, thought I'd tell you, too. So you'd know." *That you have a fag for a son*, I add in my head.

He takes a breath. "Quique, I know."

"What? You do? Mom said she didn't tell you!"

"She didn't have to. I've known for a long time. Kinda."

"But how? I—I was so careful."

His face falls. "I don't know, Quique. I guess because you're my son and I . . . You go quiet."

"Huh?"

"You get real quiet when you see a . . . stud."

"Dad." Why did he have to say it like that?

"Well, I don't know what you kids call it. A 'hot piece' then."

"Dad!"

We're both almost laughing.

"I noticed," he says. "I noticed."

For some reason I like those two words coming from him. Usually, for dudes like me discovery is always the scariest option. But with my dad? He noticed. He saw me.

"I like girls, too." I don't mean it in a posturing way, like I'm telling him my liking dudes is a "quirk" that we don't need to focus on. I want him to know that about me too.

"Hard not to," he says.

We both smile.

"You still want that beer?"

"Yeah, I do."

"And maybe some of your mom's Doritos. She thinks I don't know where she hides them, but I do."

He gets up from the couch, and I don't stop him this time. He returns with two Coronas, a sliver of lime sticking out of both, and the forbidden Doritos. He hands me a bottle, and we perform the following actions simultaneously—we push the limes into our beers, cover the opening of the bottles with our thumbs, and flip them over. Then we tip them back and slowly move our thumbs back, releasing a spray of carbonation. This is the first time I've done it successfully, and I wonder when my thumb got big enough.

My dad and I both take a sip. Then he puts his arm around my shoulders, something he hasn't done in a long, long time, and I feel secure. I feel like I belong.

CHAPTER TWENTY-EIGHT

"That's fantastic news!"

"Yeah."

"I'm glad he took it well."

"Me too."

"I understand that coming out can be incredibly scary."

"It lives up to the hype, yeah."

Is Luciana gay? Maybe she realized it during the two years I wasn't her patient. Maybe that's why she changed her hair, because every Realization™ necessitates some sort of hair transformation (I shaved my head the summer after eighth grade). I want to ask, but of course that would be totally inappropriate. Speaking of . . .

"I have to tell you something about my teacher, Mr. Chastman."

She seems mildly horrified at the beginning of my story, but a look of relief washes over her as she hears about everything he said.

"He sounds incredibly reasonable," she says at the end.

I wonder if she'd be into him. Does she like men? Mr. Chastman definitely wouldn't be into her, on account of her being a woman, but what if they hit it off platonically? WLW and MLM make the best friends. Fabiola and I are proof of that.

"He is," I say.

"Now, let's talk about what led you to download the app."

Ugh. I want to stomp my feet and whine, *But I don't wannaaaaaaaaaa.* Instead, I try to put it succinctly.

"I was lonely. Very lonely."

"I see."

That's code for *keep talking.* So I do.

"Sometimes I feel so, so alone that I think about someone breaking into my house and stabbing me and feeling flattered because they chose me. Because they paid attention to me."

Her face is somewhere between a smile and a grimace. "That's mildly concerning."

"I don't mean it."

"I know you don't. Not literally. But I do believe you can be prone to accepting harmful behavior if it satisfies the need you have for validation."

Well, duh. I could have told her that a long time ago.

"I agree," I say.

"Why do you think that is?"

I sigh. "Because I hate myself? Because I never think I'm good enough and I feel like everyone else around me is doing fine and I'm the only one struggling and then I realize they're probably struggling too but I'm too selfish to see it."

She pauses for a moment. "Let's unpack that."

This is going to take a while.

She only mentions medication again at the end of the session. She says if I feel like I don't need it, then that's totally fine, but if I realize that I do, in fact, need it, then I shouldn't hesitate to tell her.

"That's good!" my mom says in the car.

I shrug.

"It is! I don't care if you're on medication or not, but things are definitely looking good if she doesn't think you need it."

I just nod along.

I didn't mention to her that Luciana said it's very likely that I'll have another "episode" at least before the summer is over. *If we're looking at past patterns.* That's what she said. *Past patterns.* I have a well-defined history of crazy, a perfectly predictable propensity for panic. Hey, at least that sounds poetic.

I have no idea what I want to do today, or for the rest of my life for that matter, but I'll focus on today for now. I look out the car window and search my brain for effective distractions.

Hmm. That could work.

"Hey, Mom," I say. "You know what we haven't done in a while?"

"Reveal a deeply personal secret that's been years in the making?"

I snort. She and my dad have since talked about the whole *our son plays for both teams but knows nothing about sports* thing. Apparently, they've decided they're going to tease me about it until I die. I am neither ecstatic nor upset about it. It's who they are.

"No. We haven't gone to the movies in a while."

"That is true. What do you want to see?"

"I don't know. We can decide when we get there."

She drives for a little while in silence. Then she clears her throat and says, "Are you, um, would you pick a movie that . . . has . . . men in it?"

My eyebrows bunch together. "Every movie has men in it. Too many men if you ask me." Why does she look so uncomfortable? What does she mean by a movie with men in it?

"Men *together*, honey."

Oh.

She's asking me if I'm going to try to take her to a gay movie. As if there's even a guarantee that there's something like that playing at our theater currently.

"We'll pick something together," I say.

It's the only way I can think to respond.

"Okay. I'm just . . . I don't think I'm ready to . . ."

"Yeah, it's okay."

I try to stop blood from rushing to my face. It's hard. This makes me think of what I heard last night. After the baseball game, when I was trying to fall asleep, I heard my parents talking about me. This was to be expected, but something my dad said kept me up for hours.

"Is it my fault?"

The only reason I heard it so clearly is because of how high-pitched it came out. It was like a cry for help.

Fault. Fault implies blame. Was he to blame for the person I am? That's what he wanted to know. Did he mess me up?

And what my mom responded with made it so much worse.

"Is it mine?"

How did my suggestion for a little Sunday matinee lead me here? I don't feel like going to the movies anymore. Now I want to go to the beach, walk into the ocean, and keep going until I'm well in over my head, keep going until I sprout gills and fins, and make the sea my home for the rest of my life.

Although, with my luck I'd probably end up running into a group of racist, homophobic dolphins. The thought makes me smile, so I keep with it. They'd call me a "two-legged land faggot." They'd tell me to go back to where I came from. They'd be wearing *Poseidon hates fags* T-shirts and *Make the Ocean Great Again* hats.

That last image makes me laugh out loud, and my mom looks at me like I'm crazy. Which, maybe I am. But I'm surviving.

Focusing on this movie is hard for several reasons. There's of course the awkward discussion I had with my mom. There's the forced heterosexual romantic subplot. And then there's the paranoia that comes every time I'm in a movie theater and I think about the possibility of a shooting. I think about that possibility when I'm at school and the mall and stuff too, but there's something about the movie theater that makes me extra paranoid. Maybe it's the fact that movies are specifically made to distract you, to make you let your guard down.

I need to stop thinking about this, but it's a reality I can't forget. It happened in a movie theater like this in Aurora. It happened to people like me and Fabiola in Orlando. It happened to people like Saleem in Christchurch. It happened to people like Molly in Atlanta. It happened to kids our age in Parkland. It happens.

I look over at my mom, who's actually watching the movie and thoughtfully eating popcorn at the same time. I wish I could be like her right now. Immersed. But I don't allow myself that. I keep imagining a white guy (because, come on, who else would it be) wearing tactical gear with two machine guns in his hands, spraying the audience with bullets.

I wonder how I'd react. Would I scream and duck? Use my mom as a shield? Would I lunge at the guy and try to stop him? Those last two options probably aren't likely. The first is.

"What's up with you?" my mom says. "Do I have butter on my face?"

She wipes her mouth.

"No," I say. "Sorry."

We both turn back to the screen, one of us actually processing the story being projected onto it, the other only pretending.

I picture my mom in my mind, with her popcorn-eating ways, and I know—I would save her. Well, maybe I wouldn't be successful. But I'd try. I'd push her down and cover her body with mine. I know I would. I wouldn't want anything bad to happen to her. I wouldn't want her to get hurt. Even though she doesn't understand or accept me completely, I still love her that much.

And that has me thinking. How could I have let myself believe for so long that I have more in common with the villains of the world than the heroes?

For the rest of the movie, I feel inspired. If someone walks into this theater, thinking he's about to massacre a bunch of unsuspecting people, he has another thing coming. I'll fly out of my seat. He'll try to gun me down, but the bullets won't stop me, not yet. He will know fear, not me. I'd kill him before he had the chance to kill anyone else. And once I was done, I'd finally fall to the ground. My mother would come over and put my head in her lap. She would cry over me and tell me how brave I am, how proud of me she was.

I keep thinking it's actually going to happen. My heart's beating fast, and my muscles are tensed like I'm about to spring. *It's coming, it's coming, it's coming.* Something is coming.

The feeling doesn't leave me until we're both in the car, on our way home.

CHAPTER TWENTY-NINE

"Why is it always us?" I ask, my mouth full of hummus and bell pepper. Mr. Chastman always has the best snacks. "God doesn't hate anyone. At least that's what I've been taught. But if he does hate a specific group of people, why would he focus on queer people? What do we do that's so specifically bad?"

I've been marinating on this for almost two weeks, ever since seeing that movie with my mom.

"Why isn't it 'God hates pedophiles,'" I continue. "Or 'God hates abusive spouses,' or 'God hates men who make moves on their wives' family members?' Or what if we changed it to a single representative person. Like 'God hates Chris Browns?'"

"Or 'God hates Woody Allens,'" Mr. Chastman says.

"Exactly!"

I grab Mr. Chastman's bottle of wine and go to pour it into my recently emptied glass of chocolate almond milk.

"Oh, no you don't," he says, taking the bottle away.

"Oh, come on," I say. "I drink all the time. My dad gave me a beer for coming out."

"He's your legal guardian, and I'm not going to be the teacher who gives alcohol to his underage student. Also, there's still a few drops of almond milk in your glass, and the mixing would make me gag."

"Something tells me you don't have a sensitive gag re—"

"If you finish that sentence, you will not be allowed in my house again."

"Fine."

I feel my phone buzz and reach into my pocket. It's a text from Fabiola.

Molly's having a party tonight. You're coming. Where are you?

"Who's that?" Mr. Chastman asks.

"Fabiola. Apparently, I'm going to a party tonight."

"You obey her just like that?"

"Mostly." He says nothing, just drinks some of his wine. "You see, at a party hosted by one of my esteemed classmates, I can get all the alcohol I want."

"Is that so?"

He's halfway between amused and concerned.

"Don't worry, I'll be careful."

"I highly doubt that. Maybe if I were your age, I would be naïve enough to believe you."

I wait at the park because that's where I told Fabiola to pick me up. When I get in her truck, she asks, "Why are you here so late?"

I had intended on coming up with an explanation, but I got distracted trying to figure out Mr. Chastman's first name. As I left his place, I told him that we should be on a first-name basis at this point, but he didn't agree. Not that I have a clue what it is. I think he looks like a Benjamin though. Or a Brandon. Or, *ooh*, a Ronan—

"Were you meeting up with Manny again?"

Hmm. She thought of an excuse for me, but if I say yes, she'll ask for details and I'll have to lie and lie and lie. Maybe if I stay quiet right now, she'll assume that's the case and I'm being coy about it.

"You did, didn't you?"

"No," I say.

"You totally did."

"Whatever you say."

Well that was easy.

"Aren't Molly's parents really strict?" I ask when we're almost at her house. "How is she throwing a party?"

"They're at a business conference in Hawaii, and she'll have a whole week after tonight to clean up. I even offered my services."

"Cleaning or . . ."

"She ordered the full package."

"Of course."

As Fabiola pulls up to the curb, it occurs to me to ask a question.

"Have you and her . . ."

"Had sex?" she finishes, killing the engine.

"Yeah."

"No. Why do you ask?"

"I, uh, I thought you might have and not told me. Which is totally okay by the way. It's none of my business. I was just wondering."

She doesn't respond right away, and I don't dare look at her. Is she mad? Am I crossing a line? I didn't have to think this much around her before.

"We haven't had sex yet." I finally turn to look at her. "But I think we might tonight." She smiles at me.

"That's great," I say, smiling back. "Let's not keep her waiting."

We walk up to the front door, and, rather than knocking, Fabiola opens it and lets herself right in. I follow.

It's a typical party, like Manny's cousin's but with a younger and considerably milder crowd. Fabiola and I push through them, heading to the kitchen. The house is more tightly packed than Gonzo's. It seems like the whole school's here. Which means . . . I wonder who it's going to be. I know I'm going to run into one of them tonight, one of the three. But which?

"Fabiola!"

I don't recognize the voice and Fabiola's blocking my view of whoever called her name. It was high-pitched but bro-y. Which one of them has a high-pitched voice?

And then I realize it's Molly. She's wearing a black crop top with a plaid button-up over it and jean short-shorts. Fabiola was right. Her glorious thighs are on full display, and I have to stop myself from staring.

"You're finally here!"

She's carrying two red cups filled to the brim with beer, so Fabiola hugs her gingerly.

"This is for you," Molly says, smiling and handing Fabiola one of the cups.

"Thanks!"

They clink their cups and drink. It takes a while for them to remember me.

"Oh, hey, you . . . ," Molly says.

"Enrique," I say.

"I know!" She looks at Fabiola. "I just, uh, wasn't able to use my brain for a sec." She turns back to me. "Welcome!"

"Thanks."

"Fabiola's told me so much about you. And I know everyone says that, but it's really true. Sometimes I feel like I know *too* much about you."

We both laugh. "I guess that's flattering."

I like Molly, which isn't a surprise. She seems open and fun, and the way she casually snaked her arm around Fabiola's waist and kept her focus on me was impressive. But I need to get out of here.

"I'm gonna go get a drink."

"Here, you can take mine!" Molly says.

"It's okay. I'm not in the mood for beer."

Especially one she's already drunk from.

"Okay! Good stuff's upstairs, all the way down the hall on the right."

"Thanks."

"You're so nice," I hear Fabiola say as I begin making my way to the stairs.

"It's nothing," Molly says. "You guys are awesome. *You* are . . . really awesome."

I don't stick around for the rest of the conversation.

I hop up the steps, glad to be getting away from everyone. I'm not in a party mood tonight. I kind of wish I had stayed at Mr. Chastman's. I'm so comfortable at his place. I can be me.

When I enter Molly's room, there's already someone

surveying the small collection of liquor bottles and mixers on her desk. That someone is Ziggy.

If I could have chosen who I'd see here tonight, I don't think it would have been him. I probably would have chosen Manny. But I think he's at least a better option than Tyler.

"Hey, Ziggy."

He turns around, a little startled.

"Oh, hey, Enrique."

His face is hard to read.

"What brings you here?" I ask.

"To the party or to Molly's room?"

I shrug. "Both."

"Molly and I are tight. We do track together."

"Oh. What's her . . . um . . . area? Like what does she do?"

He smiles. "Hurdles. Her event is hurdles."

"Oh." Explains the legs.

"And fuck my event right?"

I laugh. "What?"

"You don't care what I do?"

I try to stop myself from blushing. "I already know."

"Really?"

"Your yearbook feature, remember?"

"Oh right . . ."

Time to change the subject.

"Whatcha doin'?" I ask, motioning to the liquor.

"Making myself a drink. Want one?"

"Sure."

"What kind?"

"I'll have whatever you're having."

"Two vodka Monsters it is."

"Please tell me you're kidding."

What the hell is wrong with him?

"Try it," he says. "You might like it."

"You know I'll do anything you say."

His resulting silence resounds in the room. I didn't mean for it to come off that sexual. It was supposed to be more playful.

He quickly turns around and starts mixing the drinks for us. When he's done, I know immediately I'm not going to enjoy what comes next. His concoction is a weird yellow color like he whipped his dick out and peed into my cup when I wasn't looking.

"Here you go," he says, handing it to me.

"Thanks. Cheers," I say, thinking about the bottles of Powerade we shared a million years ago.

"Cheers."

We clink and drink.

"You like it?" he asks.

The truth: His piss might actually have tasted better.

My lie: "It's delicious."

He smiles. "I know you don't mean that, but *I* really like it."

"Dude, I honestly don't know how."

He shrugs. "Well, at least you know you don't like it."

"Yeah, I guess."

"Do you want to head back to the party?"

I nervously scratch the back of my head. "Can we get something out of the way first?"

He must know what I'm gonna ask because he takes a

deep breath, bracing himself, and sits on Molly's bed.

"Sure."

I sit next to him. "It doesn't have to be a whole thing. I just wanna know—"

"What happened in my brain after we made out."

"Yeah."

He sighs. "Well. I, uh, sort of realized . . . as we were, you know . . . that I maybe don't—I'm not *super* into—somehow I . . ."

"Ziggy."

"I'm not into dudes."

"Oh. Uh . . ."

What the fuck is going on?

"And I know that's confusing because I invited myself over and kissed you first, but I was . . . questioning. I guess."

"Right . . ."

So he tested himself with me and decided he wasn't into guys. Totally flattering.

He must realize what I'm thinking because he says, "It's not you. I . . . don't swing that way. I mean the kissing was okay."

"High praise."

He laughs. "It was good . . . But then your tongue was in my mouth." He grimaces. "And I could feel your . . . jabbing at me." He starts miming it with his hand. "And the feel of your body hair on my chest made me want to vom—"

"I think I get it, Ziggy."

He laughs again. "Sorry."

"It's okay. You're not into dudes. I think it was cool that you . . . tested it out."

"Thanks."

"More guys should be as casual about it as you were."

"Yeah. And it should make you feel better that you made me think it was even possible that I could like being with a guy."

"Really?"

"Yeah. I still find you very charming."

We smile at each other. If he weren't straight, I'd kiss him again.

"But the thought of us naked together just—" He makes the face again.

"All right, I fucking get it."

"Sorry."

"Don't worry about it. I should have guessed you were straight. Everyone else did."

"Really? Who?"

"Um . . . people."

"Oh. Have you, um, been with any other dudes since?"

"Maybe. Why?"

He shrugs his shoulders. "Curious."

"I'm well aware."

He laughs. "Who were they?"

"I don't think I should—"

"Was Tyler Montana one of them?"

"How the hell do you know?"

He shrugs. "I saw you two together at school sometimes, and you had, like, a kind of chemistry thing. It kind of made me jealous. You can see why I was confused."

"Yeah."

"My next guess is Saleem."

"Understandable."

"But you haven't hooked up with him?"

"No."

"So it's only been Tyler?"

"Uh, yeah." I'm not trying to out anyone else today.

There's a look on his face that I can't read. "This is gonna sound weird, but would you wanna kiss again? Just a peck? So the last guy you kissed isn't that annoying ass wanksta?"

I stare at him with my mouth open. He can't possibly be serious. But he is.

So I have to ask myself, *Do I want to kiss him?*

Eh, what could it hurt? I'll do it. He doesn't have to know the last guy I actually kissed was Manny.

"Sure," I say.

We both lean in and kiss. I keep my eyes open this time, so I can imprint it on my brain.

"Yeah, no," he says, pulling away and wiping his mouth. "I thought I'd try one last time, but that proved it—I am not into this."

"Get out of the room right fucking now, so I can make myself a decent drink and be alone."

"Fair enough. See ya, Enrique."

"See ya, Ziggy."

He walks out, and I shake my head. What a fucking weirdo.

I turn my attention to the liquor. "You guys don't mind being in my mouth, do ya?"

· · ·

I end up staying in the room a lot longer and drinking a lot more than I intended. I leave only when Fabiola and Molly come upstairs and it's obvious they want the room for some one-on-one time.

I head downstairs as slowly as possible, a bottle of rum in hand. I'm drunk, but not a sociable kind of drunk. I know a lot of people here, but most of them probably don't know me. In any case, the backyard is beckoning me.

No one else is out here, thank God. But there is a tree and a tree house. I walk over and start climbing up the ladder with my unencumbered hand. Like every other kid in the world, I really wanted one of these growing up, but I never got one. Probably because we didn't have a tree. Or a backyard.

As I pull myself inside, I fully expect to happen upon an amorous couple in the middle of some salacious activity, but the small space is empty. I sprawl out on the dusty rug on the floor, eyes closed, and I hear the bottle of rum rolling away. The room is spinning, and I wonder if I'd end up breaking something if I tried to climb back down right now.

My phone buzzes, and I check it. I have a text from Tyler.
You up
I want to reply with *Fuck you*, but for some reason I type, *Yeah* instead.
Cool wanna come over
Csn't too drunk.
Where are you
Molly Pham's house
Not too far should I come to you

Sure

I accidentally drop my phone on my face and curse. I pick it up again and reread our conversation. I've already forgotten what we said.

Shit, he's coming. What did I do? Why am I so fucking reck—wait. Hold that thought. I feel like I'm gonna be sick.

CHAPTER THIRTY

The sound of someone climbing up the ladder wakes me, which means I must have passed out for a bit.

"Move over, dude," Tyler says.

With plenty of effort, I drag myself into a sitting position and Tyler climbs in.

"Was there like . . ." Oh God, I sound so drunk. ". . . a puddle of puke on the grass outside the tree house?" I could have sworn I vomited out of a kid-sized window not too long ago.

"Uh . . . no, I don't think so," he says.

"Dat's good." I remember now. Nothing came out as I retched. "Hey, you're peeling."

I point to a patch of dead skin on his nose.

He clears his throat. "Yeah, uh, I, uh, got sunburnt in Barbados."

"Oh."

"How was the party?" he asks quickly.

"Okay. Why didn't you come?"

He shrugs. "I'm not really a party guy."

"Really?" That's surprising. He's a jock. Jocks and parties go together like gays and pastel pink hats.

"Yeah, I mostly like to chill by myself or with a couple other people and smoke. You know."

"Right." Everything's swimming in front of my eyes. "So, are you high right now?"

He laughs. "As a kite."

"And you drove?"

"Nah. Like I said, Molly's is pretty close. I walked. Maybe jogged a little."

Dimples.

And just like that I've forgiven him. So far he's been nice and chill. I'm learning more about him. And I'm pretty sure we're going to kiss this time because his face is so close to mine.

"Jogged?"

"Yeah. I was hype."

"To see me."

"Yeah."

Okay, I'm doing it.

I mash my face against his. It's sloppy and gross, mostly tongue. Ziggy would hate it, but Tyler seems into it. This is a victory, more intimate than seeing or touching his dick.

Speaking of, I hadn't noticed until now, but his lengthy member is out at the moment. I realize it as he uses one of his hands to put my hand on it and the other to firmly grasp the back of my neck. Kinda hot.

I start stroking him as we make out, and his grip on my neck tightens. Then I realize he's actually pushing down, trying to get my head to his crotch.

I slip under his arm and pull away, feeling a little more sober all of a sudden. "What are you doing?"

"Don't you wanna?"

"I mean . . . I'd like the option to choose."

"I wasn't forcing you."

"You weren't exactly hinting, Tyler."

"Sorry, dude. I thought you were into it."

"I was, but . . . What do you want from me?"

"Huh?"

"Is this how things are gonna go? Every time you want your dick played with, you're gonna hit me up?"

He sighs. "I thought you were down."

I laugh. How is he this obtuse?

"Tyler, me being into you doesn't mean that I'm at your beck and call."

"My what?"

Is he that dumb or that high?

"Am I a walking mouth?"

That's putting it succinctly enough.

"Come on, dude. Did you really think we were gonna be boyfriends and that we'd hold hands at school and go to prom together?"

I'd laugh if he weren't being such a dickbag right now.

"No," I say, "and I don't expect a ring or whatever the fuck. I just don't want to feel used, and that's how you make me feel."

"Since when?"

"What the hell was last time?"

"What do you mean?"

God, this guy has a lot of questions. "Why didn't we kiss?" He shrugs. And not a lot of answers. "Why didn't you"—I cough—"at least offer to . . . uh . . . return the favor?"

"Everything you do, I gotta reciprocate?"

Sound logic and solid word choice. I guess he's only been acting dense on purpose.

"No. But I wanted . . . I don't know, *something*. Why didn't you ask me to stay and hang out after?"

"You left."

"Because I thought you wanted me to."

"I didn't say that."

"Tell me you didn't want me to go."

He's silent.

"The truth is, Tyler, I was, and sadly still am, somehow, very attracted to you. I thought you were fun and nice. And you're hot. And I probably would have gone down on you tonight if you hadn't been so . . . intent on it. But I don't feel like a person with you. I want to be with someone who makes me feel like a person. Even if we're only hooking up."

He rolls his eyes. "You're being really *dramatic* right now, you know that?"

The utter disgust in his voice jacks up my heart rate. Is this what those guys on the app meant when they put "not into drama" in their bios? They don't want someone who will call them out on their bullshit? Who demands to be treated like a human being?

"I know," I say. "It's because I'm a faggot. But you're not, right? You're just down for whatever. No labels." It seems like Tyler is trying to ignore his reality, like he's trying to bypass oppression. He doesn't want this aspect of himself to change all of his relationships, which I understand, but he's running away. "Whatever feels good, right?"

"Huh?" he says.

"The first time we—dude, can you put your dick away?" I just realized it's been out this whole time.

He starts tucking it back in.

"Look, I thought we could have some fun," he says, "but this isn't fun."

I don't say anything. Obviously, I agree, but I don't say anything.

I expect him to leave, but instead he turns to me and opens his mouth. Is he going to apologize? Take everything back? Ask to start over? I might say yes. If he begs.

"Are you sure you don't wanna suck my dick? You got me hard and—"

Oh for fuck's sake.

"Get out! Get out of my tree house."

"It's Molly's—"

"Get out of Molly's tree house."

He succeeds in getting his dick back into his shorts, and starts climbing down the ladder.

"One more thing!" I call out after him. "You're white! Really white! Like dough! So start acting like it! Put on sunscreen and talk like your equally white parents raised you to!"

He shakes his head in disbelief when he's on the ground and walks away.

When he's out of sight, I start shivering. It's like he took all the warmth with him. Then I crawl over to the bottle of rum in the corner, uncap it, and start chugging.

I don't know how long I'm up there until I hear someone climbing up the ladder again.

"Go away, Tyler," I call out. I'm so out of it I keep my eyes closed, my cheek pressed to the cold wooden floor.

"Tyler's here?" Fabiola asks. I open my eyes in time to see her head pop up in front of me.

"He was," I say.

"*Ooh*," she says, climbing in.

"Not ooh."

"Why not?" she asks, sitting next to me.

"He's a dick. Just a dick."

"A big one."

"Fabiola."

"Sorry. He sucks. He doesn't deserve you. Or me for that matter. He is unworthy of either of us."

"I mean you have Molly anyway. Wait, why aren't you with her? I thought you'd be knuckle deep—"

"You texted me."

"What?"

I tear my phone out of my pants and check my last message. She's right.

SPS, I wrote.

And then, *I mean SPS*

Shit

SPS

FUCK

S. O. S.

"Ugh, I'm sorry, Fabiola."

"It's okay, Quique. I'm always here for you. No matter who I'm dating."

"Yeah?"

She sticks out her pinkie. "Always."

I take her pinkie with mine and then, I don't know why, I start to cry. I think. I'm suddenly so tired—in addition to being dangerously drunk—that I don't know exactly what's happening. All I know is my whole body starts shaking and I'm breathing weird and I can't process anything. Fabiola pulls me in for a hug, which comforts me somewhat.

"I don't know why I'm like this," I say.

"It's okay," she says. "It's okay."

I reach for my face to check for tears and feel my cheeks, warm and wet—found them.

CHAPTER THIRTY-ONE

I wake up in my own bed, which might be a miracle, as I have no recollection of how I got here.

I close my eyes and try to relax myself back to sleep because my body is in shambles. My head is throbbing, my stomach's doing flips, and both my muscles and bones ache.

An actual hangover. This is gonna be fun.

Sleep must have managed to overcome me once more because I wake up again. I was hoping to feel better, but I realize very quickly that I don't. Like, at all. In addition to all the ailments I woke up with before, my mouth is so dry I think I might actually die of dehydration.

"Here," someone says, "stop moaning."

It's my mom. She's holding out a bottle of water. I take it and start chugging. God, this stuff is, like, bringing me back from the dead.

"Thank you," I manage to whisper.

"You're welcome. Just no more of whatever it is you were doing. You sounded like a ghost."

I didn't even realize I had been making noise.

My mom leaves the room, closing the door behind her. I hold my hand to my forehead. She closed it as softly as she could, but it still sounded like she slammed it shut. It's going to be a long day.

I end up falling asleep again. I won't describe what it feels like to wake up a third time. I'll skip past everything else, too, past the showering (which relaxes my aching muscles), the teeth brushing (a massage for my exposed skeleton!), and the—to put it delicately—explosive shitting (a small relief for my digestive system).

I curl up on the couch, not bothering to put on the TV.

"Food?" my mom asks.

I let out a whine in reply.

"Okay, okay," she says. "I get it."

I scrunch up my eyes and press my fists against my cheekbones, which is for some weird reason a slight relief. This is the worst one ever. I've gotten headaches or stomachaches the morning after I drank. But this, this is hell.

I sense something next to me, so I open my eyes and find a bottle of Advil and another water bottle hovering in front of me. This time it's my dad offering.

"Thanks," I say, taking them.

He doesn't reply, just ruffles my hair and leaves.

I fall asleep (again) and wake up (again). This time I feel significantly better, partially human. I'm about to head to the bathroom (again) when my phone starts buzzing.

"Hello?"

"Hey, are you alive?"

Fabiola.

"Yes, unfortunately."

I sit up.

"Good. Just wanted to check in. I don't think I've ever seen you like that. I've seen you wasted, but . . . I've never seen you like *that*."

"I'm sorry. I'm so embarrassed."

"Don't be. People get drunk and cry all the time. My dad does."

I take a deep breath. I'm too tired to hide.

"It's not only that, Fabiola. I'm . . . I'm kinda . . . a little bit . . . God, this is like coming out again. I'm . . ."

"Quique, tell me."

"I'm mentally unstable. Like, clinically."

She doesn't say anything, so I go on.

"I had a sort of mental breakdown the summer after eighth grade, and I saw a therapist. I thought everything was fine—or at least *pretended* everything was fine—until a breakdown I had three weeks ago."

"By 'breakdown' you mean . . ."

"I thought about killing myself."

"Jesus."

"Yeah, but I would never actually do it. I just think about it. But sometimes it feels like I might do it without choosing to, and that's . . . not great."

Silence.

Oh no. I'm scaring her. I'm driving her away. I have to backtrack or I'm gonna lose us.

"But it's not like—"

"How would you do it?"

"What? Like, how would I kill myself?"

"Yeah."

"I, uh, I don't know. I thought about riding my bike into traffic."

"Ooh-hoo-hoo. Gnarly."

I laugh. "I know, right?"

"Why didn't you tell me sooner?"

"I thought it would change our relationship. I thought you'd have to start walking on eggshells, and I know that's not who you are or who I'd want you to be."

"Fair. But I'm glad you *finally* told me, Quique. You're kind of an idiot for not saying something sooner."

"Probably. But also . . ."

"What?"

"The way you talked about Mariana always, kinda, made me feel like . . . you might see me in a similar way."

"Shit, Quique. I'm sorry. I don't. Like at all."

"It's okay. I knew what you meant by 'crazy'—"

"No, I'm still so sorry. I'll just call her a cunt from now on."

I snort. "How very gracious of you."

"You know me. Also, might I add you were much better at hiding this than you were at hiding your gay."

"With some people."

"Yeah . . ."

I look up and see my parents staring at me.

"Uh, I gotta go. Talk later?"

"Of course! Bye, Quique."

"Bye."

"Oh, and I love you."

I smile. "I love you, too."

I end the call, and my parents take their places on either side of me.

"He lives," my mom says.

"Barely."

"Do you want to talk about last night?" my dad asks.

My stomach clenches. I'm guessing that's not really a question.

"What do you guys already know?"

They laugh.

"Subtle," my mom says.

"I'm too near death to be sneaky."

"You came in at four in the morning, barely able to walk, using Fabiola as support."

"Okay." Sounds about right.

"And you kept saying, 'I'm such an idiot, a fucking idiot. Why am I such a fucking idiot?'" my dad adds.

"Ugh." Ugh indeed.

"You also kept apologizing to Fabiola for being a . . . a . . ." My dad scrunches up his face. "A . . ."

"'Cuntblock,'" my mom says.

"Yeah, that was it!"

Oh my God.

My parents both turn to me and stare expectantly.

Aw, fuck it. Telling them about last night can't possibly make me feel any worse than I actually do.

"Fabiola and I went to a party. And that's all I'll say about her. I found out a guy I thought liked me doesn't, and I made out with a guy who ended up being a jerk."

"Wait, you kissed a boy who didn't like you?" my mom asks, confused.

"No." Although I did kiss Ziggy last night and on the couch we're all currently sitting on. "It was another guy."

"Oh."

The two of them give each other a look, communicating, telepathically, *Did you know our son was such a ho? Because I didn't.*

"How was he a jerk?" my mom asks.

"Trust me." I don't want to explain.

"Well, I'm gonna be real with you: That's men, sweetie." My dad gives her a look, and she shrugs. "It's true."

"It is," I confirm.

"Then why do you choose—" My dad stops himself.

"I didn't choose to be attracted to guys, Dad."

Who the hell would? Guys are the worst.

"I know, mijo. I meant . . . Why are you going for them more than girls?"

I want to say he's wrong, that I've been just as open to the possibility of falling in love with a girl lately, but he's right. Like Arturo also pointed out, this summer, this past year, has been all about the dudes. It's not that I like guys better (though it's common for bi peeps to have a preference for one gender or another), and it's not that I don't still like girls. And I'm realizing now that it's not just the tiramisu explanation, either. It's just that . . . I think I've always been subconsciously aware that in the future, when I'm older, when it comes time for me to take relationships more seriously, to maybe start a family, I'll probably seek out women. Because that'll be easier. On my family and on myself. I guess I'm focused on guys at this point in my life because I know any relationship that begins now or in the next few years most likely won't be permanent.

And I hate realizing that. I hate that prejudice is a factor when it comes to my love life. I hate that it makes it seem like I see women as a second choice or a backup plan or a consolation prize when I could very well meet a girl one day who makes me redefine love. I want to be free. I don't want to consider what people will think of me when it comes to what I want. But that's not life. At least, not for me, not at this point in time. I hope eventually I find the courage to follow my heart when I need to, wherever it takes me.

And I wish I could tell my dad all that. Hell, maybe one day I will. But in this moment, I don't.

Instead, I say, "I don't know."

"Fabiola seems perfect for you," my mom chimes in. "Why don't you two—"

"It's not like that between us," I say. "At least . . . not for now. I love her and she loves me, but neither of us thinks that's a good idea."

"Is it because you see your father and I fighting sometimes? We—"

"No, Mom. It's not your fault." I look at my dad. "Either of yours."

They share a guilty look before turning back to me.

My mom speaks first. "Honey, we're sorry you heard that. We just . . ."

"We're worried," my dad says. "We've always been taught that two men together is wrong. And we see you, and you're— you're *so good*, Quique. And we just want what's best for you."

I sigh. "I know. I get that. But . . ." Hmm, how can I put this? "So. One time in chemistry, we used this thing called a pH indicator. It's a liquid that you pour into an unknown solution, and if the solution's acidic, it turns one color. But if it's basic, it turns another. And I've always kind of felt like that indicator. I react differently to different people. And I never know who's gonna cause that reaction. But whoever it is, I can't help it."

My parents don't say anything. Probably because that metaphor could use some work. What can I say, it's new.

"I think I'm confusing you even more," I say.

"No, that made sense," my mom says. "Kinda."

"In any case, after last night, I'm probably never getting close to a guy again. It only ends in disaster. And so does drinking. I'm also never gonna drink again."

There's a pause, and then we all laugh. I'm not good at making promises. In fact, I'm going to break one right here and now.

"Can one of you drop me off at Saleem's?"

My parents exchange a look.

"Sure," my dad says. "It's on the way to Home Depot anyway."

"Cool, thanks. Why do you need to go to Home Depot?"

He clears his throat. "Not to be a drama queen"—I absolutely hate that expression now—"but you destroyed our toilet, son."

Of course I did.

. . .

I sleep on the way to Saleem's and wake up (sadly) when my dad shakes me awake.

"We're here, mijo."

I groan before saying, "Thanks," and hobbling out of the car. As he drives off, I stand at the bottom of the stairs and take out my phone to call Saleem.

"Hello?"

"Hey, it's me. I'm at your place. Let's go swim."

"Uh, okay. Give me five minutes."

"Okay."

I take a seat on the first step. My alcohol-mangled brain didn't think to let him know I was coming. Five minutes is a long time.

I'm awakened by the sound of Saleem's door slamming shut.

"Quique, are you okay?" he asks as he comes down the stairs. He sounds genuinely concerned.

"Yeah," I say, wiping my mouth. "I was just taking a li'l nap." Fourth one today if you're counting.

"Okay . . ."

He steps down next to me.

"I might need your help getting up," I say, reaching out to him.

He takes my hands and pulls. He has a surprisingly strong grip.

"Goodness," he says, "you *reek*."

"Do I? Like what?"

"Alcohol."

"Yeah, that makes sense."

"And roadkill."

I smile, which hurts.

"Fun night?" he asks.

"No."

"I'm sorry."

"It's okay."

He looks good today. Really good. His curls are shining, his skin looks moisturized, his eyes are bright and alive in the sunlight. Maybe I'm just comparing him to me, or my corpse rather.

The next thing I know I'm hugging him.

"It's been a while," I say into his shoulder.

"Yeah," he agrees. "It has. For us."

We stay there, pressed against each other, and it feels so good. Last time it was his hand that made the world stop. His whole body makes the solar system stop. I feel like I'm being healed.

Why hasn't he pulled away? I've been waiting for the slightest restlessness on his end, but it hasn't come. In the end, it's me who breaks out of our embrace.

"Sorry," I say, "I think I fell asleep."

He laughs nervously. "You really needed that, huh."

Was it only me, Saleem? For some reason I can see through him today. At least I think I can.

We start walking to the pool.

"This . . . is an arduous journey," I say pathetically when we're halfway there.

"You'll survive, Quique."

"Will I?"

"Yes."

"In case I don't, I have a list in my pocket of the most important people in my life, and it's going to be your job to tell each of them, 'I love you,' for me one last time."

"Yeah?"

"Yup."

"Who's on the list?"

I know what you're asking right now, Saleem. It's all so clear. This morning you must have, in the words of Mariah Carey, bathed in Windex.

"Yes, you will have to say it into a mirror, Saleem."

He opens his mouth, but nothing comes out. A pleased look appears on his face before he transparently wipes it off.

"Whatever you want," he says.

We've reached the pool. It's midday, so we have company.

"Hey, boys!" the guy from Apartment Forty-Three calls out. "Great day for a swim, innit?"

"Hello," we say, "it is."

When Saleem takes off his shirt, it's like I'm seeing his torso for the first time. My eyes trace every line and every curve, and I realize it's changed. It's more dimpled with muscle and hairier. When did that happen?

"You coming in?" he asks, standing at the water's edge.

"I already am," I say. "I'm in over my head."

He arches an eyebrow. "You say strange things when you're hungover."

He's not wrong.

• • •

We're in the pool for an hour before I realize I didn't put any sunscreen on.

"Do you want me to go back to the house and get some?" Saleem asks.

"No," I say. "Let's go back to your place."

"Oh, okay."

"Wish I'd brought mine with me, boys!" Apartment Forty-Three says. "Sorry! I was just trying to get out of the house as fast as possible. You know that Christine can really—"

"It's okay!" I say, climbing out of the pool. "Not your fault!" I turn to Saleem and growl, "Let's get the fuck out of here."

If I thought the walk to the pool was bad, the climb up Saleem's steps is a superhuman task. I have to take a break halfway and lean on Saleem for the rest of the way. That might not have been totally necessary, though.

When we enter the apartment, I look around for his family.

"Baby cousin's birthday party," he says.

"Why didn't you go?"

"Well, if you're my parents, the reason is all of the summer assignments I have to catch up on. The real reason is that it's Minions-themed, and I'd rather talk to the guy from Apartment Forty-Three about his marital problems all day than have to deal with those yellow bastards."

I laugh. Did he just say bastards?

"Do you need anything?" he asks.

"Water," I say, "and Advil if you have any."

"Okay."

As Saleem opens the fridge, I look down the hallway. His bedroom door's open, and I can see his bed, which is calling to me. After a quick glance at him, I make my move.

Entering his room, I notice that not much has changed since the beginning of the school year when I pretended to leave my copy of *1984* in my locker so I could borrow his. On the left there's the bookshelf with all of his immaculate books, arranged in alphabetical order by author last name, filled with colorful sticky notes. On the right wall is the standard wooden desk in the corner with the world's last surviving personal desktop computer on it. In the corner next to the desk is a rolled-up prayer rug. The last time I was here it was laid out on the floor, and I could see that it was royal blue and sand-colored and beautiful. I walk over to the bed and trail my finger over the plush comforter, which is the same blue as the rug. It's such a sexy bed, and not just because Saleem sleeps here. And probably does other things here.

I can't resist.

"Aw, dude come on!" Saleem says, entering the room a minute later. "You're getting my bed all wet."

"Sorry," I say, hugging his pillow to my face. "I had to."

He's not actually mad. He's never mad at me.

He sighs. "Well, here's your water and your ibuprofen."

I take both.

"Where am I supposed to sit?" he asks. "You're taking up the whole bed."

After I'm done popping my pills, I scoot over and make room for him.

"Hold me," I say, closing my eyes.

"What?"

"Hold me. I felt so much better when you did it earlier."

He doesn't respond. I'm tempted to open my eyes but don't. *What is he thinking?* Then, I feel him get on the bed.

"Come here," he says.

I do.

He wraps his arms around me, and I bury my face in his chest, my nostrils flooding with the smell of his body and chlorine. I wish we hadn't put our shirts back on after the pool.

"Yes, this is good," I say. "This is nice."

He again doesn't say anything.

We lie like that for a while. For how long I'll never know. Feels like forever and a few moments at the same time. God, his heart is beating fast. I thought it was only mine that was always hammering away.

In this moment, with his heartbeat echoing throughout my body, with his smell more precious than oxygen, this broken boy has never felt more whole.

CHAPTER THIRTY-TWO

"And you still don't think he likes you?"

I look at Molly in the passenger seat. Two days ago, after I broke down with Fabiola in the tree house and she called the next morning, I realized that I wasn't losing my best friend, I was gaining a friend. And Molly's a welcome addition because she makes one of my favorite people very happy, as evidenced by the fact that Fabiola currently has her left hand on the steering wheel and her right hand aggressively planted on Molly's left thigh. For this reason, I have no problem spilling my guts in the car on the way to Saleem's.

"I don't know," I say. "Yesterday I was sure he did, but after we napped together nothing changed. There have always been moments . . . but they've never led to anything. They've just left me feeling stupidly optimistic."

Molly nods slowly and says wistfully, "The curse of the queers."

Fabiola takes her eyes off the road to give Molly a reassuring smile and a squeeze on the thigh. Molly's resulting smile could cure cancer. It's an intimate, tender moment, but Fabiola's heartfelt gesture feels like a vice around my heart. She got her happy ending. *Why didn't I?*

More importantly, why can't I be happy for them without having to feel sorry for myself?

"To be clear," Molly says, interrupting the gray thunderstorm in my head, "that was qurse with a 'q.'"

Fabiola and I laugh.

"Of qourse it was," Fabiola says.

Molly rolls her eyes but smiles. Then they share another heart-eyes-emoji look.

This time, I'm not so envious, and I'm embarrassingly proud of being able to feel positive emotions about the fact that my best friend and her girlfriend are deliriously happy. I take a deep breath and repeat to myself a thought I had recently: *Love is not a zero-sum game.*

From the moment Saleem enters the car, I try to suss out whether anything's changed between us, but I find zero evidence of that fact. His smiling normalcy could be a front, but the alternative, that he's actually unbothered and I'm a crazy person, feels all too probable. During the hour-long ride to the beach, we don't say much. He mentions a new show he's watching. He asks if Dua Lipa's singing, "I got a girl I'm trynna f***" instead of "I gotta tell them to myself." He complains that his sister's driving him crazy by leaving her clothes lying around everywhere. But he doesn't even come close to proclaiming his undying love for me that began the first time he ever saw my face. The audacity, am I right?

"I can't believe I was about to go the whole summer without a trip to the beach," Fabiola says while we walk down the main street of the quaint little beach town we frequented last summer.

"I know," Molly says. "I almost had to take your Californian Card away."

"You can take all of my cards, babe." Fabiola winks.

"Except her V-Card," I say without thinking. "That one's but a distant memory."

Fabiola hits me with the folding chair she's carrying, and I almost drop the ice chest.

"Ow! Sorry, it just came out."

"I don't mind," Molly says. "It's not like I was locked away in a tower my whole life."

"*Ooh,*" Fabiola says, sidling up to her. "Is that so?"

The two of them take the lead and begin whispering conspiratorially as we reach the sand, leaving Saleem and me to ourselves. For the first time today, I feel a tension between us in the silence. Although, it's entirely possible it's solely on my end.

As we weave through countless groups and their beach setups, I'm grateful for all of the noises that serve as a buffer between us: the squawking of seagulls, the delighted squeals of children, and the dueling speakers of almost every family here.

At one point, Saleem clears his throat but says nothing, so I decide to give voice to a question that pops into my head.

"How do you feel about them?"

"Who?" he says.

I point my chin at Fabiola and Molly. "Them."

"Oh. Like as a couple?"

After I left Saleem's place yesterday, Fabiola called and said she and Molly wanted to go the beach and that they wanted me and Saleem to come along.

"Are you gonna tell him that you two are dating?" I asked.

"Yeah," Fabiola said. "I know I didn't tell him about Mariana. But I probably should have. I trust him."

"Yeah, me too," I said. And I did.

When we hung up, she called and told him, and he didn't really react to the news that she had a girlfriend. He just said he'd bring extra sunscreen.

But right now I need to know exactly how he feels about them.

"Yes," I say. "What do you think of them as a couple?"

"They seem really happy," he says, skirting around two kids building a sandcastle.

I nod. "Yeah, but you don't think it's, like . . . wrong?"

Saleem flinches. "No," he says quickly. "Do you?"

"No, of course not."

"Then why would I?"

We look at each other, and I see hurt on his face.

"I didn't think you would. I was just asking."

I should have known he'd react this way, but no matter how much I trust anyone, it's always too easy to believe they could turn on me in a second. While Saleem and I have always been very comfortable expressing our platonic love for each other, some part of me needed to know for certain that he was okay with them, okay with Fabiola and Molly, okay with me.

"I don't think it's wrong," he reiterates. "I don't think they're wrong."

"Good. Because . . ." Oh my Lord, am I actually gonna—"I like guys, Saleem."

He stops short, and my heart begins beating dangerously fast. What is wrong with me today? My thoughts are out of control, and my tongue seems to be working independently of my brain. At this rate I'm gonna blurt out what I saw when I was seven and ran into my parents' room because it sounded like my dad was murdering my mom. (He wasn't.)

"You what?"

"I, um, I've never told you, but, yeah, I like guys."

We stand there for a long moment.

Finally, he clears his throat and says, "Thank you for telling me."

"Uh . . . you're welcome?"

He laughs, probably only to break the tension.

"Hey, come on!" Fabiola yells. She and Molly are standing several yards away where a group of teenagers are blasting reggaeton. They're just past a lifeguard stand, high up from the water. Not ideal, but it's essentially the only space available on a crowded day like this. "We found a spot!"

"Coming!" Saleem calls out.

He starts toward them, but I hang back. He seemed to take it all in stride. He was shocked, sure, but he recovered. He sounded . . . accepting. Right?

It doesn't take long for the doubt to settle in. *What if I've changed our friendship irreversibly? What if it's never the way it was before?*

I watch Saleem's figure get smaller and smaller, wondering if he's walking away from me in more ways than one.

We lay out our blankets, placing water bottles and sandals on the corners to keep them from flying away. Then Fabiola sets up the one beach chair, which Molly immediately claims, mumbling, "It's not the only thing of yours I want to sit on." Saleem goes about meticulously coating his torso in sunscreen, and I train my eyes on the waves.

"Can you put some on my back?" he asks, holding out a bottle of sunscreen.

"Sure," I say, taking it.

This is probably a really good sign that he's fine with my revelation. In order to keep things that way, I apply the sunblock as nonchalantly as possible. The smell of it (coconut) and the warmth of his skin make that a Herculean task. I'm trying my absolute hardest not to tear a hole in the netting of my swim trunks.

"Thanks," he says when I'm done.

"No problem."

"I got hot watching that," Fabiola says, lying on her stomach. "I gotta go take a dip."

She pushes herself up.

"You coming?" she asks Molly.

"Nah," Molly says. "Someone's gotta watch our stuff. Plus, I don't wanna get seaweed in my pussy."

"My delicate princess."

Molly frames her face with the back of her hands.

Fabiola smiles and turns to me and Saleem. "Boys?"

"I'm down," I say.

Saleem nods.

The water is freezing compared to the heat of the sun. I

stand at the border of the ocean and the sand, my feet chilled to the bone as the last remnants of the waves sweep over them, watching my friends as they enter the water in two characteristically different ways. Fabiola runs full speed, splashing loudly as she goes, and dives under a wave. Saleem makes steady progress, stepping slowly but surely toward the spot where Fabiola disappeared.

"Come on, Quique!" Fabiola says upon surfacing.

Saleem turns around, noticing for the first time that I've stayed behind, and I hurriedly move toward him.

"Isn't it better to get it over with all at once?" I ask him.

He seems to weigh this in his head.

"Sometimes."

"Then let's go."

"I will. When I'm ready."

"PUSSIES!"

Saleem and I both turn to Fabiola, who's now yards away, treading water.

"Can't keep her waiting," Saleem says, and before I can process what he's doing, his arms are around my neck and he's taking me down, down, down.

There's the spirit-invigorating chill of the water, the harsh scrape of salt in my nose, and somehow, more immediate, the feel of Saleem's body on mine.

"What the fuck?" I say when my head is above water again, and I've spit out all the salt in my mouth.

Saleem smiles at me with a mischievous look on his face that makes it hard to breathe.

• • •

Around dinnertime, we pack up and head back to Fabiola's truck to drop off all the beach stuff. Despite eating the sandwiches Fabiola's mom made for us about an hour ago, we're all hungry, so we decide to walk to a nearby Mexican restaurant.

I can't stop thinking about Saleem the whole way there. How his brown skin literally sparkled when we were in the water. How the hair on his face and his body grew darker, more clearly defined. How his swim trunks sagged, revealing a strip of paler skin I had never seen before.

The hostess leads us to the back of the restaurant out the door onto a clay-tile patio. She points to a metal table and we all take a seat. Saleem sits across from me, and I'm suddenly embarrassed by how desperately I want him to touch me in any way. But I don't let that feeling stop me from inching my legs forward, hoping he'll accidentally swipe me with his feet.

All throughout dinner, I'm silent because my lungs won't seem to work, like I'm still underwater. I only want to say one thing to one person, but I can't and it's killing me. What a horrible weight it is to be silent when you want to shout, to hold back when you want to reach out, to freeze when you want to melt.

"Quiqueeee, helloooo."

I snap out of it. "What?"

"Are you ready to go?" Fabiola asks.

I nod. I hadn't realized we'd already paid.

The four of us get up from the table and make our way to the front door. There's a group of tall, college-age, mostly white guys sitting at a table having dinner. As Saleem squeezes past their table, he misjudges the space between him and one of the guys, accidentally hitting the guy with his backpack. I'm so preoccupied with my own thoughts that I only see it out of the corner of my eye.

College Guy immediately stands, rising to his full height of six foot two or so.

"Watch it, you fucking Arabian."

The words barely seem to register. It's mostly the hateful look on his scrunched-up rodent face that propels me forward.

"Enrique, don't!" Fabiola yells behind me.

"What the fuck did you just say?"

I'm in his face now. Well, as close as our considerable height difference allows.

He doesn't break eye contact with me when he says, "I said he needs to watch it."

"And you need to watch your fucking mouth."

It's like it's not really me who's saying it. The real me is chillin' over by the fish tank, watching someone who is very much not me jab his finger into some douchebag's collarbone.

"Don't touch me," Douchebag says, shoving me backward.

I manage not to lose my balance, which I'm grateful for.

"Quique, he's not worth it," I hear Saleem say beside me. "Let's go."

I don't take my eyes off Douchebag. He smirks.

"Better listen to your boyfriend, fag—"

He doesn't finish the slur before my fist flies into his jaw.

I wish I could say he hits the floor, but he only staggers back a few steps, puts his hand on the spot where I decked him, and stares at me incredulously.

"Holy shit," Fabiola says.

Douchebag's look of disbelief then turns into anger, and he charges forward.

Two things happen at the same time. One, Saleem steps in front of me. And two, one of the guys at Douchebag's table leaps up and wraps his arms around Douchebag's torso, pinning his arms to his sides.

"Chill, Josh," he says. "Chill."

At this point, I see a waitress take out her phone and dial three little numbers.

"We need to get out of here *now*!" Fabiola says.

She doesn't need to say it twice.

We streak out of the restaurant and tear down the street to where Fabiola's truck is parked. Fabiola takes off before all the doors are closed and all our seat belts are buckled.

"Slow down!" Molly says. "We don't want to get pulled over."

Fabiola takes a deep breath and eases off the accelerator, but I can still see the tension in her neck and shoulders. She takes her first visible breath when we're on the freeway.

We ride in silence for a while, the sun setting over the ocean in a sickening display of ironic beauty.

"It was stupid," Molly says, the first one to speak. "*Brave*, but stupid."

"Thank you," I say.

"Can you even *imagine*," Fabiola says, looking back at me for far longer than I'm comfortable with, "if we had stuck around for the cops to show up? Whose side do you think they would've taken?"

"I know but—"

"But like Molly said, it was brave. I'm proud of you."

"Th—"

"You fucking idiot."

I smile.

Fabiola checks her blind spot before merging onto a new freeway. I, likewise, check out Saleem in the corner of my eye.

His body is stiff, his face turned toward the window. He's lightly running the fingers of his left hand over the back of his right. *What is he thinking?*

"Does your hand hurt?"

"Huh?" I say.

"I said does your hand hurt," Fabiola repeats.

"Uh . . ." Saleem glances over at me briefly. "It's fine." He turns back. "Everything's fine."

Fabiola stops at Saleem's place first. Before he can get out of the car, I ask, "Can I come up?"

He looks surprised. "Sure."

"Okay then. See ya, Fabiola. See ya, Molly."

"See ya . . . ," they say, their mouths hanging open.

They can feel it, and I can too—it's now or never.

CHAPTER THIRTY-THREE

The first thing he does, without my asking, is head to the kitchen so he can put some ice in a sandwich bag for my hand.

"Where's the fam?" I ask.

"San Diego," he says, closing the freezer door.

"Homework excuse again?"

"SAT prep." He walks over to me. "Let me see." I hold out my hand, and he frowns when he looks at it. "I thought you said it was fine."

"It is."

"It looks like it hurts."

I examine my swollen, purple knuckles. "Maybe a little."

Saleem gently takes my hand and puts the bag of ice on it. After a few seconds, he looks up and asks, "Better?"

Our eyes lock.

"So much."

He looks down at my hand again. "Why do you always come to me in shambles?"

I laugh. "What do you mean?"

"You called me when you were high and alone, you came here when you were near death and hungover, and now . . ."

"And now I expect you to fix my hand."

He smiles. "Yes."

"Why did you stay home?" I ask. "Unlike a child's birthday party, San Diego could have been fun."

Saleem shrugs. "We had plans."

"Really? You stayed because of a beach trip?"

"Not only that. Other stuff."

"Like what?"

"You punching someone, apparently." I laugh, and he lifts the ice bag. "Swelling's going down, I think."

"Yeah," I say.

"I guess this is kind of my fault."

"How?"

"If that guy hadn't, uh, if he hadn't—"

"Exactly."

"What?"

"If *he* hadn't. It was his fault, Saleem."

"True, but—"

"Don't blame yourself."

"But if it weren't for me, you'd be fine."

I look him dead in the eye. "That's not true. I'd never be fine without you."

As numb as my hand is, I can still feel Saleem's beneath mine. He looks down as I wrap my fingers around it and squeeze.

"You know why, right?"

He clears his throat but doesn't say anything.

"Saleem?"

"Mm?" he says. I think it's a yes. But he can't say it. I bet he can't say anything right now.

"Say something."

He clears his throat. "Like what?" That sounded normal. Too normal.

"Something," I say.

"Something," he tries to say casually.

But I heard it. A quaver.

I'm looking at him, but he's still avoiding my eyes.

"I love you," I say.

I hear his breath catch in his throat. He must be able to sense it, its new meaning, but my dumb ass clarifies anyway.

"Like, in a gay way."

He swallows. I continue.

"Every time I'm with you, I feel this . . . tether between us. Like there's a part of me buried in you, and no matter what, I can't get close enough to you. Do you feel that too?"

He gently puts the bag back on my hand and withdraws his. "You should go, Enrique."

Four words. Four words that aren't *I feel it too*. And they hurt like nothing I've ever felt before.

Without a word, I grab the ice bag and head to the door. As I reach for the handle, Saleem says, "Wait, I'm sorry."

I turn around. *Did he change his mind?*

"I'll drive you," he says. "You don't have your car."

Oh.

"It's okay," I say, opening the door. "I'll walk."

I'm out of the apartment before he can try to convince me otherwise.

· · ·

I throw the ice bag on the ground somewhere in the maze of Saleem's apartment complex. My hand isn't the part of me that's been damaged the most today.

For a while, the walk home is soothing, even if it takes place on the side of a desolate road without a sidewalk. There's something about making a physical effort to put some distance between me and Saleem that makes me feel like I'm accomplishing something. It's the illusion of moving on.

But soon enough, the walk is only adding to my problems. I'm dehydrated, exhausted, and, as evidenced by the sting that comes with my profuse sweating, possibly sunburnt. All I want is my bed.

As it often does, my mind begins to replay the most painful moments of the night: Saleem's words and the look on his face when I told him I love him. My hand starts to throb, and I swallow the urge to cry.

I'm alone.

And I'm probably going to die here. I could get robbed and stabbed. Eaten by an animal. Hit by one of the cars that fly by every few minutes.

Maybe I should throw myself in front of one to end all the anticipation. . . .

Oh no.

They're back. The thoughts are back.

But I'm not *really* gonna do it, right?

Why not? a voice says in the back of my mind.

Because I have people who love me.

Do you?

The voice is louder now.

I check my phone. No one's messaged me since I left Saleem's. No one cares.

It'll make things easier.

I see headlights from down the road, where it begins to rise and twist up into the hills, and I stop in my tracks.

I need to push the voice out of my head, to use something from one of my weekly sessions with Luciana to drive it out. But her voice is so soft right now. The other voice is so much louder.

Not just easier for you, easier for everyone else.

As the lights get closer, I think about how real this is, how I'm unable to predict what's going to happen when the car passes by. I don't feel like I'm in control here. Someone else is. Or *something* else is. The mental image of me diving in front of what I now see is a red sedan plays on repeat, looking almost comically like a sped-up GIF.

I take a deep breath as the car approaches and give myself one last chance to convince myself not to do it. I go the usual route, listing all the things I have to live for. Family, friends, music, TV, food, sex, roller coasters, cats, dogs, swimming . . .

And then everything goes black.

Because I closed my eyes the second the headlights were on me.

For a split second I don't know what path I chose.

And then the sound of the car racing past me fills my ears. I'm alive.

I open my eyes and stare at the empty road in front of me. I'm alive. I *chose* to be alive.

And I wish I could say it was all the things I listed that saved me, the "there's so much to live for" line of thinking. But it wasn't. The thing that saved me was the knowledge that I wouldn't always feel this way. That things change. For better or for worse. But I still want to find out what happens next. I have a morbid curiosity to see how this all turns out. That's why I'm here.

I laugh to myself (solidifying my status as a crazy person) and take out my phone.

I need a ride home.

It feels like an eternity waiting for her to arrive—both because she had been sleeping before I called and because every second that passes by is a second a cop could pull up and ask me why I'm loitering on a random street corner—but she shows up. She always does.

My mom doesn't say anything as I get in the car. I don't think she's mad; I think she's giving me time to process. And for that I'm grateful. So many small mercies today.

When we're almost home, I take a deep breath, ready to tell her about today's events, but no words come out. Instead, a lump forms in my throat, and my eyes begin to water.

"Quique, are you okay?"

I shake my head and start to cry.

"Oh, Quique."

She pulls over to the side of the road and turns off the car. "Is this about Saleem?"

I nod even though that's not the whole story. At this point, it's all I can do.

"I'm sorry, honey." She puts her hand on my back and starts rubbing. "Did you guys break up already?"

"What?" Pure shock actually managed to dislodge a word from my throat.

"Ever since you came back from his place yesterday you've been so happy. Well, maybe not *happy*, but . . . hopeful."

Ouch. She's right. After he held me, the possibility that we could be together has kept me . . . afloat. And now that I know what his response to my confession is, there's no hope. Only cold, unforgiving certainty. I should have waited forever in that comfortable limbo.

"Mom, we're not together. We were never together. We'll never be together." I give myself some time to take that in, and of all the rational, possible reactions I could have to that, my crazy ass smiles. And then I start to laugh.

"Uh, honey, are you okay?"

The look of panicked concern on her face sets me off even more. I'm laughing from the pit of my stomach, my cheeks wet with tears.

"I'm crying over someone I've never been with!" I scream between bouts of laughter. I'm mourning a made-up relationship, memories that I distorted in my head. I'm a pathetic mess.

When the laughter subsides, the pain rushes in again. What about the hug after dinner when he had to lie for me? What about that moment at the top of the drop tower? What about his mild heart attack when we were on his bed? Did that really mean nothing to him? It must have. Or it meant something different.

"I wish I could say something comforting and wise," my mom begins, "but I can't think of anything. This is gonna hurt, kid. It's gonna continue to hurt. For a while."

I'm about to make a sarcastic response about the dour nature of her words, but she continues.

"But one day it won't. And it won't be because someone else has taken his place, and it won't be because you've forgotten him. It'll be because heartbreak, like any other injury, will heal when you give it time."

I nod slowly to myself.

My mom puts her hand on the parking brake. "You ready to go home?"

"There's just one other thing."

She takes her hand off the brake. "What is it?"

"I, uh, maybe had the thoughts again."

She leans back in her seat and looks out the window.

"I'm sorry," I say. I don't want to hurt her, but I feel like I had to tell her. "I'm really, really sorry."

"You don't need to apologize to me, Quique." Her voice is wobbly, and I can't stand it. I can't remember the last time I heard her cry, and it's all my fault. "I should be saying sorry to you."

She looks at me with tears in her eyes.

"What? No. What could you possibly be sorry for, Mom?"

She looks down at her hands and begins picking at her cuticles, something she's always stopped me from doing. Even now when I start to do it, I stop, the promise of a slap on the hand in my mind, Pavlovian style.

"When you were little," she says, "you never kept things from me. You would walk over when I was balancing the checkbook or cooking and you'd say, 'Mommy, I'm sad.' And I'd ask why, and you'd just shrug."

Her eyes drift to the windshield.

"I never did anything," she says. "I didn't get you a therapist or ask you to explain. Like a good mom would've . . ."

"It's okay. You did your be—"

"No. Don't do that. Don't make this about me. I should have been better."

She looks down at her fingers, realizes what she's been doing, and throws her hands to the side like she's been caught with a bag of stolen money. I almost laugh.

She takes a deep breath. "I was just so tired. Cooking, cleaning, working, raising you. And your father." She rolls her eyes. "But I cared." She turns to me. "I did. I really cared. Do care, still, obviously. But I was just so *tired*." Her last word comes out like a plea.

"Mom, I don't think there's anything you need forgiveness for. But if you want it, I'll give it to you—I get it. I really do. And I forgive you. And I love you."

"Thank you." Those two words come out as a squeak. "You know I'd never be able to live without you, right? I just . . . couldn't."

She smiles at me, but it's a broken one, her face twisted with pain. Her meaning is clear. Count that as another reason not to hop in front of the next moving vehicle I see.

"I know, Mom."

I lean in to hug her, and she practically mauls me as a result. During our embrace, I don't think about when she'll pull away or when I'll pull away or if her snot is currently running down my back, even though it probably is. We just hold each other until we've spoken every unspoken word we can find.

"Let's go home," I say.

She wipes her face with her hand, takes a deep breath, and says, "Finally."

Later that night, when I'm about to fall asleep, my mom comes into my room with my dad.

"We wanted to say good night," she says.

"Good night," I say.

"Good night," they say.

My dad walks over and plants his hand on my face, a fittingly annoying gesture that he does to make me laugh, which I do as I slap his hand away.

"You're gonna be okay, mijo," he says.

"Thanks, Dad."

He leaves the room so that it's only me and my mom. She walks over, sits on my bed, and runs her fingers through my hair.

"Try to get some sleep tonight."

"I will. Try, I mean."

She pats my head and gets up. As she's about to leave, she turns and says, "You can tell me tomorrow how you fucked up your hand."

And with that she leaves.

I don't *feel* particularly lucky at the moment, but I know I am.

CHAPTER THIRTY-FOUR

This is it, the worst one, the worst Saleem hangover.

I stay in bed. I sleep as much as I can. I take out my laptop to watch my favorite movies. I do a little bit of my summer reading. But I don't leave my bed.

My phone blows up with messages, something I'd normally be anxiously happy about, but I don't answer. I can't tell Fabiola and Molly what happened last night because I'll have to relive it. I can't tell Manny why the winky face in his text causes a rise in my boxers but a cramp in my stomach. I can't tell Saleem why I can't bear the thought of going back to his place so we can "talk about it."

"You need to talk about it," my mom says.

"What the fu—" My mom and dad have suddenly materialized in my room. "What are you guys doing home? Don't you have work?"

"You need to talk about what happened," my dad echoes.

"No offense, but you guys aren't—"

"With Luciana," my mom clarifies.

"But—"

"We already made an appointment."

I sigh exaggeratedly.

"Stop being a child," my dad says, "and go talk about your feelings."

". . . and then they forced me to come here," I finish.

"Flattering," Luciana says.

"I know it's healthy to talk about this kind of stuff, but I don't think I'm ready. I'm still processing, ya know?"

She puts her pencil down. "Enrique."

"Yes?"

"I didn't even get a chance to say hi before you launched into a recap of what happened yesterday."

"Well, I knew you'd ask and—"

"You want to talk about it. You want to talk about it a lot, in excruciating detail. You want to rehash and question and overanalyze everything, don't you?"

"Uh . . ."

"But you're embarrassed. You've been rejected and hurt by someone you care for deeply, and you can't stand the idea of reliving everything that happened yesterday with the people who know you best."

"The thing is—"

"But that's why people like me exist. I'm here to listen to whatever you have to say, even if you keep repeating yourself and losing your train of thought. Because I get paid either way."

I laugh.

"So let me help you. You talk and I listen. I might point things out to you and lead you to certain realizations. But I'm going to listen."

She looks at me expectantly and picks up her pencil.

"You're certainly very direct today," I point out.

"I could only squeeze you in for half an hour on such late notice. Now talk."

"Did it help?" my dad asks as we leave Luciana's office.

"Yeah."

"Good."

"But now I need a favor."

"Oh God, what now?"

I realized something after my third retelling of yesterday's events to Luciana: Saleem loves me. Maybe not in the way I'd hoped, but he loves me nonetheless. And I owe it to him to hear him out.

"A ride."

He has to get permission from my mom first, but my dad drops me off fifteen minutes later.

I hike up the stairs to Saleem's with a growing knot in my stomach. Before I knock, he opens the door.

"Hey," he says, "come in."

I do.

He closes the door behind me and leads me into the living room, which is good because his bedroom would remind me of the closest I've ever felt to him, and the kitchen would remind me of last night. He sits on the end of the smaller couch, and I sit on the end of the longer one perpendicular to it. We're technically sitting next to each other, but there are two armrests between us. Fitting.

"So," he begins, "I want to start by saying sorry. I didn't mean to react that way last night, and I'm ashamed of myself."

He looks me in the eyes. "I'm sorry, Enrique."

Enrique?

I swallow. "It's okay, Saleem."

"It's not, but thank you for saying that. The second thing I want to say is I love you, and I always will."

I smile, and he does too.

"Even if I'm in love with you?" I ask.

He nods. "Even if you're in love with me."

"Good. Because I don't think that's changing anytime soon."

"Noted. We'll figure it out."

He stands up and spreads his arms, inviting me in for a hug. As we embrace, I start to process what just happened.

I used to keep Saleem at arm's length because I was so scared of how badly he could hurt me if I let him in, if I opened up to him. But here I am, intact, having laid my soul bare to him. I have another person in my life who will love me no matter what. Again, I should feel lucky.

But . . .

Saleem is my best friend, who I'm in love with, who doesn't love me back. And that really fucking sucks. I feel like I'm no longer carrying the weight of the world on my shoulders, but I'm at least carrying all of the oceans.

This hug helps, though. His arms are wrapped around my lower back, and mine are around his neck. I rest my head on the crook of my elbow and my face brushes against his facial hair.

And suddenly there's something present in this particular hug that wasn't present in all of our other ones. (Well, it was present, but it wasn't this . . . pronounced.) It's possible it means nothing, but it's also possible that Saleem wants me the way I want him but is too scared to admit it.

"Um, Saleem?"

"Yeah?" he says.

"Do you have a boner?"

He immediately pushes me away and looks down.

"Oh, *shit.*"

I put a hand over my mouth to keep from laughing.

He looks at me, horrified, but I don't know why. It's a very impressive tent. "This happens sometimes. You know how it is."

"Saleem."

"Any body contact really. I can't control it."

"Saleem."

"Pure biology. Nerve endings and—"

"Saleem."

"What?" he says forcefully.

"Come here."

"No," he says weakly.

He's putting up walls right now, erecting turrets of excuses, digging a moat where he'll drown his feelings, an elaborate fortress of denial. And I'm about to knock it all down. I inch closer to him.

"Quique."

I continue, even slower.

"Quique."

Our faces are centimeters apart.

"Quique, please."

I stop and put my hands on his face. "Please what?" I ask.

He swallows. "If you don't want me to kiss you, then say, 'Quique, don't kiss me.' But if you do . . . say that instead."

"Quique."

"Tell me."

"I can't."

"You can. Tell me what you want."

"Quique . . . please . . . please kiss me."

I don't need him to say it twice.

I kiss him and it's fireworks and sunsets and rainbows and Disneyland and unicorns and . . . yeah, I'm lying. My first kiss with Saleem is . . . unpleasant. The boy has nice, full lips, but it feels like he's just putting two of his fingers together and pushing them hard against my mouth. I pull away.

"What is it?" he says.

"You need to relax."

"How?"

"Good question."

If he initially planned on going back to being friends after my declaration of love, then he must've thoroughly convinced himself he wasn't going to kiss me, and it's going to be hard to get him to do so properly. But maybe our bodies know a way that our brains don't.

I lead him to his bedroom, our hands intertwined, and sit down on his bed. Then I pull him onto my lap. My hands move of their own accord through his hair. They're gentle at first, but before I know what's happening, they grab and pull.

Saleem starts, loses his balance, and falls onto me. I let him take me down. We both take deep, heavy breaths as he lies on top of me, our eyes locked.

"Is that what you're like?" he asks.

"Sometimes."

He smiles. "I like it."

His response catches me by surprise, as does his kiss. It's . . . better. Much better. His lips are softer and nimbler this time. He holds my arms above my head with one hand and my face with the other. He stops to look in my eyes, smiles, and then kisses me again. But before I can give in to the moment completely, I have to say something, so I gently pull away.

"Saleem, promise you won't run."

"What do you mean?"

"Promise you won't take all this back, that you won't rethink this and leave. Promise not to take 'us' away from each other."

He considers what I said. "Okay. I promise. You promise too."

I smile. "I feel like that's highly unnecessary, but here: I promise."

CHAPTER THIRTY-FIVE

It should come as no surprise that Saleem and I spend the next few hours making up for lost time. We talk, we touch, but mostly? We kiss.

A lot.

I am, of course, the more experienced one here, so I throw out a couple of moves I've learned. He's not a big fan of tongue sucking, but when I bite his lower lip, I swear I can feel his entire body split right down the middle.

He surprises me a few times with some of his own techniques, though. He was the first one to start using his tongue. I didn't want to pressure him or freak him out like I did Ziggy. But he didn't just stick it in. He used it to explore my mouth, running it over every tooth, it seemed, before our tongues touched.

I rise up at one point, his body clinging to mine, and maneuver myself on top of him. More flashbacks of what happened with Ziggy invade my mind, and I have to bat them away. I start pushing my lower half against him, slowly this time, and he wraps his legs around me. I don't feel repulsion coming from him, which is a relief. Instead he relaxes into me, moving with me like a seagull in the ocean, bobbing up and down in the waves.

"Quique."

"Yeah?"

"Stop."

Ziggy. Ziggy. *Ziggy*.

"Okay."

I climb off of him, and we both sit on the edge of his bed.

"Are you grossed out?" I ask. "Did you just realize you don't like guys?"

"No—"

"It's okay as long as you're honest with me."

"Quique—"

"Just say it. Say that was awful and disgusting."

"Shut up, Quique."

"Why?"

"It's the opposite. I, um, I need to come."

"What do you mean 'need to'?"

"It'll be . . . neater in a controlled setting. I.e., not in my shorts."

I clear my throat. "I can help you with that."

"No," he says immediately. "I, uh, think that would be moving really fast."

"Ziggy," I say under my breath.

"What?"

"Nothing. What do you propose?"

"I'm going to go . . . *relieve* myself in the bathroom."

That's the least cringe-inducing way anyone's ever put it.

He gets up stiffly, exits his room, and walks down the hall. After I hear the bathroom door close, I start thinking about what he's doing in there, and I can't help myself. I grab a couple of tissues from his desk.

• • •

By the time he comes back, all the evidence is gone. He took a lot longer than me, so I had time to stash the used Kleenex in the bottom of his wastebasket.

"Hey," I say.

"Hey," he says.

"You still wanna kiss me even after you've relieved yourself?"

He smiles. "I do."

"I think that's a good sign."

He walks over and sits next to me. We kiss softly. This is a different kind of kiss.

"Saleem?"

"Yes?"

"I don't want you to take this in a bad way, but . . . how are we going to deal with the religion thing?"

"What do you mean?"

"You're Muslim."

"And . . ."

"So how can you . . . Isn't this wrong?" What's that word he uses when he talks about alcohol and pork and stuff? "Haram?"

He nods slowly. "I mean . . . a lot of Muslims think so."

"And what do you think?"

"I don't know. Aren't you Christian? Don't Christians also . . ."

"Hate fags?"

He frowns. "That's one way to put it."

"Yeah, a lot of them do."

"So how do you reconcile that?" Saleem asks.

"I guess I don't." Which is the most succinct way I can put it. "I haven't yet."

"I guess we're in the same boat then."

"Huh. Yeah."

Thinking about the fact that so many people have used religion as a way of making people like me and Saleem hate ourselves is crushing. But then I think about my parents (who still love me) and how no one group is a monolith, that no matter what your religion is, you can still choose to love others. And I feel incredibly embarrassed that it took me so long to figure that out.

Saleem looks at me and smiles, and it makes me so unbelievably happy that I can lean in and kiss him. So I do.

"It's just . . . ," he begins. "This doesn't feel wrong."

"It doesn't."

"It did at first."

"When I asked you if you had a boner?"

"Yes."

"Not my best work."

"But now it feels right."

I reach out and grab his hand. What a beautiful hand. I bring it to my mouth and kiss it.

"When did you know?" he asks, rubbing my hand with his thumb.

"That I liked you?"

"Yeah."

"First time I saw you."

"Quique."

"It's true."

His smile, so untempered, so uninhibited, transforms him into the boy I saw all those years ago.

"And when did you know I might like you?" he asks.

"Well," I say, "I knew you liked me as a friend, obviously. For a long time, I hoped you liked me as something else but didn't actually believe you did. Or could. So I guess the first time I thought, 'Hey, maybe he's into me' was the night we skinny-dipped."

"That was a great night," he says.

"Really?"

"Yes. Strange and hard to deal with, but yes."

"Did you forget to put your trunks on on purpose?"

"I absolutely abhor the fact that the English language allows for that grammatical construction to exist."

"Answer the question."

"Actually, no. It was a split-second decision to skinny-dip."

"I see. You didn't give me anything else for a while."

"To be fair, I was across the country."

"With *Ahed* and her *voluminous curls* and her *beautiful brown skin* and her *sexy nose*—"

"Ya Allah, Quique."

"What? Am I wrong?"

"No, but . . . That made me kinda jealous."

"Wait, really?" I ask excitedly.

He coughs into his hand. "Yeah."

"Well how do you think I felt?"

He smiles. "You actually owe her."

"What? How?"

"Well, so we did kind of have a . . . thing."

"Slut."

"Quique!"

"Not her, you." He pokes me in the ribs. "Ow!"

"Anyway, we got close."

"How close?"

"We kissed."

"And?"

"And then we got realistic. We're both seventeen, living on opposite coasts. We have senior year ahead of us, and who knows where we're going to college. So we amicably parted ways."

"Holy shit."

"Yeah. And it's kinda like putting myself out there with her gave me the confidence to come back and see if you felt the same way about me as I did you."

"So why didn't you—oh. Oh my God."

The night he and Fabiola came over for dinner.

"I made you lie for me."

"Yeah." He scratches an eyebrow. "I, um, somehow I *knew* you had been *with* someone, that that was what the lie was about. And I hated it. I hated covering up for you while I had to think about you kissing someone else."

He's squeezing my hand really hard.

"But then you hugged me," I say, "before you got in the car. And it was different from your usual hugs. It was . . . weightier."

"Yeah, I couldn't stop myself."

"I'm sorry," I say. "I was hanging out with Arturo Peralta, but we didn't kiss. It's not like that with him."

"It doesn't matter if you did. We weren't together."

"We really didn't. He's been really helpful throughout this whole process. He can be partially blamed for me using my raw sexual charisma to seduce you." Saleem rolls his eyes. "Anyway, I'm sorry about making you lie."

"You apologized." He kisses me. "And said you'd never do it again." And kisses me. "And I believed you. Still do." And kisses me again; it's my favorite punctuation of his.

"But in that moment, I sort of wanted to . . . claim you. I knew you liked me. I think I've always known, but I was so scared of realizing it."

"I know what you mean. Then there was the free fall."

"Ya Allah," he says, laughing. "That was hard. So hard."

"Tell me about it. I thought I had freaked you out. I thought I had pushed you into that girl's arms. I forget her name."

"Me too."

"But I sort of knew why you were freaked out even then. I knew it meant something. Fabiola said it didn't, but I was almost sure."

"And that one day when you were a zombie, you were almost completely sure," he says.

"Yes."

"And now you're totally sure."

"Definitely."

"How?"

"I don't know," I say. "I guess I have this feeling that it's finally our time."

"Me too. I feel it too."

CHAPTER THIRTY-SIX

I tell everyone about Saleem. Well, everyone who matters and accepts us as who we are. Luciana, Mr. Chastman, Fabiola, and Arturo all have vastly different reactions.

Luciana quizzes me about the reciprocity of our relationship.

"Is it fifty-fifty?" she asks.

"No," I say.

She frowns.

"Enrique, I thought we talked about—"

"It's 100-100."

She snorts. "In that case, it's great news. I will caution you, however, about a common misconception that comes with being in a relationship. Some people believe that by finding 'the right one' they will automatically be 'cured' of their various mental illnesses, but—"

"I know about that," I say. "Saleem can't fix me. You can't fix me. Even *I* can't fix me. Completely. But I can try damn hard. And I'd be lying if I said Saleem doesn't make me try harder."

She smiles. Not a therapist smile.

"I think you guys are on the right track," she says.

. . .

Mr. Chastman and I raise a glass to the new relationship; his is full of wine and mine, of course, is filled with chocolate almond milk.

"That's great!" Mr. Chastman says after a sip. "Saleem is a wonderful boy *and*, might I say, age-appropriate."

"That he is. We can go to town on each other without breaking a single law." Mr. Chastman starts choking. "At least until he turns eighteen in a few weeks. I guess I have a thing for mature men."

"Does this mean you'll leave me alone?" he asks hopefully.

"Not a chance."

He fakes an exasperated sigh.

"I'm going to start needing actual relationship advice," I add.

"You might not want it from me," he says. "In case you haven't noticed, I'm a thirty-one-year-old high school English teacher whose student is in a relationship while he is not."

"Oh, come on. I'm sure you've been in relationships before. With like a stockbroker or something."

"Oh my God, how do you know about Brian?"

I laugh and decide to test a theory. "Would you let me drink sangria here? Its alcohol content has to be significantly lower than wine's."

"Still a no-go. Wait, why would you bring up sangria? Do you actually know Brian?"

Fabiola is of course asking about every little detail, but now that the guy in question is her friend too, I'm not as quick to humor her. I think I finally understand why she kept some parts of Molly to herself.

"Really?" she says. "All you guys did was kiss? And then he went into the bathroom to beat off?"

"To relieve himself, yes."

"Wow, you guys need to pick up the pace a bit."

"Wow. So you and Molly take your time getting to the sex part of your relationship, then pressure me to move quicker?"

She laughs. "If I knew how good it was gonna be, I wouldn't have waited so long."

They sealed the deal the night I told Saleem I liked him. I tell myself it was because of me. You know, bravery begetting bravery and such.

"Although," Fabiola says, "I think we did everything perfectly. And now it's like we're making up for lost time. When we're alone we're never not . . . occupied. When I eat stuff with my hands now, I don't even taste the food."

The sound that comes out of my mouth is alien even to me.

"Ow," I say. "I think one of my organs just burst."

"Careful now. Don't die before you and Saleem *make love*."

"Please. Even if I do die, I'll come back from the fucking dead and rock his world."

"Yas, give 'im that ghost dick. Or that *boo*ty."

We laugh.

"That reminds me," she says, "was my theory about him correct?"

"Which one?"

She mimes holding a baguette between her legs. (Not actually a baguette.)

"Oh. Well, I haven't seen it."

"So? I know you can feel it when you two are dry-humping like teenagers."

"We are teenagers."

"Whatever. Tell me."

I don't say anything. I just smile.

"You fucker! It's huge isn't it! I bet he's a grower, one of those magic growers with a dick that keeps on unraveling, like a magician pulling a never-ending scarf out of his sleeve. Is he?"

I remain silent, but this time it's not because Fabiola guessed wrong.

Arturo demands that I name my and Saleem's first adopted child after him.

"I mean you said it yourself—I was an instrumental part in getting you two together." He takes a bite of his pastrami burger. "So I deserve a namesake for my troubles."

"Chill," I say, my eyes surveying Pogo's for anyone listening in on our conversation. "We've been together a week."

"Right, you're not lesbians." I choke on my horchata. "Speaking of, is Fabiola still high on Molly?"

"One, that was a bad joke, and two, yes, they are perfectly happy."

"Ah, so it's just me who's gonna end up alone. Nice."

"Stop being dramatic," I say after a bite of my burger. "You'll find a dude at UCLA."

Arturo's eyes light up. "Like a professor."

"No, not like a professor."

"At least a senior."

"Sure."

"Guillermo's gonna be a senior."

"Ew, no. Forget about that loser. You'll find someone much better."

"Eh, I don't really care about that. For now, I'm plotting on success. I need him to see me on a billboard of some sort in the future and shit his pants."

I laugh. "You'll make it happen, I'm sure. If you stop driving like a maniac."

"Hey! I am a perfectly safe driver."

Arturo recently purchased a car. It's a used 2004 Honda Accord, but he drives it like a Maserati.

"Is that why I have seat belt marks on my chest?"

"It's not my fault that I want to get where I'm going as fast as I can."

"Right, well if this summer's taught me anything, it's that—"

"Oh no you don't. Don't you dare try to impart some 'it's not about the destination' Miley Cyrus–ass life lesson on me. I am older and wiser. Just eat your fries."

I smile and do as he says.

"Now let's circle back to my godson. I guess I can cede a little, and accept his middle name being Arturo. . . ."

The only people I'm not ready to share my relationship with are my parents. I don't think they're ready. Which is okay. Ish. Thinking about all the times they missed work to help me deal with my messy brain is enough. For now. Plus, they'll probably figure it out on their own. Eventually. That'll be a whole thing. They'll think it'll have been going on a lot longer than it actually has, but we'll cross that bridge when we get to it.

For now, there's one person I still haven't told about me and Saleem who I think deserves to know: Manny. That's why I've been parked outside his house for the past ten minutes, downing a bottle of an off-brand sports drink called Tranquilo. My parking job this time is shit, probably because I'm so nervous. Manny is the only one of my original prospects who merits my time. I know we only hooked up once, but I don't want to be like Guillermo with Arturo and never talk things out with him. I'm going to be super mature and gracious and kind about it. Maybe I should text him?

No. I can't do that to him. And plus, I already told him I'm here.

Come in, he replies. Damn it. I was hoping he'd say something like *I'm not home. Why the fuck did you show up at my house unannounced like a faggot? I love Minions!* And then I'd be able to tell him to go fuck himself and that I never want to see him again.

I sigh and get out of the car. As I walk to the house, I notice that I parked so far from the curb that if I exited from the passenger seat, I wouldn't be able step directly onto the sidewalk.

I knock and wait. Manny comes to the door shortly after.

"Quique!" he says.

We hug, the normal way, but one of his hands rests firmly on my lower, lower back. I start breathing really hard. Should I blurt it out now?

"Come on," he says, and walks in.

I shut the door behind me and follow him to his room.

"Can I use your bathroom?" I ask as he flops onto his bed. Too much Tranquilo.

"Yeah. Right there." He points to the door behind me.

"Cool, thanks."

I slip inside, lock the door, and lean against the wall for a bit, taking deep breaths. Then I walk over to the toilet and pee. The lid's already up. Very Manny.

When I'm finished, I wash my hands and stare into the mirror. *You can do this*, I tell myself. He's not in love with you. Just say it really quick and he'll say something like *It's okay, foo'. Live your life. Lemme know if you two break up.*

I take one breath and exit the bathroom.

"Manny, there's something I need . . . to . . . tell . . . you."

He's naked. Fully naked. Well, except for his long black socks.

"Come here," he says, lounging on his bed.

I swallow. "Uh . . . that's okay."

Fuck, he's hot.

"C'mon, I know you want to," he says, smiling. He knows I'm staring, despite trying my hardest not to.

"That assertion is simultaneously accurate and inaccurate."

He stops smiling. "Huh?"

"'Accurate' because, objectively speaking, making tactile contact with your skin would excite my nerve endings in a pleasurable manner"—coming up with big words helps distract me from his naked body—"but simultaneously 'inaccurate' because I have quite recently acquired a serious suitor whom I intend on being faithful to."

"Huh?"

"I'm with someone. That's what I came here to tell you."

"Oh . . . Fuck."

"Yeah."

We both stare at each other. I'm looking at his eyes now.

"I'm gonna go," I say.

"Don't," he says. I glance at his dick for a split second. "I'll put clothes on."

"Okay then."

I walk out and head to the living room. I take a seat on the couch and less than a minute later, Manny joins me, fully clothed like promised.

"That was awkward," he says, pulling his T-shirt out of the waistband of his gray sweats.

"A little."

We both laugh as he sits down next to me.

"So," he says, "I assume it's a girl."

I raise an eyebrow. "No, actually. It's a guy."

"Oh. I thought because you're bi—"

"Wait, how do you know that?"

"You like tits. I've noticed."

"You don't?"

"They're okay."

"So you're not—"

"Nah, I'm gay as fuck, dude."

"Oh."

"Anyway, who's your guy?"

"Uh . . ." For some reason I don't want to tell him about Saleem. What if Manny says something about him that sticks in my head and ruins us? Is that even possible? I think about

Saleem. No, it isn't. "My Saleem. I mean, my friend Saleem. I mean, my boyfriend is Saleem."

"Small guy? Pretty-ass eyes?"

"Yeah," I say laughing. I wasn't kidding about the eyes.

"You really like him."

"How do you know?"

"The smile on your face when you said his name."

"Oh. I didn't even realize . . ."

"That's how I know."

I nod. "I should have told you a lot earlier."

"It's okay, foo'. Live your life, ya know?"

I laugh. "Yeah. I also feel bad I didn't get to pay you back for . . . you know."

He smiles and licks his lips, and I feel really guilty for thinking, *If only we'd seen each other one more time before Saleem and I happened.*

"I got my app. I'm good."

"Mmm."

"What?"

"I still don't like the idea of you on there."

"So you get some steady dick and start looking down on me?"

"No! It's not that. It's that I—I—" He looks mad. "I'm sorry. I didn't mean—"

He starts laughing. "I'm kidding, foo'."

"Fuck you!" He laughs again. "I almost shit myself."

"Your face."

I take a deep breath. "Even if you don't want a relationship, remember that you are fucking hot and funny and hot.

And don't get with anyone who doesn't appreciate that. Also, maybe don't use it until you're eighteen."

He seems to consider this.

"Maybe I'll hit up your old dude Tyler."

"Oh God no. Talk about not being appreciative."

"I'm playin'. I only go down for brown." I laugh. "I'm actually really glad you're not with a white dude. You're guy's what? Honduran or some other shit?"

"Palestinian. Arab."

"Muslim?"

"That too."

"They get a lot of shit, ya know."

"Yeah . . ."

I feel guilty again because if it's not blatant Islamaphobia, Muslims have to deal with assumptions from "well-meaning" people like me. I have some work ahead of me.

"But you're ride or die," Manny says. "I can tell."

"Thanks. I hope so."

"Anything happens, I got your back. It's so dumb because it's always white dudes blowing up the country."

"Very true." I check the time. "Well, I gotta go."

"Your man waiting for you?"

"Yes." I don't have to see my own face to know my smile gives away how much I love the boy waiting for me at his for-the-next-week-conveniently-empty apartment.

Manny walks me to the door. "Hey, um, Quique."

"Yeah?"

"Make sure to lemme know if you two break up."

"You'll be the first one I call."

We hug and then I'm off. I have plans. So many, many plans.

"How'd it go?" Saleem asks, out of breath, stopping the five-minute kiss that started the moment he opened the door of his apartment.

"Uh . . . good," I say.

He doesn't need specifics, right? I mean he wasn't entirely on board with my "tell Manny in person" idea when I told him yesterday in the pool. Not because he didn't trust me but because he, well, maybe had guessed correctly that Manny would make a move.

"I'd obviously stop him," I said, trying to shake water out of my ear.

"I know," he said. "But I'm, uh, I don't know. I'm—"

"Jealous."

"I don't think that's—"

"It's okay," I said, wading toward him. "It's cute."

"Really?"

"Yeah." I kissed him quickly on the cheek. "And nothing's gonna happen."

But of course I was wrong, and wanting to change the subject, I push Saleem against the wall and kiss him again, hoping this kiss lasts even longer than the one before.

Manny may have been a momentary temptation, but with Saleem right here, I know the truth: I'd choose him over every other guy on the planet. They could all be in the room right now and I would pick Saleem over and over and over. Over Manny, Ziggy, Tyler, Mr. Chastman, Chris Evans, Dante Kruger, the guy from the travel (?) company commercials, Dorian Gray, Giovanni, Maurice, Oliver, every Everygay, every Better Man, and everyone in between.

Later that night, after cooking and eating a dinner together that made me pinch myself, Saleem and I sit down on the couch to watch a movie, the first two minutes and twenty-nine seconds of which are pretty good.

Saleem pushes me down on the couch and pins me with his mouth while somehow managing to get both of our shirts off (what can I say, the boy's a quick study). I keep waiting for him to dismount and take some time to cool down at any moment because that's what he did last time we got this far, but he doesn't. Instead, he reaches for my zipper.

"Saleem."

"What?"

"What are you doing?"

"Taking your pants off," he says matter-of-factly.

"You sure?"

"Never been more sure."

I let him. I also let him take my boxers off. And then his pants. And then his boxers.

This is only the third time I've seen a naked guy in person (and the second time today weirdly enough), which isn't a lot, but I've also seen countless on the Internet. And Saleem's is by far my favorite. It excites me in a way that touches my heart, my brain, my body and soul.

"Ugh," I say. "I don't deserve you. You're too perfect. But I'll fucking take it. I don't care if you're meant for some other perfect-ass Goody Two-shoes. I'm sticking my claws in you, and I'm not letting go."

"Quique, there's no way I'm meant for a Goody-Two-shoes."

"Why?"

"Because I'm really, really bad."

I laugh.

"You think I'm joking?"

"No, which makes it *so* much funnier."

"Want me to prove it to you?"

I'm serious now. "More than anything."

He climbs on top of me. "Okay then. Don't say I didn't warn you."

I may not deserve Saleem, but I don't deserve a lot of things I used to think I did. I don't deserve to feel shame, to feel lonely, to be treated like a sex object, to be ignored, to be someone's experiment. I definitely don't deserve any of that. And I'm glad I know that now. It's a feeling I hope doesn't leave me for the rest of my life.

CHAPTER THIRTY-SEVEN

As soon as the lunch bell rings, I hightail it out of my economics class, leaving Mr. Stewart with a look of disapproval on his face. (It's going to be a long year; he's already used the word "bootstraps" sixteen times this week.) I'm tearing down the hallway, my backpack swinging wildly behind me, when I have to skid to a halt in order to avoid crashing into someone who is also running.

That person is, of course, Saleem.

"Hey," I say, out of breath for two reasons: the running and his face.

"Hey," he says, also breathless.

Students stream out of classrooms on all sides, making us tear our eyes away from each other for a second before we come back.

We are two oppositely charged magnets, but in this moment, we must resist what comes naturally for fear of what would result. We remain apart despite the invisible force pulling us together. It blows.

"Lunch?" I say.

Our schedules lining up this year is a godsend.

"Lunch," he says with a smile.

I wish I could say we share our love with the rest of the

world, that we march down the halls of our high school with our chins held high, our hands firmly clasped, chanting, *We're here; we're queer; get used to it!* but we don't. There are many battles ahead in our lives, and we don't want to start fighting them just yet. We focus instead on how fun it is to sneak in moments of affection that would, if we did them in public, cause us to get into altercations with people. There's something about boys loving boys and girls loving girls that fills people with hate.

But like I said, I don't focus on that. As Saleem and I join Fabiola and Molly at our usual lunch table, I focus on our clandestine meetings: the rushed kissing behind locker doors, gratuitous ass-grabbing in abandoned stairwells, and shameless dry-humping behind the bleachers. I also focus on the raucous lunches I have with my and Saleem's fellow same-sex couple and devoted beards. We eat and laugh and joke and plan our lookout shifts for each other. It's not ideal, not anywhere close to that, but we make it an enchanted life. We bisexuals are, after all, mythical creatures.

Molly's had a boyfriend or two before and has come closer to confirming rather than denying a brief involvement with none other than Ziggy Jackson.

Things with my parents are the same. They think my sky-rocketing spirit lately is the result of my going back to school and ending my usual "summer funk." They also don't suspect anything's happening between me and Saleem because we don't do anything non-platonic if they're within a five-mile radius of our house. That and the fact that Saleem's gotten scarily good at lying. I think he's used to having a secret under his skin at all times.

I feel bad sometimes and get scared that I corrupted him. It's not only the lies. I once said the travel company guy was the human version of the purple devil emoji, but I'm almost convinced it's Saleem instead. The things I let that boy do to me and he gets me to do to him are . . . uncouth. But I like him this way. We've filled Molly's tree house with so many deliriously happy memories I've almost completely forgotten the ones I made there with Tyler. And maybe I've always idealized Saleem too much. It's like I was a toy collector, and he was an extremely valuable action figure that I hadn't wanted to break out of its plastic. But that's not the case anymore. I've taken him out, and I'm going to play with him all I want.

I try to focus in school, but it's hard. Not only because of Saleem. I still don't know what I want to do with my life. None of my classes this year excite me (not that they did any other year). I'm hoping to find inspiration when I least expect it, and I'm hoping that day will come soon.

The one thing I am happy about is having access to my school library again. Our librarian may not be as cute as the one I saw so many times over the summer, but I'm glad to be back here. I've all but abandoned *Literature* for now. I'm back to my teenage ways. For a while it was more books about white boys kissing white boys, but I recently managed to find some books about brown boys falling in love with each other. Still not as graphic as I'd like, but maybe I'm just a perv.

"Helloooooo. Earth to Quique."

"Huh?" I say.

"Dude, where'd you go?" Fabiola says.

I shake my head. "I don't know. I . . ."

I don't want to tell them about the dissociation, Luciana's psychiatric term for when I go blank. It's not like when I'm thinking really hard about something and forget I'm at the dinner table. It's when I zone out and detach, regardless of what's happening around me. Sometimes I leave when I actually want to stay in the moment. I just find myself slipping away.

I know I have to tell Saleem about it eventually. It's happened while we've been . . . together. Decent guy that he is, he always stops to ask what's going on in my head. I don't really want to tell him that the answer is quite literally "nothing."

But I will tell him. Because I want to. Because it's easy to. It's beautiful having someone to share your secrets with so that they're not secrets anymore, someone who makes you feel like your thoughts shouldn't just be your thoughts, that you should speak them into existence because you're unique and smart and cute and funny.

I'm lucky. Maybe not mentally stable, but lucky.

"I'm having a moment," I finally say.

"Well, have a moment with us," Fabiola says.

"Try to keep me entertained then."

"Dragged," Molly says.

"Don't you encourage him," Fabiola says. "You're on my team."

"I play for both teams," Molly says with a wink.

Fabiola rolls her eyes. The rest of us laugh.

But then Saleem turns to me with concern on his face. Fabiola and Molly might have noticed my zoning out, but they don't notice how it's making me feel at the moment. Saleem does.

He reaches out underneath the table and takes my hand. It's only for a second or two, but it helps. My boyfriend has healing powers I'll never understand.

I smile at him. It's a real smile and he knows that, so he looks relieved.

I'll tell him tonight. I will. And I'll tell him other things, too. How I love him and I want him. How he looks most handsome when he's wearing the shirt I told him looks best on him and not only because I'm right, but because he wears it more often now for me. How last night I had a dream he wanted to become a clown and I was trying to talk him out of it because there was no way in hell he'd get a fraction of the action he's currently getting with white makeup and a red nose on. How my heart still races every time he takes my hand. I have a lot to tell him.

Mr. Chastman's at his desk reading a book when I enter his classroom. School's over, but before I headed home, I wanted to see him. He looks up as I walk over.

"Enrique! So nice to see you for the first time since the end of last year!"

I laugh. "Likewise."

"What brings you here? Book recs? Letter of recommendation? Literally nothing else?"

I sit on his desk. "Has it gotten better?"

He drops his act. "Has what gotten better?"

"Life. For us. Since you were a kid. Has it gotten better?"

He strokes his chin and sighs. "Yes. But it's also gotten worse."

I give him a strange look, and all he does is smile. It's the girlfriend smile. I have a feeling I'll understand what he's saying soon enough.

I'm about to leave when his phone lights up on his desk, and I glance at it instinctively.

"Oh my God!" I yell, jumping off the desk. "Your name is Leroy?"

"Enrique!"

He grabs his phone and shoves it into his pocket.

"It was an accident! Mostly."

He shakes his head, disbelievingly.

"Who's Ira?" I ask.

"Enrique, forget what you've seen."

"I will, I will." I start walking backward to the door. "Just make sure to text him back that you guys *are* still on for that wine bar in Silver Lake tonight."

"Go home now, Enrique."

I throw up my arms. "Already gone."

The first thing I do when I get home is crawl under my bed. I'm not trying to hide here, like I did when I was little and the world felt too big. I'm trying to find something. After a minute of pushing stuff around and getting dust in my nose and eyes, my fingertips touch a glossy surface, and I drag it out.

I sit on the floor of my room and place the yearbook on my lap. I flip through the pages, stopping to read the messages scrawled out by my non-prospects.

Fabiola:

Keeks,

Babe what is there left for me to say? I've never been one to leave my thoughts unsaid so stuff like this is really hard. What haven't I told you? What don't you know? I guess some things bear repeating: You're a great friend. With a great butt. And I love you. I'm always here. Even if you lose your butt in some tragic accident. Maybe. No, but really I'm here til the end.

Your ride or die

Leroy Chastman:

Enrique,

I never did get your Old Man and the Sea *response paper. I know you were absent the day it was due (not suspicious at all, I might add), but I still expected you to hand it in. Especially considering the fact that you seem to harbor a strong opinion about it, which I'm basing on the fact that you roll your eyes every time I mention Hemingway. I am 100% certain that you will turn your paper in before the year is over, but I thought I'd mention it. All that being said, have a great summer. I'll see you in the fall.*

Mr. Chastman

And, of course, Saleem:

> *Enrique Luke Luna (aka 'Quique),*
> *This past year, our friendship has grown in ways*
> *that I never could have imagined and for that*
> *I am extremely grateful. You are a kind, funny,*
> *intelligent person, and I pray that you can see*
> *that as clearly as I (and most likely everyone else*
> *in your life) do. Don't ever be afraid to reach out.*
> *I'll always answer your call. Or your depress-*
> *ingly agrammatical texts.*
>
> *Sincerely,*
> *Saleem Kanazi*

I'm a sniveling mess when I'm done (because of the dust, obviously), but I still take out my phone to dial.

I don't mention the yearbook at first. I tell him everything else I need to tell him first. He says he feels bad for not being able to help with the dissociation thing. I tell him talking about it makes it better, like always. He tells me that makes him feel good.

"Oh, and another thing," I say. "I just read your yearbook message."

"What? Really? Just now?"

I laugh. "Yeah, but not just yours. I guess I sort of forgot because . . . I don't know, I figured I knew what you'd say."

"I . . . am . . . *utterly* offended."

I laugh again. "In a good way though. I knew you guys—

you in particular—would write something perfect. Maybe I didn't feel like I deserved those words."

He clears his throat before speaking in an English accent, "There's something I want to say to you, Quique, my darling Quique."

"Yes, Saleem? My beautiful Saleem?"

We do this sometimes, talk like we're in a movie adaptation of an old British novel.

"Remember when I told you about being a tiger in a cage?" he asks, dropping the accent.

"Yeah, why?"

"Well, I still feel like that sometimes."

"I'm sorry."

"But."

"But?"

"But." He's smiling. I know it. "Ever since we first kissed, I've known something, something that I still haven't told you yet."

"What is it?"

"You feel like home. When I'm with you, I'm home. Your chest is where my head belongs, and your arms are where the rest of me belongs."

I don't say anything. Because I can't.

My chest feels too tight to breathe, let alone speak.

I know how much that word means to Saleem. I know the context and subtext of it, all of its complicated history. And I can't help but feel unworthy.

"Quique? You there?"

"Yeah."

"What are you thinking?"

"You got yourself a real fixer-upper."

He laughs. "No. I don't."

A stream of tears falls down to the big, stupid smile on my face. He's wrong. I'm crazy.

"You still there?" he asks.

"Yes, stop asking that."

"Well, all I'm getting is silence from your end."

"I think . . . I think my brain's trying to take me away. I don't think it wants to deal with all the emotions you bring out in me. Even if they're good. I think it's scared. I think I'm scared."

"Let's try something."

"Okay."

"Close your eyes."

I do.

"Breathe."

I do.

"Allow yourself to feel."

I try. I think about Saleem's words, the faith he has in me, this fucked-up, selfish human being. I feel the weight of it, and it hurts. But I stop blocking the fear. And with it comes everything else. Joy and sadness and exhilaration. I kinda wanna cry and throw up and jump out a window. But I don't. I wait for him to speak again.

"Talk to me."

I open my eyes. I take another breath. I let what I'm feeling move my lips, and I say, "So when are you coming home?"

ACKNOWLEDGMENTS

Thank you, God, for everything good in my life, for your love and peace and kindness and forgiveness.

Thank you, Mom, for being my favorite person, for inspiring my love of reading, for being a writer before I was. I pray that one day you receive the inspiration and confidence that you gifted me and pick up one of your many pens as a result. I love you. (More.) (Yes, I do.) (Yes I do.) (Yes—)

Thank you, Ashley, my favorite sister/drummer, for giving me a home when I didn't have one and for making me capable of Mariah Carey lyrical references.

Thank you, Tina Dubois, for believing in my words. You continually pushed me to do better and for that I forgive you (kidding). You are a titan in this industry.

Thank you, Jennifer Ung, for saying yes the second time. Thank you for your calming energy, your vision, and your advice. Thank you for letting me keep my title.

Thank you, Amanda Ramirez, for picking up where Jen and I left off. And thank you, Alexa Pastor (+Alyza Liu), for picking up where Amanda and I left off. It feels incredibly fitting that my debut experience was as Dramatic as it was. Glad I was somehow lucky enough to have a plethora of incredible editors.

Thank you to the entire Simon & Schuster Books for Young Readers team for every step of getting this book into the hands of readers. Special shout-out to Goñi Montes and Laurent Linn for a beautiful cover. Thank you, Tamara Kawar at ICM Partners, for your insights. Thank you, George Abraham, for your careful reading of this book and your generous feedback.

Thank you to (almost) all of my teachers for your patience and knowledge. You are definitely overworked and most definitely underpaid. Specifically: Lovey Sherman, who gave me the greatest foundation a kindergarten teacher could; Jane Hara, who gave me a college scholarship twelve years after I was in her class; Mr. Sams (I'm sorry I don't know your first name), who told my mother he "wouldn't be surprised" if her son became a writer one day; Ms. Drayman, Mrs. J(amreonvit), Ms. Lobos, and Mr. Lopez, who had to put up with my middle school self (I'm so sorry); Ms. Cunningham, who taught me when I was Quique's age; Lorgia Garcia-Peña, Jamaica Kincaid, and Mark Jude Poirier, who wrote all those letters of rec; James Cañón, Victor LaValle, Heidi Julavits, Keri Bertino, and Matthew Burgess, who supported me even after I got my MFA.

Thank you to the KidLit community. So many of you kept me sane during various freak-outs. Thank you, Ryan Douglass, Adib Khorram, Abdi Nazemian, and Aiden Thomas, for the kind words and for talking shop with me. Thank you, Elizabeth Acevedo, Arvin Ahmadi, Robbie Couch (aka Robert Sofa), Jonny Garza Villa, Greg Howard, Kosoko Jackson, Leah Johnson, Jason June, Laekan Zea Kemp, Ryan La Sala, Kyle Lukoff, RaCquel Marie, Claribel Ortega, Mark Oshiro, Austin Siegemund-Broka (we've come a long way since *The Crimson*), and Nic Stone (you absolute bicon). Thank you, Adam Silvera, for being my biggest inspiration, for making me feel seen.

Thank you to the queer artists who provided me with the magic that is your music and, in some cases, gave me things to write about: Kevin Abstract (and BROCKHAMPTON), Frank

Ocean, Troye Sivan, Tyler Glenn, Lil Nas X, Moses Sumney, Sam Smith, Tinashe (hey birthday twin), The Internet, Halsey, Tegan and Sara, Billie Joe Armstrong (and Green Day), Rita Indiana, and MUNA. Special shout-out to Hamed Sinno (and Mashrou' Leila). [And Taylor Swift.]

Last and certainly not least: thank you to my friends and family. Thank you, Aunt Yvonne, for "chocolate milk li'l bit hot." You are loved and missed. Thank you to my cousins Kristen, Jackie, Jade, and Jill; my day ones Michelle Verzani (+Handsome) and Hua Chen; my brother Steven; my favorite sister-in-law Nancy Guzman; La Familia Quezada, mi familia Dominicana, Amelier, Iserbel, Damaris (Bonita), y Benito (Bombero); The Harvard Hoodrats aka Andree Franco-Vazquez, Ilian Peña-Meza, Christian Ramirez, Lymaira Reyes, Jennifer Ruiz, Lorena Trujillo-Avilez; my Columbia peeps, Jai Hamid Bashir (can't wait to hold your poetry collection in my hands, love), Veronika Kelemen (can't wait to hold your essay collection, daughter), Jessica Rodriguez (can't wait to hold your novel, babe), and Sia Shin (can't wait to hold your memoir, friend). And thank you, Minnie Meow-Aceves. One day, I will tell everyone how it was actually you who wrote this book by stepping on my keyboard every time I was writing, but for now, let me pretend it was all me.

Thank you, Melissa Quintana (+Tomás), for always knowing what to say when I was down on myself (I drink to that!).

Thank you, Dorothy Villarreal, for being so, so strong and making me stronger by association.

And, of course, thank you, Leti, for being the person I always want to share my good news with. You've always seen the best in me, and I am in constant awe of you. Te quiero. Also . . . yerrrrrrrr.

Last but not least, thank you, reader. If you see a piece of your soul reflected in this book, I love you. We'll make it.